Praise for Claire Douglas and
The Couple at Number 9

"Gripping, twisty, and hold-your-breath tense, this is Claire Douglas's best book yet."
—Tim Weaver, bestselling author of *No One Home*

"A well-plotted tale. All the characters are hiding things, and you're often waiting for the next secret to blow up. Intriguing. Twisty. Surprising. Touching. Enjoyed it."
—Dorothy Koomson, bestselling author of *All My Lies Are True*

"Secrets, skeletons, mothers and daughters—and some absolutely corking twists! A cracking thriller. I loved it."
—Eve Chase, bestselling author of *The Glass House*

"This book has everything I love: murder, a taut and fiendishly clever plot, and nail-biting tension."
—Emma Curtis, bestselling author of *One Little Mistake*

"Combines a tight, gripping plot and truly shocking twist, with beautiful writing and emotion. A thriller with a heart. One of the best I have read in a long time."
—Nuala Ellwood, bestselling author of *The House on the Lake*

"Twisty, nail-biting, and utterly absorbing, you won't be able to put *The Couple at Number 9* down."
—Louise O'Neill, author of *After the Silence*

THE COUPLE AT NUMBER 9

THE
COUPLE
AT
NUMBER 9

A Novel

CLAIRE DOUGLAS

HARPER

NEW YORK · LONDON · TORONTO · SYDNEY

HARPER

Originally published as *The Couple at No. 9* in Great Britain in 2021 by Penguin Random House UK.

FIRST U.S. EDITION

Library of Congress Cataloging-in-Publication Data has been applied for.

ISBN 978-0-06-313814-8 (pbk.)
ISBN 978-0-06-324632-4 (library edition)

22 23 24 25 26 LSC 10 9 8 7 6 5 4 3 2 1

For Elizabeth Lane, Rhoda Douglas and June Kennedy

PART ONE

1

Saffy

April 2018

I'M IN THE FRONT GARDEN, PULLING AT WEEDS THAT spill out from the borders of the driveway, like gigantic spiders, when I hear yells. Deep and guttural. The builders are in the rear garden with the mechanical digger. All morning, as I was pruning the rose bush under the living-room window, I could hear the thrum of it on the breeze, like a nagging headache. But now it's stopped. It's enough to make my heart pound and Snowy – Gran's little Westie who's lying beside me – prick up his ears. I turn towards the cottage, a film of sweat breaking out between my shoulder blades. Has something happened? I imagine severed joints and gushing blood – at odds with the blue skies and the dazzling sunshine – and my stomach heaves. I've never had a strong gut at the best of times but being four-teen weeks pregnant I'm still experiencing morning sickness – well, morning, noon and night sickness.

I stand up, mud stains on the knees of my jeans, still my usual size, although the waistband is snugger. I deliberate, chewing the inside of my cheek, inwardly berating myself for being so indecisive. Snowy stands up too, his ears pricked, and he emits one solitary bark as a builder – Jonty, the young good-looking one – suddenly appears from around the side of the house. He's running towards me, damp circles under the armpits of his T-shirt as he waves his cap in the air to get my attention, his sandy curls bouncing with each step.

Shit, he's going to tell me there's been an accident. I fight the urge to run in the opposite direction, instead shielding my eyes from the sun that beats down onto the thatched roof. Jonty doesn't appear injured but as he gets closer I can see shock on his freckled face.

'Is someone hurt?' I call, trying to keep the panic out of my voice. Oh, God, I'm going to have to ring for an ambulance. I've never phoned 999 in my life. And I'm not good with blood. I wanted to be a nurse when I was younger, until I fainted when my best friend fell off her bike and gashed her knee open.

'No. Sorry to disturb you but,' he sounds out of breath and his words tumble out in a rush, 'we've found something. You'd better come. Quick!'

I drop my gardening gloves onto the grass and follow him around the side of the cottage, Snowy at my heels, wondering what it could be. Treasure, perhaps? Some relic from the past that could be exhibited in a museum? But the yells. They weren't of joy at the discovery of something precious. They were laced with fear.

I wish Tom was here. I don't feel comfortable dealing with the builders while he's at work: they constantly ask questions, expecting me to make decisions I'm worried will be wrong, and I've never been very authoritarian. At twenty-four Tom and I are only three years out of university. All of this – the move from the flat in

Croydon to Beggars Nook, a quaint village in the Cotswolds, and the cottage with views of the woods – has been so unexpected. A surprise gift.

Jonty leads me to the back garden. Before the builders came it had looked idyllic with the mature shrubbery, the honeysuckle snaked around the trellises and the rockery in the corner filled with velvety pansies in a burst of pinks and lilacs. Now there is an ugly orange digger surrounded by a huge mound of un-earthed soil. The other two builders – Darren, mid-thirties with a hipster beard, who, by his confident stance, is the boss, and Karl, around my age and as stocky as a rugby player – stare down at the hole they've made in the ground, hands on hips, their heavy boots sinking into the soil. They whip their heads up in perfect synchrony when I approach. They're wearing match-ing shocked expressions, but Karl's eyes are flashing with some-thing akin to excitement. I follow his gaze and notice a glint of ivory among the soil, protruding like broken china. Instinctively I reach down and grab hold of Snowy's collar to prevent him from darting into the hole.

'While we were digging we found . . . *something*,' says Dar-ren, folding his arms across his dirt-streaked T-shirt.

'What is it?' Snowy strains against my hand and I tighten my grip.

'Remains.' Darren's expression is grim.

'Like . . . an animal?' I ask. Darren and the others exchange a look.

Karl steps forwards confidently, almost gleefully, kicking up dust from the ground as he does so. 'It looks like a hand . . .'

I step back in horror. 'So you're saying . . . they're human?'

Darren regards me with sympathy. 'I think so. You'd better call the police.'

2

BY THE TIME TOM ARRIVES HOME TWO HOURS LATER I'M pacing our tiny kitchen. It looks like a relic from the 1980s with its farmhouse units and the scenes of fat-cheeked pigs and sheep on the wall tiles. We've managed to squeeze in our oak table from the flat, although we can pull out only two of the four chairs. Not long after we moved in, in February, we'd sat with the architect, a short balding man in his sixties called Clive with a good local reputation, planning the back of the house: the kitchen would be extended and span the width of the cottage, with Crittal doors leading out into the large garden. And, to be honest, it's taken my mind off my pregnancy, which I still feel jittery about even though I've had the twelve-week scan and everything looks okay. But I'm blighted with what-ifs. What if I miscarry the baby? What if it doesn't grow properly, or comes too early, or I have a stillbirth? What if I can't cope when the baby is born or suffer post-natal depression?

The pregnancy hadn't been planned. It was something Tom and I had spoken about, loosely, after perhaps a wedding, but we'd been busy starting up our respective career ladders and saving for a deposit to buy our own flat. Babies and weddings had been for when we were older. For when we became proper grown-ups. But I'd been ill with a stomach bug, had forgotten to take extra precautions. And that one slip-up had resulted in this. *A baby*. I'd be a young mother but not as young as my own mum had been.

Snowy is stretched out in his bed by the oven, head on his paws, watching me as I pace. From the leaded window I can see the hub of activity in the back garden. A white tent has been erected over half of the lawn, and police officers and men in forensic suits come and go, along with another officer, a camera slung around his neck. Fluorescent yellow tape has been put up around the tent and it flaps in the slight breeze. It has *CRIME SCENE DO NOT CROSS* printed along its length, and it makes me feel nauseous every time it catches my eye. It might look like a scene from an ITV crime drama but its presence drives home the reality of the situation. I'd been surprised (and, actually, a little bit proud) of myself for how quickly I'd taken control of things after I'd recovered from the shock. First, calling the police and then, after we'd given our statements, sending the builders home, saying I'd let them know when they could resume work, even if my heart still pounded the whole time. Then I'd called Tom at his office in London; he'd said he'd be on the next train home.

I hear Tom's Lambretta pull up on the driveway; he's always wanted one and treated himself to the second-hand moped when we moved here to get back and forth to the station. It's cheaper than running two cars, and all the spare money we had saved is going on this extension.

I hear the front door slam. Tom rushes into the kitchen, concern etched all over his face. He has his glasses on, the trendy black-rimmed pair he bought when he started his new job in the finance department of a tech company over a year ago. He felt they gave him more gravitas. His sandy-blond fringe falls over his face and he's rumpled in his linen shirt and blazer over jeans. It doesn't matter what he wears, he still manages to look like a student. He smells of London – of fumes and trains and takeaway lattes and other people's expensive scents. Snowy is circling our legs and Tom bends down to pat him distractedly, but his attention is firmly on me.

'Oh, my God, are you okay? What a shock . . . the baby,' he says, straightening up.

'It's all fine. We're fine,' I say, palms on my stomach protectively. 'The police are still outside. They've interviewed me and the builders, and now they've set up crime tape and a tent and everything.'

'Fuck.' He looks past me at the scene from the window and his expression darkens for a few seconds. Then he turns to me. 'Have they given you much info?'

'Not much, no. It's a human skeleton. Who knows how long it's been there? It could date back a few hundred years for all I know.'

'Or to Roman times,' he says, smiling wryly.

'Exactly. Probably been here before Skelton Place was even built. And that was . . .' I frown, realizing I can't actually remember.

'1855.' Of course Tom would know. He only has to read things once to remember them. He's always the first to answer a general-knowledge question on game shows and he's forever looking up facts and trivia on his phone. He's the opposite to me: calm, pragmatic and never overreacts. 'It looks like serious shit, though,' muses Tom, his eyes still fixed on the scene in the garden. I follow his gaze. Someone has turned up with two ca-daver dogs. Do they suspect more bodies? My stomach twists.

Tom turns back to me, his voice serious. 'Not what we ex-pected when we moved to the country.' A beat of silence before we break into nervous laughter.

'Oh, God,' I say, sobering up. 'It feels wrong to laugh. Somebody died after all.'

This sets us off again.

We are interrupted by the clearing of a throat and we turn to see a uniformed policewoman standing at the back door. It's one of those stable-style ones, so the top part is open and it frames her, like she's about to perform a puppet show. She's regarding us as if we're a couple of naughty school kids. Snowy starts barking at her.

'It's okay,' murmurs Tom to Snowy.

'Sorry to interrupt,' says the officer, not looking sorry at all. 'I did knock.' She pushes open the bottom half of the door so that she's standing on the threshold.

'That's fine,' says Tom. He releases Snowy, who instantly darts over to the police officer to sniff her trousers. She looks vaguely irritated while gently pushing him away with her leg.

'PC Amanda Price.' She's older than us by about fifteen years with a dark bob and intense blue eyes. 'Can I just confirm you are the owners of this property? Tom Perkins and Saffron Cutler?'

Technically my mother is but I don't complicate things by saying so.

'Yes,' says Tom, widening his eyes at me. 'This is our cottage.'

'Right,' says PC Price. 'We'll be a bit longer, I'm afraid. Is there someone you can stay with tonight, maybe for the week-end?'

I think of Tara, who currently lives in London, and my school-friend Beth, who's in Kent. Tom's friends are either in Poole, where he's originally from, or Croydon. 'We haven't lived here long. We haven't made friends in the area yet,' I say, and it brings home how isolated we are, in this new village in the middle of nowhere.

'Parents nearby?'

Tom shakes his head. 'Mine still live in Poole and Saffy's mum's in Spain.'

'And my dad lives in London,' I say. 'But he's only got a one-bedroom flat . . .'

She frowns, like this is all information she doesn't need. 'Then may I suggest a hotel, just until Sunday. The police will pay your expenses for this inconvenience. It's just while the crime scene is being secured and the excavation is completed.'

The words 'crime scene' and 'excavation' make me feel sick.

'When can the building work resume?' Tom asks.

She sighs, as though this is a question too far. 'I'm afraid you won't be able to use the back garden until the excavation and removal of the skeleton has been completed. You'll have to wait until you hear from the SOCO. A scenes of crime officer,' she clarifies, when we look at her with puzzled expressions.

'So you think this is a crime?' I ask, throwing Tom a concerned look. He tries to smile at me in reassurance but it's more of a grimace.

'We're treating it as a crime scene, yes,' she says, as though I'm incredibly stupid, but she doesn't offer any further information and I sense it would be fruitless to ask.

'We've only been here a few months,' I say, feeling the need to explain, just in case this stern police officer thinks we might have had something to do with it, like we're in the habit of hiding dead bodies in our garden. 'It might have been here years . . . centuries perhaps . . .' But the look on her face makes me falter.

PC Price purses her lips together. 'I'm not at liberty to say anything further for now. The CSI have requested a forensic anthropologist to confirm the bones are human and we will keep you updated.' I think of the hand that Karl claims he saw. It doesn't sound like there's much doubt. There follow a few beats of awkward silence before she goes to leave. Then she pauses, as though suddenly remembering. 'Oh, and please can you be out of here within the hour.'

We watch her step out into the back garden, into that gruesome world of police forensics, and I fight back tears. Tom reaches for my hand silently, as though he's lost the ability to offer words of comfort.

And it suddenly hits me that this is really happening. Our dream home, our beautiful cottage, is now a crime scene.

Luckily the Stag and Pheasant in the village has a room for us to stay in and they allow dogs. We turn up with one overnight bag each, which Tom insists on carrying while I take Snowy on his lead.

The landlady, Sandra Owens, regards us questioningly. 'Aren't you the new owners of the cottage up at Skelton Place?' she asks, as we hover in the bar area. We've only been in the pub once since moving to Beggars Nook and that was for Sunday lunch last month. We'd been impressed with the tasteful pale green Farrow & Ball-painted walls, the rustic furniture and delicious home-cooked food. It had, apparently, undergone a huge makeover when the Owenses took it over five years ago.

I don't know what to say. Once the news gets out it will be all over the village.

'We've run into a bit of bother with our build,' says Tom, pleasantly but noncommittally, 'so thought it best to move out for a few nights, just until it's sorted.'

'Right,' Sandra says, although she doesn't look particularly convinced. She's in her late fifties and attractive with her high-lighted bob and elegant wrap-dress. It won't be long before she finds out the truth but neither of us wants to tell her about it tonight. Fatigue has set in and it's not even seven o'clock yet, still light. I just want to crawl into bed.

She shows us to a double room, which is small and cosy with views of the woods from the back window. 'Breakfast is between seven thirty and ten,' she says, before leaving.

Tom is standing by the tea-making facilities, looking out of the window at the trees in the distance. 'I can't believe this,' he says, his back to me.

I stretch out on the bed – it's a beautiful four-poster with a quilted bedspread in inky tones. Normally this would be such a treat for us. We haven't had a holiday for ages – all our money over the last five months has been put aside for the extension – but it's tainted, overshadowed by the excavation back at the cottage. Every time I think of it I feel sick.

Snowy hops onto the bed next to me, laying his head on my lap and looking up at me with his soulful brown eyes. 'I can't believe we've been turfed out of our own house,' I say, as I stroke Snowy's head. Then I pull my cardigan around myself. It's turned chilly, or perhaps it's the shock.

Tom flicks the switch on the little plastic kettle, then comes to join us on the bed. The mattress is softer than ours at home. 'I know. But it will all be okay,' he says, with a return to his former optimism. 'We'll be able to resume our building work soon and everything will be back to normal.'

I snuggle into him, wishing I could believe him.

*   *   *

We resist the urge to walk past the cottage. Instead we spend the weekend either in the pub or on long walks through the village and woods.

'At least it gives me the weekend off decorating,' says Tom, on Saturday, taking my hand as we amble through the village square. He's done so much to the cottage already since we moved in: taking up the threadbare carpet on the stairs, painting the living room and our bedroom a dove grey, sanding the floorboards. Next he wants to strip the wallpaper in the little bedroom ready to decorate before the baby arrives, although he put off doing this until my twelve-week scan so as not to tempt Fate.

When we eventually return on Sunday after lunch, with our bags at our feet, like visitors in our own home, my heart sinks. There are police cars and vans still parked on our driveway. Another uniformed officer – a middle-aged guy this time – informs us that they should be done excavating by the end of the day, and we're allowed in the cottage but not the garden until they've finished. I wonder if they've searched inside. The thought makes me uneasy: I hate to think of the police rifling through our things. When I voice this to Tom he assures me that they would have said if they were going to do that.

Tom and I spend the rest of the afternoon hiding in the living room. 'What must the neighbours be thinking?' I say, standing at the window and sipping a decaf tea. I think of elderly Jack and Brenda next door. A hedge obscures their property from ours, but she's definitely the curtain-twitcher type, and when Clive put in the plans for the kitchen extension they opposed them.

A small crowd has gathered at the end of our driveway, only partly hidden by the police vehicles.

'I bet they're journalists,' says Tom, over my shoulder, his fingers clasping a mug. 'You might want to ring your dad and get some advice.'

My dad is the chief reporter on one of the national tabloids. I nod grimly. I feel as exposed as if someone has ripped the roof right off our house. 'This is a nightmare,' I mutter. For once Tom doesn't offer any assurance. Instead his face is grave, a muscle throbbing near his jawline as he stares out of the window, sipping his coffee in silence.

I ring Dad later to ask his advice. 'You don't fancy giving your old dad an exclusive,' he deadpans.

I laugh. 'I don't know anything! It might turn out to be hundreds of years old yet.'

'Well, if it's not I should warn you, as soon as the police confirm a crime and have identified the body, you'll be swamped by press.'

'Should we move out?' Although as I say this I have no idea where we'd actually go. We can't afford a hotel. I wish Dad lived closer. Or Mum, but she's even further away.

'No. No, don't do that. Just be prepared, that's all. And if you need anything – information or advice – let me know.' I can tell he's in the newsroom by the sound of phones ringing in the background and the general hubbub of conversation and activity.

'Will you be sending someone down here?'

'I expect we'll use a press agency for now. But if you're going to talk to the press, remember me, yeah? Seriously, Saff, if you're unsure about anything – whether it's the police or the reporters – then come to me first.'

'Thanks, Dad,' I say, feeling reassured. My dad has always had the ability to make me feel safe.

The next morning the police take down the tent and crime tape and Tom and I stare in horror at the huge hole left in the garden. It's four times bigger than it was when the builders left it. Tom asks his boss if he can work from home for a few days, and we spend them trying to avoid the smattering of journalists that still hover.

And then, on Wednesday – the day Tom returns to work – the police call.

'I'm afraid it's not good news,' says the male detective with a gruff voice, whose name I instantly forget.

I stiffen, waiting.

'Two bodies have been found.'

I nearly drop my phone. 'Two bodies?'

'I'm afraid so, yes. All the bones were recovered and forensics could determine that one was a male and the other a female. We could also work out the ages of the victims based on the bone formation and maturing. Both victims were between thirty and forty-five.'

I can't speak, nausea rising.

'Unfortunately,' he continues, 'the female victim died of blunt trauma to the head. We're still trying to ascertain how the man died. The decomposition of tissues makes this more difficult. With the female skeleton it was more obvious due to the fracture to the skull.'

I squeeze my eyes shut, trying not to imagine it.

'That's . . . that's awful.' I can barely take it in. 'Are . . . are you sure there aren't any more?' I suddenly have visions of the whole garden being dug up to reveal a mass grave and shudder at the thought. Other 'houses of horrors' as the press luridly describe them, come to mind – 25 Cromwell Street and White House Farm. Will our cottage become as infamous? Will we be stuck here for ever, nobody ever wanting to buy it? My heart starts to beat faster and I swallow, trying to concentrate on what the detective is saying.

'We had cadaver dogs at the site. We are confident there are no more bodies.'

'How . . . long have the bodies been there?'

'We can't be sure for definite, not yet. The soil in your garden is more alkaline based and the conditions, therefore, have preserved some of the clothing and shoes, but we think no earlier than around 1970, and by the decomposition, no later than 1990.'

Goosebumps ripple over my skin. Two people were murdered in my house. *In my idyllic cottage.* Everything suddenly takes on a dark, surreal quality.

'And, of course, we have to speak to everyone who occupied the house between 1970 and 1990,' he continues. 'I'm afraid, being the previous owner of the cottage, we will need to speak to Mrs Rose Grey.'

The room tilts.

Rose Grey is my grandmother.

3

May 2018

I CAN'T STOP THINKING ABOUT THE BODIES. IT'S ON MY mind when I take Snowy for his daily walks around the village, when I'm watching TV with Tom, when I'm working on a project in the tiny room with the 1970s flowered wallpaper at the front of the cottage that I use as an office.

It didn't take long for news to get around the village, and even though it's been more than ten days since the excavation, people are still speculating about it. They won't yet know the latest information, about how and when the victims died, but while I was in the corner shop earlier, I heard old Mrs McNulty gossiping about it to one of her elderly friends – a stooped woman wearing a headscarf and pushing a checked bag on wheels. 'I can't imagine the Turners being responsible,' she'd said. 'They'd been there years. Mrs Turner was very mousy.'

'Although,' Mrs McNulty lowered her voice, her beady eyes

flashing with excitement, 'wasn't there all that business a few years ago? With his nephew and the stolen goods?'

'Oh, yes, I remember that. Well, they did leave in a bit of a hurry,' said Headscarf Woman. 'When was it now? Two years ago? And I heard they left the cottage in a bit of a state.' She lowered her voice. 'Hoarders, apparently. Although they kept the garden nice. Mrs Turner liked to plant bulbs.'

'And now those youngsters have turned up.'

'I hear they've been given the cottage for *free*. Inheritance apparently.'

'It's all right for some.'

I could feel my cheeks burning. I put the tin of baked beans back on the shelf and left the shop before they noticed me.

Now I grab my cardigan from the back of the chair. It's cooler today, the sun struggling to poke through clouds, and I bend over Snowy's bed to kiss him on the top of his fluffy head. 'See you later, mister.'

I'm knocking off work early today, like I do every Thursday, to visit Gran. I feel a lurch of guilt when I think of how I ended up missing my visit to her last week because of the swarm of press outside our house. Yet today won't be like all the other Thursdays. Today, when I sit opposite my grandmother I'll be wondering what happened all those years ago. How did two people end up dead and buried in her garden?

My battered yellow Converse trainers crunch over the gravelled driveway as I dart to my Mini. I'm wearing denim dungarees with the bottoms turned up. They feel so much more comfortable now my tummy is expanding. I'm sixteen weeks pregnant and have a small bump. Although it doesn't look like I'm pregnant, more bloated. I've tied my dark curls back with a matching yellow scrunchie. My mum always turns her nose up at my collection of scrunchies. 'They're just so . . . *eighties*,' she says, rolling her eyes. 'I can't believe they've made a comeback.' I haven't seen her since Christmas and that hadn't gone very well, thanks to her rude boyfriend, Alberto. The weeks are flying by and I still haven't told her she's going to be a grandmother. Every time I think about telling her I imagine her disappointment.

As I get behind the wheel I notice a man standing in the lane, partially concealed by our front wall, staring up at the cottage. He's stocky, with a face like a bulldog, maybe mid to late fifties, wearing jeans and a waxed jacket. When he notices me he moves away. Was he taking photos of the cottage? He must be another journalist. Most of them have given up for the moment – until there's new information to be had. But every now and again another will pop up, like the weeds in my front garden. On Saturday, as we made our way down our driveway to take Snowy for a walk, a journalist sprang out in front of us, obscuring our path and taking a photo of us. Tom was furious, and swore at him as he scuttled back to his car.

I pull out of the driveway and continue slowly past him, making sure to give him enough room so he doesn't have to press himself against the hedge, but as I do I notice him shooting me such an intense look that it shocks me. From the rearview mirror I see him getting into a black sedan parked further down the hill, next to number eight.

Tom came home from work yesterday saying he'd spotted a piece about the bodies in the garden in a copy of the *Sun* that someone had left on the Tube. It had a sensationalist heading that played on the skeletons at Skelton Place, accompanied by the photo the journalist took of us on Saturday, with startled looks on our faces. 'Oh, God, Tom,' I'd said, my face flushed with fear. 'They're going to say we're Wiltshire's answer to Fred and Rosemary West!'

He'd laughed properly then. 'No, they won't. It happened at least thirty years ago. We weren't even born.'

But my gran was.

I push the thought of the man from my mind as I continue down the hill, passing the Stag and Pheasant at the bottom. Instead I think again about how peaceful Beggars Nook is with its beautiful old Cotswold-stone buildings. I drive through the village square, taking in the market cross, the pretty church, the corner shop, a café and the one boutique selling trinkets, cards and slouchy expensive clothes. All walkable from the cottage and in a dip, surrounded by the woods and the thick oak trees that stretch up to the sky. It gives the impression that the village is hidden from the rest of the world. I cross the bridge and continue down the long, winding lane, pretty stone houses either side, until I get to the farm at the end. So different from built-up Croydon. So safe. Or so I'd thought. Now I'm not so sure.

The murders must have happened before Gran bought the cottage back in the 1970s. I know she went on to rent it out for decades after she moved to Bristol – we found out this detail only recently after she went into a care home. Mum and I had been a little surprised. As far as we'd been aware Gran had only ever owned one property: her red-brick terrace in the Bishopston area of Bristol where Mum grew up and where I spent every summer. Gran, who, before the dementia took over, loved to bake and tend her plants, was calm and practical, never raising her voice. Not like Mum who has a short fuse and no filter, although she's mellowed a bit now. Those summers with Gran, in her Bristol house with the large garden and adjoining land at the end, were my sanctuary, a break from my mum and the drama that always seemed to surround her.

I'd loved Gran's fat black Labrador with the grey whiskers, Bruce (Mum never wanted us to get a pet. Too smelly, she said but Gran's house never smelt), and the old-fashioned, comfy sofas with white cotton slips on the arms that Gran would wash and starch every week. The butterscotch sweets she had in a tin at the top of the cupboard and the garden with the wired fence that separated it from her neighbours. The warm, musty smell of the greenhouse and the tomato plants inside. It was comforting to see Gran in the greenhouse tending those plants, talking to them softly to encourage them to grow. I love my mum dearly, but she was – and still is – so high energy, so effusive and demonstrative, with her colourful clothes and over-the-top personality, that she sometimes makes me feel exhausted. I've always felt more of an affinity with Gran, both of us loving nature and the outdoors, slightly reclusive, preferring our own company to crowds of people.

Gran made me feel normal when I admitted I'd rather stay in and watch *EastEnders* than go out and play with the other kids in the street and that it was okay not to have to be out there and loud all the time. My mother was always telling me when I was a kid that I was 'too quiet' and 'too shy' and asking, 'Why don't you go and mix with the other girls in your year instead of just sticking with one friend?' But Mum is a social butterfly, fluttering from one group of friends to another with an ease I have always envied, even if I don't want it for myself. As a result I felt awkward and uninteresting growing up, never knowing what to say. Until I met Tom at university. Tom made me feel I could be myself and I realized that, with him, I was capable of being witty and fun.

The traffic builds up as I head towards Bristol. The care home Gran lives in is off a dual carriageway in a town called Filton.

It was nearly a year ago when I started to realize something was very wrong with her. It started off innocuously enough.

Gran was always a little forgetful, forever saying, "Ere, have you seen my bag?' or 'Where did I put my glasses?' in the Cockney accent she'd never lost despite leaving London in her twenties. She was always so independent and practical. Even up until last year she was strong and able-bodied enough to get on a train to visit me in Croydon, following a map – she had an old-fashioned mobile phone and an *A-Z* that was dog-eared and always in her handbag – her little Westie, Snowy, in tow. She refused to let me or Tom pick her up at the station despite us constantly offering.

The first sign was the two birthday cards she sent me, one a few days after the other, as though she'd forgotten about sending the first. Then, when she came to stay with us a few months later she'd seemed more forgetful. Snowy's name slipped easily from her mind, and she forgot to walk or feed him until I had to remind her or did it myself. And then, after she'd been staying with us a few days, she'd turned to me and Tom one evening while we were watching TV and said, "Ere, where have the other couple gone?' It had sent a shiver of fear down my spine. Because there was no other couple. Gran had been sitting with us all evening. And it broke my heart to realize that, at times, Gran had no idea who Tom or I was, her memory fading in and out like the radio with a bad signal.

On that visit it was obvious that Gran was finding it hard looking after Snowy so when I offered to keep him with me she agreed. I'd cried behind my sunglasses as I watched Gran get on the train without her beloved dog, pulling her wheelie suitcase, and I didn't stop worrying until she rang later to say she was home safely.

But just three days afterwards Gran called me in a panic to say she'd lost the dog and I had to remind her gently that Snowy was living with me and Tom now.

The final thing that really did it, that made me ring Mum and tell her everything, was when one of Gran's neighbours, Esme, contacted me.

'It's your gran, lovely,' she'd said. 'She left a pan on to boil dry. It was lucky I'd popped over – she could have burnt the house down.'

When I confessed my concerns to Mum, she flew back from Spain and whisked Gran off to the doctor. After that things happened quickly – but Mum always got things done, she was just that kind of decisive person – and a private nursing facility was found for Gran, not far from where she'd lived in the Bristol house with the garden that I will always think of as home.

I pull into the spacious car park outside the front of the huge grey Gothic-looking building called Elms Brook, which makes it sound more like a retreat than a care home. Although Mum said it used to be an asylum with bars at the window. But it was nice, Elms Brook. It was mid-range price wise, although Gran still had to sell the house to pay for it. I swallow a lump in my throat when I remember how I'd felt packing up her things and clearing out her home.

It was in one of my grandmother's more lucid moments, last November, when she told me and Mum about the cottage. This was the first time we even knew of its existence.

'It's in your name, Lorna,' Gran had whispered, leaning forwards in her high-backed chair and holding on to Mum's hand. 'I transferred the deeds ten years ago.' And I had marvelled at Gran's astuteness. By putting the cottage in my mum's name it wouldn't have to be sold to pay for Gran's care.

Afterwards, as Mum and I stood outside the care home saying goodbye, Mum, shivering in her bright orange coat, had turned to me and said, 'I always knew my mother was a wily thing, squirreling her money away. She would have bought that cottage as an investment.' She blew on her hands. 'Anyway, I don't want it. It's yours, if you'd like it. I know you hate living in a city.' And it had shocked me because, for once, I felt my mother really understood me.

'But you haven't even seen it,' I'd protested.

'What do I want with a cottage in the middle of nowhere?' And I could see her point. A cottage in the countryside would be too mundane for Mum. No, she needed sunshine and san-gria and exotic men who weren't much older than me.

Mum had flown back to San Sebastián without even visiting the cottage. She couldn't have been less interested in it. Which helped ease my guilt for accepting the offer. A free house. No mortgage. It meant the sort of financial freedom Tom and I had never expected in a million years, especially not in our mid-twenties. It meant I could give up my job in Croydon and go freelance, surrounded by idyllic countryside. A dream come true.

But now I revisit that conversation. Ten years ago Gran had transferred the deeds into my mother's name. Why? Was it purely for financial reasons? To avoid inheritance tax? Or be-cause she knew a murder had taken place?

But, no, that's ridiculous. There's no way Gran would have any knowledge of this. I know it like I know I love black coffee and peanut-butter sandwiches and the velvety patches of fur on Snowy's ears and the smell of cut grass.

I take a deep breath and hold on to the steering wheel as though to steady myself. I can never predict when I visit which Gran I'll get. Sometimes she'll recognize me, at others she acts like I'm one of the staff, and each time it's like losing her all over again.

As I get out of the car I notice a black sedan slowing down on the road so that it idles past me. I can't be sure but it looks like the same car that was parked near the cottage earlier. The driver's face is turned towards me as it coasts past. It's a man but I can't make out his features. Is it the same guy as earlier? Is he going to pull into the car park too? Then the car speeds up and drives off down the road. I stand for a moment staring after it, wondering if I'm worrying about nothing, or if this is something to be concerned about.

4

GRAN IS SITTING IN THE DAY ROOM BY THE BAY WINDOW that overlooks the manicured grounds, a coffee table in front of her and an empty chair opposite. The sun has come out and it streams through the net curtains, highlighting dust motes that dance around her head, like little orbs. My heart contracts with such love that my eyes smart. Seeing her here makes me ache with longing to go back in time to how it used to be: Gran bustling around her little kitchen making endless cups of tea the colour of treacle, or in the greenhouse showing my teenage self how to plant radishes.

Gran's head is bent. She's lost the plumpness to her face, the skin now hanging loose around her jowls, her cheekbones prominent. Her snow-white hair – it once used to be a beautiful coppery red, from a bottle Gran always claimed – is fluffy, the texture of cotton wool. She's pushing the pieces of a jigsaw around the table and, for a moment, it takes me back to when I was a kid and we'd sit together in companionable silence in the evenings, as the sun went down, trying to work out the best way to construct the puzzle.

I stand in the doorway for a few minutes, just watching. The room is too warm and smells musty, like roast dinners and over-boiled veg. The carpet is the kind you'd find in an old-fashioned seaside guesthouse, all red and gold swirls.

'Rose is having a good day,' says a voice from behind me. It's Millie, one of the carers, and my favourite. Millie is a few years younger than me with the kindest face and widest smile I've ever seen. She has short spiky black hair and piercings half-way up both ears.

'Oh, I'm so pleased. I've some news for her.'

Millie raises an eyebrow. 'Ooh. Good, I hope?'

I touch my stomach self-consciously and nod. I don't want to think of the other thing. The bad news. The bodies.

Millie squeezes my shoulder encouragingly, then moves on to help an elderly man, who's trying to get out of his chair. I make my way to the end of the room, weaving past some of the other residents clustered around the television and the old man reading a newspaper upside down in the corner, until I reach Gran.

She looks up as I approach and, for a moment, confusion flits across her features and I have to swallow my disappointment. She doesn't recognize me. Today is not a good day after all.

I slide into the chair opposite. It has such a high back that I feel like I'm sitting on a throne. 'Hi, Granny. It's me, Saffy.'

Gran doesn't speak for a few seconds, continuing to move around the pieces of the jigsaw even though she hasn't started making the picture. The box is propped up at the end of the table. A black Labrador puppy on the front surrounded by flowers. 'Let's find the edges first,' she always used to say, her weathered hands, the result of many hours' gardening, nimbly seeking out the right pieces. But now there is no method, Gran instead just moving the pieces around aimlessly, her fingers gnarled and wrinkly.

'Saffy. Saffy . . .' she mumbles, not looking at me. And then her head shoots up and her eyes sparkle with recognition. 'Saffy! It's you. You've come to see me. Where have you been?' Her whole face lights up and I reach out and touch her frail hand. She's seventy-five but since she was admitted into the home she's looked much older.

I know I haven't got long before Gran's mind slips back in time. It never ceases to amaze me how much she remembers about the past but can't recall something as recent as what she had for breakfast.

'I'm pregnant, Granny. I'm going to have a baby,' I say, unable to keep the joy and fear out of my voice.

'A baby. A baby. So wonderful. Such a gift.' She clutches my hands, a little too tightly. 'You lucky girl. Is . . .' Her eyes cloud and I can tell she's having trouble assessing her memories. 'Is Tim happy?'

'Tom. And, yes, he's over the moon.' Gran had doted on Tom, before the dementia diagnosis. She couldn't do enough for him whenever she saw him. She used to send him little care packages: a homemade cake, some sloe gin she'd brewed herself, rhubarb she'd grown in the garden because she knew he loved it and I didn't. 'You need to feed him up,' she used to tell me. It was a generation thing, I would remind myself. To keep your man happy. Not that I remembered Gran ever having a man. My granddad died before Mum was even born.

Gran's face darkens. 'Victor wasn't happy. Oh, no, he wasn't happy at all.'

Victor? I'd never heard her mention a Victor before. She

told me my granddad had been called William, not that she ever spoke about him. Even Mum didn't know much. But I don't want to interrupt Gran's flow by asking questions so I stay silent.

'He wanted to hurt the baby,' she says, her face crumpling.

'Well, Tom would never do anything to hurt the baby. Tom is a nice man. You love Tom, remember?'

Her expression changes again. 'Oh, yes. Tom is lovely. Tom likes his fried breakfasts.'

I smile. Gran always made Tom a full English every time we stayed. 'That's right.'

How am I going to bring up the subject of the remains of two dead people in the garden? Should I even bring it up? Maybe it's best to leave it for now. But then I think of the police who will need to interview her at some point knowing she owned the cottage for so many years, even if she did have tenants. If I've already told her about it, it will be less of a shock when the police speak to her.

'And . . . we love living in Skelton Place,' I begin tentatively.

Her face clouds over. 'Skelton Place?'

'The cottage, Gran. Beggars Nook?'

'You're living in the cottage at Skelton Place?'

'Yes. Mum wanted to stay in Spain. You know what she's like. She loves the sun. So Tom and I are living there. And it's so generous of you . . .' I've told her all this before, of course.

Gran starts moving the pieces of the puzzle around aimlessly again and I'm afraid I've lost her. I have to say something now, quickly, before she retreats back into herself.

'And the weird thing is . . . we started digging up the garden to build an extension and we found two bodies . . .'

Gran's head shoots up. 'Bodies?'

'Yes, Gran. Buried in the garden.'

'Dead bodies?'

'Um . . . Yes.' Is there any other kind?

'At Skelton Place?'

I nod encouragingly. 'A woman and a man.'

Gran stares at me for such a long time that I'm afraid she's gone into some sort of catatonic state. But then her eyes mist over as though she's remembering. She suddenly grabs hold of my hands again, disrupting the pieces of the jigsaw puzzle so that some of them fall to the floor. 'Is it Sheila?' she whispers.

Sheila? 'Who's Sheila, Gran?'

Gran snatches her hands away, a film of confusion over her eyes, like cataracts. She looks like a frightened child as she shrinks further into her seat. 'Such a wicked little girl. That's what they all said. A wicked little girl.'

'Who? Who's a wicked little girl?'

'That's what they all said.'

I need to change the subject. Gran is getting agitated. I lean over and pick up the pieces of jigsaw from the carpet.

'The gardens here are lovely,' I say, when I straighten up, looking past Gran and out of the window. 'Are you still able to get out there every day?' Gran's mind might be going but there is nothing wrong with her physically.

But Gran is still mumbling about Sheila and a wicked little girl.

I reach across the table and take Gran's gnarled hand tightly between mine. 'Gran. Who is Sheila?'

Gran stops her mumbling and looks directly at me, her eyes focusing. 'I don't . . . know . . .'

'The police will want to talk to you at some point, but only because you owned the cottage and . . .'

A flash of panic flits across Gran's face. 'The police?' She looks wildly about her as though expecting them to be behind her.

'It's okay. They'll only want to ask you a few questions. Nothing to worry about. It will only be a procedure. Something to tick off their list.'

'Is it Lorna? Is Lorna dead?'

I swallow my guilt. 'No, Gran. Mum is in Spain. Remember?'

'Wicked little girl.'

I release Gran's hand gently and sit back in my chair. Gran is mumbling to herself again. I'm not going to get anything more from her today. I should never have mentioned the bodies. It was unfair. Of course she's not going to know anything about them. Why would she? Instead I reach over and help Gran with the jigsaw in companionable silence, just like we used to do when I was a kid. Edges first.

5

Theo

THEO PULLS UP ONTO THE DRIVEWAY, PARKING HIS OLD Volvo next to his father's black Mercedes, which looks like a hearse. The old, rambling house looms over him like something from a horror film, eclipsing the sun and causing him to shiver. He hates the place. Always has done. His friends thought it was impressive when they visited, which was rarely – he tried to keep them away as much as possible – but the depressing grey stone and the ugly gargoyles that peer down from the roof as if they're about to swoop still give him the creeps. The house is much too big for an elderly man living by himself. Theo doesn't understand why his dad refuses to sell it. He doubts he holds on to it for sentimental reasons. A status symbol, he imagines. Theo has never felt the need to show off about what he's got. Not that he's got much in the material sense, but that's not how he measures his self-worth anyway. Another thing his dad doesn't understand.

He lets himself into the cavernous hallway with the wood panelling and the winding staircase that he has hated with a passion since his mother's death, and the deer heads on the wall. Those heads gave him nightmares as a kid. He breathes in the familiar smell of woodsmoke and floor polish. His dad has a housekeeper, Mavis, who comes in every few days to do the cleaning and his washing but she's not due in until tomorrow.

'Dad! It's Theo,' he calls. There's no answer so he darts upstairs to the study, which is at the front of the house, the rubber soles of his trainers squeaking against the polished floor. His father spends a lot of time in his study, doing what, Theo can only imagine. He's been retired for years.

He opens the study door and he can tell instantly his dad is in one of his moods, anger seeping off him. His large face with the familiar flat nose that Theo has inherited is redder than usual. Even the bald spot on the top of his head is pink, poking through the remains of his wispy white hair.

When he acts like this Theo thinks his dad is a prick. He actually thinks his dad is a prick most of the time even when he's not behaving like a spoilt child rather than the seventy-six-year-old retired consultant that he really is. He wonders what's set him off now. It doesn't take much. Mavis has probably put one of his golfing trophies back in the wrong place. Theo is grateful he doesn't have to live with him any more.

Theo has only popped over to check on him. Like he does every week. Because even though his dad hasn't been the best father, or the best husband, he feels a sense of duty. And he knows it's what his mum would have wanted. Theo is the only family his dad has left. And sometimes, when his dad forgets to act like a total dickhead, in his more vulnerable moments, like when they sit side by side watching a film together on the sofa and he falls asleep, his face looking peaceful and old with his chin resting on his chest, he feels a rush of fondness towards him. And then his dad will wake up and turn back into his grumpy, demanding self and the sympathy Theo had been feeling, just moments before, evaporates.

Despite all this Theo tries to cut his dad some slack. He understands that losing his wife – Theo's mum – fourteen years ago was devastating. Caroline Carmichael had been only forty-five when she died, and so vibrant, so caring. Her loss has left a gaping hole in their lives. Not that his father would admit to any feelings. Showing vulnerability is a weakness, according to him. He prefers to hide his emotions behind his gruff exterior. Despite this, Theo has always felt a grudging respect for him. He's a brilliant man. Exceptionally clever and hugely talented in his field. Even now, after retiring, he still writes papers for medical publications.

Theo clears his throat. His dad is so busy slamming drawers and opening and shutting cabinet doors that he doesn't hear him at first. Theo has to repeat the action several times before his dad looks up.

'What do you want?'

Charming, thinks Theo. He's had a bastard of a day, helping his brother-in-law, Simon, move house and he's on a late shift at the restaurant tonight. It's not a fancy enough restaurant to impress his dad, even if it is in one of Harrogate's premier streets, but, still, he enjoys working there as head chef. He feels grubby after hauling the furniture from the van and needs a shower before starting work at 6 p.m.

'Just thought I'd look in, make sure you're eating properly. I've made a couple of lasagnes for you to freeze.' He holds up the carrier bag to illustrate his point.

His dad grunts in response before turning his back on Theo and continues rifling through a drawer.

Theo runs a hand across his chin. God, he needs a shave. Jen hates it when he has stubble, says it scratches her face when he kisses her. He steps further into the room. 'Can I help?'

'No.'

'Okay. Right. Well, I'll dump these in the freezer and then I'll be off. I'm working tonight.'

His dad doesn't say anything, his body a question mark as he bends over a drawer. Theo can see the outline of his shoulder blades through his polo shirt. He always dresses smartly – that's one thing Theo can be grateful for. He showers every day, splashes on the same Prada aftershave he's used for years and dresses in his favourite uniform of chinos and a smart Ralph Lauren top with a V-neck cable-knit jumper if it's cold. If his father ever let himself go he would begin to worry.

'Make sure you eat the lasagne. Keep your strength up.'

'You fuss too much. Like your mother used to.'

He has an image of his lovely mum, running herself ragged in a fruitless attempt at keeping his dad happy. There had been an eighteen-year age difference between his parents. Friends at school had thought his dad was his grandfather. It used to embarrass Theo, although he probably wouldn't have minded if his dad had acted like a kindly grandfather. Nevertheless his friends had been impressed when his dad occasionally picked him up from school in his expensive car.

Just as he's about to leave the room his dad stands up, brushing down his chinos. He's tall, even taller than Theo, with the same long limbs and rangy physique. Theo has to concede his dad is still handsome and fit for his age, from regularly playing golf at the club. 'I'm going to look downstairs,' he says, brushing past Theo. He doesn't say what he's looking for. 'Are you staying for a cup of tea?'

Fuck. Now Theo is going to feel obliged. 'A quick one. I've got to work tonight.'

'Yes, you've said.'

His father had wanted him to go to medical school, follow in the family size-eleven footsteps. He thinks Theo's job as a chef is little more than a hobby. It still riles Theo when he thinks about it so he tries not to.

'I'll go and put the kettle on,' promises Theo, but his father doesn't reply, slamming out of the door, the soles of his brogues clipping on the lacquered parquet.

Just as Theo is about to leave the room something catches his eye on his dad's desk. It's immaculate, as everything in the study always is, even after all the rummaging, but left on the padded dark green leather insert is a newspaper clipping. Theo wonders if it's anything to do with his mother. His dad has obsessively kept everything that ever mentioned her name while simultaneously never wanting to talk about her death. He goes to it and picks it up, confused when he sees it isn't about his mother at all. It's dated last week and is a small article, only a few paragraphs long accompanied by a photograph, about a young couple from a Cotswold village in Wiltshire who found two bodies in their back garden. SKELETON PLACE screams the headline. The names of the couple are underlined in red as well as another – Rose Grey. Underneath the article someone has written, *Find Her.*

6

Lorna

IT'S RAINING HEAVILY AND LORNA CURSES UNDER HER breath as her umbrella spoke suddenly springs free of the fabric so that it concertinas over her head, no longer providing adequate cover for her freshly cut hair. And now her hair, which took the stylist – the strapping Marco – for ever to blow-dry into a sleek finish, will fluff out to resemble the shape of a bell. She'd wanted to look nice for Alberto, make an effort for their date tonight. After nearly two years together she fears things have become stale between them; she works during the day while he's out late supervising the bar he owns. She can just imagine him flirting with the young women, pretending he's Tom Cruise from *Cocktail*. Why, oh, why does she always choose the wrong men? Too young. Too handsome. Too egotistical. She'll be forty-one in three months' time. She should know better. But, no, she won't think negatively. That's not her style. And, anyway, he's promised to take the night off from the bar so they can go dancing. Maybe they can get some of their fire back.

She's only wearing a light linen blazer over the boring hotel uniform (off-white blouse and dark green knee-length skirt, although she's paired it with a bubblegum pink scarf) as it was hot when she left her apartment this morning. Her wedges are rubbing her heels. By the time she makes the ten-minute walk back to the apartment she shares with Alberto she'll be drenched. But she keeps up her stride across the busy plaza, trying to ignore the scraping of flesh on her heel. She dares not stop or someone will careen into the back of her. Not that she's complaining. She loves the hustle and bustle of San Sebastián. The sea is rough today: angry white waves roll towards the shore and some fool is surfing in the froth. Despite the bad weather a group of holidaymakers are perched on the beach, determined not to let the showers put them off.

It's been a hard day at work. The hotel where she's a receptionist has started to get busy as it always does at this time of year. They've had quite a few families from the UK this week, some of whom have complained about the weather, not expecting to leave an early-May heatwave in England for spring showers in Spain. She'd pointed them in the direction of the indoor aquarium. She understood their disappointment – they'd come on holiday for the sun and the beach and the outside tapas restaurants. She'd felt the same when she first moved here, surprised that it does indeed rain in Spain. But she loves it here, loves their little apartment with its own courtyard in a beautiful old building off a cobbled street in the Old Town. And the food. She could eat paella and prawns and squid, not to mention the *pintxos*, every day.

She touches the ends of her wet hair. All afternoon, while sitting behind her desk watching the hotel residents come into the lobby, drenched and disappointed, she'd been looking forward to getting her hair done, and now it's ruined.

After another five minutes' walk through a maze of crowded streets and tall stone-coloured buildings with their black wrought-iron balconies rearing up at either side of her, she's reached her apartment. She lets herself through the enormous front door into the lobby. She continues down the long, thin hallway, passing the glass lift that goes up to the second floor, and enters through another door at the end of the corridor. It leads across an open-air courtyard to two maisonettes perpendicular to each other: hers and Mari's. You'd never know from looking at the front of her building that all this was hidden behind.

Mari, a petite woman in her late fifties with waist-length dark hair, is standing at her threshold banging dust from a rug. '*Buenas noches*,' she calls, as Lorna walks carefully across the courtyard so as not to slip on the rain-slicked terracotta tiles. Lorna smiles and waves back, aware that she must look like a drowned rat. She lets herself into her own front door. It leads straight into the dining-living area, with wooden stairs that go up to a mezzanine level where the en-suite bedroom is. The kitchen and cloakroom are at the rear of the apartment, looking out onto the backs of buildings where there is also a concrete basketball court covered with graffiti. Sometimes she can hear the local kids playing out there, or listening to music late at night. It's comforting, makes her feel she's not alone while Alberto is working.

She peels off her wet blazer and kicks off her shoes, bending over to examine her heel where a blister has formed. She pads into the galley kitchen to put the kettle on. She's tempted by the bottle of white wine she has in the fridge but decides against it. Later she can let her hair down in a way she hasn't for ages. She leans against the counter while she waits for the kettle to boil and checks her watch. It's nearly six. She should have enough time to straighten her hair before Alberto gets home. He promised to be back by seven.

She notices two wine glasses in the sink. She was sure she washed up before she went to work this morning. She never leaves a mess – the kitchen's too small for that. It would make her feel stressed to see it cluttered. She'd left Alberto in bed, one tanned arm flung across his face this morning. He wasn't due at the bar until 4 p.m., he'd said. So what had he been doing all day and, more importantly, with whom? She picks up the wine glasses and examines them for lipstick marks. There is nothing and she replaces them in the sink. She's being ridiculous, she decides. This is where madness lies. She's not normally like this. She's usually trusting. Too trusting as it turns out – her last boyfriend, Sven, had left her for someone else after eighteen months together. She'd been living in Amsterdam then, had left England when Saffy met Tom. After she broke up with Sven she didn't want to stay, and had decided to find a place in Spain instead. Within months she'd met and fallen in love with Alberto. Tall, ripped, tanned Alberto, six years her junior. She'd thought she'd feel younger but it has the opposite effect.

Her mobile vibrates on the worktop and she leans across to get it. Saffy's name flashes up on screen and Lorna feels a lurch of happiness, followed by a quick stab of guilt. She hasn't seen her daughter since Christmas and she misses her.

'Hi, honey,' she says into the phone.

'Mum.' Saffy sounds hesitant and straight away Lorna's antennae twitch. She stands up, picturing her daughter's beautiful and slightly anxious face.

'Is everything okay?'

'Yes . . . well, no. Something odd has happened.'

No small talk. She loves that about her daughter. She always gets straight to the point.

'O-kaay.' Lorna braces herself for the many catastrophes she tries not to worry about befalling her only child while she's living so far away. Her stomach tenses.

The line crackles and Lorna moves into the living room as Saffy speaks. Did she just say something about dead bodies?

'. . . ten days ago, in the garden, while the builders were digging . . .' She sounds young.

Lorna sinks into her lime-green armchair, her mobile still pinned to her ear, her stomach dropping. 'What?' Her mouth falls open as her daughter fills her in. And why is she only hearing about this now? Saffy said this happened ten days ago.

'The police are going to want to speak to Gran, although I haven't heard anything about it yet,' says Saffy. 'Do you know the exact date she bought the cottage? I know Gran told us it was sometime in the 1970s, but she might have got it wrong.'

Lorna tucks her legs underneath her. The rain has soaked through to her blouse and she feels cold and damp. 'I have no idea. I didn't even know about Skelton Place until she told us about it last year. As far as I know she never lived there herself.'

'You've got the deeds, haven't you? It should say on there when Gran bought it.'

Lorna frowns. 'I have them somewhere, yes. I'll dig them out. But the police might already have this information.'

'Even so, I'd like to know,' says Saffy. 'And the list of tenants.'

'You might be better off speaking to her solicitor . . . I'll see if I have their details.'

Saffy shouldn't have to be dealing with this alone. Lorna knows how close she is to her gran. They share a bond that Lorna never had with her mother. She loves her, of course, but they've always been so different. Her mum kept herself to herself, never wanting to socialize or get involved, and as a result Lorna found herself rebelling at a young age. Drinking and partying at fourteen, pregnant at fifteen. Her mum had called her a wild child, resignedly, sadly. Saffy was the greatest gift Lorna could have bestowed upon her to make up for it. A quiet, studious daughter, who preferred staying in on a Saturday night to going out partying. It had warmed her heart to see how much they loved each other. And it had broken it, mostly for Saffy, when her mother was diagnosed with Alzheimer's.

'I'll come to England,' Lorna says suddenly. 'Can I stay with you at the cottage? I'd love to see it.'

'Coming over? But . . . you don't have to. There's no need.'

Lorna swallows her disappointment. 'I want to see you. I miss you. And I haven't seen Mum for a while either. And I can help you sort things out.'

'Mum . . . I don't think it's as easy as that.'

'I know. But I'd like to be there. Especially if the police are sniffing around, asking questions and disrupting you. I'm happy to stay in a hotel . . .'

'No, it's not that. Of course you can stay here. We have a futon.' A pause. 'Will you be bringing Alberto?'

Lorna thinks about the two wine glasses in the sink and leans back against the chair's soft cushions. 'No. We could do with some time apart, to be honest.'

'Oh, Mum.'

'It's okay. Things are fine. We're off out tonight. But he's busy, with the bar . . .' She lets her words hang in the air. Her daughter is smart and more sensible than she ever was at that age. She won't be fooled. When had their roles reversed? It should be Saffy ringing her about boyfriend troubles. Instead she's been with Tom for four years when Lorna can barely keep a relationship with a man for four minutes.

'What are you up to tonight?'

Her daughter laughs totally unselfconsciously. 'The usual. Staying in with a takeaway and watching Netflix.'

Lorna smiles into the phone. She suddenly longs to be there. With her daughter, eating fish and chips off plates on their laps and watching a box set. 'I'll fly home Saturday morning. Is that okay?'

'I'll pick you up at Bristol airport. Just text me when you know times.'

They say goodbye and Lorna climbs the wooden stairs to her bedroom to change into a slinky red dress that she knows is Alberto's favourite. He calls it her Jessica Rabbit dress because it accentuates her bust. As she tries to fix the damage to her hair she mulls over the conversation with her daughter. Two bodies buried in the garden. A man and a woman. A memory, hazy and warped, flits through her mind – a flash of a garden, darkness punctuated by fireworks exploding into the night sky – but before she can grasp hold of it, it floats away, like the seeds of a dandelion on the breeze, out of reach.

7

Saffy

I SPOT MUM STRAIGHT AWAY. SHE'S STRIDING THROUGH Arrivals at Bristol airport in an unnecessarily large floppy straw hat and pink cropped jeans that show off all her curves. She has a wristful of bangles and huge dangly earrings that catch the light when she moves. She looks like a chandelier. Men stare at my mother. It used to embarrass me when I was younger: Mum's exuberance, her naturally flirty nature and cleavage that was always on display. Plus she was so much younger than the other mums at the school gates. But not now. The two of us living in different countries has made me realize how much I miss her. I wonder if it's because I'm about to become a mother myself. I'm not sure how Mum will feel about being a gran at forty-one. Will it make her feel old? I swallow my worries. I can't be thinking about that now. I've got too much else on my mind.

Like the phone call yesterday evening from the detective.

When Mum spots me, a wide smile lights up her whole face and she click-clacks towards me in her heeled sandals, pulling a leopard-print suitcase behind her.

'Honey,' she cries, wrapping me into a hug. She smells familiar, of Tom Ford perfume and coconut sun cream. 'It's so lovely to see you.'

'You too. Looking well, Mum.'

Mum holds me at arms' length to assess me. 'So do you,' she says, and I have to laugh to myself at the surprise in her voice. 'You look like you've filled out a bit. It suits you. You know I think you're too skinny.' And then she looks around. 'Where's Tom?'

'He's waiting by the car with Snowy.'

She links arms with me. 'It'll be lovely to see him. Now, tell me about these skeletons. It all sounds so unbelievable, doesn't it?'

I open my mouth to speak but Mum continues, 'I mean, as long as the police don't go charging in there upsetting your gran with lots of questions. Let me know the name of the police officer you're dealing with and I'll find out exactly what they're planning to do. I'll . . .'

I can feel a headache coming on. I love her to bits, but my God she never stops talking.

I let her natter on as we walk to the car. Tom is leaning against the Mini, a bemused smile on his face that he always seems to adopt whenever Mum is around. Snowy is sniffing the ground by his feet.

'Tom!' Mum exclaims, running over to him and enveloping him, her jangle of bracelets almost catching his ear. He glances over her shoulder at me with raised eyebrows and I stifle a laugh.

'Lovely to see you. Good flight?' he says, removing himself from her embrace.

She waves a hand dismissively. 'Cramped. I was squashed between two very large people but,' she shrugs, 'I'm here now. And I have to say the weather is nicer than it is in San Sebastián at the moment.'

I watch as Mum climbs inelegantly into the back seat while Tom takes her suitcase and puts it into the boot. We've said, with the baby coming, we should really change the car to a four-door. But with the extension, money is tight.

'I'm excited about seeing the cottage,' Mum says, sitting forward and holding on to the back of Tom's seat as I drive out of the car park. 'After I spoke to you on the phone I found the deeds and gave the solicitor a quick ring . . .'

Of course she did. I bet Mum was on to it the minute I ended our call. But I'm grateful I didn't have to do it.

'Apparently your gran bought the cottage back in March 1977 and she lived there until she rented it out in spring 1981. Then she bought the house in Bristol.' She says all this without pausing for breath.

'So you would have lived in the cottage for a bit?' I ask, surprised. 'Can you remember it?'

'Hmm . . . No, not really. I would have been three when we left. But maybe seeing it again will jog my memory.'

'Well, it's a bit old-fashioned inside,' I explain. 'Especially the kitchen, although Tom's making excellent progress on the rest.' I flash Tom a smile. 'Unfortunately the spare room still has bright yellow walls.'

Mum laughs. 'That will suit me down to the ground. So tell me more about your gran.'

I glance at Mum in the rearview mirror. She's taken her hat off and her dark brown eyes are bright with excitement, but there's something else too, a pain that she's trying to hide. I wonder what's really going on with her and Alberto. I always get the sense that my mother is running away.

I open my mouth to speak, hoping I'm not interrupted this time. 'I had a call from a detective last night. A DS Matthew Barnes. He sounded nice enough but he said he's spoken to the manager of the care home, Joy. She advised the police that it would be better for Gran to be interviewed at Elm Brook, a place where she feels safe. And that either you or I should be there too. They deem that she's able enough mentally to be interviewed because she has some lucid moments and seems to remember a lot from the past so it might be helpful.'

'I'll come too,' she insists.

'Okay, great. Um . . . how long are you planning on staying? What about work?'

Mum makes a *phut* noise through her mouth. 'I've taken a week off. I think this would be classed as extenuating circumstances, don't you?'

'I . . . well, yes . . . but it's only a formality. They have to speak to everyone who occupied the property during those twenty years.'

'I know. But it would be lovely to spend some time with you, honey. I haven't seen you properly since Christmas.'

And what a nightmare that was, I think. And to be fair it wasn't Mum's fault. It was more that moron she calls a boyfriend, who was rude, dismissive and acted like he'd rather be anywhere else, preferably on a beach in Spain, than spending the day in our tiny flat in Croydon. And in the past when I've spent time with Mum she always gives me the impression she, can't wait to go back to her hectic life.

Out of the corner of my eye Tom is staring straight ahead with a keep-me-out-of-it expression on his face.

I turn onto the Long Ashton bypass. There's nothing I can say. And it's not like I don't want to spend time with Mum, but at the moment I just don't have the energy for her . . . well, *energy*. She never says it, she doesn't have to, but I know she disapproves that I've settled down so early. When Tom and I moved in together a few years ago she tried to talk me out of it.

And when I told her we were saving for a deposit to buy a house she warned me about 'tying myself' to a mortgage 'too young'. It's obvious that having me at sixteen had ruined her teenage years. Something she certainly seems to be making up for now, judging by her Facebook photos.

'You can stay as long as you want,' I say, trying to ignore the dragging feeling in the pit of my stomach.

Forty minutes later we've arrived in Beggars Nook.

Mum draws breath for long enough to gaze out of the window at the Cotswold-stone buildings. 'What a stunning place. Strange name. Kind of eerie. I dunno, though, it's familiar but that could be because it reminds me of those pretty villages in *Agatha Raisin*. How far away is the nearest town?'

I mentally roll my eyes. Trust her. She's probably already planning a day out shopping. This village will be too remote for her. 'Chippenham, seven or eight miles away.'

'Eight miles. Wow.' She glances around with a slightly panicked look in her eyes, like a pony that's on the verge of bolting.

We head through the centre of the village, and as we pass the main square she gasps. 'What's that?' she says, pointing to a cube-shaped stone construction with open sides and a roof with a spire on top. It sits to the edge of the square, where the three main streets converge, and in front of the church. It's a very striking landmark, with stone steps surrounding all four sides.

'That's the market cross,' says Tom, his face lighting up at his chance to be able to impart a fact. 'I looked it up when we first moved here. It dates back to the fourteenth century. They're quite common in market towns and villages, apparently, although I've never seen one as lovely as this.'

Mum is frowning at it. 'I . . . I remember this . . .'

'Really?'

She blinks. 'It's very hazy. But I've seen it before. I . . .' She shakes her head. 'It's so frustrating but it's like the image is there, in my mind very briefly, and a feeling.' She places a hand on her heart and I can see, from my rearview mirror, that she's closed her eyes. 'This feeling . . .' Her eyes snap open. 'But then it's gone.'

'I read once,' says Tom, 'that our memories are forever evolving, so we only remember the version of the memory we last recalled rather than the original event.'

I roll my eyes and laugh. But Mum remains unusually stony-faced, her nose pressed up to the glass, like an expectant but slightly hesitant child. I glance at Tom and he shrugs. I continue up the hill until we reach the rank of twelve properties that's known as Skelton Place. I pull onto the shingle driveway, which fans out to greet us, relieved that there aren't any journalists hanging around today. It's been two weeks since the bodies were discovered so I'm hoping they've now moved on to another story.

'Gosh, the woods are quite bleak, aren't they?' says Mum. 'They encompass the whole village. I feel like I'm in *Little Red Riding Hood*.'

'They can be, especially on a dull day,' I say.

'I'm surprised the cottages don't have names,' says Mum. 'Look at all that beautiful wisteria. And the thatched roof. Nine Skelton Place is so . . . I don't know.' She gives a small shudder. 'Sinister-sounding.'

I know what she means, even though it niggles me that she's finding fault with everything. It's not exactly a pretty name. It doesn't seem to go with our little property. The cottage isn't very big, and it wouldn't have been worth as much as Gran's house in Bristol, but I've never lived anywhere so beautiful, so quaint and postcard perfect. The wisteria is out in full force at the moment and wraps around the front of the house, like a dusky lilac feather boa. And from the driveway you can't see the massive hole in the back garden.

By rights it should be Mum who's living here, with whatever toy-boy has taken her fancy this time, not me and Tom. I'd offered to pay Mum some money from our savings. She refused. As far as I'm aware Mum doesn't own another property. She rented the flat where I grew up in Bromley, Kent. She said she didn't like being tied down but to me it's always seemed a little . . . *irresponsible*.

We still haven't got around to transferring the deeds into my and Tom's names. I'd been meaning to broach the subject with Mum before we started work on the kitchen extension but I haven't quite managed it yet. Just like I haven't quite managed to bring up the subject of my pregnancy. I'm aware it's a running theme.

I step out of the car and stretch. My back aches and I feel nauseous. I take in deep lungfuls of country air as Mum and Tom climb out, Mum giggling as her heel gets tangled in the seatbelt and Tom laughing along as he helps her. Tom is so good with people. So patient. I know he'll make an excellent father. 'It's a bit pongy around here,' she says as she steps onto the driveway. 'Is that manure?'

I grimace at Tom. As I walk around the car to join them I see someone hovering by the hedge at the end of our driveway. I freeze. It's that man again. The one I saw the other day lurking by the cottage, and the one I'm sure I saw driving past Gran's care home.

'Tom! That man . . .' I begin but Tom has noticed him too. He hands Snowy over to Mum.

'Bloody journalists,' he mutters under his breath.

'Why are they still hanging around when the police have no

new information?' I cry. The police haven't released the information about the cracked skull yet.

'Oi,' he shouts, stepping forward. But the man disappears behind the hedge. I watch as Tom darts down the driveway in pursuit. 'Hey! Wait!' When he reaches the entrance he stops, looks back at us and shrugs. 'He's gone.'

8

Lorna

LORNA WATCHES AS TOM HURRIES TOWARDS THEM. WHEN he reaches Saffy he drapes an arm protectively around her shoulders, and she feels a pang of envy at the bond they obviously share. It was the same with her and Euan, once. But having a baby when they were both still kids themselves took its toll on their relationship. Saffy looks cute in her oversized dungarees, biting her lip. She was always doing that as a kid. Lorna was forever telling her to stop.

'That was weird,' Tom says, sounding out of breath. 'He must be a journalist but why run away when I confronted him? Why not ask us questions?'

Lorna hands him the dog lead with relief. She's never had an affinity with animals.

Saffy's face is pinched with concern. 'I've seen him before. The other day,' she says. She already knows her daughter will be making more of this. Her imagination running wild. Her little worrier. When she was four she got it into her head that a monster or dragon could get into their flat, and Lorna had sat on the edge of Saffy's bed, every night for a few months, convincing her it wasn't possible.

'Honey, it will just be another reporter,' she says, squeezing Saffy's upper arm gently. 'It's only to be expected. Come on, I'm excited about seeing inside this cottage.'

Saffy glances back towards the road, her big brown eyes darting about, like a scared puppy's, but then she turns to Lorna, her mouth in a tight line and nods.

Tom lets them in through the arched front door and into a small hallway with beams overhead and stripped floorboards. He stands back to allow them over the threshold first. She notices that Tom's head is only inches away from the beams. He has a proud look on his face and she remembers Saffy's words in the car. 'It looks gorgeous, Tom,' she says, glancing around at the Farrow & Ball-painted walls and the sanded floorboards.

'So the living room's through there,' says Saffy, pointing to a wooden door to their left, 'and at the end of the hallway is the kitchen. It's small, but there's room for a table. Just about. And . . .'

But Lorna has turned instinctively to her right, to the room just before the stairs. She pushes the door open and a flash of memory explodes in her mind. A sewing machine. The sound of a pedal, the clack-clack-clack. She blinks rapidly. When her vision clears she can see there is no sewing machine. Just a desk and a computer under the window, the walls decorated with ugly brown and yellow old-fashioned paper.

'My study,' says Saffy, from behind her. 'We haven't got around to decorating it yet. I don't think this wallpaper has been changed in fifty years!'

Lorna turns back to her daughter, a smile plastered to her

face. A sewing machine. Her mother never had one in the Bristol house. 'It's cute,' she says. 'It'll look lovely when it's painted.'

Saffy throws her an uncertain smile as though sensing something has unnerved Lorna. 'And then upstairs,' she indicates the staircase – bare boards: were they like that before? – 'there are three bedrooms. The master bedroom at the front, then a small double and a single overlooking the back garden where we'll put the ba–' She She stops, a horrified expression crossing her face.

'The what? Were you . . .' It suddenly dawns on Lorna. The roundness to Saffy's face, the slight weight gain. '. . . were you about to say *baby*?'

Saffy's cheeks turn fuchsia and she nods, looking guilty. 'Yes. I'm pregnant.'

Lorna reels. Pregnant. Shit. She's still so young. Still *her* baby. Lorna feels a thud of disappointment. Saffy's only twenty-four and has barely lived. Has she learnt nothing from Lorna? She was always telling her to wait until she was older and had her career established before marriage and kids.

'I . . . Wow, that's wonderful news, honey,' she manages to say, swallowing her true feelings. 'Congratulations.' She wraps her daughter in a hug although Saffy feels tense in her arms. Is she that unconvincing? She pulls away to address Tom, who's standing awkwardly by the front door, still clutching her suitcase, Snowy sitting at his feet, his head cocked to one side looking up at her. 'You too, Tom. Wow.' She turns back to her daughter. 'How far along? Have you had the three-month scan yet?'

Saffy nods, a blush creeping down her neck and towards her blue and white striped T-shirt. 'Yes. I'm seventeen weeks now. The baby's due on the thirteenth of October.'

Seventeen weeks. It means Saffy would have known for a good two, perhaps even three months. Lorna can't help but feel hurt that she hadn't come to her straight away. Lorna had hidden it from her own mum, of course, but that was because she'd been not quite sixteen when she'd found out, Euan only a year older. Lorna had been five months gone before Rose had noticed. The wild-child only daughter of quiet, strait-laced Rose Grey had done what the neighbours had been predicting for years. Got herself knocked up when she was still in school. Everyone called her Pramface. Not that Lorna regretted any of it. She might have split with Euan when Saffy was only five, but they'd made a good go of it, moving in together, getting married, though divorced a few years later. But he'd remained a big part of Saffy's life: she'd spent every other weekend with him in his little London pad when she was growing up, and Lorna knows the two of them remain close. Neither Lorna nor Euan ever remarried, and Lorna kept his surname.

Lorna had envisaged the day she'd become a grandmother. She knew she wouldn't be old, because she'd been such a young mother. But she'd expected to be older than forty-sodding-one. What will Alberto think?

This all goes through her mind at speed. And then she pulls herself up. She's being selfish. This isn't about her. It's about Saffy and Tom and their baby. 'I'm so pleased for you, honey. Truly I am.'

Saffy seems to sag with relief. 'It wasn't planned but . . .' She lets out a nervous laugh. 'Well, you know.'

Lorna laughs too. 'I do. Have you . . . have you told your dad?'

'Not yet. I wanted to tell you first.'

She tries not to feel gleeful that at least she knows before Euan. 'Well, come on then. Let's get the kettle on and then you can show me where the bodies were buried. A sentence I never thought I'd say.'

Tom announces he's going to walk Snowy around the block to give them time to catch up and disappears out of the front door. Why does she have the feeling he can't wait to get away? Although Lorna feels relieved she's got her daughter to herself for a bit.

The kitchen is small and old-fashioned, and as soon as Lorna walks in she heads straight for the window. Through the glass she can see the mess in the garden: the abandoned digger, the dug-up patio slabs, the huge hole in the ground, and the dense woods, a brooding backdrop. It gives her the heebie-jeebies. She senses Saffy at her shoulder but she doesn't turn. It feels as though some-one is gently blowing on the back of her neck, and she shudders. At the end of the garden, just before the woods, there is a large tree with purple flowers and a thick branch that looks like an arm reaching towards the house. She takes a sharp breath.

'What is it, Mum?' Saffy asks.

'That tree . . .' She shakes her head. The purple petals. She used to put them in her bucket and mash them with water. She remembers that. 'I played in that garden,' says Lorna. 'It's very familiar to me. I think . . . I think the tree might even have had a rope swing once. I used to pretend to make perfume with its flowers.'

She feels Saffy's warm hand squeezing her shoulder. 'Wow, Mum.'

Lorna turns to her daughter. 'Are you happy to stay here? Knowing this happened?'

Saffy looks pale and a little tearful. 'I . . . We haven't got anywhere else to go. And before this I loved it here.'

Lorna swallows the sudden lump in her throat. 'I know.'

'And it happened a long time ago, didn't it? Not as long ago as I was hoping.' She flashes a watery smile. Then her eyes go to the window. 'I wonder who they were.'

'Maybe the police will find out through dental records. Can we go outside? I'd like to take a closer look.'

'Now the police have finished we can. I'll grab the back-door key. Hold on a sec.'

Saffy moves slowly, her shoulders hunched, and Lorna longs to wrap her in a cuddle.

'Here we go.' Saffy is back and Lorna moves out of the way so she can open the stable door. They venture into the garden together. The sun is going down now and the trees cast shadows on the lawn.

They make their way over the uneven ground to the gaping hole – it's very deep, and as they get closer Lorna can smell the damp soil. 'The police have checked there are no more bodies?' she asks. She feels like she does when she occasionally visits a graveyard, aware of all those corpses below her feet even though she knows these bodies have been taken away.

Saffy nods. 'They had special dogs here. There are no more, don't worry . . .'

Lorna places her arm around Saffy's shoulders. 'Come on, let's have that cup of tea and then you can show me my room.'

Later, after Tom comes back with Snowy and they cluster around the little wooden table in the kitchen for dinner – Saffy pulls it out from the wall so there's room for Lorna – she broaches the subject of the baby again.

'So have you thought of any names yet?'

'Not really,' says Saffy, through a mouthful of bolognese.

'Will you find out the sex?'

Saffy glances across at Tom. 'No. We want it to be a surprise.'

'*You* do,' says Tom, good-naturedly. 'I wouldn't mind finding out.'

'I just think it will be a nice surprise.'

'But if we find out, we'll know what colour to paint the nursery!'

Saffy rolls her eyes. 'Ever the practical one,' she says fondly. 'We can paint it a pale grey.'

Lorna tries not to grimace. What is it with grey? What happened to colour?

Saffy reaches across the table, takes Tom's hand and squeezes it. Her daughter is more like her dad when it comes to being demonstrative but the love she has for this man shines from her. It slams home even harder what Lorna is missing with Alberto. In fact, with any of the men in her past, apart from maybe Euan. But they'd been so young.

Saffy puts down her knife and fork, a glazed look in her eyes. 'I keep thinking about Gran. She should be here, with us.'

'I know, honey,' Lorna says gently.

Her daughter's eyes well. 'Do you think she's happy in that place? I worry that she's unhappy and doesn't understand why she's there. That she has moments when she's scared. Do you think we could bring her here to visit?'

'It might confuse her. And she's well looked after there. It's a good care home, I did my research.' Saffy has always lived too close to the well, as Lorna used to put it. She was such a sensitive kid. Once on a holiday to Portugal when she was nine she burst into tears at a restaurant when she saw the lobsters in a tank ready to be eaten. It took her days to get over it. She'd worry for hours about a homeless man on the street, or a stray dog.

'But . . . it's not *her* home, is it?'

'Being here must remind you of her.'

Saffy's face crumbles. 'It does. And I miss her.'

'I do too.' Lorna realizes, with a jolt, that this is true. When

Saffy was born her mother doted on her only grandchild and the two of them have always been exceptionally close. Lorna was pleased they loved each other so much – and she tried, she really did, not to mind being the third wheel when they were all together. They were so alike – she could see that. But while her mother let their differences create a wedge between them, Lorna has always vowed never to allow that to happen with Saffy.

'Why don't you show me where the baby's room is going to be?' Lorna suggests, hoping to cheer Saffy up.

Saffy's face brightens and she leads Lorna into the hallway and up the stairs. 'We're going to get a runner up here but we can't decide on one. Maybe natural wool . . .' she shrugs '. . . or something.'

At the top of the stairs they turn into the little bedroom. It's no more than eight feet by nine, with a fireplace on the left wall, but Lorna can see it would make a perfect nursery. It's empty at the moment, other than a few boxes stacked in the corner. The carpet has been ripped up to expose the floorboards and the wallpaper is faded. But as soon as Lorna steps into the room she's overcome with a sense of déjà vu so strong she has to hold on to the windowsill.

'What is it?' asks Saffy, alarm in her voice. 'Are you okay?'

'It's just . . .' Lorna turns towards the window, which overlooks the back garden. She can see the purple tree from here. It only stayed purple in the spring and then the leaves would turn green, falling off in the winter. They used to carpet the lawn. She turns and reaches out to touch the wallpaper. She remembers. She remembers lying in bed in this very room and trying to decipher face shapes in the rosebuds on the wallpaper.

Lorna turns to her daughter. 'I think this used to be my bedroom.'

9

Theo

THE GRAVE IS LOOKING BARE. THE YELLOW ROSES THAT
Theo placed there last week are already brown and wilted. The
hot weather must have speeded up their decay.

'Your dad hasn't been again, then?' says Jen, at his shoulder,
voicing what he's thinking.

'Are you surprised?' he asks, trying to keep his voice light.

Theo's wife raises her well-groomed eyebrows in answer.
She squeezes his arm gently but doesn't say anything. He knows
she doesn't like his father – and why would she after the way he
is with her? – but she never bad-mouths him. She hands him
a bouquet of brightly coloured blooms that they bought on the
way here. 'I'll leave you alone for a bit . . .'

'You don't have to.'

'I know you like to talk to her.'

He flashes her a small smile. 'You think it's weird.' He'd told
her once, early in their relationship, then instantly regretted it.
He didn't want her to think he was some sad mummy's boy.

'Of course it's not weird. I just wish I'd had the chance to
meet her.'

'She'd have loved you.' And she would have. Everyone does. Jen is instantly lovable with her effervescent personality and her warm nature. Straight away she puts you at ease.

His wife reaches up and kisses him. She has to stand on tiptoe. 'I'll be over there, reading the old graves.'

'Now that *is* weird . . .' He laughs.

'Hey! It's interesting!' She throws him a smile over her shoulder as she wanders off towards an old cracked tombstone with a huge angel perched on top.

He watches her go in her long swishy summery skirt and tight T-shirt. Her shoulders are pushed back, her walk confident, the knot of strawberry-blonde hair on top of her head wobbling as she strides away towards the older part of the cemetery.

Then he turns back to his mum's grave. 'She's being brave, Mum,' he says. 'She's still not pregnant and I know she's worried. We've been trying for nearly a year.' He wonders if he'd have been so honest about this stuff if his mum was still alive. He stoops to take the dead roses out of the vase. The foetid smell of the rank water rises up his nostrils and hits the back of his throat. He shoves them into his plastic bag ready for the compost heap and replaces them with the fresh bouquet.

Theo visits every Saturday – mostly without Jen as she's usually working at the beauty salon in town and only gets one Saturday off a month – and each time he hopes to see something other than his decaying flowers from the previous week, something to show his dad has visited. That he actually cares. But for years there has been nothing. It happened gradually over the first year or two, he supposes, looking back, his dad's lack of interest. He suspects that his dad no longer visits the grave because he finds it too emotional. If he doesn't visit he can pretend it hasn't happened.

Theo kneels down on the dry grass and traces his fingers

along the date on the headstone. *Wednesday, 12 May 2004.* To-day is the fourteenth anniversary of her death. How can it be fourteen years, he wonders, when it still feels like it happened yesterday? Theo had been away at university in York when he got the phone call that changed his life. He'd been nineteen. And despite the heat of the day he shivers when he remembers. His father's deep, commanding voice, thick with emotion at the end of the line. *She's fallen,* he'd said. *She's fallen down the stairs and she's dead. I'm so sorry, son. I'm so sorry.* Theo had been standing at the student-union bar with a group of mates jostling either side of him, the mobile in his hand, unable to comprehend what his dad was telling him when everyone around him was drinking, jolly and singing. *You need to come home.* He'd taken the bus straight away, thankful that the bender he'd been envisaging had just begun and he'd had the chance to drink only half a pint. He remembers the journey from York to Harrogate clearly even after all these years. He remembers hoping that his dad was confused and had got it wrong, even though he knew there was nothing wrong with his sharp mind.

At the hospital he'd looked broken. Diminished and old. *What am I going to do?* he'd said over and over again, his face grey. *What am I going to do now?*

Theo never went back to finish his medical degree. Instead, for the remainder of that academic year he stayed with his dad in the ugly mansion he's always hated and tried to find memories of his mother in its every corner. But all he could see when he closed his eyes at night was the image of her falling down that fucking elaborate oak staircase, then lying crumpled and broken at the bottom. She'd been there all day, apparently, until his father came home from work and found her. His dad said she'd died instantly, but to this day Theo doesn't know whether to believe it. He still tortures himself that she lay there, on that beeswaxed parquet, in pain and unable to move to get to a phone for help. She'd died while Theo was busy shagging his first girlfriend in his cramped room in a shared student house in York. That September he changed his course to catering and hospitality, much to the derision of his dad. But he knew his mum would have been happy for him, would have told him life's too short.

The cemetery is quiet but Theo still lowers his voice as he talks to his mum. He describes the article he found in his dad's study two days ago. 'I think Dad is trying to find someone,' he says, picking at the grass with his fingers. It feels like straw. He's been unable to stop thinking about it. He'd memorized the two names from the paper. Saffron Cutler and Rose Grey. *Find Her.* But which one and why?

For the years after his mother died his dad has remained an enigma to Theo, hiding part of himself, refusing to talk about anything important. In those months after her death the two of them had rattled around in that house and he'd thought, naively he realizes now, that they could provide comfort to each other. Maybe even become closer. But instead, after that first night at the hospital and his dad's rare outpouring of emotion, there had been nothing. Just silence. His dad had gone back to work after the funeral, leaving Theo to wallow in loneliness and grief.

He knew his parents' marriage had been far from perfect. Looking back now, he can see his dad was possessive. The way he demanded his mum change her outfit if he thought she was wearing something 'too tarty' as he put it. Theo had never thought his mum looked tarty. Jen would, quite rightly, slap Theo's face if he ever said anything like that to her. He smiles at the thought of his feisty wife. His little firebomb. But his mum would just sigh good-naturedly, then go and change into something more nun-like to please her husband. She very rarely went anywhere with friends – in fact, he can't remember her having any female friends. His parents would go out to dinner with other couples – older couples from his dad's work – stuffy galas and dinner parties. But his mum never went far without his dad.

What she did in the house all day while his dad was at work he doesn't know, but she never had a job. Once, when he was about sixteen, he came home from school early to find her crying at her dressing-table. Her eyes were all puffy and he was sure he saw an angry bruise on her shoulder that she hurriedly covered with a cardigan when he walked into her bedroom. When he asked if she was okay she'd said, in a rare moment of honesty, 'I feel like a prisoner.' And then she'd given him a watery smile and told him she was just being silly, that it was hormones and to ignore her. But it had left Theo with an uneasy feeling for days. He'd watched his parents more closely. They were so unlike how his friends' parents were with each other. *It's just his way, sweetheart. Your father is a brilliant man. He works so hard. He just gets a little stressed sometimes.* But he never saw his dad raise a hand to her. If he had he would have thumped him.

'There is so much I wish I could ask you,' he says now. 'And I promise, if I'm ever lucky enough to be a dad I won't be emotionally cut off, like *him*.' He stands up and dusts off his jeans. 'See you next week. Love you, Mum.'

Then he strolls off to find Jen, who is standing by a huge tombstone dating back two hundred years with about ten members of the same family inscribed on it. He comes up behind her and wraps his arms around her waist. 'All done,' he says.

'Shall we go and get a coffee now?' she says, turning to him. She frowns. 'What is it? You look . . . worried.'

'I don't know. Something doesn't feel right. About Dad.

About that article.' He'd told Jen all about it after his shift that night.

'Why don't you just ask him about it?'

'My dad isn't like yours.' His father-in-law is the polar opposite: warm, kind, fun, loving.

'I know, but if you confront him about this he can't wriggle out of it. Theo,' she says softly, 'you know I love you, but where your dad is concerned, you ... I don't know ... pussyfoot around him.'

He laughs. 'Pussyfoot!'

'Yes, pussyfoot. It's like you're scared of him.'

'You've met my father!'

'Yes. He's formidable. I'm not gonna lie.' His wife is being diplomatic. Even Jen's effusive and bubbly personality couldn't win his father over. He's never told Jen this but after he first brought her home his dad said she was common. It was the only time Theo had stood up to him after his mum's death. He told him he loved her, and if he ever heard him say or do anything nasty to her he'd never speak to him again. His dad had looked shocked, then muttered something about it not lasting. But here they were, five years later and married for the last three.

'He won't tell me the truth. Dad should have been a politician.'

'There must be someone you could ask. I know your grandparents are dead, but ... a cousin perhaps?'

He takes his wife's hand and they walk out of the cemetery together. He doesn't know his cousins. It's hard for Jen to understand because her family is huge and they all get on. 'I'll start by asking him. And if he doesn't give me what I want, I'll find out for myself.'

'Good. And I'll help. It will be a distraction.' She smiles but her eyes are too bright.

It feels as if someone is squeezing his heart. 'Jen . . . we could go and see someone. Get some tests?'

She shakes her head, a blonde curl falling into her eyes. 'Not yet. I'm not ready to face that yet. Let's just wait for now.'

He kisses her hand in response, his mind already slipping back to his father and the newspaper article. *Tomorrow*, he vows. *Tomorrow I'll find out who my dad is looking for, and why.*

10

Lorna

It's too dark and quiet, and Lorna is finding it difficult to sleep on the hard futon, knowing her daughter and her boyfriend are on the other side of the wall. She still finds it difficult to get used to the thought of her only child having sex and now carrying a baby. *A baby.* She can't believe she's going to be a grandmother.

She misses the sounds of San Sebastián – the occasional laughter and screeches of teenagers, the thrum of music from a neighbouring tapas restaurant. The comforting noises of city life, not this God-awful silence. Then her mind wanders to Alberto. She turns onto her side and reaches for her phone on the pine bedside cabinet. It's gone midnight. Spain is an hour ahead. She expects he'll still be at the bar, the proverbial night owl.

She sits up, trying to shake the image of her boyfriend surrounded by a flock of scantily clad women. There's no point lying here trying to sleep – she's suffered from insomnia in the past and all the advice she's read on the subject says to get up. She throws on her hot-pink kimono and opens the bedroom door quietly so as not to wake Saffy and Tom and pads down the hallway towards the little bedroom. She's drawn to it, that bedroom, that insight into her past. She pushes the door open, wincing as it creaks before continuing into the room.

There are no curtains at the window and a shard of moonlight illuminates a patch of black varnish stuck like tar to one of the floorboards. She stands at the window that looks over the garden. The hole in the ground looks even more ominous in the dark. The woods, thick and dense, line the back boundary. She forces her brain to remember more. *What happened here?* she whispers to her reflection. But it just stares back at her, like a ghoul with big curly hair and wide haunted eyes. She turns away from the window, to survey the room. Her bed was in that corner, by the door, where the boxes are now. Yes, yes, she remembers. It had a white iron frame and a colourful crocheted throw with large yellow daisies, and underneath she kept a pair of red patent shoes, like Dorothy's in *The Wizard of Oz*. She hasn't thought about those shoes for a long time. They had been her favourite. Where did they go when they moved to Bristol? And the iron bed frame and the crocheted throw?

The wallpaper is faded in parts, yellowing in others. The fireplace looks like it needs renovating, and there is a thick layer of dust on the wooden mantelpiece. The past tenants obviously didn't use this room. Saffy and Tom will have their work cut out if they want to turn it into a nursery. She turns back to the window. A cloud moves across the moon so that for a few moments the woods and the garden look bleak and sinister.

She should go back to bed and read. She's got Marian Keyes's new one ready to begin. She wraps her kimono further around her body. She's cold now and shivers slightly.

Just as she's about to turn and leave, something bright catches her eye. A flicker of light between the trees in the woods. She presses her nose to the glass and cups her hands around her face. Her heart picks up speed. It looks like torch-light. Is someone there, watching the house? She blinks, not taking her eyes off the dot of light, the surrounding halo-like beam moving between the darkness of the trees. And then just as quickly it vanishes. She stands there for a further ten minutes, straining to see, but there is nothing.

The next morning, Lorna doesn't mention it to her daughter. She knows she'll only worry and that's the last thing she wants. Instead, after she's dressed and had breakfast – one of Tom's fry-ups that she notices Saffy pushes around her plate – she says she'd like to walk in the garden.

'I'll come with you,' says Saffy, making to get up from the table. Tom already has his old decorating clothes on, saying he wants to make a start on painting the banister in the hallway.

'No, it's okay. You finish your breakfast. I'll see if anything jogs my memory.'

'Oh . . . okay. Good idea.'

The sun is bright this morning although there is a chill in the air and dew on the grass as Lorna steps onto the lawn, the dampness seeping into the sides of her sandals. She takes a deep breath of the unpolluted country air. It smells more refreshing this morning, like washing after it's been on the line. She ignores the hole in the ground and carries on until she reaches the end of the garden, with the beautiful purple tree. She wonders what it's called. She makes a mental note to ask Saffy. She turns back towards the cottage to make sure her daughter isn't watching and steps onto one of the low thick branches, just enough to give her a leg up so she can hop over the wall. The action is so natural she must have done it before. She holds on to the trunk for support as she jumps down on the other side.

The ground there is higher, with little pathways ahead snak-

ing through the trees, dotted with bluebells. Lorna surveys the
spot where she saw the light last night. She's not sure what she's
expecting to find. Footprints, perhaps? Although the ground
is too dry. And then she notices something. A patch of bluebells has been flattened, as if someone recently stood on them.
She moves closer, her eyes scanning the ground and then she
glimpses something else among the trampled flowers. Three
cigarette butts.

She hadn't been imagining it last night. Someone had crept
through the darkness and into the woods. Someone had been
watching the house. Watching *them*.

PART TWO

11

Rose

Christmas Eve, 1979

THE VILLAGE NEVER LOOKED PRETTIER THAN IT DID THE evening I first met Daphne Hartall.

Warm white lights were strung up between lamp-posts along the high street and twinkled against the inky sky; the church choir stood on the stone steps of the market cross and sang 'Silent Night' in front of a huge Christmas tree, and a few rickety stalls had been set up around the edges of the village square. Melissa Brown, who owned the only café in Beggars Nook – imaginatively named Melissa's – was open late to serve hot drinks and mince pies. The smell of roasted chestnuts and mulled wine filled the air.

And that Christmas you were old enough to appreciate the magic of it all.

'Mummy. Drink?'

I looked down at you. Your little snub nose was red with the cold and the pink scarf I'd knitted you was up to your chin. It was already dark and not quite tea-time.

'Why not?' I smiled, clasping your soft woollen hand in my own. 'What about a hot chocolate?'

You squealed in excitement, trying to pull me across the square.

And that was when I saw her.

The woman who was to change my life. Although, of course, I didn't know that yet.

She looked sad. That was my initial thought. She was standing alone by the market cross, blowing on her bare hands as she watched the carol singers. She was wearing a thin olive-green velvet coat with colourful patches stitched onto it and her cord flares were too loose around her thighs. She was thin, I observed, her collar bones sticking out from her shirt. A crocheted beret was pressed down onto long blonde hair parted in the middle, and she had a large bag over her shoulder. She was new to the village, I could tell. She had that look about her. And I made it my business to watch out for newcomers – even while keeping myself to myself. I had to. For my safety. And for yours. This backwater village in the depths of the Cotswolds was where people came to hide. And I recognized a kindred spirit when I saw one.

'Mummy,' you urged, tugging on my hand.

'Sorry, Lolly,' I said, pulling my gaze away from the stranger and following you into the café. Your huge brown eyes lit up when Melissa handed you the hot chocolate in a white polystyrene cup, whipped cream swirled on top. I laughed and told you that you'd never manage it all. Then we stood just outside the café, fingers curled around our warm cups, you licking the cream off the top of the hot chocolate and me searching for her among the knot of people gathered by the Christmas tree. I could see her moving through the crowd, her shoulders hunched against the cold, her eyes darting about as though afraid. She looked like a hunted animal. Was that how I'd looked when I came to the village three years ago, pregnant with you and desperate for a new start?

'Hold on a sec, sweetheart. I just want a quick word with Melissa.'

I let go of your hand to step inside the café. Melissa Brown was a large woman with a greying bob, parted in the middle and pinned at the sides, somewhere in her forties, old-fashioned in both her outlook and appearance. She had never been married and had lived in Beggars Nook all her life. As a result she knew everything about everyone. Well, mostly everyone. I knew she thought of me as an enigma because she'd said it to me on many occasions. *Dear Rose*, usually said when my hands were clamped between her large, clammy ones. *You're such an enigma.* This was often uttered after I'd avoided one of her many questions. But she had always been kind to me and had tried to involve me in village life.

The café was quiet. Most people were still gathered by the market cross or perusing the stalls filled with colourful tinsel and garish decorations. You'd already persuaded me to buy one: a little gold fairy to put on top of the tree.

'Melissa,' I said, lowering my voice even though it was just me and her in the café. 'You don't know who that woman is, do you? The thin one in the crocheted hat?'

Melissa wiped her hands on her flowery apron and stared in the woman's direction. She shook her head. 'Never seen her before. She could be from the next village. Oh, and before I forget, Nancy said someone was interested in the ad you put up in her window. You know, for the lodger?'

Nancy worked in the local shop and was Melissa's younger

sister. I'd kept the advert vague on purpose, asking Nancy to take details of any interested parties so that I could get in touch with them, rather than give out my own information. I didn't even put my name on it. I couldn't risk it.

'That's great.' I already knew that if a man had enquired I'd never get in touch.

I'd made a mistake with my last lodger. She had been the right sex, but she'd asked too many questions. Wanted to be friends. So she had to go.

'I'll ask Nancy to pass their details on to you – tomorrow, if you like?'

I nodded but I was already distracted, moving away from the counter, towards where I'd left you by the open door.

I froze. You'd gone.

I'd turned my back on you for just a few minutes. It was foolish of me. I never normally let you out of my sight. But I felt unusually safe in that moment, you see, surrounded by a collective Christmas cheer and villagers who didn't really know me but whom I'd been watching for the last three years, from afar, to see whom I could trust. They all seemed honest, hardworking folk. Salt of the earth. And I thought I could trust you, that I'd instilled it in you since you could walk to be careful, to stay near me. Not to wander off. But you were just a little girl. Only two and a half. A little girl mesmerized by the glitziness of Christmas.

You'd gone.

'Lolly!' I cried, unable to keep the panic from my voice. I stepped out of the café and onto the street. My eyes scanned the pavements and the square, the group of carol singers, who had finished their rendition of 'Silent Night' and begun to disperse. It had been a minute, two at the most. You couldn't have got very far. Yet I couldn't see you anywhere. I couldn't see your little red coat or your pink scarf or the bright patterned bobble hat. Blood rushed to my ears.

'Are you okay?' I could hear Melissa's voice behind me but it felt distorted, like I was under water.

'She's gone! Lolly's gone!' I cried. 'I can't see her. I can't see her anywhere.'

People were milling about, laughing, talking, sipping mulled wine. I wanted to scream at them all. GET OUT THE WAY! WHERE IS SHE? WHERE'S MY CHILD? I could feel tears at the back of my eyes, panic pressing on my chest.

He's taken you. That's all I could think, over and over again, replaying like a horror film in my mind.

I pushed past people, calling your name. I could sense that Melissa was behind me, trying to calm me, but I couldn't process what she was saying. I was in a panic. A blind panic – I've heard people call it that, and that's exactly how it felt. I was blinded by fear.

I pushed through people, Melissa on my tail. I heard her asking them if they'd seen a little girl in a red duffel coat.

And then there you were. I saw you through the crowds, holding the hand of the mysterious woman I would come to know as Daphne Hartall. You were smiling but had dried tear tracks on your cheeks.

I rushed over to you, almost snatching you away from the tall, thin woman and bending down to your level, hugging you to me, breathing in your familiar sweet smell. 'Thank God, thank God, thank God.'

'I'm so sorry,' the woman said. Her voice was husky. 'She looked lost so I said I'd help her find her mummy.' I noticed she was clutching your polystyrene cup, the rim sticky with chocolate.

I stood up, holding on to your hand. Never wanting to let go of it again.

'See?' said a voice behind me. It was Melissa, her large bosoms rising up and down as she gasped for breath. 'I knew . . .' pant, pant '. . . she'd be fine.'

'Thanks, Melissa. I'm sorry . . . for the overreaction.'

She nodded, her hand pressed to her chest, and said it was no problem and that she'd better get back to the café. But she threw me a strange look over her shoulder as she went. I knew what she was thinking – that I was an over-protective mother. Hysterical.

There were a few beats of awkward silence and then the woman said, 'I'm Daphne.'

'Rose. And this is Lolly.'

She smiled and it lit up her whole face, making her seem less severe, less angular. Now I was closer to her I could see the tips of her long eyelashes were blue. 'Yes, she told me that. An unusual name.'

'It's Lorna. But she finds it hard to say. She called herself Lolly and it's stuck. Well, thank you again.' I hesitated, wondering if I should ask. 'Are you new to the village?'

She nodded. 'I'm staying in one of the rooms over the Stag and Pheasant. But I'm looking for lodgings. Something more permanent. At least for a while.'

I wondered if it was her who had enquired about my ad.

'I might be able to help you there.' I smiled at her. She smiled back shyly, flashing her small white teeth. This was serendipitous, I thought. We were supposed to meet.

How wrong I was.

12

Saffy

MUM IS UNUSUALLY QUIET ON THE DRIVE TO SEE GRAN. She stares out of the window as we pass the village square and the market cross and the café – the Beggars Bowl. Beyond, the church's spire glints in the bright sunshine. It's rained overnight and the air has a fresh, newly laundered feel, making everything look brighter and sharper. Is she thinking about Alberto? She hasn't mentioned him much. I spent most of yesterday afternoon showing her around the village as we reminisced about Gran, Tom discreetly lagging behind with Snowy. Mum instinctively seemed to know her way to the café, and when she walked up the crumbling stone steps of the market cross she said she had a feeling of déjà vu.

'This,' she said, pointing to a small building by the church. 'I'm sure this was a playschool or Sunday school or something.'

I'd booked us in for Sunday lunch at the Stag and Pheasant, knowing she'd love it there as it's won awards for its food – my mum is the biggest foodie I know. She seemed unusually on edge as we walked around the cobbled streets, and kept asking about how easy it was to access the woods at the back of the cottage. Mum is very rarely on edge. She's a happy-go-lucky kind of person, always looking for the bright side of a situation. When I asked her what was wrong she'd shaken her head, nearly knocking herself out with her huge earrings, and linked her arm in mine. 'Nothing, my sweet girl. I love being here with you. Now, show me where that lovely gastro pub is. I could murder some roast beef.'

'Are you okay?' I ask now, as we head out of the village and towards the M4.

She turns to me, flashing a dazzling smile. But beneath her expertly applied makeup she looks tired. 'Of course. Why?'

Because you're not chatting nineteen to the dozen as usual. 'You're just a bit . . . *quieter* than usual,' I say instead, wanting to be diplomatic.

'I'm wondering about your gran, that's all. Is she going to be lucid enough for this interview today?'

The sun goes in suddenly and everything is gloomier. 'I'm worried about that too. I don't want her to feel frightened but at least they're doing it at the care home. And it's good that you're not leaving until Saturday so you can see Gran again before you go.'

Mum fidgets in her seat and adjusts her top. She's wearing a tight, bodice-style denim blouse that strains across her chest slightly, white jeans and tan-coloured heeled sandals. Her toe-nails are freshly painted in fuchsia. I haven't done mine since Christmas. Not that it matters as I live in trainers, even in this heat. If I ever don sandals they're my trusty Birkenstocks, which Mum has always deemed *downright ugly*. 'I'm thinking of staying on a bit longer.' She pauses. 'If you don't mind?'

I wonder what's made her decide to lengthen her stay. I'd thought a week would be more than long enough for her. Surely by then she'll be pining for Alberto and the beach. 'Of course I don't mind,' I say, although that's not strictly true. Mum's personality fills the cottage somehow so that everything feels even smaller. She can't help but take over — cooking for us, even if we're not hungry, or, just as we're about to unwind on the sofa, she'll ask me to fetch some clothes that she can put in the machine. I feel guilty when she starts washing up and feel I have to help, even though Tom and I would usually leave it until the next day, preferring to chill out in front of the TV. Tom is great with her, but I could see the strain on his face as she talked at him last night while he was trying to watch *The IT Crowd*. 'What about your job?'

'I can take some of it as unpaid leave. Anyway, they owe me lots of holiday.'

'Okay. You know you can stay as long as you want, but I do need to work. I've got a deadline,' I say, which is true and hopefully means she'll know I haven't got time to sit around chatting all day.

She reaches out and pats my knee fondly, her bracelets jangling. 'You don't need to worry about me. Just do the things you'd normally do and pretend I'm not here.'

I want to laugh. That's just not possible with my mother. 'Will Alberto mind?'

She waves a ringed hand dismissively. 'Leave that to me. It'll be fine.'

I force down my worry. I can't help but think Mum is running away from her life in Spain, from the problems she's no doubt having with Alberto. It makes me feel guilty that I have Tom and a baby on the way when Mum has never really been able to settle.

She emits a sharp laugh, which makes me jump. 'Darling, you look so serious. Stop worrying.'

'I'm not.'

'You're chewing your lip again. You always do that when you're worrying. I'm a grown woman. I'll be fine. You don't need to worry about me . . . I need to worry about *you*.'

I frown. 'Why do you need to worry about me?'

'I meant . . .' She twists the ring on her index finger. My dad gave it to her. It's a sapphire, and beautiful, and even though they split up years ago she never takes it off. 'It's just in general, you know. That's a mother's job.'

Why do I get the feeling there's something she isn't saying?

The sun bursts from behind a cloud, bright and blinding, and I have to pull the visor down. But Mum is right. I am anxious. I'm anxious about throwing up my decaf tea and half a piece of toast, about seeing the police, about Gran's interview. About what she'll say.

When we arrive, Gran is sitting in her usual chair in the corner of the day room. Sun streams through the glass and it feels too hot and airless in here. The French windows are firmly closed and Gran is wearing a pink jumper. She must be boiling.

She's not doing a puzzle today. Instead she just gazes out of the doors, deep in thought, at the gardens beyond. I wonder what she's thinking about.

'Gosh,' says Mum, putting a hand to her throat. 'She looks so much smaller and thinner than when I last saw her.' Her voice catches.

I swallow my nerves and check my watch. It's just gone ten. The police said they'd arrive about ten thirty.

Joy, the manager of the care home, a thin, officious woman in her late fifties, strides over to where we're hovering in the doorway.

'Rose is having a good day,' she says. She smiles but it

doesn't reach her eyes beyond her horn-rimmed glasses. She always has an air of harassment. 'I'll let you know when the police arrive. I don't want them coming in here and distracting the other residents.'

Mum nods, thanks Joy, and we wander over to Gran. There's a cane two-seater sofa next to her and we squash onto it together.

Gran doesn't look up as we join her, continuing to gaze off into the middle distance. She has her false teeth in. I'm so used to seeing her without them that the effect changes her face shape, accentuating her jaw and making her look sterner, somehow.

'Hi, Gran,' I begin, shifting my weight towards her. I'm sitting closest to her.

Mum leans across me and reaches out her hand to take Gran's. 'Lovely to see you, Mum. You're looking well.'

But Gran turns and frowns at Mum. Her face is blank. 'Who are you?'

My heart sinks.

'It's me. Lorna. Your daughter.' Mum's voice wavers.

Panic flutters across Gran's face. 'I don't have a daughter.'

My eyes fill with tears at Mum's crushed expression and I blink rapidly to stop them spilling over. That's not going to be helpful to anyone. Mum quickly recovers. 'Of course you do. And a granddaughter.' But she retracts her hand from Gran's.

Gran turns to me, a spark of recognition in her eyes. 'Saffy!'

I smile, trying not to look at Mum. 'Hi, Gran.'

'How's that lovely man of yours?'

'He's good.'

'I hope you're still feeding him up.'

I laugh. Mum has slumped against the back of the sofa, utterly dejected.

'It's not a Thursday. You usually come and see me on a Thursday.'

Sometimes I'm shocked by how switched on Gran can be. And at others it's like someone has snuck into the care home late at night and wiped her memory. It seems all the more cruel that she can't remember Mum when she's so lucid about other things. 'It's Monday, you're right. But today the police are coming. Remember last week I told you about the bodies in the garden?'

Gran stiffens and Mum leans forward expectantly.

'Why do the police need to see me?'

'They just want to ask you a few questions, that's all, because you used to live in the house.'

She narrows her eyes.

'Just try to answer them as best you can. You . . . you spoke about a Sheila last time. And a Victor.'

'Sheila. Wicked little girl.'

Who is this Sheila she keeps mentioning? As much as I'd love to know more I need to get her to focus on the topic in hand. 'Can you remember living in the cottage, Gran?'

Gran straightens up. 'Of course I can. I'm not fucking stupid.'

I'm taken aback. Gran has never spoken to me like that before and I've never heard her swear. 'I know you're not stupid,' I say softly.

Mum's voice cuts across us. 'I think we should leave the questioning to the police, honey.'

'I'm not questioning her,' I say, throwing Mum a look. Even though I know I am. But Mum doesn't understand how to handle Gran. And I do. The three of us fall into a terse silence.

I know Mum is silently brooding that Gran forgot who she is. And I appreciate how hurtful that is, but she does it to me sometimes. Mum hasn't been to see Gran very often since she was admitted to the home. I should have warned her it can be like this.

'Jean hit her,' Gran says suddenly, breaking the silence.

I lean towards her. 'Who's Jean?'

'Jean hit her. Jean hit her over the head and she fell to the ground.'

I hold my breath, not wanting to interrupt her flow. I can sense the tension radiating from Mum.

Could it be possible that Gran does know something about the bodies after all?

We wait . . . one beat, two . . . Next to me Mum opens her mouth and I shake my head at her. *No*, I plead silently at her. *Don't speak.*

'I didn't know what to do. Everyone said she was wicked. Everyone said she was bad for what she did. Victor was trying to hurt us.'

I lean forward carefully so as not to put her off her stride. 'Gran . . . are you saying someone called Jean killed the woman at Skelton Place?' I turn to glance at Mum, horrified.

'Victor . . . Sheila . . .'

I rub my temples. I can feel a headache coming on. Gran is confused and so am I. It's just the dementia talking, I tell myself. Before my last visit I'd never heard her mention these names.

Thankfully Joy walks over to us at that moment. 'The police are here,' she whispers, looking around to make sure the other residents haven't heard. 'I think you should all come with me.'

13

Lorna

THEY FOLLOW JOY INTO A ROOM JUST OFF THE HALLWAY, WHICH HAS a fireplace and flocked wallpaper in duck-egg blue. Saffy is holding her gran's arm and Lorna's heart is silently breaking. Breaking not only at the sight of her mother looking so much older than the last time she'd visited six months ago, but the shock that she doesn't recognize her. She knows she hasn't been to visit as much as she should. It's been hard from Spain. That's what she's always told herself, anyway. Yet deep down she acknowledges she could have done it more often if she'd really wanted to. It's only a ninety-minute journey by plane. But it had been easier not to think about her mother, fading away in the care home, her brain scrambled. It had been easier instead to focus on ridiculously buffed and unsuitable toy-boys. Now the guilt eats her up. She's been a terrible daughter.

The two floral armchairs positioned either side of the fireplace are occupied by men, both in open-necked shirts, smart trousers and a sheen of sweat on their faces. It's even hotter in here than it is in the day room. The older of the two – mid-forties, Lorna suspects, with receding hair, blue eyes and a chiselled jaw – stands up when they enter. The younger man – late twenties, short and stocky with spiky hair the colour of dirty dishwater – remains seated. He's drinking what looks like a chocolate milkshake from a see-through Starbucks cup.

'I'm DS Matthew Barnes,' says the older one, shaking their hands across the coffee table. 'And this is my colleague, DC Ben Worthing. We're from Wiltshire Police CID.' Ben nods to them all. She notices his gaze lingers on Saffy.

DS Barnes returns to his seat and Joy fusses around them all, ushering them into chairs opposite the officers, taking their coffee and tea orders. Lorna and Saffy flank her mother, who looks small in the chair and very confused, her fingers knitted together in her lap, her eyes darting between the two men, like a nervous child's. Lorna reaches out and takes her mum's hand for reassurance. She's relieved when Rose lets her.

'Now, I don't want you to worry, Rose,' says DS Barnes, kindly. 'This is an informal chat. We're just gathering information at this point. Like we're doing with everyone connected to the property.' He has a notebook and pen on the table in front of him. He opens the notebook and takes off the lid of his pen, ready.

Her mother doesn't say anything, instead staring ahead, sipping the tea that Joy kindly brought in.

'So, first, can I just have some information, Rose? Like your date of birth?'

Her mother suddenly looks panicked, lowering her mug. 'I . . . um . . . July . . . no, August . . . 1939, I think . . .'

'You were born in 1943, Mum,' pipes up Lorna. She turns to DS Barnes. 'The twentieth of March 1943.'

'Oh, yes, yes, 1943. In the middle of the war, you know.' Her mother takes another sip of her tea and smacks her lips together. Lorna glances over her head at Saffy, who stares back at her anxiously.

This is surely going to be a disaster. How can they proceed with this when her mum can't even remember her own date of birth?

'And you've been diagnosed with Alzheimer's?' asks DS Barnes.

Her mother doesn't say anything so Lorna adds, 'Yes, last summer.'

Saffy fidgets in her seat. Lorna notices she's hardly touched her glass of water.

'Thanks, Lorna,' says DS Barnes, nodding to her without smiling. 'So, Rose, my notes say you began proceedings to rent out the cottage in April 1981.'

She shakes her head. 'I . . . don't know.'

He refers to his little black notebook. 'We know that your first tenant was in June 1981. A couple who rented the house from you for ten years. We've already spoken to them. But before that you lived at the property for nearly four years. Did anyone live there with you?'

'I . . . had a lodger.'

This is news to Lorna. She sits up straighter. She notices Saffy does the same.

'A lodger? Male or female?' asks DS Barnes.

'A female lodger. Daphne . . . Daphne Hartall.' She says the name almost with relish, like she hasn't said it in a very long time and enjoys the way it forms on her lips.

Her mother has never mentioned a Daphne before.

'Can you remember what year this was?' says DS Barnes.

'I think 1979. No. 1980 . . .' She slurps her tea noisily, some of which sloshes onto her pink jumper. Saffy's hand hovers near the mug, ready to help her with it. 'The last year I was in the cottage.'

'And how old was Daphne?'

'She was ... she was the same age as me, I think. In her thirties. Or ... maybe forty ... I ...' her eyes dart from side to side '... I can't remember exactly ...'

'And what happened to her?'

'I ... don't know. She left. We lost touch.'

'Were you friends?'

'Yes. Yes, we were friends.' She sounds grumpy now. The way she'd sounded with Lorna when she used to ask about her dad.

'And did either of you have any ... male friends around that time?'

Her mother moves suddenly and a splash of tea jumps from the cup and dribbles down her front.

Saffy is wearing a pained expression. 'Here, Gran, let me take the mug,' she says, relief flooding her face when she has it safely in her hands and has lowered it to the table.

'Rose ...' prompts DS Barnes. 'Male visitors?'

Her mother shudders. 'No. No, we were scared – Victor.'

Lorna frowns. Victor again. Who is this Victor?

'Why were you scared, Rose?' DS Barnes asks gently.

'Victor wanted to hurt the baby.' She touches her soft stomach as though remembering what it was like to be pregnant. *Does she mean me?* wonders Lorna. *She can't mean me. She told me my dad died before I was born.*

Her mother was always so over-protective when Lorna was growing up, insisting on meeting her from the school bus every evening, when all her friends were allowed to walk home by themselves. She never let her wander far, always making sure that she knew where Lorna was going and what time she'd be back, and if she was ever late she'd ring around her friends' parents and it was so embarrassing that Lorna made sure she was always back on time. Is that why? Because she was scared of a man called Victor?

DS Barnes frowns. 'Who is Victor? Can you remember his surname?'

She shakes her head. 'It's all such a long time ago now . . .' She turns to Saffy and says, 'I don't want to answer any more questions. I want to watch *Bargain Hunt*.'

'Oh, Gran,' says Saffy, taking her hand. 'It won't be long now, will it, Detective?'

DS Barnes nods. 'Just a bit longer, please, Rose. Can you remember any more about Victor? Did he ever come to the cottage?'

'No. I don't know. I . . .' she blinks rapidly '. . . I can't remember.'

'Is there anything else you can tell me about Daphne?'

'No. Like I've already said, she lived at the cottage with me for a while. A year, I think. And then left. Moved on. Yes . . . yes, she moved on.'

'And did you have any other lodgers around that time?'

'No. Oh, yes, yes, I did. Before Daphne. But she didn't stay long.'

'Can you remember her name?'

'No . . .'

DS Barnes takes a deep breath. 'Okay. Well, we'll need to look into that. And did you ever witness anyone being hurt at the cottage?'

'Jean hit her over the head.'

Lorna's heart sinks.

DS Barnes glances across at his colleague and then back at her mother. 'Jean? Who's Jean, Rose?'

'Jean hit her over the head and she didn't get back up again.'

DS Barnes uncrosses his legs, his face passive, but Lorna can see the twitch of excitement at the corners of his mouth. 'Jean hit Daphne over the head?'

'No.'

'Then who?'

Confusion flits across her mother's face. She looks tired, dark circles around her eyes. 'I don't know.'

'I think my mother has had enough now, don't you?' Lorna cuts in. This feels wrong to her. How can anything her mother says be believed?

DS Barnes nods in defeat. 'Okay.' He turns to Lorna. 'But if your mother remembers anything else, anything, no matter how insignificant it may seem, please let us know.'

Lorna stands in the corridor and watches as Saffy and Joy accompany her mother back to the day room. She's chattering away about *Bargain Hunt* and she can still hear her voice as she rounds the corner: strong Cockney accent even after all these years. There doesn't seem to be any lasting damage but she's still furious with DS Barnes. She wants to give him a piece of her mind.

She hovers in the hallway until he exits the room, Ben Worthing close behind. She hoists her handbag over her shoulder and marches up to him.

'Was that really necessary? She's an old woman with dementia, for crying out loud. I hope you didn't take her talk of this Victor and Jean seriously. She's confused, that's all. She doesn't know what she's saying.'

DS Barnes looks taken aback by her outburst. 'We have

to interview everyone who lived at the property during that time frame,' he says calmly. She can't imagine him ever raising his voice. 'This is a serious crime and we need as much information as we can get hold of. But, yes, I understand that Rose has dementia. I won't be taking everything she says at face value. However, there could be something in what she's saying, and I wouldn't be doing my job if I didn't investigate that.'

'My mother won't know anything. You said you spoke to the people who rented the house from her. Did they shed light on any of this?'

He sighs. 'Not at the moment. But, like I've said, we're just trying to ascertain as much as we can at this stage about who was living at the property and when. We are also working hard to identify the bodies. Once we know who they were and when exactly they died, it will be easier to −'

They are interrupted by the gurgling sounds of liquid being sucked through a straw and they turn in time to see DC Worthing polishing off his takeaway milkshake. Lorna glares at him and he has the grace to look shamefaced. 'I'll meet you in the car, Guv,' he says, scuttling out of the building.

Guv? Really? She rolls her eyes. DS Barnes notices because he says, deadpan, 'He's new. I think he's watched too many episodes of *The Sweeney*.'

Her lips twitch but she refuses to laugh. He's not getting off that lightly.

She shuffles her feet. One of her sandals is rubbing her recent blister. 'So what happens next?'

He gives her a long look that she can't read. She wonders if it's pity. 'We'll be in touch.'

14

Saffy

WHEN WE GET BACK TOM IS STILL AT WORK SO MUM SAYS
she'll start on dinner and I take Snowy for a walk. It's still warm,
the sun flickering through the trees. As I stroll past number
eight Brenda Morrison comes scurrying out, still in her sheepskin slippers. 'Oi, I want a word with you!' she says, scowling.

I stop and try to smile politely, turning towards her. I've
never taken to Brenda, or her husband, Jack. Neither made us
feel particularly welcome when we moved in. Not to mention
them opposing the build. They're always complaining about
something: the position of our rubbish bin, the sound of the
builders drilling, Snowy barking in the garden.

'How are you, Brenda?' I ask.

'Not good. I'm fed up with those journalists coming over
all the time. Last week there was one in our back garden, taking
photos over our fence. It's just not on. It's making my Jack's acid
reflux play up.'

'I'm really sorry – I hate them being here too.'

'We've lived here nigh on thirty year and have never known
the like.'

'I don't know what they're hoping to achieve. There's no new information and there might not be for some time,' I say. DS Barnes said earlier about trawling through missing persons between 1970 and 1990 to try to identify the bodies. It could take months.

'And I've also had the police here last week asking questions,' she bulldozes on, as though I haven't spoken. 'And I can tell you what I told them – we've been living here over thirty years, and if two people had been murdered and buried in the garden next door, well,' she folds her arms across her chest, 'we'd have seen. Nothing gets past me.'

That doesn't surprise me.

'Thirty years? So you arrived here in . . .'

'1986. Bought it from a lovely old couple. They wanted to move to a bungalow near their son.'

'You didn't know my gran? Rose Grey? She wasn't living here then, but she was the landlord. I don't know if she ever came over or . . . ?'

But she shakes her head. 'Nope. When we moved in a Beryl and Colin Jenkins lived in your house and I don't remember meeting any Rose Grey.'

Snowy pulls at the lead and I bend down to stroke him. 'And after them was it Mr and Mrs Turner?' I ask, recalling Mrs McNulty's conversation in the corner shop.

Brenda glares at me, and just when I think she'll refuse to say, she leans towards me, and I can tell, despite her prickliness, she's enjoying having a gossip. She pulls her cream cardigan further around her skinny body. 'The Turners – Valerie and Stan – moved in around 1988 or 1989. Had a dodgy son. Always getting into trouble.'

'Do you remember the son's name?'

'Harrison. Yes, that's it, I remember because of George

Harrison. He was a wild one. Felt sorry for his mum and dad. They were older. Stan had very bad arthritis.'

'Have you told the police this?'

'Of course I have. I told them last week.'

I hope they've looked into the son. I make a mental note to ask DS Barnes.

'Anyway,' I say, trying to sound cheerful, 'there are no journalists right now. Maybe they're having a day off.'

But she harrumphs and scurries back inside, without saying goodbye.

Later, I recount my conversation with Brenda to Tom as we stand side by side at the sink, washing up our dinner things before Mum insists on doing it. She's already rearranged the cutlery drawer. I filled him in on our visit to Gran when we were eating.

Mum's gone up to her room to attend to her blistered feet. I don't know why she insists on wearing heels everywhere. A silvery salmon skin sticks to the oven dish and I take out my frustration by scrubbing hard. I'm desperate for a dishwasher but God knows when we can start the building work again. It looks like it'll be a long time before I have my dream kitchen. Even though the garden is no longer being treated as a crime scene and the police have said we're allowed to continue with our renovations, the builders can't come back for a few months because they've now started on another job. I can't help wondering if that's an excuse.

'The son could be an interesting line of enquiry for the police,' says Tom. 'Maybe his parents helped him cover it up.' I notice a fleck of white paint in his hair. He came home from work and instantly changed into his decorating clothes, saying, 'I can just get in another lick of paint before dinner.' The banister is nearly finished and then he wants to start on the little bedroom. But something stops me . . . Every time I go in there I feel strange. It's only been since the bodies were discovered and I know it's because the back window looks onto the garden and the gigantic hole. It's just a reminder of what happened, that's all. I know I'll get past it. Once all this is over.

'Gran mentioned a Jean and Victor today,' I say. 'I think she's just getting confused but,' I sigh, 'for the first time it made me wonder if she knows something about those bodies. Like she's trying to remember something. But after speaking to Brenda . . .' I let my words hang in the air.

DS Barnes told us as we were leaving that the woman who sold the house to Gran, back in 1977, is long dead. She had no children but a sister whom they have spoken to. He added that they were following up with the two families who rented the house from Gran in the years between 1981 and 1990 but didn't mention the Turners' son. He also said they will be looking into Daphne Hartall and the other lodger. It sounds like they're working hard to identify the bodies but he did say it would be a long process due to the state of decomposition. It sounds like a mammoth task.

'It must be so hard for your gran. And hard to know if what she's saying actually means anything or is just ramblings due to the dementia,' says Tom, as he dries a plate. It nearly slips from his hand.

'Careful! That's one of our only unchipped ones.'

He pulls a face. It's a running joke how clumsy he is. On the night we first met at uni in Bournemouth he'd walked me back to my student digs after I'd had too much to drink. I could tell he was kind straight away: he took care of me, fetching me water and making me toast to nibble. I remember looking at him, as he'd crossed my shabby living room with a tray, and feeling a pang of fondness for him, this hot, slightly geeky guy with the floppy blond hair who was trying to impress me, when he tripped over the rug and the plate and mug went flying across the room. He froze in horror, his eyes meeting mine. Then we both cracked up and it broke the ice.

Since then he's slipped on wet decking when we went to look around our first rental property with the estate agent, fallen over a tree stump and broken his ankle on a romantic walk in the woods, and only last year tripped over Snowy and put his back out for a week. Not to mention all the glasses and plates he's dropped over the years. He says he's not coordinated because he's never got used to his long limbs and lanky frame. 'Like a puppy German Shepherd that's growing too fast,' he'd joke.

Tom sets the plate carefully on the laminate work surface and picks up the oven dish from the rack with an exaggerated care that makes me laugh.

Mum rushes into the kitchen. She looks flustered. 'I've just had a great idea,' she says. 'Why don't we look through your gran's things? All this talk of a Jean and a Victor. It's got me curious.'

'Her things?' I say, taking the tea-towel from Tom to wipe my sudsy hands.

'Yes. You know, the stuff we boxed up when we were packing her Bristol house.'

I frown. 'We gave a lot of it away to charity. Her furniture and things.'

'Yes, yes, but we kept her personal stuff, didn't we, her admin and so on?' She sounds impatient. I nod, remembering the envelopes and boxes of papers that were stuffed into her sideboard and we couldn't be bothered to look through, telling ourselves we'd do it at a later date. But then we forgot and Mum went back to Spain. 'What did you do with it all?'

'I . . .' I try to think. 'It could be in the spare room or in the attic now. We still have a lot of unpacking to do.'

Mum raises an eyebrow at me as if to say, 'But you've been living here months!' I know she would have had it all done in the first week. 'Okay, then. We need to find the boxes and go through them.'

My heart falls. 'What – now?' I was looking forward to a packet of Minstrels in front of the telly and a light-hearted rom-com, something funny to take our minds off everything that's been going on.

Her face softens. 'I'm sorry, honey. I know you must be tired. I'd forgotten how knackering the second trimester is. Just show me where they are and I'll go through them.'

I'm tempted, I'm not going to lie. But I can't let her do it by herself. It wouldn't be right. 'It's fine. I'll help. Come on.'

I throw Tom an exasperated look over my shoulder. He smiles in sympathy and says he'll put the kettle on.

We find them in the attic. The two large boxes the furthest away, crammed into a corner under the eaves. Tom has to come up to help lift them down the ladder. Then the three of us sit on the floor, with a hot drink beside us, and sift through them, Snowy with his head resting in Tom's lap.

'God, your gran kept a lot of crap,' he says, as he sorts through a pile of old receipts.

'Look at this.' I hold up a tan leatherbound book. 'It's a book of poems. It looks ancient.' I open it. The pages are yellowing and smell musty. 'Oh . . . wow.'

'What?' asks Mum.

I gently peel a pressed flower from between the pages. 'It's a pressed rose.' It's dry and crispy but the burnt crimson colours are still vivid. 'Someone she loved gave her this.' I place the flower carefully back in the book and hand it to Mum. 'They're love poems.'

Mum's eyes glisten as she takes the book and turns it over in her hands. I know how she feels. Gran has always been so private, never talking about her past, her lovers, her husband. It's hard to imagine she had a life before she was a mother and a grandmother. A life in which she'd received a pressed rose in a book of poems. A life in which she was in love. 'Maybe my father gave it to her,' says Mum. 'What about old photos? Do you have any in your box?'

'She always did have a sparse amount,' I say, remembering how I'd asked once to see some of my granddad and she proclaimed that she hardly had any, that people didn't take that many photos in her day, which I found hard to believe. She didn't grow up in Victorian times. 'Have you ever seen any of your dad?' I say to Mum, who's still staring at the little book of poetry. She puts it on the floor next to her feet, reluctantly.

'No, never. She said they'd got lost in a move.'

'So you know nothing about him?'

'No. Not much. She didn't like to talk about him, said it upset her too much.' She continues ferreting in the box. 'She said he'd died before I was born. A heart attack. We never visited any grave.'

I think of the man buried in the garden. For one awful mo ment I wonder if it could be my granddad. I shake the thought from my mind. That's ridiculous. I can't start doubting Gran now. And that book of poetry, the dried rose. They must have been in love once.

'Did you ever meet any of your dad's family?' I ask Mum.

She shakes her head. 'No. Your gran always said his parents had died young, like her own, and they were both only children.'

'And you knew nothing else about him?'

Mum looks up from the box and ponders this. 'Not really. I suppose I gave up asking. She never seemed to want to talk about him.' She turns back to the box and then gives a shout of joy, making me jump. She's holding a brown A4 envelope in her hand. 'There's photos in here!'

I crawl over to where she's sitting by the window. 'Let me see.'

She pulls out a pile in different sizes and starts flicking through them. Most are of Mum in various stages of growing up, in the garden of the house in Bristol, but then she pulls out five or six square ones. 'Look at these,' she says, handing them to me. I'm sitting almost on top of her, so eager am I to see the rare photos. They look like they were taken with one of those old Polaroid cameras and are of Mum when she's really young, no more than two or three years old. Most are of her sitting cross-legged in what looks like the garden here, the cottage just visible in the background. One is of her and a much younger Gran, slimmer than I've ever seen her and dressed in flared trousers and a stripy tank top.

'Oh, my God,' says Mum, staring at another photo. I peer over her shoulder. It's of Mum again as a little girl and she's standing in front of the cottage, the frothy lilac wisteria visible above her. Bent down next to her is a woman I don't recognize. They aren't close up, so it's hard to distinguish features but it's not Gran. Mum turns to look at me, her brown eyes wide. 'Who is this woman? Do you think this could be Daphne?'

'Maybe.' I take the photo from her and flip it over. On the back are the words *Lolly, April 1980. 9 Skelton Place*. I frown. 'Who's Lolly?'

'Me,' says Mum. 'It's how I referred to myself. I couldn't say Lorna, apparently.'

'I've never heard Gran call you that.'

Mum chuckles. 'I probably told her off for it. That would have been the sort of thing that embarrassed me, I reckon, as I got older.'

I hand the photo to Tom, who glances at it, then lets out a bark of laughter. 'Nice pageboy haircut, Lorna.'

'Mum used to cut it. That fringe!'

I scoot back to the box I was looking through and pull out an envelope, hoping to find more photographs. Instead I find a yellowing newspaper clipping. 'What's this?' I say, as I slide it out. I'm worried it's going to disintegrate in my hands, it's so old. 'It's from January 1977 in a newspaper called the *Thanet Echo*.'

'What?' This time Mum scuttles over to me and we both read it at the same time.

A BROADSTAIRS WOMAN WHO HAS BEEN MISSING FOR OVER A WEEK IS THOUGHT TO HAVE TRAGICALLY DROWNED.

Sheila Watts, 37, was last seen on New Year's Eve at her local pub, the Shire Horse. Late-night revellers said she joined them at the beaches of Viking Bay to continue celebrations

Witnesses told police Miss Watts was on the beach at just after midnight and was spotted getting into the sea. Her clothes were found on the shore although Miss Watts wasn't seen again.

Alan Hartall, 38, a neighbour of Miss Watts, said, 'Sheila was a bit of a loner. Kept herself to herself, although I got to know her quite well. Because it was New Year's Eve she decided to join us for a drink in our local and then came with us to the beach. She was the only one who got in the sea. We were busy drinking and had forgotten all about her. It was only when she failed to return home that I realized what must have happened and alerted the police.'

Coast Guards have scoured the bay to no avail and local police issued a statement to say they believe Miss Watts died of death by misadventure.

I turn to Mum. 'Sheila! Do you think this is who Gran was talking about today?'

She looks as puzzled as I feel. 'Maybe she knew her.'

'In Broadstairs? But I thought Gran was from London.'

'I think she lived all over before I was born.'

I pass the piece to Tom, who reads it. The fading light from the leaded windows casts a shadow on one side of his face. It has the effect of making his nose look crooked. He hands me back the article. 'This has to be important,' he says, glancing from me to Mum and voicing what we're all thinking. 'Why else would you keep an article for forty years?'

15

Theo

THEO HAS BEEN WATCHING HIS DAD CLOSELY SINCE HE stumbled upon that newspaper article last week, finding excuses to pop over to the soulless mansion in between shifts, plucking up the courage to broach the subject of the couple in Wiltshire. His dad has never been open with Theo at the best of times, but lately every time Theo turns up at the house his dad acts as though he's an intruder, questioning him on why he's come over. Just once Theo would like his dad to look even a little bit pleased to see him. But he's promised Jen he'd ask him. Jen, who wouldn't be afraid to ask her warm, open family anything.

So here he is again, Tuesday lunchtime, before he starts at the restaurant. Why is it so bloody hard to broach the subject with his father? He's a grown man. But when he's around him he feels like that unsure teenager again, obeying his mother's wishes to keep his mouth shut, to do what his father says so as not to upset him. To keep things on an even keel like she always did. To stop his father getting angry.

'I don't need any more food,' his dad snaps, when Theo

walks into the kitchen with his trusty cool-bag filled with a chicken curry and a cottage pie. 'I've got a freezer full of them. I eat at the golf club most nights anyway.'

Honestly, Theo doesn't know why he fucking bothers. God, he'd love to tell his father where to go. But even though his mum has been dead for fourteen years he can't bring himself to do it. She'd be disappointed in him, he knows it.

'Actually,' says Theo, dumping the bag on the table. 'I came here to ask you something.' His heart pounds beneath his T-shirt. He imagines Jen behind him, encouraging him to continue.

'What's that, then?' His father has one of his golf clubs in his hand and is buffing the end of it with a rag. He'd tried to teach Theo golf once, when he was thirteen. He bought him a set of his own irons and taught him the name of each one. Theo had hated every minute of it, but kept it up for more than a year to please him. But when his father realized Theo was never going to be any good, he lost interest in teaching him.

Theo takes a deep breath. 'Last week when I came over I found a newspaper article on your desk. It was about this couple from Wiltshire who were doing some kind of renovations and found two skeletons in their garden. You'd underlined two women's names and then there were the words, "Find Her".'

His father stops polishing his club but doesn't look up. Instead his muscular shoulders tense, and the tendon in his neck bulges. 'Have you been snooping around my things?'

'No, of course not.'

His dad stands up, golf club still in hand. For a wild moment Theo wonders if he's going to smack him with it. His father is looking at him now. His blue eyes are icy. 'Then mind your own fucking business.'

Theo tries to hide his shock. His dad hasn't spoken to him like that in years. 'Who are you trying to find?'

'Did you not hear me?' His dad moves two paces towards him. His face has darkened. The old familiar fear resurfaces in Theo.

I'm not that scared little kid any more, he reminds himself.

'Why won't you talk about it? Maybe I can help?'

His dad lets out a nasty-sounding laugh. 'You?'

Why are you such a prick? thinks Theo. But he stands his ground. Refuses to move back towards the door. 'Yes, me. Do you know the couple from Wiltshire?'

'Of course not.'

'Then why the article?'

He puts the golf club down, leaning it against the kitchen table, and Theo lets out a small sigh of relief. 'I just used it to write on. Not that it's got anything to do with you.'

He's lying. His dad must think he's an idiot.

'So what does *Find Her* mean?'

'Why does everything have to have some hidden meaning with you? What is it you really want to ask me, huh? What is this really all about?' He stares at Theo, his mouth set hard. 'I'm a grown man, and I don't have to run everything I do past you. Do you understand?'

Theo stares back. *What are you hiding, Dad? Because I know you're hiding something.* 'I'm not playing games,' says Theo, trying to keep his voice even. 'I'm asking you about that article, that's all. You've seemed very preoccupied lately, like something's troubling you.'

'The only thing troubling me is *you*,' he snaps.

Theo takes a deep breath. There's no point in arguing with his father when he's in this mood. He holds his hands up. 'Fine,

I'll leave you to it, then.' He picks up the bag from the table. 'I take it you don't want these?'

His dad scowls in response.

'Then I'll take them. Jen and I will eat them.' He marches out of the kitchen with the bag and doesn't look back until he's behind the wheel of his Volvo. He half hopes his dad will follow him, to apologize. But, of course, he doesn't. Theo dumps the cool-bag on the passenger seat and sits for a few minutes without turning on the ignition, guilt raining down on him, as it always does. Was he out of order? Should he have handled it differently?

Your dad's just old-school, his mum used to say gently. *He's not very good at showing his emotions. But he loves us.* He was never sure if she was trying to convince him or herself.

Theo knows he shouldn't be surprised his dad hasn't revealed anything. After his mum died Theo had tried talking about her, but his dad had refused to be drawn. Burying his grief under even more layers of bitterness and anger, like a well-cooked lasagne.

And now this. This extra mystery. The two dead bodies in a Wiltshire garden more than two hundred miles away. And the words *Find Her* in his father's sprawling handwriting.

It finally hits him that he'll never get answers from his dad. It's been too many years. Too many unanswered questions. He's just going to have to do some digging of his own.

But where to start? he thinks later, much later, after his shift at the restaurant has ended. Jen is fast asleep upstairs but he is still buzzing. His body is dog tired, his feet ache after standing up all evening, but his mind is too active and he can't switch off.

Google, he thinks. He'll start there.

He goes to his laptop, which lives on the dining-room table in their two-bedroom Victorian terrace, the glow of the screen the only light in the room. It reflects back at him from the French windows that lead to the garden.

He starts off typing in 'Saffron Cutler'. A few articles pop up about the bodies found in her garden, but nothing that wasn't in the cutting on his dad's desk. He continues scrolling. Lots of news stories from someone called Euan Cutler, who writes for one of the red tops. Rose Grey is also a dead end – he has no clue which of the many Rose Greys could be the one referred to in the article he found.

Then he types in his father's name.

A number of entries pop up. His dad is a very eminent man. It takes Theo a while to sift through it all, and he almost gives up. He doesn't know what he's expecting to find. There's a page detailing his long and successful medical career and then he notices another article about a private practice set up in 1974. It's accompanied by a grainy black-and-white photo of his much younger father standing with another man at some black-tie do. He peers more closely at the screen. There is a caption underneath: *Practice partner Larry Knight.* That's strange, thinks Theo. As far as he's aware his dad never had a partner at the small private clinic he used to run, and which he sold when he retired six years ago.

He types his dad's name and 'Dr Larry Knight' into Google. A few articles from a range of medical journals pop up. It sounds like they parted ways about four years after setting up the clinic. Theo wonders why. His dad has always been an enigma to him – there is so much about his past he doesn't know. Maybe Larry Knight might give him some answers. He realizes he's grasping at straws. There's nothing here to link his dad to the bodies in Wiltshire. But maybe Larry Knight might give him some insight into what his dad's life was like before he met Theo's mum; he might even know Rose Grey.

He rubs his eyes. He's exhausted yet wired at the same time. He can't tear his eyes away from the screen even though there is no new information there.

He blinks away his tiredness but his dad's name swims in front of him.

Dr Victor Carmichael.

16

Rose

January 1980

Daphne moved in with us on New Year's Day. She turned up on the doorstep just after lunch, her blonde hair in a French-style plait, shivering in her thin coat, armed with just a rucksack and the clothes on her back.

I often wondered, in the days and weeks that followed, why a woman who, I assumed, was in her mid to late thirties had no other worldly possessions. It seemed to me she had left her last location in a hurry.

Was it rash of me to invite a stranger into our home? I didn't think so. Not then, anyway. Then she was nothing more to me than a lodger, someone to pay rent so that I had another source of income rather than squandering the last of my parents' inheritance. From her demeanour on Christmas Eve, I sensed she was as desperate as I was to hide away. And I was willing to bet my life on it that it was for similar reasons: running from a man.

That first evening was a little awkward. I showed her

around the cottage and to her room so she could dump her stuff. I saw the cottage through her eyes: the unvarnished floorboards that I still hadn't got around to carpeting, except in your bedroom (pink, like you wanted); the tatty kitchen with the brown tiles; the fireplaces instead of radiators; the old Rayburn range that was always on, and where I boiled water in a cast-iron kettle.

'What do you use this for?' asked Daphne, pointing to the door on the left as we descended the stairs.

'Nothing at the moment,' I said, leading her into the empty room, with the brown and yellow patterned wallpaper left from the last owner. 'It's not a very big room. I think it was probably a front parlour or something.'

She frowned. 'I suppose you could use it as a dining room.'

'True, but we have the table in the kitchen.'

'Or a playroom for Lolly?'

'She usually plays by me in the front room. Or up in her bedroom. But . . .' I hesitated, glancing at her '. . . you're welcome to use it. For whatever you want.'

Her face brightened and she turned to me, her eyes widening. 'Really? That would be great. Although,' her face fell, 'I don't have my sewing machine any more.'

'You sew?'

'I made my own clothes before . . .' She blushed. 'Anyway, I'll save up and buy another.'

I wondered if she'd made the patched green coat she was wearing. It certainly had a homemade look about it.

'You might be able to get one second hand. I can ask around.'

'Thank you.' She lifted her eyes to mine and held my gaze longer than was comfortable. Her lashes were tinted with blue mascara, a fleck of which had landed on her pale cheekbone.

She had a very small black dot on her iris that looked like a beauty spot.

I lowered my gaze first. 'Right. Well, I'd better see to Lolly,' I said, turning around and going back upstairs.

Later, after I'd tucked you up in your little iron-framed bed, Daphne and I sat side by side on the brown corduroy sofa, like a nervous couple on a first date. She was still wearing her coat and a pair of navy platform boots that looked like the toes had been coloured with pen under her flared jeans. I'd poured us both a glass of Babycham that Joel, the landlord of the Stag and Pheasant, had given me for Christmas, and we sat and watched the flames and logs spit and crackle in the open fire. The smell of smouldering wood and firelighter fuel was heavy and intoxicating. The radio was on and Blondie's 'Heart Of Glass' was playing in the background.

I could see Daphne taking in the modest living room with the pink and blue flowered wallpaper I'd put up myself when we first moved in and the fringed floor lamp in the corner that clashed.

'I hope it's not too basic for you,' I said to her. 'At least we have an indoor bathroom. The last owners put it in.'

Daphne smiled enigmatically, casting her eyes around the room. 'I've lived in worse,' she said, and I tried not to feel offended. I'd made it as homely as I could for you.

'It was cheap.' I smiled and shrugged, trying to look nonchalant and not like I was secretly proud of owning my home. Something nobody else could ever take away. My security. 'I didn't want to spend all the money I had on a property.' I'd ignored the estate agent's warning about the ridges on a thatched roof having to be replaced every ten years. It seemed so far away. I might have moved by then.

She raised one of her thin pencilled eyebrows. 'It must be hard being a single parent.'

I nodded. Better than the alternative, I thought, although I didn't say that.

'Did your husband leave you this cottage?'

I hesitated. She thought I was a widow. What to tell her without giving anything away? You have to understand, Lolly, that I had always been so honest. Before. Telling people everything – the cost of a new top, how much I earned, who I was going out with – whether or not they actually wanted to know. But I'd learnt the hard way to keep my mouth shut.

I nodded and sipped my drink.

'How long ago did your husband die?'

'When I was pregnant,' I replied. I felt terrible for lying.

'How awful,' she said, playing with the stem of her glass. She glanced at my hand, noting the absence of a wedding ring. I didn't want to admit there had never been a ring.

'Have you . . . ever been married?' I asked her instead.

She shuddered. 'God, no. I'm never getting married.'

'Really?'

'I don't understand why anyone would want to tie themselves down to a man.'

Was it because she'd also been treated badly? Or had I got her wrong? Maybe she was just a bit of a free spirit. Or a hippie. Maybe she believed in free love. She was attractive with large hooded eyes, an elfin face and long, dyed-blonde hair, the brown roots visible. I was sure she'd have no shortage of male interest. I'd always thought of myself as reasonably attractive, not stunning or a head-turner, or anything like that, but natural, unthreatening. I could see that Daphne was more striking. 'Um . . .' I cleared my throat. 'I know this is a bit delicate, and we probably should have talked about this before you moved in. But . . . with

Lolly and everything . . . I think it's better there are no . . .' How could I put this tactfully? '. . . overnight visitors.'

She stared at me for a few moments, then let out a loud laugh. 'Oh, Rose! Look at you, you've gone red. I promise I'm not going to be entertaining men in the bedroom. Honestly, men are the furthest thing from my mind.'

I sipped my drink in relief.

'Do you mind if I smoke?'

I shook my head. 'I try not to smoke around Lolly if that's okay.'

She looked a little surprised but shrugged. 'That's fine. I'll go into the back garden.' She placed her drink on the side table and stood up. I followed her into the kitchen and through the back door. She stood on the patio outside, shivering in her ribbed polo neck and thin coat, and I felt so guilty that I told her we could stand in the doorway. She handed me a roll-up. We stood in silence, puffing on our cigarettes as a fine layer of ice coated the paving slabs in front of us.

'Thank you,' she said eventually. 'For agreeing to rent me a room. I think this will work out well.'

I didn't know if it was the alcohol, or the nicotine, or a combination of both, but I suddenly felt confident that she was right. We both wanted the same thing, I could already tell. Peace and quiet. Anonymity.

Standing there with her on that first day of a new year, a new decade, I never dreamed, in a million years, that her baggage, her past, would put us in danger.

17

Lorna

THE NEXT MORNING LORNA OFFERS TO TAKE SNOWY FOR a walk to give Saffy some space. Even though it's been only four days, Lorna can tell by her daughter's slightly harangued expression that she is getting under her feet. The more Lorna tries to be helpful around the house, the more Saffy looks like she's sucking a sour boiled sweet. She'd thought, hoped, that this *gruesome discovery* would bring them closer together. She knows it's selfish but now Saffy is pregnant she fears the gap will widen even further between them.

She realizes she made mistakes when Saffy was growing up. Lorna had been happy for her mother to take over. She'd shipped Saffy off every summer so that she could have a break, act like the teenager and then the young woman she'd been at the time, going to clubs and pubs, and, when she and Euan finally split up, hooking up with unsuitable men.

And now Saffy finally needs her. Really needs her. Even if she doesn't yet know it.

She leaves Saffy in her depressing little study, hunched over her computer, and steps outside into the sunshine. She takes deep breaths, then coughs as the smell of the countryside hits the back of her throat. The skies are cloudless; she's wearing a light top with her jeans and sandals. She probably should have brought flatter shoes. Heels aren't the best for the slopes and inclines of Beggars Nook.

As she treads over the gravelled driveway with Snowy, she notices a large van parked up. A young, well-dressed woman in a purple suit and dark hair that doesn't move in the breeze is talking to a camera on the pavement.

'This might look like just another idyllic Cotswold cottage,' she is saying, into a microphone, in a sepulchral tone. 'But looks are deceiving. Two bodies have been found here at Skelton Place.' She turns to indicate the cottage and Lorna freezes, not sure whether to keep walking or stay still. The journalist's face lights up when she sees her. 'And here is one of the owners now.' She moves towards Lorna. 'It must have been a shock to discover the bodies,' she says, thrusting the microphone into Lorna's face.

Lorna bristles. 'This isn't my house.'

'Oh.' The reporter looks thrown and then professionalism kicks in. 'I gather you're not Saffron Cutler?'

'No, I'm not.'

'I understand this cottage used to belong to Saffron's grandmother. Is that correct?'

'No comment,' says Lorna. 'Now, if you'll excuse me –'

'Cut!' shouts the cameraman. He's standing in the road and an irate driver beeps for him to move. He strides to the pavement but doesn't apologize or acknowledge the driver.

The reporter looks daggers at him before fastening her gaze back on Lorna. 'It would be great if we could interview you for our news segment. Heleana Phillips, pleased to meet you.' She extends a hand but Lorna doesn't take it.

'There's no story here,' snaps Lorna. 'We know nothing about the bodies. It happened years before my daughter lived here.'

Heleana pushes a lock of her sleek hair behind her ear. 'Well,' she says, in a soothing voice that Lorna suspects is put on to cajole, 'I think this is a very interesting story. It's not every day that two bodies are discovered, now, is it? Are you sure there aren't any more?'

'Quite sure,' says Lorna, gently pulling Snowy to his feet and moving away. She notices a few of the elderly ladies who live across the road have clustered together on the pavement and are watching the scene with disapproving expressions, arms folded across their chests. Lorna understands that this Heleana and the other reporters are just doing their job – she's used to it, after all, once living with Euan – but she wishes they'd bugger off. Particularly for Saffy's sake: she notices how her daughter hides away when they're outside, like a prisoner in her own home.

Lorna stalks off down the hill in her unsuitable shoes, ignoring Heleana's calls. Her heart is beating fast but she doesn't slow until she reaches the Stag and Pheasant at the bottom of the slope. Then she stops to catch her breath before continuing through the village square. It opens up like a scene from a pop-up children's book, and as she passes the market cross and the quaint little church, she is besieged by that diaphanous memory again. It floats frustratingly out of reach. The market cross is so familiar to her that she finds herself heading there. She sits on one of the cold steps, surveying the rest of the square. And it hits her. A memory, struggling to solidify in her mind. She remembers walking through this square, flanked by two women, each holding one of her hands. Her mother . . . and someone else. Someone faceless. The woman in the photograph, perhaps? It's more of a feeling than a memory and it instantly makes her feel melancholy, a bit like grief.

What is it about this place? she wonders, getting to her feet. When she's here she feels enveloped in a sadness she can't explain, as if a cold mist has descended over her, covering her like a veil.

This won't do, she thinks. She needs to snap out of it. To remember why she's here. She mentally ticks off all the things she wants to buy: ingredients to make a traditional Spanish paella for Saffy and Tom tonight. She heads over the little bridge to the shop at the end of a row, tying Snowy to a post. She's getting used to him now. She'd even go as far as saying she feels some affection for him.

The corner shop doesn't have all the ingredients she needs, so she has to improvise. As she walks around the narrow aisles, she notices a few stares from other customers. She ignores it. She's used to being stared at. She pays and then, with Snowy, ambles to the little café on the corner, the Beggars Bowl.

The café allows dogs so she takes Snowy inside. It's cramped, with just enough room for two round tables towards the back. There is an elderly man with a shock of white hair in front of her talking to the young guy who's serving behind the counter, and she just catches the tail end of his conversation.

'. . such a quiet place but now there's journalists everywhere and coppers – one came to my door last night asking questions. It was dinner time. Who comes knocking at dinner time? I ask you! This is what happens when youngsters come in and over-develop their houses . . .' He falters when he notices Lorna. He raises his white, craggy eyebrows at her, but doesn't continue his tirade. Lorna's tempted to tell him not to stop on her account but she doesn't want to make things worse for Saffy. She's the one who's got to live with these villagers after all.

The man takes his cup from the guy behind the counter, nods at her without smiling and leaves the café.

'What can I get you?' asks the young guy. If he knows who she is he doesn't let on and she's grateful. She orders a latte and makes small talk while he's preparing it. She learns that his name is Seth, he grew up in the village, his aunt used to own the café and that he's off to do a degree in engineering at Nottingham in October. She's smiling to herself as she leaves with her precious latte. He's the first friendly person in the village she's encountered since she arrived.

As she slows down to sip her coffee she hears someone clearing their throat at her shoulder. She turns to see a man in his late fifties, wearing a checked shirt and jeans. Short, greying hair and narrow eyes that seem to be assessing her for longer than is polite. She stops walking and Snowy plonks himself at her feet.

'Hi,' he says, smiling pleasantly. 'You live at nine Skelton Place, don't you?' He has a northern accent and there is something about his posture and tone that screams ex-military.

'No. I'm just visiting,' she replies.

'I'm not from around here either,' he says, surprising her.

'Oh. Right.' Then it occurs to her. 'Are you a journalist?'

He looks taken aback. 'Oh, no . . . no. I'm just visiting too. The name's Glen.' He holds out a hand and she feels it would be impolite to refuse to shake it.

'I'm Lorna.'

His handshake is firm. 'I heard about the bodies up at Skelton Place. Everybody in the village is talking about it.'

'Yes, I can imagine.'

He grins at her, still holding her hand. She wonders if he's trying to chat her up. He must be a good fifteen years older than her at least. She supposes he's quite handsome in an older-man kind of way, although there is a hardness to his face. She retracts her hand.

'Anyway,' she says, 'I need to get back. Nice to meet you, Glen.'

'Nice to meet you too,' he says, but he stays where he is.

As she walks away she's sure she hears him call out, 'Say hello to Rose.' But when she turns he's heading towards the woods. She frowns at his retreating back, wondering if she should run after him and ask if he knows her mother. But she decides she must have misheard.

When Lorna reaches the cottage she's relieved to see that Heleana and her crew have left. She rings the doorbell and Saffy lets her in with an air of distraction.

'Hi, honey,' she says, unclipping the lead from Snowy's collar. Saffy bends down to kiss his head, then returns to her study. On the screen is a mock-up of a book cover with the name Leon Bronsky in huge red letters across the top and a sinister-looking china doll on fire underneath. Lorna's read some of his books: they're exceptionally dark. 'Did you create this?'

Saffy nods. 'His publisher's employed us to do his cover and marketing. Posters, headers for magazine ads, that kind of thing. A rebrand. He's moved into horror. It's a good commission. He's a huge deal.'

Lorna winces, imagining how much more gruesome this book must be. 'Did you have to read it?'

Saffy laughs. 'Yep. It gave me nightmares.' She pushes a curl from her face, eyes still trained on the screen and the creepy cover. 'I'm glad the reporters have finally gone.'

'Me too. One of them cornered me earlier. But don't worry,

I didn't say anything.' She holds up her carrier bag. 'Bought groceries for tonight. I couldn't get everything I wanted but I'll manage to make a paella of sorts.'

Saffy grunts in answer, her brow furrowed as she concentrates on the screen. Lorna decides it's best to leave her to it and puts the shopping away in the kitchen. Afterwards, she wanders into the living room. They were too tired to finish looking through the boxes last night and Tom had to get up at the crack of dawn for work.

Lorna settles down to continue what they started yesterday. She can see a layer of dust on the skirting board and resists the urge to go and find a cloth. She slips off her sandals and curls her feet underneath her on the hardwood floors, trying to decipher if a bunch of papers is important or just receipts when her mobile rings.

It's Alberto.

Her stomach drops. She's been trying to ring him for days. He sent her a few cursory texts when she arrived but every time she called his mobile it went straight to voicemail.

'*Mi tesoro*, I've missed you,' he says, as soon as she answers. 'When you coming home?'

'I've missed you too.' She's not sure if it's true. 'I'm staying until the weekend, at least.'

'The apartment is lonely without you.' She doubts that. He's usually at his bar until late. But, still, he sounds like he's missing her. Maybe her suspicions about him are wrong.

But he doesn't ask after Saffy or her mother, she thinks, with a stab of disappointment. 'I'm needed here right now. Saffy's pregnant . . .' She recounts everything that's happened since she's been in Beggars Nook but she suspects she's lost him somewhere along the way because he sounds bored when he replies.

'As long as you come back soon, *mi amor. Me muero por verte.*'

'I can't wait to see you too,' she lies, ending the call with a heavy heart.

She spends the next hour sifting through her mother's papers, hoping to find anything else of interest, some more photos maybe. Perhaps of her father. Most of the time she didn't think much about her dad but there were occasions when she missed having a father around. She remembers once at school when she was about ten, they'd had to do a general knowledge quiz – over a full week they were tasked to see who could come up with the most facts – but the library was in town, and without a car to get there she could use only the old-fashioned encyclopaedia her mother had in the house. Her best friend, Anne, won because her dad took her to the library every night for a week to help her find what she needed. She had felt jealous of Anne then, with her doting father and his Mini Metro. Lorna had come last in the quiz.

Her hand brushes the newspaper article about Sheila that they'd found yesterday. She scans it again, wondering why her mother chose to keep it. Had Sheila been her mum's friend? Had she always hoped to get to the bottom of what had happened to her? It sounds like a straightforward case of drowning to Lorna. And then she notices it. And is surprised they didn't realize it yesterday.

Alan Hartall, 38, a neighbour of Miss Watts, said, 'Sheila was a bit of a loner. Kept herself to herself, although I got to know her quite well.'

Alan Hartall. Wasn't that the same surname as her mother's lodger, Daphne? Is that why her mum had kept the article? She stands up and rushes out of the room across to Saffy's, barging in without knocking.

Saffy looks up. 'What now, Mum? I'm already behind, thanks to reporters knocking on my door for most of the morning.'

Lorna slams the article down on the desk in front of her. 'Sorry, honey, but look at this,' she says, indicating the line. 'Alan Hartall. Same surname as Daphne.'

Saffy turns to her mother, her eyes alight. 'Oh.'

'We need to investigate it. It could be a link to finding Daphne if they're related.'

'It's forty years ago. Alan Hartall could be dead now.'

Lorna mentally rolls her eyes. Typical response from her pessimistic daughter. 'And if not he'll be around your gran's age. We need to try. He might be able to tell us about this Daphne.'

'Yes . . . but . . .' Saffy takes a scrunchie from her wrist and ties her hair back with it. 'I'm not sure what the point would be, Mum. It's doubtful Gran was even living here when the murders happened.'

'I know, but Daphne might be able to shed some light on things. The police are questioning everyone who lived here. And,' she swallows, 'it would be nice to meet someone who knew your gran. Back when she was young.'

'We should leave it to the police,' says Saffy.

'They're taking ages.' Lorna begins to pace the small room, frustration building. Now she's had the idea she can't let it go. 'They have so many people to speak to. Past tenants, old lodgers, and even if they do find and speak to Daphne they won't tell us much, will they? If Daphne is still alive it would be fascinating to speak to her, wouldn't it? She knew your gran. Lived here with her. With *me*. It can't hurt. She might know something about this Sheila. She's obviously important or your gran wouldn't have kept that newspaper clipping. Maybe they were all friends . . .'

'I've already asked Dad to look into Sheila and the drowning.'

'Oh. Right. Did you . . . tell him about the baby?'

Saffy nods. 'He was surprised. But happy, I hope.'

'That's great.' Lorna lingers by Saffy's desk until her daughter gives a resigned sigh.

'Okay. How do we go about this?' she asks.

Lorna claps her hands together. 'Right, well, I think maybe you should contact your dad again, if you don't mind? He can get on the electoral roll through his newspaper and find out if there are any Alan Hartalls still living in the Broadstairs area. But don't worry about it yet. You're working.'

Saffy hands Lorna back the article. 'I'll give him a call later – let me just finish this.'

'Great.' Lorna gives Saffy a quick hug, then retreats back into the living room.

It's not a lot to go on, she thinks, as she continues rifling through the box. But it's all we've got for now.

18

Saffy

I walk into the living room, mobile in hand. Mum is sitting on the sofa clutching one of the mustard cushions to her chest. She looks up when I enter, her dark eyes sparkling with excitement. 'And? Did you speak to him?'

'Yep. Dad said he'll try to find out what he can tomorrow. He's not in the newsroom this afternoon.'

Mum jumps up from the sofa. She goes to the window. Her feet are bare and tanned and she keeps hopping from one to the other. Her energy is almost visible, like the glow the kids had in the old Ready Brek adverts that Mum made me watch once on YouTube. 'I feel like I need to be doing something more to find Daphne.' She touches the chunky necklace at her throat, threading the aqua beads through her fingers for a few moments, then turns to me, her eyes flashing. 'I'm going to London.'

'What? Why?'

'I'll go and visit your dad. I haven't seen him since your graduation. It would be nice to catch up.'

That's the weird thing about my divorced parents. They

still like each other. They spent the whole time at my graduation drinking and laughing with one another, and when I told
Tara they were actually divorced she'd been shocked. I've often wondered if they'd met later in life, instead of as teenagers,
would they have stayed together?

'Dad might not be able to find anything on Alan Hartall,' I
say. 'The most he'll have is an address and you can get that over
the phone.'

'I know, but it will give me something to do. Get out from
under your feet. You've got work to do and I'm just hanging
around here, not being useful. I'll catch the train tomorrow.
Would you mind giving me a lift to the station?' Before I can
answer she's whipped out her mobile from the back pocket of her
jeans. 'There's a train tomorrow to Paddington at . . .' she peers at
the screen more closely '. . . nine twenty-eight a.m.' She looks up.
'Not too early for you?'

Mum still assumes I haven't progressed from my teenage
self, lounging around in bed until noon. 'It's fine,' I say. I think
it's a mad idea but it will get her out of the house for the day
and give me some space to finish the book design for my boss,
Caitlyn. She wasn't happy with my last mock-up. I'm worried
I'm losing my touch. I've been too distracted by the move, the
baby, Gran, my mum. And, of course, the small matter of the
dead bodies.

'Stop chewing your lip,' she says, as she breezes past me. 'I'll
put the kettle on.'

Mum is already dressed and applying her makeup at the kitchen
table when I get up the next morning. Tom was out of the house
by 6 a.m. It's a long commute for him every day and I think the
novelty of it is starting to wear off. He was late home last night
due to train delays, and fell into bed, exhausted, wrapping his

arms around my stomach and conking out more or less straight away.

'You look smart,' I say, which is true even if her outfit is something I'd never wear. She has on a fitted black and white tweed jacket with big brass buttons, her favourite skin-tight cerise jeans and a low-cut white T-shirt with the same chunky necklace as yesterday. I feel underdressed in my baggy dungarees and lemon T-shirt.

'Thank you.' She beams at me over her compact mirror. Then she puts it down and frowns. 'Are you okay? You look a bit . . . peaky.'

'I'm fine. Just feel queasy in the mornings.' Her perfume is giving me a sickly headache. Although it's not just that. I feel a little uneasy about being in the cottage all day on my own. I'm used to it, usually. And I've been yearning for some time without Mum hanging around. But now she's actually going – and with Tom in London too – it's hit me that I'm actually going to be alone. In this eerie cottage with the spectre of the two bodies lingering.

I try not to look out of the window as I fetch a glass of water. Tom thinks we might have to hire a different building firm. The sooner that hole has been covered the better. Every time I look at it I get the creeps.

Mum pushes her chair back. 'Sit down, honey. What can I get you? Toast? Crackers to nibble on?' I've noticed she's already washed up and put away last night's things. I feel like I'm a guest in her house, which, I suppose, technically I am. She's even fed the dog. Something I thought she'd never do.

She fetches me some crackers and I sink into a chair, while she fusses around me. I'm too tired to object. Anxiety furs my insides. I feel like I'm the one getting the train to London. What might Dad unearth? This is surely opening a can of worms.

'So, what's the plan?' I say, putting down the cracker. It's not helping.

'I'm meeting your dad for an early lunch.' She checks the slim gold watch on her wrist. 'Right, we'd better get going. Now, are you sure you're okay to take me? I'm happy to get a taxi.'

I stand up. 'It's fine, Mum. Come on.'

She chats all the way to the station. By the time we've arrived I've got a massive headache. She's still talking as she gets out of the car. 'I'll ring you later to keep you updated. I'll get a taxi back so don't worry about picking me up. I'll –'

A car behind me beeps. 'Mum, I'm not supposed to have stopped here.'

'Okay, I'm going, I'm going.' She shuts the passenger door and waves and blows kisses as I pull away.

It's peacefully quiet on the drive back to the cottage.

I let myself in and decide to call Dad. He picks up on the second ring.

'Hi, sweetheart. I was going to ring you but thought it might be a bit early.'

It's nine thirty. What is it with my parents? 'Just wondering if you've had any luck with Sheila Watts?' I ask.

From his breathing it sounds like he's walking. I like the thought of him striding through the streets of London with perhaps a takeaway coffee, his notebook tucked away in his jacket, on his way to a job. My big, handsome dad. 'Well, actually, I did find something,' he says.

I stand up straighter. 'Oh, yes?'

'In Archives I found a file on her.'

I gasp. 'Really? What was in the file? Was it the same Sheila?'

'I imagine so. I'm up to my eyes finishing off a big story, so I only flicked through it. It didn't look like much, I'm afraid. I'm surprised it hasn't been shredded. A lot of stuff in Archives has just been forgotten about. But it might be useful. I can take some photos of it and ping them over to you?'

'That would be great.'

'I've got to go. I'm at a job, but I'll email you later.'

'Thanks, Dad.'

I end the call intrigued to see the file.

I need to clear my head before I start work so I decide to take Snowy for a walk. He circles my legs eagerly while I retrieve his lead and clip it to his collar. Before leaving the house I peer through the small section of glass in the front door to make sure there are no journalists outside. When I see the coast is clear I open the door and step onto the driveway. Pulling my jacket on, I head for the narrow lane a few houses down that leads to the woods behind the Skelton Place properties. Mum thinks the woods are creepy and oppressive, but to me they're beautiful and tranquil. I love the woody aroma of the trees, the damp earth, the bluebells that provide a violet carpet at this time of year, and how the sun sparkles through the leaves. I feel I can properly breathe out here, no pollution, just nature.

I trudge deeper into the woods where the trees are so dense it's hard for any sunlight to get through and I shiver slightly in my thin jacket. Snowy pulls on his lead as we pick our way over snaking pathways and gnarled tree roots sticking out of the ground, like a network of pipes.

I'm so engrossed in my own thoughts that I don't hear anyone behind me at first.

And then a twig snaps.

It's so loud it makes me jump and I whip my head around.

A man is standing a few feet away. I recognize him as the one outside the house the other day, the one I'm sure followed me to Gran's care home last week.

Heat rises to my face and my mouth goes dry. Snowy stops sniffing the tree trunk to stand next to me, his ears pricked forward.

The man has on a waxed jacket and thick boots. He looks like he should be on some posh estate with a hunting rifle in his hand. 'Hi,' he says, smiling.

I nod to him and continue walking.

'Saffron, isn't it?'

I stop. Who is he? Is he a journalist? I turn to him, trying to keep my voice even. 'Look, if you're a reporter I know nothing more about the bodies that were found in my garden. I'm as clueless about all this as you are. It happened way before my time.'

He holds up his hand. 'I'm not press.'

'Oh.' I don't know what else to say. I feel the first prickle of unease. The woods are deserted as far as I can tell and I'm sickeningly aware that I'm alone with this strange man.

'Actually,' he says, 'the name's Davies. I'm a private detective.'

'A – a private detective?' Why would a private detective be following me into the woods? Why didn't he just knock at my door?

'I wasn't following you,' he says, with a little chuckle as though he's read my mind. 'I thought it might be a bit too early to come calling so I decided a walk in the woods was in order. They're so beautiful.'

I frown at him. 'Um . . . who hired you?'

'I'm afraid I'm not at liberty to say.' He gazes around the woods as though this is just a casual conversation, one he isn't particularly bothered about, but I can tell by the tension in his body it's an act.

'Right. Well, I know nothing, I'm afraid, so . . .' I begin to walk off.

'Wait!' he calls, even though he doesn't follow me. I stop and turn towards him. 'It's your grandmother I really need to speak to.'

'My grandmother? Why?'

'It's . . . Well, it's a personal matter.'

'My grandmother is in a care home. She isn't up to speaking to anybody.'

A shadow passes over his face, making him look less amenable. 'Is she ill?'

'She has dementia.'

He rubs his hand over his stubbly chin. 'Oh. That makes things a lot more difficult. A lot more difficult indeed. You see, my client really needs some information from her.' His tone is colder now, all pretence at friendliness gone.

My heart quickens. 'What kind of information?'

'About something that happened a long time ago.'

'I see,' I say, although I'm completely thrown.

'How long ago did your grandmother move out of the cottage?'

'Years ago. She hasn't lived there in a very long time.'

'Do you remember what year?'

'Not exactly, no.' I'm not telling him anything. He seems to consider this for a moment. Snowy starts pulling on the lead impatiently. 'Look,' I add, 'I really don't know anything. My mum and I didn't even realize Gran had this cottage until she went into the care home. I honestly can't help you.'

He moves towards me, reaching inside his jacket. 'Can I give you this?' He pulls out a small cream business card. I reach out and take it from him. *G. E. Davies. T&D Private Investigators* is typed along the front and underneath a mobile number. 'My client is looking for something your grandmother has. My client is certain that she's held on to it for a number of years.'

I think of the two cardboard boxes full of her stuff and vow to go through them again. 'What kind of thing?'

He sighs, looking frustrated. 'Some kind of file. Paperwork.'

'What is this all about?'

'I'm just following orders, Saffron.' He lowers his voice, even though there isn't anybody around, and fear ripples through me. I take a step back. 'My client says this file is very important. It belongs to my client and my client wants it back.'

'Even after all these years?'

'Yes, especially after all these years. So if you find it call me. If it gets into the wrong hands it could cause all sorts of problems for your grandmother. Okay?'

'I . . . In what way?'

'It's complicated. But it's very important. You do understand that, don't you?'

I nod.

'Good. Then I hope to hear from you.'

He turns away. I stand and watch him negotiating the pathways, stepping over thick roots, until he's rounded the corner out of sight.

19

Theo

LARRY KNIGHT'S HOUSE IS A RED-BRICK EDWARDIAN DE-
tached in one of Leeds's affluent suburbs with two ball-shaped
miniature trees in square metal planters at either side of the
black-painted front door.

Theo manages to find a space outside, under a huge shed-
ding cherry tree, its petals already coating the pavement. It's a
beautiful evening: the sun is low in the sky, casting striated ice-
cream colours across the horizon, and the road is quiet, apart
from the tweeting of birds and the far-off sound of children
playing.

It had been a bit of luck, Theo felt, tracking down Larry. After a lot of ringing around he'd finally got hold of a clinic he was
listed under, and was told, as he'd expected, that he had retired.
Just as he was about to hang up, the receptionist revealed the
business was now in the capable hands of Larry's son, Hugo.
He left a message and Hugo called him back to say he'd speak
to his father. Then, just a few hours later, Larry rang him and
agreed to meet face to face. So here he is now, on this unfamiliar street in Leeds. On a beautiful Wednesday evening.

He's only a few minutes late but he suspects Larry has been waiting for him because the door swings open before he's even had a chance to press the bell. An elderly man, who has made up for his receding hairline by growing a white bushy beard, stands on the threshold. He's wearing a cardigan over a shirt that pulls at the belly. He's got kind blue eyes that crinkle at the edges when he smiles, which he does the moment he sees Theo. 'Good gracious,' he says. 'You're the spitting image of your dad at the same age.'

'Hopefully that's where the similarity ends.' Theo laughs to lighten his words.

Larry looks surprised but moves back to allow him over the threshold. Theo stands in the large hallway. The walls are adorned with a vast collection of family photos, all in different sizes but somehow complementing each other. He casts his eye over them. Family holidays in exotic locations; wedding photos; windswept children on beaches in welly boots; grandkids snuggled under checked blankets on squashy sofas; even the family pets are framed. It couldn't be more different from the house he grew up in where the only photo on the wall is of his dad receiving a golfing award back in 1984.

He turns to the old man, to Larry Knight. He can see why the partnership with his dad didn't work out. They are polar opposites. Theo feels a sudden pang for what his childhood could have been like if he'd been brought up in this family, with siblings in wellies, building sandcastles on winter beaches, a home full of dogs and cats and guinea pigs and hamsters. A house bursting with love and laughter, not fear and intimidation. A life documented on hallway walls. He wants all this for him and Jen if they're ever lucky enough to be parents.

Then he thinks of how sad Jen looked when he left her this evening. How she'd sat on the sofa with a hot-water bottle pressed against her stomach, her lovely pale green eyes shining with tears she was trying not to shed. Another period, another chance missed. He hadn't wanted to leave her but she'd insisted. 'As long as you bring me back some Maltesers,' she'd said good-naturedly, as he kissed her goodbye.

'You have a lovely home,' Theo says now, meaning it. Two ageing Golden Retrievers with grey whiskers come waddling up to him and he bends to pat them.

Larry smiles in response. 'Come on, then,' he says, clapping Theo on the back, like he's known him for years. 'Let's go through to the sitting room. Do you want a cup of tea? Marge,' he bellows, before Theo's had the time to answer. An older version of the woman cuddled up to Larry in the photos appears in the hallway. She's tall with high cheekbones and shoulder-length white hair and looks smart in a silk blouse and navy trousers.

'This is Theo, Victor's boy.'

'Hi, Theo,' she says, grasping his hand warmly. 'Good to meet you. Cup of tea?'

Theo says he'd love one, then follows Larry into a cosy room at the front of the house. He perches on the edge of the sofa while Larry sits in an armchair, one of the Retrievers at his feet. The other dog sits beside Theo on the sofa and rests her head on his lap.

Larry chuckles. 'Bonnie likes you.'

Theo strokes her head. 'I love dogs. Hopefully one day my wife and I will get one.'

'Well,' says Larry, hands on his large stomach, 'I was surprised to hear from you. I haven't seen Victor in . . . gosh . . . years. How is he doing?'

'Okay, thanks. He's retired.'

'How is your mum? I went to their wedding . . . What must it have been now? Thirty-five years ago.'

'My mum . . . she died fourteen years ago. An accident.'

Larry's face falls. 'I'm sorry to hear that. She must have been young.'

'Yes. Too young.' Theo swallows. 'I know it must seem strange, me asking to meet you, but . . .' He looks across at the kind-faced man, with the large, happy family, and knows he can be honest. 'I found something of my dad's and it's raised more questions than answers.'

'Okay.'

'You and my dad had a clinic together. Back in the 1970s.'

'Yes, that's right. A private practice. We worked together for years.'

'And I was wondering . . .' He pauses when Marge comes in with two mugs. He takes one from her, careful to keep it away from Bonnie's head, which is still resting on his leg.

'And you were wondering?' Larry prompts, when Marge has left the room.

Theo concentrates on pulling his thoughts together. 'I don't know, really. This all started after I found a newspaper article on my dad's desk.' He hesitates. 'Have you heard of a Rose Grey?'

Larry thinks about it. 'I don't recognize the name.'

'Saffron Cutler?'

Larry shakes his head.

'My dad is so secretive. He never even told me he used to have a business partner.'

Larry regards Theo patiently over the rim of his mug, waiting for him to get to the point.

'Why did you and my dad decided to part ways?'

Larry looks regretful. 'Yes. That was a bad business.'

Theo's heart quickens in anticipation . . . and also dread at what Larry might reveal. 'Did my dad do something wrong?'

'Um . . . well, nobody knows for certain. Of course Victor always maintained his innocence. But there was a complaint from a young woman. I'm sorry, this won't be easy to hear.'

Theo braces himself. Whatever it is, he knows he's probably imagined it.

'A woman complained that Victor was inappropriate with her. During an examination.'

His heart sinks. Out of all the different scenarios he's been envisaging, this one hadn't occurred to him. 'Don't they have to have nurses in the room with them?'

'This was the 1970s,' Larry says, by way of explanation.

'Did the woman press charges?'

'She went to the police. But it was her word against his.'

Theo can just imagine how a woman, forty years ago, would have found it harder to be listened to, to be believed.

A white-hot anger rises within him at the thought his dad could be capable of something so awful, and he takes a sip of his tea to try to extinguish it. He can't get emotional about this, not now. Not yet.

'Do you remember the woman's name?'

Larry thinks for a few moments. 'I can't remember. I want to say Sandra, but I might be wrong. Sadly she killed herself a year later.'

The tea curdles in Theo's stomach. 'Oh, God, that's *awful.*'

Larry nods gravely. 'I know.'

'Did you ask my father to leave the clinic after that?'

'I wanted to believe him . . .'

'But you didn't?'

He sighs. 'It wasn't just that. There were other things.'

Theo's always known his dad could be a control freak and a bully, but he'd believed he was a brilliant doctor. His dad might have been a bit shit at home but in his job he helped change people's lives.

'Were there more complaints?'

'Not of that nature, thankfully.' Larry sips his tea.

'But you said there were other things?'

'Well, we just stopped . . . gelling, I suppose, in the months after the accusation. I think we wanted different things. Your father, as you surely know, is a very ambitious man. I . . . I suppose I wanted a quieter life.' Theo senses there is more that Larry isn't saying.

'Did you keep in touch?'

He nods. 'A little over the years. We'd end up at the same conferences. He met Marge a few times although he never brought your mother to those things.'

That doesn't surprise Theo. His dad always liked to keep his work and home life separate, apart from the odd occasion his mum had to have some of his colleagues over for dinner.

'I followed his career. I was pleased to see he was doing well. I hoped . . . I really hoped . . . that there had been a misunderstanding between Victor and the young woman.'

'When was the last time you saw him?'

Larry narrows his eyes. 'Ooh, let me think. It must have been a good fourteen to fifteen years ago now. Yes, that's right, it was at a conference in the autumn of 2004.'

'That would have been a few months after my mum died.'

Larry looks troubled. 'Ah . . . he didn't say, but I didn't speak to him for long. We had a quick conversation, but about work.'

Bonnie decides she's too hot on the sofa so jumps down and flops at Theo's feet instead. He leans forwards to put his mug on the coffee table. 'Can I ask you something?' he says.

'And please give me your honest answer. Don't worry about my feelings.'

'Of course,' says Larry.

'Do you think my dad was inappropriate with that young woman? Do you think she was telling the truth?'

Larry's face clouds. 'Ah, well, that would only be my opinion. No charges were ever brought against your father, you have to understand that. And at the time I really wanted to believe him.'

'I know . . . but do you now?'

Larry is silent for a while. Theo can almost see his brain weighing it up. Eventually he says, 'We'll never know for certain. But my heart tells me that the young woman wasn't making it up. Whatever happened in the clinic that day, the woman really believed your father had acted inappropriately.'

Theo goes cold.

He'd come here for answers but now he has more questions than ever.

20

Rose

January 1980

I WAS SO USED TO IT JUST BEING YOU AND ME THAT IT felt strange at first having someone else in the house, sharing our only bathroom, our small kitchen, having to be extra polite about which of the four TV channels to watch. It felt like having a permanent guest and it was hard to relax. I felt the same about our last lodger, Kay, and those feelings had never gone away. I hoped to get a job when you were old enough to go to school, but until then the only way I could earn money was by renting out a room in our home.

However, unlike Kay, you took to Daphne straight away. She was like an aunt to you, and even though she was quiet with me, she chatted away to you, as if she was more comfortable in the presence of children. She sat for hours on the sheepskin rug in the front room with you, playing with your Sindy dolls. She even knitted your favourite doll a jumpsuit, in sage green and cream. You loved it.

I assumed she might stay in her room more often but every evening she came and sat with us, handing me a cup of tea even though she'd only just got home from a shift at the pub. Every week she brought back logs for the fire. She was thoughtful.

Daphne had a cash-in-hand job as a cleaner at the Stag and Pheasant so was out most afternoons, and you went to playschool three mornings a week. We usually sat down to dinner at the same time – Daphne liked to cook stews in one of my old brown casserole dishes that had been my parents'. Most days there was one bubbling on the stove, and sometimes, if she was feeling extra creative, with dumplings. That was mainly what she ate that winter: thick meaty stews. 'It's cheap and easy,' she said, chopping the carrots so professionally I wondered if she'd ever worked in a restaurant. She spent ages in the kitchen in her baggy jumpers with holes at the wrists that I suspect she'd knitted herself, slicing up whatever meat she could get her hands on from the butcher, standing at the counter with one leg bent, like a flamingo. 'Oh, I've had so many different jobs over the years,' she'd said, when I asked. 'What haven't I done?'

Even then, at the beginning, when things were good, when I was oblivious to what lay ahead, something about Daphne intrigued me. Apart from that first night, we seemed to have forged an unspoken agreement not to talk about our pasts. But I found myself wanting to know more about her, yet realizing if I probed too deeply she might do the same with me, and that I might reveal things that could put us in danger.

What or who was Daphne running from?

But in those weeks, those first few weeks in particular, I felt more secure having another grown-up in the house. I felt cared for, and it was a lovely, unusual feeling. Something I hadn't felt since Audrey.

It was a cold winter. Our leaded windows were opaque with

condensation and there was a fine layer of frost on the internal glass. The stone floor in the kitchen was like stepping on an ice-rink – we could even feel it through our socks – but it was cosy in our little cottage, just the three of us, away from outsiders. Safe.

A few weeks after Daphne moved in, when you were in bed and we were sitting watching *Hart to Hart* on TV, she asked if I'd like to go to the pub with her one night. The most socializing I did was at the odd WI meeting with Melissa or when I helped out at the local church while you were at playschool, and even then I worried about whether it was too much, whether I was being too complacent.

'Could Joyce and Roy babysit?' she suggested. 'We wouldn't have to be back late.'

Joyce and Roy were the kind elderly couple who lived next door, a cottage similar to this but without the thatched roof. They doted on you and sometimes looked after you when I took part in the church bell-ringing twice a month. I trusted them. They weren't gossips, didn't ask too many questions, had one son a bit younger than me, whom they rarely saw, and no grandchildren of their own. They gave you presents at birthdays and Christmas, skipping ropes with hand-painted handles and Weeble sets, and when Joyce was in her front garden pruning her roses she always stopped to say hello, her face lighting up when she saw it was you.

I felt bad asking them to look after you just so that I could go to the pub. But Daphne looked so excited at the prospect, with her gap-toothed smile, her hair messily hanging down over her shoulders. She was the only other woman my age in the village whom I knew. What harm could it do to go out for one evening? To have a few drinks and act like normal women in our thirties, instead of two hermits?

So I said yes, and when I asked Joyce and Roy the next day they were delighted to help. They came over the following evening – a Friday – with a tube of Smarties for you, and I said you could stay up a little later to be with them. But my heart still felt heavy as I waved goodbye on the doorstep, you standing between them, Roy in his brown big-buttoned cardigan and Joyce in her floral dress, the light from the hallway spilling out onto the driveway. And then, when Joyce closed the front door, we were plunged into darkness. The air was so cold our breath fogged in front of us and frost sparkled on the ground. We clutched on to each other as we negotiated the hill into the village without slipping. Daphne was wearing her velvet patch coat, a black polo neck and flared burgundy cords, a long scarf wrapped around her neck, and I had changed into a long flowered dress and boots under the thick sheepskin coat I'd bought in a charity shop five years ago. I tried not to feel jittery, just the two of us in the dark, tried not to think about being watched from the hedgerows, telling myself nobody would think to look for me in Beggars Nook. I tried instead to concentrate on Daphne, my lodger, the person who – despite all the promises I'd made to myself after Kay – was becoming a friend.

'Are you sure you want to go to the Stag and Pheasant when you work there?' I said.

She shrugged. 'I don't mind. It's warm. It has alcohol. And it saves us having to drive anywhere.'

I hated driving, although I did it occasionally, when needed. But just knowing my mum's Morris Marina was parked outside the cottage gave me extra security: I could escape quickly with you if we ever had to.

The pub looked Christmas-card pretty from the outside. It still had a string of fairy lights draped around the doorway, and the square stone-mullioned windows were steamed up but

I could see the outline of people jostling inside. We were hit by a cacophony of noise when we entered, and the smell of stale alcohol mixed with peanuts. A group of older men were standing in the corner playing darts and someone had put 'Don't Bring Me Down' by ELO on the jukebox. Joel, the landlord, looked up from behind the bar as we walked in. He smiled kindly at me, like he always did. And I saw his expression darken slightly when he noticed Daphne. I wondered why. My antennae twitched and I was reminded again that I didn't really know Daphne. I couldn't let my barrier down. It was exhausting, the constant being on alert, like one of those guards at Buckingham Palace, but I'd been doing it for four years. Usually Joel was so good-natured, one of life's jovial types, laughter lines bracketing his mouth when he smiled, which was often. Late forties, handsome in a rugged, earthy way with a warm West Country accent and a love of Aran jumpers. And he had been kind to me in the past. When I first came to the village, pregnant with you and scared of my own shadow, he'd helped me when I mistakenly thought I was being followed because a man – who turned out to be Mick Bracken from the farm at the edge of Beggars Nook – was innocently walking his dog behind me on land that I now knew to be his. Joel had sat me down on one of the bar stools, made me a cup of coffee and waited for me to stop shaking. He never asked any questions, never tried to make me tell him what or who I was so afraid of. He was just a reassuring presence. I often wished he was my type.

'How can I help you, ladies?' Joel asked, from behind the bar.

'What do you want to drink? My treat,' said Daphne, reaching into her fringed bag for her purse. 'It's a thank-you for letting me lodge with you.' I spotted the look that passed between her and Joel and it gave me an uneasy feeling, as if they knew something that I didn't.

I asked for a dry white wine and Daphne had the same, and we went to sit in the corner by the fire, on the other side of the pub to where the men were playing darts.

'Do you get on with Joel?' I asked, trying to sound casual as I shook off my coat. He had his back to us, filling a glass with an amber-coloured spirit from a bottle on the wall.

'I suppose. Why?'

'I just felt there was . . . I dunno . . . tension between you.'

She pushed her hair back from her face. She had more makeup on tonight than usual, lots of blue eyeliner. It made her eyes look huge. Was she hoping to pick someone up? I wanted to laugh at the thought. Joel was the only eligible man there. She lowered her voice and leant across the table. I could smell the wine on her breath. 'He made a move. Not long after I arrived. He was very insistent, forcing himself on me.'

'What?' I spluttered in horror. I had occasionally suspected that Joel might have a soft spot for me, but he'd never acted upon it. And he had never made me feel uncomfortable.

'Yep. I was vacuuming the carpet down here, after afternoon closing, and he came up behind me. Wrapped his arms around me really tightly so I couldn't get away and nuzzled my neck. Pressed himself against me.' She pulled a face of disgust. 'I could feel . . .' she shuddered '. . . everything.'

'Oh, my God.' I was an even worse judge of character than I'd thought. I would never have thought that of Joel. He always seemed like the perfect gentleman.

She sat back in her chair with a self-satisfied grin and folded her arms across her chest. 'I know.'

'W-what did you do?'

'I pushed him away. Told him if he ever tried anything like that again I'd chop off his cock.'

I nearly choked on my wine.

'And he's been making my life difficult ever since. He obviously doesn't like being rebuked. Urgh. Honestly, I'm so pissed off with men thinking they can pull this crap on women. Well, not me.'

I couldn't help but admire her feisty attitude – so at odds with the nervous, jittery woman I'd witnessed on Christmas Eve. But it cemented everything I thought I knew about her past. She had been a victim of a cruel, misogynist man, like I had.

She reached out and took my hand. 'We have to stick together, you and me, Rose. It's a shit world out there. We need to look out for one another.'

I glanced over to where Joel was now serving a couple of old blokes at the bar, chuckling at something they said, and my stomach dropped with disappointment. I had been taken in by him but he was the same as the others.

He must have sensed me watching him because he turned to me, flashing me a warm smile.

I didn't smile back.

21

Lorna

SHE SEES HIM BEFORE HE SEES HER. A BIG BEAR OF A MAN. HE'S sitting in the corner of the restaurant, a pale blue shirt straining across his broad shoulders, his dark hair ruffled and a hint of stubble on his handsome face. Her stomach flips.

Euan Cutler. Her one-time husband, lover and best friend.

His head is bent over a spiral-bound notepad, chewing the end of a pen, and as she is led over to him by an over-effusive waiter, she spots ink stains on his index finger. It takes her back to when they were first married and he'd started his journalism course, always scribbling away in the corner of their tiny flat.

He looks up as she approaches and puts down the pen. He has one of those faces that appear stern, a little intense, like a boxer before a fight, until he smiles, when his features instantly soften. 'Lorna!' He stands up. At six foot two he towers over her. He bends down to kiss her cheek. He smells like he always does, of musky aftershave and laundry detergent, at odds with his ruffled appearance.

She slides into the seat opposite. They wait until they've been handed their menus and ordered their drinks before they speak.

'You're looking well,' he says.

'You too.' And it's true, he does. Still broad but leaner, less tubby around the belly. And even though he has lines around his eyes, at forty-two he still has a boyish quality.

'How's it going, living in Spain?'

'Good. You know me. Itchy feet.'

He laughs. 'Sounds about right.'

'What about you? Met the woman of your dreams yet?'

'Too busy working.'

'Sounds about right,' she quips back. They hold each other's gaze.

'I'm sorry to hear about Rose,' he says, breaking eye contact.

'About the dementia or the bodies?' she asks, trying to make a joke but he doesn't laugh.

'It must be hard for you and Saffy.'

She fiddles with the napkin on her lap without meeting his eye. 'It's like we've lost her but she's still alive. When I went to see her she . . .' her voice cracks '. . . she didn't recognize me.'

He reaches across the table and takes her hand. 'Rose was good to me . . . even after we split.'

Lorna nods, ashamed that a lump has formed in her throat. She's tried so hard, this week, to be strong for Saffy, to remain upbeat and positive. 'It's difficult because she gets confused and I don't want Saffy to worry because of the baby.' She looks up at him. 'What do you make of that, then? Grandparents in our early forties.'

He grins. 'It was to be expected, I suppose. Saffy was never going to play the field. She was born a grown-up, that one.' He takes his hand from hers.

'Such a serious little girl,' she agrees, and they smile at each other, remembering their shared history.

They fall silent and their eyes lock for a few seconds until Lorna pulls her gaze away. She needs to be proactive and practical. That's what she's here for, after all. She bends down to retrieve the newspaper clipping from her bag, then pushes it across the table towards Euan.

He smacks his hand onto it but doesn't pick it up. 'Before we get into all this let's have a look at the menu. I'm starving and I can't take longer than an hour and a half.'

'Oh, God, of course.'

He chuckles. 'And you know what we're like once we start talking.'

The waiter appears at the table with their drinks, and Euan orders a steak and Lorna the fish.

'Now that's out of the way, let's have a look,' he says, picking up the article. 'The *Thanet Echo*. That paper's still going.'

Lorna explains their findings. 'It sounds like this Sheila woman killed herself.'

Euan frowns. 'Or death by misadventure. Anyway, I've already spoken to Saffy about this. I found a file.'

'Oh, really? On Sheila?'

'Yes. Not much, but I've promised Saffy I'll email it to her later.' He hands the clipping back to her. 'You don't think your mother knows anything about the bodies in the garden, do you?'

Lorna takes the article and puts it back into her bag. 'It's doubtful. It's just . . . it's probably the ramblings of an old woman, but her talking about Jean hitting someone over the head and saying it was Sheila. Then finding this clipping. And the link between Alan Hartall and Daphne Hartall. It's got me intrigued, that's all.'

He laughs. 'Maybe you should have been a journalist!'

'I'm surprised your lot haven't been down to Skelton Place to check it out,' she says, taking a sip of diet Coke.

'We've used a press agency and we've run a story, of course. But it will be more interesting if and when the victims are identified and when the police have an idea who is responsible. Then, I'm afraid, there will be even more of a swarm. Just warn Saffy, would you?'

The waiter is back and Lorna's stomach rumbles when the sea bass is put in front her. It looks delicious. She takes a bite. 'And have you any contact details for Alan Hartall?' she says, with her mouth full.

Euan cuts into his steak. He obviously still likes it cooked to within an inch of its life. 'Only addresses. All ex-directory. I found two Alan Hartalls living in the Broadstairs area but I have no idea of their ages.'

'I'm going to head there this afternoon.'

He looks up from his steak. 'It's an hour and a half on the train.'

'I know.'

'A lot to do in one day. You'll be careful, won't you?'

She laughs. 'I doubt Alan Hartall, whoever he is, will be dangerous. He'd be an old man now.'

But Euan doesn't laugh. Instead he runs one of his large hands over his stubble. Something he always did when he was anxious. 'Even old men can be dangerous.'

It's gone four by the time Lorna arrives in Broadstairs. Her train back to St Pancras is at 6.30 p.m. It doesn't give her much time to try to find the right Alan Hartall. And as she stands there, in front of the station with the faint whiff of chips and sea air, she falters. *Is this completely mad?* This wild-goose chase for an Alan Hartall who could long be dead or moved away?

The first address is in Pierremont Avenue, a five-minute walk from the station, according to Google Maps, which she has up on her phone. She follows the little blue dot, her heels clipping the pavements, past unremarkable houses until she arrives there. It looks like a long road with houses in varying degrees of attractiveness and eras. She could be anywhere, she thinks, but apart from the cries of seagulls she doesn't feel as if she's in a seaside town. The blue dot flashes in front of a 1970s-style house with a skip at the front. She hesitates, righting her jacket and pushing her shoulders back. She feels anticipation sizzle through her. Buoyed by hope, she marches to the front door and knocks loudly. It takes a while before someone answers: a woman around her age in leggings and a baggy T-shirt who looks harassed. A little girl is clinging to her leg.

'Sorry to bother you,' Lorna begins.

'If you're selling something, I'm not interested,' says the woman, without smiling.

'No, I'm trying to find someone,' Lorna says quickly, before the woman can shut the door on her. 'An Alan Hartall.'

She shakes her head. 'Sorry. No Alan Hartalls live here. We've only just moved in.'

'Do you know anyone called Alan Hartall?'

The woman looks irritated now. 'No.' The little girl starts to cry. 'If you'll excuse me . . .' She doesn't finish her sentence before the door is closed in Lorna's face.

Lorna lets out a long sigh. This is a waste of time. Why did she ever think the Alan Hartall who was friends with Sheila Watts would still be living here?

Hoisting her bag further up her shoulder she wanders out of the gate and stands by the wall, tapping in the other address she has. It looks like it's by the sea. At least if she has no luck there she can wander down to the beach, maybe grab a coffee and bask in the late-afternoon sunshine. Thank goodness the two places are close to each other.

God, she's hot. She takes off her jacket and threads it between the straps of her bag. The sun burns the back of her neck. She glances down at her mobile. The next address is at the end of Wrotham Road and, as she heads down the street, she can see a haze of blue in the distance. The sea. This is more like it, she thinks, excitement bubbling up inside her. This address is a converted flat in a large red-brick Victorian building. She buzzes Flat C and waits, mentally keeping everything crossed that she'll get some kind of lead.

But nobody answers, even though she rings the bell three times, then holds the button down for at least ten seconds. The disappointment is acute. What does she do now? Put a note through the door hoping that Alan Hartall still lives here? Hoping it doesn't get picked up and thrown away by a resident in one of the other flats?

She's rummaging in her bag, trying to find a pen and something to write on, when she hears a crackle of the intercom and a man's voice: 'Hello.'

Adrenalin ripples through her. 'Hello. Is this Alan Hartall?'

'Yes?' His voice sounds croaky. Old. 'Who is this?'

She can hardly believe it. Can it really be *the* Alan Hartall?

'My name is Lorna. I hope you don't mind me coming over out of the blue like this, but I'm trying to find the Alan Hartall who knew a Sheila Watts, back in the 1970s.'

'Right,' says the disembodied voice. 'Are you police?'

'No, no, nothing like that. Just . . . it's someone I think perhaps my mum used to know as well. Did you know a Sheila Watts?'

There is a pause, just the crackling of static. She wonders if he's even heard her. 'Hello,' she says again. There is no answer.

Has she said something wrong? Maybe he's got the beginnings of dementia too. Maybe he's hard of hearing. Or . . .

Her thoughts are interrupted by the main door swinging open. On the other side of the threshold stands a man in his seventies with a white thatch of thick, wiry hair. He's holding a walking stick but he looks sprightly, in jeans and a T-shirt.

He has hazel eyes, a large nose and bushy eyebrows threaded with silver. 'You knew Sheila Watts?' he asks.

It is him. It has to be, she thinks. 'Yes! Well, no . . . not exactly. My mum did, I think. I found a clipping in her things about Sheila's death.'

'Yes, that was a sad business. She seemed a nice girl. Not that there's much I can tell you about her. I didn't know her that well.'

Lorna hesitates, wondering how best to ask the next question. 'Actually, it's a long story but I'm also trying to find another person my mother knew. A Daphne Hartall. I wondered if she was any relation to you.'

He looks confused, his bushy eyebrows bobbing up and down. 'Daphne Hartall's my sister.'

'Daphne Hartall's your sister?' She knew it! She knew it couldn't be a coincidence. Hartall is too unusual a surname.

'Why do you ask about Daphne?' There is pain behind his eyes when he mentions her name.

Lorna shifts her weight from one foot to the other. How can she even begin to explain it all? 'Your sister used to lodge with my mother, back in 1980. And I think they must both have known Sheila Watts. I think maybe my mum lived here in Broadstairs too at some point. Did you know her? Rose Grey?'

He shakes his head, looking confused. She doesn't know if she's making any sense.

'Anyway, really, I just wanted to speak to Daphne. To find out about my mum. She has dementia now and . . .'

Alan clears his throat. 'Hold on,' he says, his bushy eyebrows drawn together. 'You said your mum knew Daphne in 1980?'

'Yes, they lived together. In Wiltshire.'

He clicks his tongue, his face impatient. 'No, no. Something isn't right about this. Daphne was Broadstairs born through and through. Never left. And . . .' his eyes moisten '. . . Daphne died. At thirty-two, of cancer. Back in 1971.'

22

Saffy

As I let myself into the cottage I feel shaky after the conversation with the private detective. Who is he working for? And what sort of information does he think Gran has? I wonder if it's something to do with Sheila. But I dismiss the thought straight away. The private detective only turned up since the bodies have been found, so it must be something to do with that. But what? Does Gran know more than she's capable of telling us?

I go to switch the kettle on, annoyed when I see Mum has moved it to the other side of the microwave. I move it back while Snowy chews a toy at my feet.

A knock on the door makes me jump.

I freeze. Oh, God. It's him. That private detective. He's followed me home. Does he know I'm alone? Is he going to force his way in here and make me search the house? My imagination goes into overdrive and I have to tell myself to calm down. Snowy leaps up and trots down the hallway, barking. I go to the living-room window and peer out, trying to see who it is, my heart thumping. Maybe it's just a reporter, I think, *actually hope*, for once. An unfamiliar car is parked on the driveway next to my Mini, some big blue sedan. Is it the private detective's car? If he tries to get in I'll call the police. But no, wait, there are two men outside. I recognize them as the police detectives from yesterday.

With relief I go to the front door and wrench it open. They must have news. Why else would they bother to visit instead of ringing? My throat goes dry.

'Hi, Saffron,' says the older one, DS Barnes. He holds up his badge unnecessarily. 'May we come in?'

'Of course,' I say, moving aside. I show them into the living room and offer them a drink, which they both decline.

DS Barnes sits on the sofa and DC Worthing perches on the edge of the armchair. They are both imposing in the small room but I instantly feel safer having them here. For a few seconds there is silence, broken only by the birds chirruping outside.

I sit at the opposite end of the sofa to DS Barnes. He angles his body towards me. I can see the spider-web tattoo on his arm. He notices me looking and pulls at the hem of his shirt sleeve. 'Is Mrs Cutler here?'

'Um. No. She's . . . she's in London today.' Now they're here I can ask them if they have any updates on the Harrison Turner that Brenda mentioned.

A flash of concern crosses his face. 'We have bad news, I'm afraid.'

I nod, steeling myself. 'Okay.'

'We've identified the male body in the garden.'

My mouth goes dry. 'Right,' I say, wondering why this would be bad news. Unless I knew him. But that's not possible. And then I think of Gran and my stomach turns over.

DS Barnes reaches for his little black book in the inner

pocket of his suit jacket and flips a few of the pages over. 'Does the name Neil Lewisham mean anything to you?'

I shake my head. 'Never heard of him.' *Just get to the point.*

'Well, as you can imagine, it has been a difficult job trying to identify both of the bodies, considering they died a long time ago. But we've gone through a list of people who were reported missing from 1975 to 1990 in the south-west of England in particular, and in the thirty to forty-five age range. A thirty-nine-year-old man called Neil Lewisham was reported missing in April 1980 by his wife. Although he was from Surrey, what alerted us to him was that his wife said in a statement taken at the time that he was going to visit someone in the Chippenham area before he disappeared. This, of course, was followed up back in 1980 but came to a dead end. Unfortunately his wife has since died so we spoke to his son, who agreed to a DNA test. The DNA matches.'

I feel like someone has knocked the breath out of me. 'So, you're saying he died in this house . . . while my gran was living here?'

'It looks that way, yes. He was last seen at Chippenham station on the seventh of April 1980. He hasn't been seen since and he never tried to access his bank account. So we can assume he died on, or around, the seventh.'

'Are you definitely sure it's this man? The DNA . . . I mean . . .' I frown. 'How?' The flesh would have decomposed by now, surely.

'We can extract DNA from bones and teeth. His son is a match. It's definitely him.'

I feel sick. Gran was living here when he died. 'I . . . I can't believe this.'

DS Barnes shuffles in his seat. 'I'm sorry,' he says, holding my gaze, his eyes sincere. Then he turns to the notebook in his hand, tapping his pen on the page. 'We're still trying to identify the other body. For now,' he continues, 'all we can do is look into missing females around that time period and for anyone with a possible connection to Neil Lewisham. Now we have a date it will narrow the time frame at least. It might take a while but we have a team working on this. Plus a number of officers have been making door-to-door calls in the village, asking residents if they lived in Beggars Nook at the time and what they can remember. We also have officers doing background checks on this house to see if anyone has ever reported a disturbance taking place here, or anything else. And we are working on the victimology.'

'Victimology?'

'Yes, on Neil Lewisham. Information on the victim, essentially. To see if we can find out why he was killed. I just want to reassure you that we're doing everything we can.'

I swallow down nausea. 'What does this mean . . . for my gran?'

He flicks away an imaginary piece of lint from his trousers and avoids eye contact. 'Well, we'll need to speak to her again, to see what she can remember. We're also trying to locate the whereabouts of your grandmother's two lodgers. A Kay Groves and, of course, Daphne Hartall.'

I don't tell him that my mum is currently in Kent trying to find Daphne herself.

'What about these other people that my gran mentioned? Victor and Jean?'

'Yes, that's harder without surnames.'

I look across at the younger detective. He is scribbling something in his notebook and looks up when he senses me watching. He gives me a sympathetic smile.

'There's something else,' I say, turning my attention back to Barnes. I retrieve the card that the private detective gave me and hand it to him. 'A man stopped me in the woods today.' I explain our conversation. 'He seemed very agitated by the end, like he really wanted this information, whatever it is. He said his name was Davies.'

DS Barnes frowns at the card. 'I'll look into it,' he says. He scribbles the number in his notebook, then gives me back the card. 'If you do find what you think he's looking for please call me. I advise against calling him.'

'Okay.' I nod, and as I do so I have an out-of-body experience, like I'm looking down at myself talking to CID about my gran. Two months ago I would have panicked at the thought of having to talk to the police without Tom by my side.

'We'll need to speak to Rose as soon as possible,' he says, standing up, and DS Worthing follows suit. 'I'll ring the care home and arrange it and let you know.' I show them out. As I watch them drive away I realize I didn't get to ask about Harrison Turner after all. It seems pointless now anyway.

Gran was the one living here when Neil Lewisham was murdered.

Her words pop into my mind. *Jean hit her over the head.* Are her ramblings not as innocuous as I'd first thought? Have all her mentions of Jean, Victor and Sheila been her way of trying to tell me what really happened forty years ago?

23

Lorna

'She died?' Lorna reels and holds on to the wall. 'Back in 1971? But . . . but that can't be right.'

'I think I'd know when my sister died,' Alan replies curtly.

'Of course. I didn't mean . . . I'm sorry . . . I just don't understand.'

He stares at her, his bushy brows furrowed. His face softens. 'You look a bit pale. Do you want to come in for a glass of water?'

Lorna's parched but she remembers Euan's words. *Even old men can be dangerous.*

'Um . . . no, you're okay. Thanks. I'll . . . Is there a café here somewhere?'

'Down at the front.' He points towards the sea. 'There's a great place by the beach.'

'Thank you.'

He assesses her quietly. 'What did you say your name was again?'

'Lorna. Lorna Cutler.'

'I don't really understand what all this is about,' he says, more kindly now.

She pulls her bag more firmly over her shoulder. 'I don't either,' she says, sighing. 'It must be a different Daphne Hartall . . . the Sheila connection, though.'

He falls silent, as though thinking something through. 'Do you fancy some company at the café? We could get a drink and you could tell me all about it. I did know Sheila Watts so I might be able to help.'

She brightens. She's not being irresponsible by walking to the café with him, is she? In broad daylight in a public space?

'That would be lovely,' she says.

'Come on then.' His eyes twinkle at her and she smiles at him in a rush of gratitude. He closes the door behind him and they walk towards a main road. This is more like it, thinks Lorna, as they cross the street, heading through some pretty gardens and past a bandstand as they follow the path down to the sea front. People are meandering along in shorts and T-shirts, eating ice creams and enjoying the gorgeous May weather. Alan talks about his walking stick and his dodgy hip that needs replacing. But he's surprisingly steady on his feet, walking faster than her. She has to keep trotting in her heels to keep up with him.

He leads Lorna to a funky little coffee shop with music and tables set outside on a terrace overlooking the beach. People are milling about, some drinking pints and others sipping cappuccinos in huge colourful cups and saucers.

'What would you like? It's my treat,' she says, waving away his offers to pay. 'It's kind of you to talk to me.'

'It's my pleasure. I'm happy to have the company.' He grins. He has a dimple on his left cheek. He says he'd love a beer and Lorna decides to order a glass of wine. It's not like she has to drive, she tells herself. She can get a takeaway coffee afterwards to drink on the train.

Alan has found a table at the corner of the terrace, overlooking the bay and the ice-cream-coloured row of beach huts. She sits next to him and takes in a deep breath of the sea air. She could live here, she thinks, with the sun on her back, the music, the hustle and bustle. She suddenly yearns to be back in San Sebastián.

Alan thanks her for his pint and takes a long glug, the froth settling on his top lip. 'This has hit the spot.'

She laughs. The wine and the sun and the music have made her feel giddy and helped ease her disappointment at finding out Daphne died before she could have become her mother's lodger.

'So tell me,' he says, putting his pint down on the wooden table, 'what's all this got to do with Sheila Watts?'

Lorna explains about the bodies found in the garden, the article about Sheila, her mother's lodger also being called Daphne Hartall. She pulls the newspaper clipping from her bag and hands it to Alan. 'And then I saw this, your quote in the paper.'

He scans it and hands it back to her. 'I haven't got my glasses on. Would you mind reading it?'

She does as he asks, making sure to read slowly and clearly – she's often accused of being a fast talker. When she gets to the end he's looking out to sea, as though half expecting to spot Sheila on the beach.

'She was a strange one,' he says, his gaze still on the far distance. 'A bit of a loner, you know. But we were friends.' He turns back to her. 'She lived in the flat below mine. Not where I live now. In Stone Road.'

Lorna has no idea where that is but she nods along. 'But you didn't know a Rose Grey?' she clarifies.

He shakes his head. 'No, no, definitely not.'

'I just don't understand why my mother would have kept an article about Sheila Watts unless she or her lodger knew her.'

Alan takes a noisy slurp of his beer in answer.

On the beach below she watches as a teenage boy frolics in the sea with a brown Cockapoo. She lifts her eyes back to Alan. 'What happened the night Sheila died? Can you remember?'

'It was New Year's Eve. A group of us went to the local pub, then decided to see in the new year at the beach. Sheila didn't know any of my friends but she tagged along. Like I said, she kept herself to herself, really. She'd only been in Broadstairs for a few years. She was originally from London, I think. She said she travelled around a lot.'

'My mum was from London. Maybe they knew each other before Sheila came here.' A breeze has whipped up from the sea and Lorna puts her jacket back on. They are sitting in partial shade now.

'Maybe. Anyway, that night Sheila was particularly quiet. She hardly spoke in the pub. She sat morosely in the corner, drinking. Although she didn't act drunk. I asked her a few times what was up. Like I said, we weren't close as such, but I'd got to know her a bit over the two years she was my neighbour. Sometimes she'd come up to my flat for a cup of tea. We'd talk a lot. Deep talks, really. About my sister dying and how she'd lost someone too. She didn't say who. The night Sheila died she seemed jittery and on edge. Personally I always wondered if she was an ex-junkie. Very thin. Paranoid.'

'Paranoid? About what?'

'Convinced she was being followed. I often wondered if she owed money to her dealer or some such.' He laughs. It's deep and throaty like he's getting over a bout of bronchitis. 'I'm probably reading more into it all now, with hindsight. But she was cagey. That's the right word.'

'So what happened when you got to the beach that night?'

'Sheila wandered off by herself. I asked her if she wanted any company but she shook me off, told me she was feeling maudlin, that she always did around New Year, and that she'd like to be on her own. Me and my mates were sitting and drinking and then I noticed Sheila was stripping off and getting into the sea. Mad, if you ask me.' He shudders. 'Bloody cold, the sea in December.'

Lorna grins. 'I can imagine.'

'I sat with a couple of my mates, sinking a few cans. We all got drunk and we forgot about Sheila. It was only later, when we started walking home, that we realized she wasn't with us. My mate, Phil, and I ran back down to the beach, where she'd left her clothes but couldn't see her in the sea. It was like she'd just been,' he grimaces, 'swallowed by the water.'

'And that was when you raised the alarm?'

'Yes. She obviously drowned. Maybe she'd drunk more than we knew. We felt terrible.'

'That's awful,' says Lorna, and despite the heat of the day, she feels goose bumps pop up on her arms. The sea, as much as she loves it, has always terrified her. It's like a mighty beast, and you never know what mood it's going to be in. It deserves respect. 'Do you think it was an accident or suicide?'

'I honestly couldn't say,' he replies. 'It was sad, really, afterwards like. Nobody came to clear out her flat. I don't think she had any family. So I did it. And she hardly had any belongings. Just clothes left behind and food in the cupboards and fridge. It was a furnished flat. Nothing belonged to her. There were no personal items. No clutter, no mess. Nothing, really, that gave any clue as to what kind of person Sheila Watts had been.'

'What about a purse? Or keys?'

'The keys to her flat were in the trousers she'd left on the beach. No purse, or handbag. The police at the time suggested they might have been stolen when she was in the water. There were a few people on the beach that night.'

An idea begins to form in Lorna's head, like a photograph being developed. 'Do you think she could have faked her death?'

Alan sits back in his chair, his mouth an O shape. 'That's a bit of a leap.'

'It's just . . .' She's trying to arrange all the images she has in her head into some kind of picture that makes sense. 'It's weird that my mother has this newspaper clipping about Sheila, and her lodger was called Daphne Hartall. It's not like Daphne Hartall is a common name, is it? It's too much of a coincidence. There must be a link.'

'What are you trying to say?'

'I could be so wide of the mark here. But . . .' her heart flutters with excitement '. . . isn't it possible that the Daphne Hartall my mum knew and the Sheila Watts you knew could be the same person?'

'You think Sheila faked her death and stole my sister's identity?' He sounds incredulous.

'People do. Did she ever seem particularly interested in Daphne?'

'Well,' he rubs his chin, 'yes, I suppose, now you mention it. And there was one thing that niggled at me. After Sheila died, I was tidying away Daphne's things that I kept in a little box on my bookcase, and I couldn't find her birth certificate, but that could just be down to me being disorganized . . .'

'Do you think Sheila could have taken it?'

He looks troubled. 'Maybe. She had the opportunity.'

'And what a perfect way to disappear if someone was trying to find her.'

The more she thinks about it the more convinced she is.

Sheila Watts and Daphne Hartall are one and the same.

24

Rose

February 1980

AS THE DAYS WORE ON I BECAME EVEN MORE INTRIGUED
by Daphne. She was so strong in some ways, and in others there
was a vulnerability about her that brought out my maternal side,
even though we were around the same age. I wanted to protect her, just like I wanted to protect you. This slim, attractive
woman who, I was now certain, had been terrorized by a man,
just like I had.

After our night out at the Stag and Pheasant the previous
week, and her Joel revelation, I felt even more certain that we
should stick together. Men, it seemed, couldn't be trusted. Even
Joel – a man I thought was kind and dependable – was really a
predator waiting for the right time to pounce. We sat up late most
evenings discussing women's rights. 'Why do men think it's okay
to pat your arse and call you "darling"?' she said, hugging her
knees, the sleeves of her chunky jumper pulled over her hands.
'It's 1980 not 1950.'

She was so right-on. So modern. So different from me: I had lived there, in the back of beyond, for the last three years.

And she was so easy to live with. She seemed to sense when I wanted it to be just you and me, tactfully staying in her room or going for a walk to the village. She'd managed to procure a second-hand sewing machine – a bulky old Singer with a foot pedal – which she set up in the little room across the hall. I'd often hear its whirr as she ran up patterns, or mended her jeans with patches. She wanted to make you a pretty summer dress and came home one day with a roll of printed yellow fabric. You were delighted at the prospect. She was capable and self-sufficient, with all these useful practical skills, and I admired her for that.

It was a cold winter, February even worse than January. Ice crusted the grass and fog rolled over the woods so that they were barely visible from your bedroom window. It unnerved me, made me concerned about who could be watching the house. Daphne must have felt the same: one evening when you were in bed and we were standing in the kitchen, smoking and huddled against the range for warmth, she said, 'It's strange.' Her gaze went to the window as she exhaled a plume of smoke. She'd been at work that day – she refused to give up her cleaning job just because Joel had made a move on her. 'To think this place could be our sanctuary or our undoing.'

Her words chilled me. 'What do you mean?'

She turned her gaze on me, intense and unnerving. 'We think we're safe hiding here, away from the world, away from danger, but the danger could be here anyway. Trapped in this place, with us.'

I'd never told her I was hiding but it was like she knew. That she could sense it. Perhaps because she was doing the same.

'In this house?' I asked, puzzled and a little freaked out. What was she trying to say?

'No, in this village. We can't escape it, Rose. Don't you see?'

I stubbed out my cigarette and wrapped my arms around myself. 'Don't say that,' I said, in a small, frightened voice.

'Those woods,' she said, in the same strange tone. 'Are they keeping others out or trapping us in?' Her eyes flashed and I could see that she was scared.

'We're safe here,' I said firmly, to convince her or myself, I couldn't tell.

She turned to me, her lips puckering round the cigarette as she took a drag, her eyes fixed on me but not saying anything for a few seconds. Then, 'I know we haven't talked about our pasts. And that's good. We shouldn't have to. Our future starts here.'

'Exactly,' I said, in a jovial voice, trying to cheer her up. 'And . . . we can protect each other, can't we? Have each other's backs?'

She nodded, her eyes still on mine. Then she stubbed out her cigarette against the sink and walked over to where I was standing by the back door. Her face was so close to mine that for a crazy moment I wondered if she was going to kiss me. But instead she moved a lock of hair away from my face. 'Thank you,' she said softly. 'I feel the same. Ask no questions, tell no lies.'

I could feel heat rising up my neck to my face. Then she took a step back, clearing her throat, and walked towards the cooker. 'You're so kind, Rose,' she said, with her back to me, her shoulders hunched. I could see the outline of her spine through her jumper. 'If I'd met you years ago things could be very different now.'

I went over to her and gently placed my hand on her shoulder. 'At least we've found each other now,' I said. 'No man can ever hurt us again.'

If only that were true.

The next morning I dropped you off at the little church playschool. You were wearing your favourite yellow wellies and the pink and red bobble hat I'd knitted for you. It was a frosty morning, ice coating the pavements, and we had to step carefully so as not to slip. The sky was dull and colourless. I nodded a hello to other parents clutching the hands of their little ones as we made our way across the village square. Parents I'd never bothered to get to know. When we reached the market cross you had to run up and down the steps, like you did every time you saw it. When you got to the top you spun around, as though you were on a medieval stage. 'Where's Daffy?' you said, as I helped you down the steps, worried you'd slip. You were only two and a half and some words were difficult for you to say. Daffy, like the duck. After you incorrectly pronounced her name the first time it just stuck. 'Daffy pick me up?'

I loved that you had taken to Daphne but I wasn't sure I trusted her enough yet to collect you from playschool. She wouldn't know who to look out for. If he came for us. I'd told myself regularly over the last three years that he'd never find us. How would he know where to look? But that still didn't stop me worrying. He was a clever man. A rich man. He would no doubt have his ways, his spies. I could never relax, never stop looking over my shoulder.

'Maybe one day, honey, but not yet, okay? And she'll be at work anyway.'

Your face fell until you saw your teacher, Miss Tilling, and then you ran over to her, your dark curls – so like his – flying out behind you.

I made sure Miss Tilling had ushered you inside the classroom, like I did every morning before leaving. When I was satisfied that you were safe I walked away, stopping at Melissa's café to get a hot chocolate. Melissa seemed very interested in Daphne and wanted to know all about her. I was careful not to say too much. Melissa was one of the biggest gossips in Beggars Nook, and if Daphne was trying to keep a low profile I owed it to her to be discreet.

Melissa looked bored when she realized she wasn't going to get any interesting titbit from me, turning away to serve the next customer. As I stepped out of the shop I bumped into Joel.

Joel who, before now, had been my saviour. A reassuring presence. The first man in a long while I had trusted. Who, after that first time we met, had always looked out for me, asked if I needed anything. When the snow came the year before, he knocked on the door and offered to clear my driveway. He was the one I called when I had a burst pipe. I'd let him into my small life. But when I imagined him feeling up Daphne and making her life hell when she turned him down, it made my skin crawl.

I was about to walk past him without speaking but he stopped me. 'Hey, Rose. I haven't seen you much lately, how are you doing?'

I'd noticed since Daphne moved in that he hadn't been over to offer any help or even to see how I was. A guilty conscience, I decided.

'I'm fine,' I replied curtly.

He looked crestfallen. He had a checked scarf pulled up to his chin and wore a black wool Crombie. The tip of his nose was red. Despite my anger with him my treacherous heart betrayed me and I felt myself softening when I remembered how kind he'd been to me.

He looked troubled. 'Have I done something wrong?' He dug his hands into his pockets. 'I get the feeling you're cross with me.'

Then Daphne's words floated into my head, reminding me that he was just like the rest of them. 'Daphne told me what you did,' I said.

'I . . . What?' He looked genuinely confounded. 'Sorry, you've lost me.'

'She said you gave her . . .' I lowered my voice even though we were a good twenty feet away from the coffee shop '. . . unwanted attention.'

He laughed. 'You're joking, right?'

'Do I look like I'm joking?'

His face fell. 'Daphne's lying. I'd never do anything like that.'

'Why would Daphne lie?'

'I don't know. I . . .' He looked down at his booted feet, kicking at a bit of ice on the pavement. A redness crept up his neck. 'But it's not true.' He lifted his eyes to mine. 'I'm not lying, Rose, I promise you.'

I'd always thought of him like a protective big brother. But no. No. I couldn't believe any of what he was saying. This was what had happened before. It had started with the charm, the promises, then the lies and control, culminating in fear, intimidation and abuse.

I had known Daphne for only two months, but I knew she wouldn't lie about something like this.

'I need to go,' I managed. As I went to walk off he grabbed my wrist.

'Hey,' he said softly. 'We can't leave things like this. We're friends, aren't we?'

I stared pointedly at his fingers circling my wrist and he let go, dropping his arm to his side.

I stalked away, convinced I was right about him. About all men.

I was so sure Daphne wouldn't lie to me.

Now, sitting here after everything that has happened, writing this to you, I wish with all my heart I could turn back the clock.

25

Theo

THEO CAN'T STOP THINKING ABOUT HIS CONVERSATION with Larry as he gets into his car. The windscreen is littered with cherry blossom, like confetti, and he turns on his windscreen wipers, although they miss where they've collected in the groove above his hood.

A young woman accuses his father of sexual assault and less than a year later she's dead.

Theo turns on the ignition and fiddles with the satnav to tap in his home address. He's just about to pull away from the kerb when he sees Larry hurrying towards him. He winds his window down.

'I've remembered her name. The woman who accused your dad. It's not Sandra. It's Cynthia. Cynthia Parsons. She was twenty-three.'

Twenty-three. He didn't think it was possible to feel even more shit about all of this.

Theo thanks him, and waves goodbye, watching Larry getting smaller and smaller in his rearview mirror as he turns out of the street. He suddenly hates his dad with a passion. He grips the steering wheel tightly, imagining that the faux-leather beneath his hands is his dad's sinewy throat. But then Theo releases his grip. He hasn't got a violent bone in him. He's so fucking angry with his dad, but he knows he could never hurt him: if he did, that would make him no better than his father.

The woman could have lied. The idea pops into his head and he wants to believe it – oh, how he wants to. But he can't. He thinks of her, Cynthia, struggling to make her voice heard in the mid-1970s when a man like his father would have held all the power. If he refuses to believe her now he's no different. For a mad second he's actually relieved his mum is no longer around to hear about it. What would she have done if she knew? Would she have had the strength to leave him?

Arctic Monkeys' 'R U Mine?' comes on the radio and he turns it up loud, trying to drown his thoughts. What should he do next? There is no point in confronting his dad about it. It's not like he'll suddenly turn around to Theo and admit it. He'll just get angry again, then defensive and nasty.

And then another thought pops into his head.

If his dad is capable of sexually assaulting someone, what other terrible things has he done?

Jen is sitting up in bed watching *Friends*. He'd popped into the garage to buy her a giant bag of Maltesers on his way home, like he promised, and her eyes light up when he walks into the bedroom dangling them enticingly, making sure he's plastered a cheerful mask over his anxious face before entering the room.

'Perfect,' she says, her knees sinking into the mattress as she reaches up and throws her arms around his neck. He climbs onto the bed and lies fully clothed next to her.

'How are you feeling?' he asks, as she settles down and opens the packet, shoving a handful into her mouth.

'Better now,' she mumbles, through the Maltesers, offering him one. He shakes his head.

She pauses the telly, even though it's an episode they've both seen umpteen times and one of Theo's favourites – the one when the girls lose their apartment to the boys in a bet. Jen could probably quote it verbatim. Comfort telly, she calls it, and she's right. It's not lost on him that it's the episode when Phoebe finds out she's pregnant.

'Well?' she asks, swallowing her mouthful. 'How did it go?' Concern flashes in her eyes. 'You seem sad.'

He shrugs. 'I'm not a good actor, am I?'

'What did Larry say?'

'More evidence that my dad is a total fucking tool. Not that I should need it.'

'Oh, babe.'

He glances at her, his beautiful wife, and suddenly he doesn't want to tell her. He doesn't want her to look at him and remember that he's related to a man who is capable of something so sick. He doesn't want to tarnish what they have, their innocent, uncomplicated life in their Victorian two-up-two-down with their dreams of babies and dogs. He thinks again of the photographs on Larry Knight's wall, of the future he so desperately wants with Jen and their unborn children, and the spectre of his father threatening to blacken it all.

But he can't keep this from her. He refuses to be the kind of man who hides things from his wife. He's not his father.

He tells her everything.

Later, after they've hugged and demolished the chocolate and made promises to each other that they won't let his father's sins destroy their lives, Theo has an idea.

'I think we should go to Wiltshire. Meet these people who

own that cottage. My dad is interested in one of them for some reason. I need to know why.'

'Are you sure?' says Jen. 'Maybe it's best to keep the past buried.'

He swivels his leg out of bed so that he's sitting on the edge with his back to her. '. . . I just can't.'

He feels her hand on his shoulder. 'Is this about your mum?'

Theo turns to look at her. 'I keep wondering about the day she died.'

'What about it?'

'It was an accident. That's what everyone said. But what if he did something to her?'

'Like what? Pushed her?'

'He pushed me down the stairs once.'

'Oh, babe . . .'

'I'm not telling you that for sympathy.'

Jen brushes her strawberry blonde hair away from her face. 'I know you're not. You said your dad was at work when it happened.'

'I just can't stop thinking that he could have pushed her and gone to work as though nothing had happened. You know how angry he gets. Maybe he hadn't meant to do it. And then pretended to find her when he arrived home. She . . .' His voice catches and he pauses, embarrassed. He hasn't cried since his mum died. 'She'd been dead for hours by the time he got home, the police said at the time. But if he's capable of assaulting a woman when he's supposed to be examining her, if he's capable of pushing a child and hitting my mum . . .' He thinks about Cynthia Parsons committing suicide. Larry told him she'd jumped from a multi-storey car park. There is no doubt about it: his father is responsible for her death even if he didn't actually push her.

Jen rubs his back. 'You can't think like that, babe,' she says gently. 'You said yourself your mother's death destroyed him. I know your dad had – has – a temper, but he had a very stressful job and unfortunately he took his frustrations out on you and your mum. But I've no doubt he's always loved you both.'

He nods, a lump in his throat. He remembers the shock and devastation in his dad's face the day it happened.

'Finding out about Cynthia has just changed . . . everything.'

They fall silent, Jen still stroking his back. Then, 'Let's go,' she announces. 'Let's go to Wiltshire and look these people up. And if they can't shed any light, well, it would be nice to have a weekend away. I think we both need it, don't you?'

26

Saffy

AFTER I'VE SHOWN THE DETECTIVES OUT I CALL MUM but it goes straight to voicemail. I don't leave a message. She promised to ring me when she was on the way home and it's not yet 5 p.m. I wonder if her lunch with Dad was productive and if she managed to find out Alan Hartall's address. She did say she'd let me know her plans. Typical of my mum. She's so flighty, she probably hasn't even considered I'd like to know when she's coming back.

I'm at my desk when a knock startles me. I go to the front door and peer through the glass. A smartly dressed woman in a polka dot blouse stands on the other side. I pull the door open a crack. 'Yes?'

'Saffron Cutler?'

'Yes.'

'Hello, my name is Nadia Barrows and I'm from the *Daily Mail*. Would it be possible to –'

'I'm not interested. Please go away,' I say firmly, closing the door before she can respond. I go back into my study. From the window I can see a pack of about five reporters clustered together at the end of my driveway. Neil Lewisham's name must have been released already. They'll want to quiz me about Gran, I bet. There are no blinds or curtains at the study window. Can they see me? This is a nightmare. I don't want to have to be dealing with this on my own with Tom at work and Mum out of the house. I put my head in my hands and groan, nausea sweeping over me. I feel Snowy brush against my legs and I bend down to pat his head. He can always sense when I'm stressed.

My phone buzzes by my ear and I lift my head. A text from Dad flashes up on the screen. *Hi, sweetheart. I've emailed you the file on Sheila Watts. Saw your mum at lunch. She looked well. I have a couple of addresses for an Alan Hartall in Broadstairs so she headed there xx*

I don't reply. Instead I click open my emails, suddenly filled with adrenalin.

As promised Dad has taken photos of the contents of Sheila Watts's file. There's not much: a few articles from various different regional newspapers in the Kent area about her drowning, and a few sheets of what looks like paper torn from a lined notepad. I can't make out the writing; it's all dots and symbols. I recognize it as shorthand. I've seen Dad use it when taking phone messages. I scroll down. The last photograph is of a press clipping from a national newspaper – the same one Dad works for. The piece was written in 1978 and isn't about Sheila but a crime that dated back to the early 1950s. I scan it, not understanding the relevance. Maybe it was put into Sheila's file by mistake. I sit back in my chair, disappointed. There's nothing new here. Unless there's something in the shorthand notes. I'm just about to close the email when something about the last article catches my eye. The by-line. I peer closer. The piece was written by a Neil Lewisham.

*   *   *

I call Dad straight away. By the sound of the phones ringing in the background and the general hub of activity I can tell he's still in the newsroom. I start to recount everything in fast, breathless sentences, until Dad interrupts me to say he's just heard from a 'source'. Of course he has. 'Your gran could have been away when it happened,' he says. 'Just because he died when she was living in the property doesn't mean she necessarily knew about it. Not if she had a lodger.'

'I know. Weirdly, though, an article in the file you sent over is written by the same man,' I say, goose bumps popping up along my arms when I think about it. 'It sounds like Neil Lewisham worked for the *Mirror* back in the late 1970s.'

'I thought the name sounded familiar,' he says. 'Although he would have worked here well before my time. I'll see what I can find out. He might have been a freelancer. Is the article about Sheila?'

'No. It looks like some kind of round-up thing. It doesn't mention Sheila's name. Oh,' I say, suddenly remembering. 'Would you mind deciphering the shorthand in photo four for me?'

'Yes, I saw that. Unfortunately it looks like Pitman. I can only do Teeline shorthand. But I'll ask around. Some of the older guys here might know it.'

'Thanks, Dad.' I feel a stab of remorse. 'I'm sorry to ask you for this. You must be shattered. When do you finish?' I wish he'd find himself a nice girlfriend. I worry that he works too much.

'You never have to be sorry to ask me for anything,' he says softly. 'And I'll be leaving soon. Oh, and Saff, if you get any more bother from any reporters just tell them Euan Cutler at the *Mirror* is your dad. That'll shut them up!'

I end the call feeling better. I stand up and glance out of the window just in time to see the three remaining journalists walking off down the hill.

I call Mum's mobile again but there's no answer. It's the third time I've rung since the detectives left. Anxiety gnaws at my insides. She always picks up when I call. What if something's happened to her? What if she met up with an Alan Hartall and he's not an old man at all but a psychopath? Mum is so gung-ho, she wouldn't think of the dangers. She believes she's invincible. Gran used to tell me stories of how Mum hitchhiked back from town when she was a teenager and I know she was only telling me these things as a warning, to keep me safe, but she needn't have bothered. I would never have been so irresponsible.

I leave a voicemail asking Mum to call me urgently, that I have news.

But by 8 p.m. she still hasn't got in touch.

The sun is going down, the remaining rays glinting through the woods out at the back. The inside of the cottage looks dark and gloomy, but it's too early to switch on the lights. Tom texts to say he's on the 18.34 train so he should be back here within the next half an hour. I go to the kitchen, make a Red Bush tea, and lean against the ugly kitchen units, comforted that I have Snowy, who has lain across my bare feet. I'm beginning to feel uneasy here now. That's the reality of it. Not just the bodies – although that's bad enough – but the private detective earlier and his insistence that Gran has some kind of information that his client wants back. I've looked through Gran's boxes again but there's nothing that would be important enough for some-one to hire a private investigator.

Gran. As he's got nothing from me he might go to her. I

slam down my mug so that liquid slops over the side onto the counter and retrieve my mobile from my pocket. I call the care home.

'Elm Brook, Joy Robbins speaking.'

'Joy, hi, it's Saffy here, Rose Grey's granddaughter.'

'Oh hi, Saffy, how are . . . ?'

'Has anyone tried to contact you about Gran? A Mr Davies perhaps?'

'Um . . . no, I don't think so. Why?'

'I've had a few people asking for information on Gran. A man approached me saying he was a private detective and I just wanted to make sure he didn't bother you or Gran, or come to the care home to visit her.'

'Oh, right . . . How strange. But don't worry,' she says, her clipped, curt voice reassuringly officious. 'We don't let just anyone come in to visit.'

'Thanks. And would it be okay . . . if someone does turn up asking to see her, to contact me first?'

'Of course.'

'Thank you. Also, how is Gran? I'm coming to visit her tomorrow anyway but . . .'

'She's fine. A bit confused today. She kept calling me Melissa.'

'Melissa?'

She laughs. 'I must remind her of someone she once knew, that's all. A lot of the residents do it. See you tomorrow.'

As I end the call there is a bang at the front door and I nearly drop my phone in fright. Then I hear the key in the lock, Tom's voice greeting Snowy, and I feel weak with relief.

This is ridiculous. I'm a jittery mess. Being in the house alone all day has made me feel nervy.

Tom still has his helmet on, which he looks faintly ridiculous in, and his expression changes to shock when I hurtle into his arms.

'Hey, what's wrong?'

I lead him into the living room. He perches on the sofa to take off his helmet. His hair is plastered to his head. He watches me without speaking while I pace the room, the words falling fast from my mouth. When I've finished he stares at me, his eyes flashing furiously. 'Who the fuck does this Davies bloke think he is? I could kill him.'

'Tom . . .'

'How dare he frighten you like that?'

'I'm more concerned about who he's working for. He wouldn't tell me what kind of information Gran is supposed to have.' I sigh. 'I don't know, it just feels like it's snowballing. Something bigger is going on here. Are we just blundering on, getting ourselves deeper in the shit without knowing the full picture? And now Mum has gone tearing off to fucking Broadstairs to meet a man who may or may not be the real Alan Hartall and I haven't heard from her, and our back garden is a crime scene – and don't get me started on those journalists. I can't step out of the front door without being accosted. I feel like I'm under house arrest!' I'm out of breath after my rant and sink onto the sofa next to him, my head in my hands, my shoulders shuddering. 'I wish we'd stayed in Croydon,' I say, through my fingers, tears falling down my cheeks and plopping onto my jeans. 'I'm sick of it all, Tom. This was supposed to be a new start for us. For the baby . . . I don't even want to go in the little bedroom any more knowing it looks out onto the garden. Seeing that hole where those bodies were . . .'

Tom pulls me against him, the cool leather of his jacket

pressing against my cheek. 'I'm going to take a sickie tomorrow. I'm not leaving you here alone.'

I sit up in shock. Tom has never once taken a day off work sick. Not even when he had food poisoning and had to take a sick bag on the Tube with him.

'Tom, you can't . . .'

'I think I'm owed it, don't you? And I don't want you to be alone tomorrow. I can get on with decorating. And I'll call the builders, find out when they can come back and continue the build. If they mess us around again, we'll get someone else. Then we won't have to look at the hole any more.'

'Mum should be back . . .' The thought of Mum makes me feel queasy with worry again. 'What time is it?'

Tom checks his watch. 'Just gone eight thirty.' He stands up, shrugging off his jacket. 'It's not like Lorna to forget to call, is it? She's usually always attached to that phone.'

'I know,' I say, picking up my mobile and trying her number again.

It goes straight to voicemail.

By ten o'clock she's still not home.

Every time I hear a car, which isn't often, I run to the window, hoping it's a taxi, but nothing.

'Do you think I should call the police?' I say to Tom, who's sitting in front of the television watching *The Wire* on box set, although neither of us can concentrate.

'The police won't do anything. Haven't you got to wait twenty-four hours or something before they'll look into an adult's disappearance?'

I take a deep breath, pushing down panic. I don't know what to do with myself – my body oozes with nervous energy.

I know Mum is a free spirit and I never worry about her when she's in Spain. But something doesn't feel right about this. I know she would have rung me – after all, this is a journey we're on together.

I pull back the grey flowered curtains that we'd taken from our Croydon flat and don't quite fit the window. It's dark outside. There isn't even a streetlamp to light the way, the moon a sliver of a crescent in the sky, half obscured by a cloud. The night seems heavy and oppressive, like a thick blanket curling around my car and Tom's bike, making innocuous shapes menacing.

'Come away from the window,' says Tom, gently. 'I'm sure she's okay.'

'Then why wouldn't she have phoned?' I wail, my hands clenched by my sides.

I can't shake the feeling that something bad has happened to her. Something that's connected to all this.

What have we got involved in?

27

Lorna

LORNA FINDS HERSELF A WINDOW SEAT ON THE TRAIN back to London, clutching her caramel macchiato, grateful that nobody has occupied the space next to her so she can stretch out. She's shattered and a little tipsy. She shouldn't have had that last glass of wine.

Now it's gone eight and she still has to get from London to Chippenham. She leans her head against the glass as the train pulls out of the station, watching the sun cast purple and peach streaks across the sky, reflecting on her conversation with Alan and her suspicions that Daphne and Sheila are the same person. She can't wait to tell Saffy.

She sits up straighter. Saffy! She hasn't called her all day. Damn it, she'd promised she'd ring on her way home. She rummages in her bag for her phone. Where is it? She has so much crap in her bag: old receipts, business cards, a notebook, two pens, her purse and makeup. But it doesn't matter how much she searches, it's not there. She flops back against the seat. She must have dropped it or did she leave it on the table when she left? She groans, startling a man in the seat opposite. Her whole life is on that phone. She doesn't know any of the numbers by heart. Who does any more? She suddenly feels naked and vulnerable without it and inwardly curses the modern world, the advances in technology that have made her so dependent on a stupid little machine. She fights the urge to scream. What is she going to do now? She just hopes there's a taxi rank outside the station in Chippenham or she'll have a long walk back to Beggars Nook. It's at least five miles. And without her phone she won't know the way.

There's nothing she can do about it now anyway, she thinks, as she watches the Kent countryside whizz past her. She has no choice but to drink her coffee and try to relax.

It's gone eleven by the time her second train pulls into Chippenham station. She hopes Saffy and Tom aren't too worried about her. She feels a stab of guilt that she's probably keeping them up because she hasn't got her own key.

The station is deserted: the other three passengers who disembarked with her have melted away into the dark night. She shivers in her tweed jacket and pulls it around herself, aware of her heels echoing on the empty platform. She walks fast, wanting to get home now, back to Saffy, to tell her everything she's found out today.

At the entrance there are no waiting taxis. Just an empty strip of road. What is she going to do now? Could she ask to borrow someone's phone? A young guy she recognizes from the train is waiting by the exit, a briefcase at his feet, headphones on and red Nike trainers, at odds with his business suit. His head is bent as he scrolls through his phone.

She sidles up to him, aware she must look a bit manic. He removes his headphones as she gets closer. 'Excuse me? Can I use your phone to call a taxi?'

'Sure,' he says, without smiling. 'I'll call one. I've got a number in my phone. Where do you want to go?'

'Beggars Nook.'

He laughs. 'Beggars Nook? Where the hell is that?'

She forces a smile. 'It's a little village nearby.'

He calls the taxi firm, then places his hand over the mouthpiece. 'Name?' he whispers.

'Lorna,' she whispers back, not sure why she's whispering too. He gives her a strange look.

'It will be with you in ten,' he says, as he ends the call.

'Thank you, I'm so grateful –'

'Got to go, my lift's here,' he says, jogging towards a Fiesta that has just pulled up. She watches his car drive off, aware she's completely alone now.

Thankfully she doesn't have to wait long before the taxi arrives. She sinks into the back seat, with relief. It takes just fifteen minutes to get to Beggars Nook. 'What number?' he asks, as he drives through the village towards Saffy's cottage.

'Nine Skelton Place. Just up here somewhere,' she says, waving vaguely. She can't remember exactly where it is on this hill. She pays and gets out, the taxi driving off into the distance, the rear lights winking then disappearing as it rounds the bend, leaving her in total darkness. She feels she's being swallowed by it. Why are there no streetlamps? She begins walking up the hill. Yes, it's not far, she tells herself. There's the lane that leads to the woods and the postbox. It's two houses up from that.

She hears footsteps behind her and the back of her neck prickles. There was nobody around when she got out of the taxi.

It happens so quickly. A hand reaching from behind and over her mouth. Another arm clamping her chest, like a steel safety bar on a fairground ride. And she's thinking that this

can't be happening in a little rural village like Beggars Nook.
She can't even scream – his hand is pressed down too firmly on
her face. She tries to kick out but his arm tightens so that she
can barely breathe.

He drags her backwards towards the lane. Towards the
woods. She tries to fight against it, to dig her heels into the
pavement, but he's too strong. The heel on her sandal snaps and
comes off. She's so frightened she wants to pee. Stay calm, she
tells herself. Stay calm, stay calm.

They're in the lane now, between two houses hidden behind
high hedges. Nobody will be able to see her.

'Listen,' he growls, his breath hot against her ear, 'if you do
what I say I won't hurt you.'

He's going to rape me, she thinks. *As long as he doesn't kill me.
Don't kill me*, she silently pleads. She can't leave Saffy. She's
about to be a grandmother.

'I need information on Rose Grey.'

She's so shocked that, for an instant, she forgets to be frightened. This isn't some random attack. He knows her mother.
She recognizes his voice.

She can only nod.

'You need to ask her where she's buried the evidence. It's important. If you don't ask her I'll hurt your daughter.'

Oh, God. Not Saffy. No.

'Anything,' she mumbles against his palm.

'I'm going to take my hand away now. If you scream I'll
come back. If you go to the police I'll know. And you don't
want me to pay Rose a little visit, now, do you? I know where
her care home is.'

Blood pounds in her ears but she nods. He removes his
hand from her mouth but he still clamps her from behind with
his arm so she can't see his face.

'I need your phone number,' he says.

'I've . . . I've lost my phone.'

'A likely story.'

She wants to cry. 'I have. You can check my bag.' It's still on her shoulder, pinned there by the weight of him.

'Then ring the number on the card. Your daughter will know which card.'

He releases her so hard that she falls forward, her knees crashing against the pavement and she cries out in pain. She hears his retreating footsteps heading down the lane towards the woods but she doesn't dare turn around until he's gone.

She gets to her feet. Her legs are like jelly and there is a hole in the knee of her jeans, blood and grit darkening the edges. She hobbles out of the lane and turns left, stopping to pick up her broken heel on the way. She's trembling all over. The bushes and hedges that obscure the other properties would also hide crime, she thinks, as she limps home. She could have been raped and murdered right here on this street and nobody would have seen a thing.

She's relieved when she spots number nine, the light in the living room still on, seeping through the ill-fitting curtains at the window. She hobbles over the drive, her unheeled shoe sinking into the gravel. Before she's even got to the door it's thrown open, her daughter standing there, a mixture of horror and relief on her face.

'Mum!' she cries, throwing herself at her. 'Oh, my God, we've been so worried. Are you okay? What's happened?'

She manages to nod as Saffy ushers her into the house and on to the sofa. Tom is standing by the fireplace and the look on his face when he sees her is so horrified that she fights the urge to laugh hysterically.

'He . . . he grabbed me,' she says. 'This fucking bastard

grabbed me. He must have been waiting . . . I lost my phone.
I'm so sorry I didn't call.'

'Oh, my God! Don't worry about that now,' says Saffy, sitting next to her and taking her hand. 'Your knee is bleeding.
Are you okay? Who grabbed you?'

'I think it was the same guy from yesterday. Glen, he said
his name was.'

Saffy frowns. 'From yesterday?'

She swallows tears. She can't cry. She has to be strong for
her daughter, who looks petrified. 'He stopped me when I was
taking Snowy for a walk. Seemed pleasant enough . . . but as I
was walking away I heard him say something about your gran.
I thought I'd misheard him but . . .'

Tom starts pacing. 'This is fucking unbelievable. We need
to call the police. Saffy, what's the number for DS Barnes?'
He's already got his mobile in his hand.

'No!' cries Lorna, standing up. She wobbles on her one heel
and has to sit down again. Her nail varnish has chipped, and
her feet are dirty. 'We can't contact the police. He said he'll
know. He said . . . he said he knows where your gran is living.'

Lorna tells them everything – almost everything anyway.
She omits the part where he threatened to hurt Saffy. She
doesn't want to scare her any more than she needs to: all this
stress and worry can't be good for the baby. 'He said something
about Gran burying the evidence. And that he wanted to know
where.'

'The evidence?' Saffy's face pales. 'Is that what he said? Paperwork that Gran has?'

'I . . . I don't know. I don't think he mentioned paperwork
but I can't remember. He wanted me to ask your gran. He mentioned a card,' says Lorna. 'I didn't know what he was talking
about.'

Saffy inhales sharply. 'That wanker. It's the same guy.'

'What do you mean?'

'I met someone earlier. He said he was a private detective and he'd been hired by someone to find a file or paperwork or something that Gran has. He tried to be all nice at first but I was feeling increasingly uneasy as the conversation progressed. He . . .' She shudders. 'He was quite intense. I felt afraid by the end. As he was leaving he gave me his card. It said G. E. Davies . . . Glen. It's got to be the same man.' She goes to the coffee table and picks something up. 'Here,' she says, handing it to Lorna.

'He can't be a legitimate private detective,' says Tom, still pacing. 'Not if he's grabbing women in the street.'

Lorna takes the card from her daughter. It looks crude and unprofessionally done. She hands it back. 'He specifically said *evidence* . . .'

Saffy pulls at her hair, looking stressed. 'The police came today,' she says, and Lorna listens as her daughter tells her about their visit. 'When they were leaving I gave them Davies's number and they said they'd check him out. We should tell them about this too.'

Lorna can't take it all in. Finding out her mother lived here when at least one of the murders took place, and now this. It must be connected somehow. She bends over and takes off her shoes. She'll have to see if she can glue the heel back on.

'What the hell was Rose mixed up in?' Tom stops pacing, his arms folded, fixing Lorna with a furious gaze, like it's her fault. She's the parent here: she needs to take charge.

'Let's all go to bed,' she says, standing up. 'I'll come with you to the care home tomorrow, honey. See what we can find out.'

'Mum . . .'

Lorna holds up her hand, looking from Saffy's anxious face to Tom's angry one. 'You both need to get some rest,' she says, in her most authoritarian voice. 'We'll talk about it tomorrow.' She limps out of the room and climbs the stairs, her knee aching with the movement. Fury builds inside her. How dare this man threaten her family. Tomorrow, she thinks, she'll buy some panic alarms and some pepper spray. If that man comes anywhere near her daughter again she'll kill him.

28

Rose

February 1980

THE DAY AFTER I RAN INTO JOEL IN THE VILLAGE SQUARE the snow came.

You woke me up, scrambling into my room and jumping on my bed, an angel in your long white nightie. 'Snow! Snow!' you cried, shaking me awake and dragging me to the window, the wooden floorboards cold underfoot. You looked so cute, your big brown eyes wide with delight and your hair in dark tendrils around your shoulders. Thick dense flakes were falling fast and settling onto the layer already on the ground. The sky was a perfect pearly white and gave the impression the world was wrapped in a quilt.

'No playschool today! I'm not going out in this,' I said, climbing back into bed and snuggling down.

You clapped your hands excitedly. 'Snowman!'

'Yes, snowman. But later.'

Daphne appeared at the bedroom door then, dressed in

many layers with thick socks pulled up over pyjama bottoms, which ballooned over the top giving the impression she was wearing old-fashioned breeches. Her long fair hair was a messy halo around her face. 'It's bloody freezing,' she said, blowing theatrically onto her hands.

'Snow! Snow!' you sang, grabbing her hands, pulling her around, like you were playing a game of ring-a-roses. Daphne threw her head back and laughed and, as I watched the two of you, I felt my heart burst with happiness. The three of us, in that little cottage, cosy and safe, cocooned from the world.

We didn't need anybody else.

We lit the fire in the front room and Daphne made hot chocolate, heating milk on the stove, while I rummaged in cupboards making sure we had enough food for the next few days, just in case we couldn't get to the shops. I bought most of my food in the grocery store but once a month I was forced to drive to the big Safeway on the roundabout, two miles or so out of the village. Luckily I'd only gone the week before.

'We've got lots of tins of beans and spaghetti hoops,' I announced. 'And I froze some bread yesterday.'

'We've still got batches of my homemade soup,' Daphne said, handing me a mug of hot chocolate.

You were already sitting at the kitchen table slurping yours noisily, your little legs swinging. Under your nightie I could see you'd pulled your bright yellow wellies onto the wrong feet. 'Lolly, sweetheart, you need to get dressed before we can go outside.'

'Daffy,' you said, standing up.

'You're a big girl now, you can get dressed by yourself,' I said, rolling my eyes at Daphne but she flashed you a beatific smile.

'Of course I'll help,' she said, taking your hand. 'Come on, Princess Lollipop, let's find lots of warm clothes to put on.'

She always called you Princess Lollipop and you loved it. You loved her.

Daphne spent hours with you that day, building a snowman in the garden. I watched for a bit out of the window, laughing with you both every time the head fell off, which it did, often. 'It's harder than it looks,' mouthed Daphne. The snow continued to fall onto your hats, lingering on your hair so that it looked like tiny white flowers were entwined in your plaits.

Bracing myself I reluctantly went outside too. I hated the cold but Daphne didn't seem to feel it. And neither did you, even though your mittens were sopping wet and your nose and cheeks red. By now the snow was nearly up to the top of your wellies. Daphne didn't own a pair so she was wearing her tatty platform boots, which didn't look very waterproof.

'We just need to find some currants and a carrot for the eyes and nose,' she said to you once she'd finished, standing up, hands on hips, to admire her handiwork. You ran inside, finally emerging triumphantly with a small shrivelled carrot and two fat sultanas.

'You both look frozen to the bones,' I said. The snow had slowed now, only the occasional flake floating to the ground. 'Come on, I'll make beans on toast.'

Later, while you played with your teddies in your bedroom, Daphne and I sat with a cup of tea by the fire, her fingers still red raw from the cold. She stretched out her legs on the sofa, resting her feet in my lap.

I stiffened, embarrassed at her familiarity. Daphne, however, was totally unselfconscious.

'Tuck your legs up here,' she said, tapping my ankle. I hesitated, then swung my legs up so that my feet rested against her thigh. 'See? That's more comfortable, isn't it?'

I smiled back. It was. It felt like the kind of thing you'd do with a sister, that's all. Completely natural. I didn't need to feel awkward about it. I relaxed into the position, smiling at her over my mug.

I had known Daphne less than two months but she had effortlessly blended into our lives. And now here we were, at ease with each other. We could sit in companionable silence, not feeling the other had to talk. We seemed to know what the other was thinking or feeling and acted accordingly. I suddenly realized that she never annoyed me. She was interesting and clever and independent and fun. She was kind and thoughtful, the way she played with you and knitted outfits for your teddies and dolls, or brought back little gifts, like your favourite sponge cake or fir cones from the woods that she sprayed silver and placed on the windowsill. She spent hours bent over her sewing machine to make you clothes. Last week she'd turned up with a Swiss cheese plant that was so big it obscured her head as she carried it through the door. It now sat in the corner by the fireplace. I didn't have the heart to tell her I was terrible with plants – they almost always died on my watch.

'Do you have any sisters?' I asked, forgetting our rule of no questions. I felt her stiffen but she shook her head, much to my surprise.

'No.'

'Me neither. And your parents?'

Daphne sipped her drink. The fire crackled in the hearth. All I knew about her was that she'd grown up in south London, not that far from where I'd lived with my parents, but moved away when she was eleven. Since then, she said, she'd lived 'all over'.

She shook her head. 'Long, boring story. I'm the black sheep. You know how it is?'

I didn't, but I nodded anyway.

She turned away from me, not saying anything else, just staring into the fire, her eyes huge and sad.

After a few minutes she fixed her eyes on me again, something changing in her expression. 'I've always kept myself to myself. Other places I've stayed, other people I've lodged with, I've kept at arm's length. But you . . .' her eyes softened '. . . you're the only person I've let myself get close to, Rose. For a long, long time. I hope you don't make me regret it.'

I felt myself blush. 'Of course I won't. But can I ask? Why me?'

'I don't know. I feel like we're the same.'

She was right. I felt that too: both self-sufficient, determined to be strong, but also damaged. She was the first person I had let myself grow close to since I'd run away that terrible night three years ago. And I got the feeling it was the same for Daphne.

As an only child I'd never known what it was like to have a sibling, but the closeness I felt with Daphne in that moment was how I'd always imagined it would be. I glanced at her and her eyes locked with mine. My stomach fluttered. I felt more for her than sisterly affection, I knew that really. The more I got to know her, the deeper my feelings became. I felt my cheeks grow hot at the thought that she might be able to tell.

She smiled at me. 'And also . . . with Lolly. With the three of us, it's like the family I wish I'd had.'

'Me too,' I said, my voice full of emotion.

We smiled at each other shyly and she reached over and took my hand in hers, squeezing my fingers gently. In that moment I knew I'd do anything for her: I wanted to look out for her and protect her. I'd never felt that way about another person apart from you, and maybe Audrey. Looking back now, I realized I was falling in love.

Then you came bounding into the room with a Barbie half dressed. You thrust it into Daphne's lap. 'I can't do,' you wailed. And Daphne laughed and pulled you onto her legs while she dressed the doll for you.

It was the most perfect day. The three of us huddled on the sofa, happy and safe, the fire roaring and the snow falling softly outside.

I wish we could have stayed that way, I really do.

PART THREE

29

Theo

ON THURSDAY MORNING THEO UNEXPECTEDLY FINDS himself alone in his dad's study and an opportunity presents itself to him that is too good to pass up.

The chance to snoop.

It's not the kind of behaviour Theo has ever indulged in before. He's not the type. He's never looked through Jen's phone, or tried to hack into her emails, like some of his mates have done with their other halves. Mutual trust is so important to him. And he knows Jen feels the same.

My dad is a potential pervert who is hiding something, he tells himself in a bid to ease his conscience.

Theo hadn't planned to go to his dad's today, especially after his visit to Larry yesterday, but guilt had gnawed at him about their argument and even though he'd lain awake most of last night, fury and disappointment grappling for prime emotion, guilt still found a way of slipping in, like a piece of shell falling into a bowl when cracking an egg.

Jen had given him a knowing smile when he said he was popping over to his dad's before work. 'He's still your dad,' she said softly, before kissing him goodbye. But when he arrived there was no answer, just Mavis, the housekeeper, on her way out. 'He's at the golf club,' she'd said. 'He won't be back until later.'

Theo had held up his backpack. 'I've got food for him,' he lied. 'Don't worry, you go and I'll let myself out.'

'You're a good son,' she said, patting his cheek fondly, then scuttling off down the driveway to catch her bus.

Now, standing in his father's study, he feels like the worst son in the world. Even as a kid he knew never to come in here without his dad's permission. It was off limits and a fate worse than death if he ever dared defy his father's orders. Not that he ever did. He hadn't been interested as a boy: it was full of his father's boring work stuff and ugly golfing trophies. But now . . . now his heart beats with anticipation. His dad refuses to tell him anything, yet he knows this room must be a vault for his many secrets.

Theo glances around the study, at the wood panelling on the walls, the built-in shelves and display cabinet, the desk with its dark green padded insert. Where to start? What to look for? It smells in here, a musky expensive scent mixed with polished wood. It's ludicrous, really, but Theo's always felt his dad just smells *important*.

He goes to the built-in bookshelves on the far wall, behind the desk. Underneath the shelves on either side there is a set of cupboard doors. The same cupboards his dad had been rummaging through last week when he was in one of his tempers. Theo bends down and pulls open one of the doors. Neatly stacked is a pile of Lever Arch folders. He pulls one out and skims through the pages; it looks like old tax accounts. He shoves them back, making sure to keep them in the right order. He's certain that's the kind of thing his dad would notice. He tries the other cupboard but it's locked. Damn it. He didn't even think about that. Why would his dad lock it unless it was something he didn't want anybody seeing? Mavis isn't even allowed in here to clean. He tries the desk drawers instead. Surprisingly they aren't locked but they contain nothing exciting, just some receipts held together with a bulldog clip, a pack of Bic pens, a fancy fountain pen, some certificates from the golf club and a bottle of pills. He picks them up, examining the label. Blood-pressure medication. He didn't even know his dad had high blood pressure. He replaces the bottle. There must be something, he thinks, his eye going again to the locked cupboard. He has to get in there, whatever the consequences. He opens the desk drawer again and finds two large paperclips, which he bends into a V, shoving the end of one into the lock. He'd tried this once, with a bunch of mates, years ago at school to get into the display cabinet that held all the sporting medals: they'd wanted to play a prank on one of the rugby team. He remembers having to push down on the end of one, while jiggling the other. 'Come on, you piece of shit, open,' he says through clenched teeth. Finally he hears a pop and feels a release and the cupboard springs open. He sits back on his heels, shocked that he's actually managed to do it.

And then his heart falls. The cupboard is empty. All that effort and his dad has locked a fucking empty cupboard. He looks around as though this is some prank and his dad is at the door laughing at him. But no, he's alone. Why would his dad lock an empty cupboard? Unless, he thinks, gathering his thoughts, his dad has moved whatever was in there to somewhere more secure. He peers into the cupboard, gently pushing on the shelves within. The bottom one creaks under his hand. He inspects it more closely: it's loose, more like a panel than a shelf. He pushes it and the top comes off, revealing a sort of hidden section underneath. Theo's heart pounds. Something's there: a small pile of newspaper cuttings with a black A4 flexible folder placed on top. He reaches for the cuttings. They are all dated from 2004 and are from local newspapers about his mum's accident. He understands why his dad might want to keep them, but why hide them? Perhaps he just forgot about them, he thinks, putting them back.

Then he turns to the folder. It has clear plastic sleeves. He flicks through it. Each of the fifteen-odd sleeves has a photograph loose at the bottom. Nothing more than that. He takes out the first. It's in colour, muted autumnal tones, and is of a woman around his age, and it looks like she's unaware the photo has been taken. She's heavily pregnant. By the style of her hair and clothes it looks to be from the late 1960s or early 1970s. He turns the photograph over, expecting maybe a date or a name, but it's blank. He flicks through the rest of the folder and it's the same: photographs of women, taken unawares. But nothing else. The latest photo looks more recent. Maybe ten years ago, fifteen at a push. Definitely the twenty-first century. Why has his dad got a folder of these random women?

An appalling thought suddenly hits Theo. Perhaps his dad molested them and has now become obsessed with them. Stalking them? A myriad different hideous scenarios flits through his mind, like a storyboard for a horror film, and he snaps the folder shut. No, he reasons. That can't be it. If his dad was a serial sex offender wouldn't at least some of these women have come forward and made a complaint? As far as he's aware nobody has, apart from Cynthia Parsons. He wonders if one of the women was her. He opens the folder again and goes back to the first photo. If only he had some other names to go by. He reaches for his phone in his back pocket and, he's not sure why, but he takes snaps of the first five photos.

The crunching sound of gravel under tyres makes him jump and he stands up to look out of the study window. His dad is pulling his Mercedes onto the driveway next to his old Volvo. *Bollocks.* He'd thought he had more time. His dad will see his car and know he's here. In the house. Alone. Something he hasn't done since moving out properly after university.

He shoves the folder back on top of the newspaper cuttings and drops the shelf on top, slamming the cupboard door shut, his heart hammering so hard he can feel the pound of it in his ears. He dreads to think how apoplectic his dad will be if he catches him in his study. He tries to relock the cupboard but no amount of wriggling of the paperclip works. Sweat breaks out on his forehead. He has no choice but to leave it and hope his dad thinks he just forgot to lock it.

He goes to the window again. His dad is standing in the driveway frowning at Theo's car, his hand stroking the back of his head. Then, he looks up at his study and Theo has to duck. Shit, was he seen?

He crawls on his hands and knees away from the window and exits the study, running down the elaborate staircase, his trainers squeaking on the parquet as he races into the kitchen. He can hear his dad's key in the lock. Theo grabs himself a glass of water and sits at the island, trying to catch his breath and make it look like he's been sitting there the whole time.

The soles of his dad's expensive brogues echo in the hallway. And then he's there, filling the doorway, all six foot three inches of him.

'What are you doing here?' he growls.

'Mavis let me in. I wanted to see you to – to apologize for the other day.'

His dad eyes him warily, as though unsure whether to believe him.

'She told me you'd be back soon.' The lie slips surprisingly easily from Theo's tongue but he blushes anyway, like he used to do at school when he was caught out by a teacher.

His dad goes over to the kettle and switches it on. He looks tired. There are new lines under his eyes and he places both hands on his lower back and does a kind of stretch.

'Are you all right for food?' asks Theo.

'Of course I am. I'm a grown man. I can look after myself. I did do national service.'

Christ, thinks Theo, mentally rolling his eyes, *not that old chestnut*. His father had been in the last cohort to do national service and, growing up, he never let Theo forget it.

He watches as his dad makes himself a cup of tea; his tanned arms are sinewy in his polo shirt. He's always felt he knew just the kind of man his father was. Strict, old-fashioned, brilliant, old-money, educated and controlling. But not a pervert.

Or a stalker or psychopath.

Are you those things, Dad? he silently asks.

Theo wonders, as he surveys him pressing his teabag against his mug, whether he has ever loved his father. He'd pitied him, yes, felt a sense of duty towards him, felt responsible for him after his mother died. But love? He's not sure. Maybe when he was a kid, when he was still full of hope that his dad might care about him, become the father he'd always wished for. He realizes, with a jolt, that he doesn't like his dad. He's cold and he's hard and Theo is fed up with trying to make excuses for him in his own mind.

He could walk out of here now and not look back. And if it wasn't for the fact that he'd worry his mum would be disappointed in him, then he would. He doubts his dad would give a shit if he never visited again.

'Right,' says Theo, jumping down from the bar stool. 'I'm off.'

His dad turns to him, surprise on his face. 'You don't want a cup of tea?'

He hesitates. Does his dad want him to stay? He's as hard to read as a stone statue. Is it a peace offering? And then he remembers Larry's words, the complaint of sexual misconduct by Cynthia Parsons. He remembers his mother's red eyes and the bruises she hid. He remembers how he'd cowered as a kid when his dad was in one of his ranting moods. But then he looks into his father's blue eyes, the whites of which are yellowing with age, and he feels a twinge of compassion. He's an old man. He's probably lonely. 'Go on, then,' he finds himself saying.

30

Saffy

TOM PULLS A SICKIE THE NEXT MORNING, LIKE HE PROM-
ised last night, even though I tell him there's no need.

'I just want to make sure he doesn't come back,' he says over
breakfast. It's raining – for the first time in weeks – and the cottage feels cold and damp. The windows need replacing, not that
we can think of that at the moment with everything else going
on, not to mention the expense. It's going to cost enough to
get the extension done, but a draught is seeping through the ill-
fitting frames and I shiver in my pyjamas as I nurse a Red Bush
tea – the only thing I can stomach – at the kitchen table. I'm
exhausted after spending all night tossing and turning and worrying about Mum and that man who calls himself Glen Davies.

'I don't want you to get into trouble on our account,' I say, as
Mum walks into the room. She has a handful of clothes in her
arms. I haven't even had the chance to talk to her about how
she got on with Alan Hartall yesterday.

'Can I use the washing machine?' she asks. 'I'm running out
of things to wear. Thank goodness I brought an extra pair of
shoes with me. Can't believe my favourite sandals are broken.'

'Give them to me and I'll fix them,' says Tom, standing up and taking his empty plate and cup to the sink. He's got his paint-splattered jeans on with holes in the knees. He wants to make a start on the little bedroom. I know it's his way of trying to get me excited about the baby and the house again. To try to take my mind off everything else. I can't bear to admit to him that I'm feeling less and less at home here with each passing day.

My phone vibrates next to me and my dad's number flashes up on the screen.

'Did your mother get home in the end?' It's the first thing he says when I answer.

'Yes.' I glance at Mum, who looks up at me. 'She lost her phone. It's all . . . it's all okay.' I don't want to worry him by mentioning that Mum got assaulted and threatened on her way home.

'Is that your dad? Can I speak to him?' she says, getting up and taking the phone from me before I've even replied.

She cups it to her ear. 'Euan? Yes, it's me.' She wanders out of the room and into the hallway so that I can no longer make out what they're saying.

'Rude,' I say to Tom, and we laugh, uneasily, as he slides into the chair next to me.

She returns five minutes later and hands me back my phone. She doesn't tell me what they talked about. Instead she makes herself a cup of tea and joins us at the table. 'I've had an idea,' she announces. 'I think we should go to Spain. You can stay with me for a while.'

I nearly spit out my tea. 'You're joking?'

'I don't think it's safe to stay here.'

'But what about our jobs? And Gran? We can't just . . . *leave*.'

'There are nursing homes in Spain,' she says. 'We can take Gran too.'

'If we go,' says Tom pragmatically, 'all our problems will still be here when we get back. We can't run away, Lorna.'

That's the trouble with Mum. She's spent her whole life thinking it's the answer to everything.

What exactly is she running from this time? Is there something she's not telling me?

Mum fills me in on her visit to Alan Hartall as I'm driving us to visit Gran. Tom has stayed at home with Snowy to guard the cottage, saying he's going to strip the wallpaper in the little bedroom. A sadness passed across Mum's face when he said it. She'd remembered the wallpaper. It had been hers when she was little, a link to the past.

As we were leaving I made sure to give Tom DS Barnes's number just in case there's any sign of Davies lurking around the house. When I get home later I'll call him myself to report what happened to Mum. Davies can't get away with attacking women in the street.

'So I think Sheila Watts stole Daphne Hartall's identity. I'm sure the woman who lodged with your gran is one and the same.'

'And she lied to Gran?'

She shrugs. 'I don't know. We could try asking her about it when we get there. Anyway, I've asked your dad to see what he can find out about Sheila Watts and Daphne Hartall.'

'I've already asked him about Sheila,' I say, explaining about the file and how I'd found Neil Lewisham's name on an article relating to a different case. 'We need to go to the police, really,' I say, knowing Mum won't agree. 'DS Barnes might be able to sort all this out.'

'Who is Davies working for and what does he know?' she says. 'Urgh, it's a mind fuck.'

'Mum!'

'Well, I'm sorry but it is. And trying to get anything from Gran is like pulling teeth.'

It's raining hard, the windscreen wipers on my Mini squeaking as they work overtime. I've had to crank up the heating because I could see Mum shivering in her thin jacket. She refused to borrow any of my or Tom's raincoats. Her dark curls, so like mine but shorter, have frizzed.

When we arrive Gran is sitting in her usual chair by the glass doors that overlook the garden; I think, as I always do, that she must miss pottering around in her greenhouse, tending her radishes and planting bulbs in her garden. The sound of the rain drumming on the Velux windows, coupled with the tropical heat, gives the room a cosy feel. She's wearing a green jumper I bought her for Christmas two years ago. In front of her is an unfinished jigsaw puzzle, the one we've done before with the picture of the dog. Her hair is thinning and fluffs like cotton wool around her face. I feel a lurch in my heart when I see her looking so small and vulnerable, like I do every week.

She smiles at Mum and me as we sit down in the chairs next to her. But it's a polite smile. The type you give strangers. 'Can I help you?' she asks. I feel Mum tense next to me.

'Gran, it's me, Saffy.'

Her eyes light up. 'Saffy!'

'And your daughter, Lorna,' says Mum.

'Lolly!'

I wipe a tear that has seeped out of the corner of my eye, hoping nobody has noticed. I've never heard her call my mum by that name before and I wonder if she's regressed into the past, to when Mum was a little girl.

'Yes,' says Mum, the relief evident in her voice. She takes Gran's hands in hers. 'It's Lolly.'

'I'm sorry, Lolly,' says Gran, her face crumpling. 'I'm so sorry.' Tears run down her crinkly cheeks and my heart feels like it's going to break.

'Why are you sorry?' asks Mum, kindly, her eyes full of concern as they flick to mine and then to Gran again. 'You don't have to be sorry for anything.'

'Are the police coming back?'

'Now don't you worry about the police. I'll handle them,' says Mum, firmly, producing a tissue, magician-like, and handing it to Gran. She always seems to have one about her person, goodness knows where in her tight outfits. Gran takes it and wipes her tears away.

'Mum,' she hesitates, throwing me a worried look, 'can I ask you if you remember a man called Neil Lewisham?'

Gran blinks up at Mum with her big eyes but doesn't say anything.

'What about Sheila Watts?' probes Mum.

'Sheila Watts?'

'Yes. You mentioned a Sheila before, remember?'

Gran turns to me, still dabbing at her cheeks. 'Jean hit her over the head. Jean hit her over the head and she didn't get back up again.'

'Jean hit Sheila?' I ask.

'No. Jean hit Susan. Susan died,' she says, sounding impatient now, like we should know what she's talking about.

Susan? Who the bloody hell is Susan?

'Is Susan the body in the garden?' I ask gently, not wanting to spook her.

'I don't know if she's in the garden,' she says, frowning, shredding the tissue in her hands. 'I don't know where they put her.'

'Who's they, Gran?'

'The people who came to take her away, of course. They weren't just going to leave her there bleeding, were they?'

From the corner of my eye I see Mum's perplexed expression.

'So Susan is dead?' I ask. My stomach is clenched with anxiety. Gran's memory is like a stained-glass window that has shattered: the fragments mean nothing in isolation, but everything if they were put in the right order. 'Do you remember her surname? This Susan?'

'Wallace. Her name was Susan Wallace.'

I hear Mum's sharp intake of breath.

'And you're saying Jean killed Susan Wallace and buried her in the garden.'

Gran shakes her head, looking distressed. 'No, no, no, not buried her. No. But Jean hit her over the head. She hit her over the head and she died.'

'And this happened in 1980 when you were living in the cottage?' says Mum, leaning forwards.

'I . . . I don't know . . .' Gran starts wringing her hands, the tissue now disintegrated in her lap. 'I can't remember when it happened. I . . . It's all so foggy.' Her face creases, and then she looks at me. 'Here, who's that?' she says suddenly, out of the blue, as though the conversation never took place. She's pointing at Mum.

'It's Lorna. Your daughter,' I say, my heart in my feet.

'Oh, yes . . . yes . . .' She turns away from us to look out of the rain-spattered window.

I glance at Mum. 'I think we've lost her.'

31

Rose

February 1980

WE SPENT A GLORIOUS FEW DAYS SNOWED INTO THE COT-
tage. I could have lived that way for ever, just the three of us,
cut off from the world. We watched black-and-white films on
the telly and ate Daphne's homemade soup and I made a cake
especially for you. It was like having a second Christmas. But
on the fourth day I was dismayed to see that the roads were
clearer, just sludge left behind, banked by mounds of snow,
tinged yellow. I took you to playschool, the pavements slippery
under our wellies, the snow compacted into ice.

When I got back inside the cottage Daphne was putting on
her thin patchwork coat, her long hair tied back in a ponytail.

'Where are you going?' I asked in surprise.

'Work. I can't stay off for ever,' she said, pressing her crocheted hat firmly over her head. 'As much as I might want to. I
don't want Joel to sack me.'

I was surprised he hadn't already, after she'd turned down his advances. I was still trying to reconcile the Joel I thought I knew to the Joel Daphne talked about. But then, as I'd come to realize, I had always been so naive in the past about men. I could no longer trust my own judgement.

I did wonder if Joel was scared of what Daphne might do if he dared sack her: she could be feisty and determined when she wanted to be. I'd seen the way she'd chastised the bin men after they'd left one of our rubbish bags behind, and shouted at one of the village youths for kicking a pigeon.

It felt strange and empty in the house without her. And I found myself counting down the hours until she returned, distracting myself by loading the washing machine, mopping the kitchen floor, then ambling back to the village square to pick you up from playschool. The corner shop was open but Melissa's café was still closed.

I knew Daphne finished her shift at 5 p.m., just before the pub reopened for the evening. She was usually home by five thirty.

But five thirty came and went and she still wasn't back.

It was dark by then, although the reflection from the snow diluted it. It was a clear night and I could see the stars in the sky and the shadowy shape of the woods encompassing us.

'Where Daffy?' you asked, as I grilled our fish fingers. Usually Daphne would eat with us and you looked longingly at her empty chair and the placemat she always used, the one with big purple flowers.

'She should be back soon,' I said, trying to keep my voice light when really I felt heavy with dread. What if something bad had happened to her? What if Joel, angry at her rebuttal, had hurt her? My past experience flashed through my mind and I shuddered at the thought she could be going through something similar.

After waiting a further hour I couldn't bear it any longer. I took you over to Joyce and Roy's house and asked if they could look after you until I got back. They were delighted to have you, as I knew they would be, even though I didn't want to leave you. But I couldn't stop thinking that Daphne was somewhere, in trouble. And then I trudged through the dirty, slushy snow to the pub. It stood out like a beacon against the dark woods behind, its fairy lights strung outside and the amber-yellow glow beaming from the windows, reflecting onto the pavement. The nearby river looked black and menacing and I had visions that Daphne had fallen in. *No*, I told myself. *She had no need to walk over the bridge. That's the opposite direction from Skelton Place.* I shivered in my coat as I walked nearer to the pub. I tried to peer through the leaded windows, but it was hard to make out features, just shapes of people clustered around the bar. I thought she might have stayed and had a drink, although she usually came straight home. To us. And then I wondered if maybe she fancied Joel after all, despite what she'd told me. I felt a thud of disappointment in her then. After everything we'd said, the promises we'd made about men. About not needing them in our lives. How, from now on, we would stick together. I thought, I'd *hoped*, she was like me.

I took a deep breath to steady my nerves, ready to confront Joel.

'Rose.'

I spun around. A figure lurked by the bushes near the bridge.

A woman stepped out of the shadows but she didn't look like Daphne. She had short hair cut in a chestnut brown pixie crop.

I gasped as she stepped into the light. It was Daphne. Her long blonde hair was all gone.

'What are you doing? What have you done to your hair?' I hissed.

She looked terrified. 'It's a wig. I carry it in my bag with me,' she said, looking about her furtively. 'He's found me, Rose. I think he's found me.'

32

Theo

IT'S BUSY IN THE RESTAURANT, AS IT ALWAYS IS ON A FRIday night, and Theo has barely time to think as he prepares garlic chicken, sautéed potatoes, and his signature Beef Wellington. He usually thrives on the fast pace, the adrenalin surging through him as he prepares dishes and shouts orders at the younger staff. Politely. He's no Gordon Ramsay. But tonight he's got a headache, which he knows is down to lack of sleep; even though his father had actually been cordial to him when he'd caught Theo in his kitchen yesterday, making small talk over a brew, he couldn't get Larry's words and those weird random photographs out of his head. He's just grateful that tomorrow he's going to the village in the Cotswolds with Jen to try to find out more about the bodies and the possible link to his dad. The thought of that keeps him going. If nothing else it will be a chance to get away with Jen.

He's run off his feet for the whole five hours of his shift and it only starts to calm down after 10 p.m. He begins clearing up, his mate Noah chattering away about the movie he saw last night, when Isla, one of the waitresses, comes up to him. 'A customer wanted to compliment the chef,' she says, smiling broadly, almost proudly, like he was a chef at a Michelin-starred restaurant. This has only happened once to him – although Perry, the other chef, has had it a few times. Luckily Perry's not working tonight, so Theo knows the customer must definitely mean him.

The restaurant is small, only ten or so tables, arranged in a linear fashion, two abreast. Isla takes him along the aisle, between the tables, most of which are still occupied by groups of people halfway through their food. On the one in the corner, by the floor-length windows that look out onto the high street, an older man in a familiar Ralph Lauren shirt and chinos is sitting alone.

Theo freezes. It's his dad.

'Here he is,' says Isla, with a ta-da gesture. She claps Theo on the back. 'We're very proud of our chef.' She twinkles and then, thankfully, she moves away without realizing that the customer is Theo's father.

'What . . . what are *you* doing here?' Theo asks. His father's plate is empty. Table eight – the order was shellfish. He's surprised. His dad is very much a traditional roast-dinner kind of man. It must have been up to his high standards if he's polished it off.

'Can't a father come to the restaurant where his son is the chef?' He sits back in his chair and folds his arms across his broad chest. 'Good work, son. I enjoyed it.'

Theo blinks, unsure if he's heard correctly. 'It's just I've worked here for two years and this is the first time –'

'I wanted to see it for myself,' he says, looking around. 'Very nice.' He has a rictus grin on his face. Theo knows it's not fancy enough for his father so why is he even pretending? Why has he really come?

Theo shifts from one foot to the other. 'I'm, well, I'm glad you like it, but I need to get back to the kitchen now.'

His dad nods. The harsh restaurant lighting makes him look sallower than normal. Just as Theo is about to walk back to the kitchen he says, 'I did love your mother, you know.'

Theo stops, his heart thudding.

'I know you think I didn't.'

'I've never said that,' Theo says, flummoxed.

'I wasn't always the best husband.' His shoulders are set back, rigid. 'I know my faults. But I would never have hurt her.'

Theo remembers the bruises his mother tried to hide and knows his dad is talking utter bollocks about hurting her. He wonders if he really believes what he's saying. Has he rewritten history in his own mind as a way to live with the terrible things he's done? Or maybe he did love her, in his own warped way.

'Her death was an accident.'

Theo goes cold. His dad knows. He knows he's been in his study. He's found the unlocked cupboard. Why else would he be here now talking about his mum?

'And Cynthia Parsons?' It's out before Theo has even registered what he's saying. He flinches. He shouldn't have brought that up here. He's at work. This is too big a conversation to be having on a five-minute break.

The colour drains from his father's face. 'What do you know about Cynthia Parsons?'

'I know she made a complaint against you,' says Theo, his voice low so as not to alert the other customers. It must be an odd sight, him in his white chef's coat talking so intently to an old man. The other customers will think his father is making a complaint. It could look bad.

'That was a long time ago.'

'Sexual assault,' Theo spits, unable to keep the disgust out of his voice.

'You know nothing about it,' his dad growls. 'And I'd appreciate it if you come to me in future, rather than sneaking around behind my back.'

'Sure,' says Theo, shrugging, trying to look unruffled, when his heart is racing and his palms sweating at the thought of having it out with his father after all this time. 'Because you're so forthcoming with information. I've tried asking you before but you're never straight with me.'

'It saddens me that you feel you have to snoop.'

Theo folds his arms across his chest. Should he deny it? There's no point.

'I know you've been in my study,' says his dad, in the same deathly calm voice. 'You left the cupboard door unlocked.'

'Why do you have a file of random women and a bunch of newspaper reports about Mum?'

His dad stares at him, his face impassive. And Theo suspects that he probably rehearsed exactly what he'd say before he got here. 'The newspaper reports are old, from the time of your mum's death. I'd forgotten all about them. And the file is just patients I've helped, over the years, that's all. You wouldn't understand, not being in the medical profession yourself, but you get attached to people you've helped. I wanted to remember them.'

Something doesn't add up. 'Then why hide both under lock and key?'

His dad makes a *pff* sound with his mouth. 'Oh, give up on the *Colombo* act, for goodness' sake. You're making something out of nothing. I just forgot about them. You know I retired years ago.' He crosses his legs, looking at Theo with a smug expression.

Theo pushes back his hair, feeling flustered. He can't allow his dad to wiggle out of this. Not now he's here. Not now he's brought this up.

'So Cynthia was lying, was she?'

His father adjusts the knee of his trousers. 'It's complicated. I did nothing wrong. She had a boyfriend, she got hysterical and tried to make out I'd acted inappropriately. I wasn't with your mother then. It was before we met. I don't need to force women to be with me, Theo.'

Theo wants to believe him but he doesn't. He's being too nice, too helpful. Like he's been backed into a corner.

'Then why the newspaper article on your desk with the words *Find Her* scribbled on it? Why –'

'*Why, why, why?*' he spits. 'I thought I'd come here, be nice, try to explain. But no, it's not enough for you, is it? Nagging. Just like your mother.' He gathers up his jacket and stands up.

'Look, Dad, this is a conversation to have in private. I get off in half an hour. I could come over and –'

But before he can finish his sentence, his dad pushes past him, and Theo loses his footing, stumbling into the table behind him, which thankfully is empty.

His father rounds on him, not looking the least bit guilty for hurting his son. 'Don't go through my fucking things again! Got it?' he hisses. The restaurant falls silent, faces tilted towards Theo as his dad slams out of the door.

33

Saffy

IT'S LATE FRIDAY AFTERNOON AND I CAN HEAR MUM in the living room on the phone to Alberto. She's had to use my mobile. Her own phone should turn up in the next day or so – she'd managed to track it down by calling the café in Broadstairs where she'd lost it. Luckily some good Samaritan had handed it in to the bar staff. It sounds like she's telling him she's staying on for another week, and as much as she can bug me, with her fussing and high energy and incessant chatter, I'd miss her if she left tomorrow. The thought of the long days in the cottage alone, the press outside, circling like a pack of wolves, and some shady private detective lurking in the woods, makes me feel panicky. It doesn't help that my days are filled creating book covers for sinister novels. And there is still so much we don't know, about Gran and the past and those dead bodies. About Sheila and Jean and Susan. It's obvious Gran knows something and it's getting scrambled in her mind, like that game she used to play with me when I was little, where the top part of a cartoon body doesn't go with the bottom part. I constantly have this feeling of low-level anxiety and I'm not sure if it's my hormones or this whole situation – maybe a mixture of both – that's causing it.

I rang DS Barnes last night and told him all about Glen Davies's assault on Mum. She tried to stop me, saying he'd threatened her about going to the police, but it was the right thing to do.

I plaster on a smile when Mum appears in the kitchen where I'm making tea. I hand her a mug, which she takes distractedly. I've finished work for the day, not that I've managed to get much done with Mum popping her head around my study door every hour asking if I'm okay, or if I need anything.

'I don't think he's very happy,' she begins, sipping her tea thoughtfully. 'I think he's going to move out.'

'What? Because you're not at his beck and call?'

She grimaces. 'No. Not just that. There's been something missing for a while now. And him, my life there, it just seems a million miles away right now. And I can't leave. Not yet. Your gran knows something about this – that's obvious – and we need to get to the bottom of it all. Find out what she knows, or if she's protecting someone.'

'Will your boss mind you taking another week off?'

'My boss will be fine. He owes me loads of holiday. Saffy,' her voice is stern, 'leave it to me. I can't go back to Spain yet. Not until all this has been sorted out.'

I sigh. 'But it might never be sorted out.'

'Of course it will,' she scoffs. Because things always are in my mum's world. She makes sure of it. 'If your gran knows something about the bodies, who they are and who killed them, then fear would have kept her quiet all these years. The police will understand that, I'm sure.'

I turn away, my hands gripping my cup, feeling nauseous. From the kitchen window I can see the hole – the dug-up grave.

The gruesome discovery that started all this. Even the cocky builders don't want to come back, and I don't blame them. So we're stuck with it for a while, the reminder that two people were murdered here. I wish so much we'd never planned the fucking kitchen extension. Then we would have been in blissful ignorance and none of this would be happening.

I go to bed early – it's not even ten o'clock. I've been feeling sick all day and I don't know if it's the pregnancy or because I'm stressed.

I lie soaking in the bath for a bit until the water turns cold. I'm nearly eighteen weeks pregnant and I can see the swell of a bump underneath the water. My belly button has changed shape, protruding more than normal. I step out of the bath carefully and dry myself, then pull on my most comfortable pyjamas. I climb into bed, the duvet lovely and cold against my skin. I can hear Tom and Mum downstairs chatting. Their voices are indecipherable but I know they're probably talking about Gran. That's all our conversations are about at the moment. I turn onto my side and pull my knees up towards my stomach. This should be such a happy time, looking forward to the baby's arrival, doing up the house. But now everything feels tainted and grey. I roll onto my back and glance around the room. Was this Gran's room when she lived here? She must have had her bed pointing this way too, facing the little cast-iron fireplace on the far wall and the window that overlooks the driveway on the right. Despite how tired I feel I get up and go to the window, pulling aside the curtains, wondering if Glen Davies is still lurking about outside.

I feel a tightening across my abdomen, then a sensation like I've wet myself a little bit. I get up and dash to the bathroom, my heart pounding, heat rising to my face in panic as I pull down my pyjama bottoms and sit on the loo. Oh, God, oh, God . . .

I can't breathe. A smear of red in my pyjamas. Blood. There shouldn't be blood. 'Tom!' I cry.

I hear him thud up the stairs. He races into the bathroom. 'What is it? What . . .' he must see the shock and devastation on my face because he helps me gently off the loo. 'Go and get dressed. We need to get to the hospital.'

I pull on an old pair of navy jogging bottoms I haven't worn in years and a jumper that doesn't match. Mum appears in my doorway, her face ashen. 'Is it the baby?'

'I don't know, I don't know,' I cry, scraping my hair back into a scrunchie, my throat dry. 'It's still so early, Mum. I'm only eighteen weeks.'

She folds me into her arms as I cry, more like a whimper of fear, and I'm thankful, so thankful, that she's here.

The journey to the hospital is a blur. Tom drives too fast, and Mum comforts me in the back. 'Do you think I'm having a miscarriage?' I say over and over.

'I don't know, honey, I don't know.' She smoothes my hair back from my face and I'm reminded of all the times she did that when I was a kid, when I woke from a nightmare, or when I was ill. And I remember Gran doing it too, when I stayed with her in the summer, how she'd let me climb into bed with her if I woke up scared in the night.

'It's not a lot of blood, more when I wipe, you know . . .' I say, trying to remain hopeful.

'Let's wait and see what the doctors say.'

We're unsure where to go so head straight to A and E but they send us to the maternity wing. They must have phoned ahead to say to expect us because a kind-faced nurse greets us and ushers me onto a ward where two women, both in different stages of pregnancy, recline on beds, strapped to machines. The smell of disinfectant is cloying. I'm too terrified even to cry as the nurse instructs me to lie on the bed. My palms are clammy as I hold Tom's hand. After I explain about the blood, the nurse scuttles off and returns moments later with an ultrasound device. She pulls the thin blue curtains around us, her demeanour calm. My face is burning but my body is cold with dread. Tom looks ashen. Mum hovers on the other side of the bed, for once not knowing what to say. The nurse, Gail, pulls up my jumper and I fold the waistband of my jogging bottoms down so that she can get to my abdomen, my hands trembling. She flashes me a cheery smile but I can tell by her face that she's concerned, her expression set in concentration as she stares at the screen while moving the probe slowly across my stomach. My chest feels tight and I glance at Tom and I shake my head sadly. *We've lost it.*

Then Gail looks up at us all with a wide smile and I want to cry with relief. 'Baby's heartbeat sounds fine,' she says. 'You could have a UTI, which might be causing the spotting. I'll take a urine test, but still be careful and keep an eye on things, and if there's any more spotting, call us straight away.' Gail strides off to get a vial for me to pee in and then Mum and Tom are hugging me, both at the same time.

By the time we get home, armed with a course of antibiotics, the infection having been confirmed, and a number to phone if there are any more issues, it's gone midnight.

We let ourselves in, Tom and I still giddy with relief. 'I've never been so frightened,' I say, as we step into the hallway. It's put everything into perspective and from now on I'll be doing everything in my power to protect this pregnancy. I cup my stomach defensively, silently vowing to keep the baby safe whatever the cost.

I expect Snowy to come bounding over to us, but there's no sign of him.

'It feels cold in here,' observes Mum. She's only wearing her little tweed jacket over a fairly skimpy blouse, but she's right: there's a draught coming from the back of the house. Tom switches the light on, walking down the hall towards the kitchen. When he pushes the door open I hear him gasp. 'What the fuck?'

Mum glances at me in concern and the elation I'd been feeling just moments before melts away, replaced by unease. *Snowy.* I pick up my pace. Tom is standing in the middle of the kitchen with alarm on his face. The back door is wide open. Snowy is nowhere to be seen.

Everything has been turned out of the drawers in what looks like a hurry so that pens, old receipts, council tax bills and everything else we'd just stuffed into whatever spare drawer was available are scattered over the floor.

'Where's Snowy?' I cry, looking around frantically.

Mum runs into the living room, then back to us again. 'You'd better call the police,' she says, her voice tight. 'It looks like you've been burgled.'

'Wait,' says Tom, picking up a knife from the wooden rack by the microwave. 'Call 999 and stay here. They could still be in the house.'

34

Rose

DAPHNE WAS SKITTISH AND ON EDGE AS I GUIDED HER home. The strange wig looked unnatural on her, as if a wild animal had landed on her head. Her eyes kept darting to the hedges as though she was half expecting someone to jump out.

'Joel told me a man came into the pub asking about me,' she said breathlessly, as we walked as fast as we could. I wrapped an arm around her, trying to comfort her but I could feel her body trembling. She seemed so vulnerable, like when I first saw her on Christmas Eve. 'He's finally found me. Maybe I should leave, Rose. Maybe I should move on.'

Dread descended over me. I didn't want her to go. 'You can't jump to conclusions. Not yet. Not until you know more,' I said, trying to pacify her, even though I knew that if it was me I'd want to run away too. 'Don't go back to your job at the pub. Lie low for a while.'

She nodded, her shoulders hunched around her ears.

'It will be okay,' I said, over and over again as we strode home through the dark. I wish I'd been right.

Daphne was too scared to leave the house. She seemed on edge every time there was a knock at the door or a movement on the road outside. Her face was pale and drawn, and she smoked even more than usual. I spent hours trying to reassure her and, as the days passed, I felt I was getting through to her and that maybe she would stay.

And then one day, while you were at playschool, she came to me while I was dusting the living room.

'I need to cut this off. It's too identifiable.'

Her hair. Her beautiful thick straw-coloured hair. The hair I envied. The hair I dreamed about running my hands through.

I stopped what I was doing. Her big deep-set eyes were pleading. 'Will you help me? I don't want to go to a hairdresser.'

I stepped away in horror. 'You are joking? You want me to cut your hair?'

'Please.'

How could I refuse when she was looking at me like that? I wanted to help her. To keep her safe. To keep the three of us safe. But I was no hairdresser. I trimmed your fringe once and made a right mess of it – it was still growing out.

'I've got a box of dye too. Chocolate brown. It was the only colour they had at the corner shop. I bought it a few weeks ago, just in case. He's less likely to recognize me with hair like that. I've had long blonde hair most of my life.'

My heart sank. 'Are you sure about this?'

'Positive.' She stepped forward, so close I could see the faint freckles on her nose, the flecks of green in her irises. My heart fluttered. And then she reached for my hand. 'Come on,' she said, leading me out of the room and towards the stairs. 'Let's do it now before you have to pick Lolly up.'

It didn't look too bad. Better than I'd thought it would. When I was growing up, my neighbour had been a mobile hairdresser and I used to watch, fascinated, when she cut, using her two fingers as a kind of ruler against the scissors. The style really suited Daphne's elfin face, even if I did have to keep going back to even it out. She didn't care, though. She seemed totally disinterested in how she looked. I understood. I was the same since leaving my old life behind. It was about survival.

But when you saw it you cried. 'No, Daffy. Boy!' you said to her, your little face crumpling. You always did this after I changed my hair too. Daphne looked devastated and I told you off for being rude. You ran to your room in a fit. I assured Daphne you'd get used to it. And, of course, you did.

By that weekend, the first in March, the snow had almost melted, leaving only remnants on high ground, like discarded white washing. On Saturday Daphne left the cottage for the first time in a week, more confident after changing her hair. When she returned she announced she had found another job.

'At the farm,' she said, as she shuffled out of her coat. She kept her stripy scarf wrapped around her neck. The cottage was still ridiculously cold and the weather seemed a few degrees chillier than it had been the previous week. I had the fire on in the front room but it still made little difference unless you were sitting right in front of it. I kept meaning to install central heating – it just never seemed like the right time to employ strangers, to let them into our cottage, our safe house, plus there was the expense.

'But that's a bit of a trek,' I replied. The farm was on the other side of the village. 'What kind of work will you be doing?' I asked, as she handed me a mug. It was so cold in the kitchen that I could see the steam rising.

'Odd jobs. Grooming the horses, mucking out, that kind of thing. I prefer being with animals to people. Apart from you and Lolly, of course.' She sipped her tea, regarding me over the rim of the mug, and my heart melted.

So Daphne went to work at the farm. Trudging the mile and a half there and back every day, her crocheted hat pressed down on her new hair, whatever the weather, coming home smelling of horses and straw but happy, cheeks flushed, eyes bright. Free, like a tiger released into the wild after being kept at a zoo, roaming around the farm, happy to be outside rather than cooped up in the pub, felt up by landlords and leered at by drunken customers. I was relieved to see she appeared less anxious about being found.

'Why don't you do it too?' she said, after she'd been there a few days. 'It would be fun working together. I'm left to my own devices a lot, can keep my head down. It's so nice not having anyone asking questions. The farmer, Mick, is gruff, lets me get on with it. There's another guy there, Sean. He's new too, handsome, if you like that kind of thing.'

But it was hard for me to get a job. You weren't due to start school for two more years.

'Maybe when Lolly starts school,' I replied.

I had calculated I had enough in savings to do a few repairs on the house with some left to tide me over until then. I didn't charge Daphne that much for her room – after all, the cottage was hardly luxurious – and she paid a third of the food bill. But she was good with money, I'd noticed. She was frugal, always making sure to buy bargains wherever she could; tins at the corner shop that were going cheap because of their sell-by dates, not to mention the money she saved me on clothes for you by knocking up patterns on her sewing machine.

By now I knew I had feelings for Daphne. Feelings that I hadn't had since my last relationship, with Audrey. I'd not allowed myself to get close to anyone after she hurt me like she did. But I couldn't help the way I felt about Daphne. I had no clue if she felt the same. Sometimes, when she touched my cheek, or came up too close, or lifted her feet into my lap when we sat on the sofa, I wondered if perhaps she did. But I was too scared to do anything about it, not wanting to cross that line. Not wanting to make her leave.

We were so happy that we forgot to be on constant alert, even though we should have been. We should have been extra careful when we realized somebody was looking for Daphne. But as the weeks passed, and there were no further sightings of a male visitor to the village, we were lulled into a false sense of security, naively thinking her disguise would keep us safe. Like a haircut and colour was enough to hide her. How stupid we were.

We should have been prepared, but we weren't.

So when he turned up at our front door that blustery evening in early April he caught us off guard.

35

Lorna

'WELL,' SAYS ONE OF THE TWO UNIFORMED OFFICERS, walking into the living room where Lorna and Saffy sit, side by side, hands curled around mugs, adrenalin and fear keeping them awake even though they're both exhausted. They're still wearing their coats. The two policemen have been combing the house for the last twenty minutes. 'It looks like nothing has been taken. No jewellery, no electronics. This is a strange break-in.'

Lorna exchanges a glance with her daughter. This, she is certain, is the work of that bastard, Davies. The contents of her mother's boxes are strewn across the floor. He was obviously looking for the 'evidence' that he seems convinced her mother has buried here in the cottage. If there is any such thing, she wonders if he's found it. Maybe then he'll leave them alone.

Earlier, after Tom had established that nobody else was in the house, Saffy had urged him to go and look for Snowy. 'What if whoever has broken in hurt him?' she'd said, her eyes huge and sad in her white face. It broke Lorna's heart. After everything Saffy has already been through tonight, this was the last thing she needed. She's devoted to that bloody dog. Tom waited until the police arrived before leaving them. He's been gone for over fifteen minutes now and her daughter has been chewing her lip ever since. She looks utterly drained, thinks Lorna, with dark rings around her eyes. It's past one o'clock in the morning. Lorna wishes she could shield Saffy from all of this. She was never particularly strict, not like her own mother had been. She let Saffy watch PG-13 films when she was ten. She didn't mind if she wanted to stay out late (not that Saffy ever did) or eat chocolate muffins for breakfast or drink wine at Christmas. If Saffy asked her a question about what was happening in the world – on third-world famine or paedophile rings – she always gave an honest answer, however brutal. She remembers her mother once saying to her, when she was younger than Saffy, already married to Euan and living more than a hundred miles away in Kent, *I'll never stop worrying about you. However old you are.* And Lorna tried not to think like that when Saffy was a teenager, knowing what it was like to be stifled by a loving but fundamentally over-protective mother. But now. Now she's more worried about her daughter than she's ever been. She finally understands what her mother meant all those years ago.

'If I was you,' says one of the police officers, red-haired, good-looking, a bit like the actor Damian Lewis, 'I'd replace that back door in your kitchen. It's not very secure. The intruder got in by kicking the lock. It was on the floor. I've put it on the side in your kitchen. Someone will have to fix it. With the woods out back . . .' He shakes his head, tucking his notebook into the pocket of his uniform.

'I know but we hadn't bothered because we were going to have an extension built,' Saffy says.

'Well, I'd at least change the locks. And consider a burglar alarm.'

Lorna's heart sinks. They won't be able to rest easy until that door is changed.

The red-haired officer and his sidekick finish off the tea that Lorna had prepared, then leave. Lorna feels vulnerable once they've gone. Like sitting ducks.

'We're going to have to tell DS Barnes,' says Saffy, in a small voice. 'We both know this wasn't a burglary.' She looks young, huddled in her big coat.

'The police will do it. I gave them his name,' says Lorna. She gets up and gathers the mugs from the coffee table, carrying them into the kitchen.

The back door, which Lorna had managed to close by wedging a newspaper underneath it, is suddenly thrown open, letting in a gust of wind and rain. Saffy squeals in fright and Lorna springs away from the sink to stand in front of her daughter, ready to defend her against any intruder, but it's Tom. It's just Tom. His hair has darkened in the rain and it lies flat against his head. He has Snowy on a lead. Lorna puts her hand to her racing heart and takes a deep breath.

Saffy rushes into his arms. 'Thank God! I was getting so worried.' Then she bends down to kiss Snowy's wet head. 'Oh, my boy, my lovely little man.' Lorna can't help but wince: she can smell the dog from where she's standing.

'Found him sniffing around the woods. He seems fine. Totally unhurt,' says Tom, unclipping his lead. Then he pushes the back door against the wind, cramming a chair up against it to stop it flying open. 'This will have to do for now.' He reaches for the lock on the worktop. 'But I'm going to have to reattach this. I've got some screws in my toolbox.' He strides out of the room, holding the lock.

Saffy grabs a holey old towel from a peg and uses it to wipe

Snowy's paws. He has mud splattered up his legs but he licks Saffy's face affectionately, happy to be home.

Tom strides back in with his toolbox. 'I'll get on with this,' he says, taking out his electric drill.

'We'll have Brenda over in a minute to complain about the noise,' says Saffy.

'If she turns up, I'll give her a piece of my mind,' says Lorna.

'What if he comes back and kicks it in again?' Saffy asks. 'I don't know if I'll be able to sleep, knowing someone's been here, rifling through our things. I feel so . . . violated.'

'I doubt he'll be back tonight,' says Tom, a screw between his teeth.

'That's right.' Lorna hopes she sounds more confident than she feels. 'Come on, honey, you need to get some sleep. We'll sort everything out in the morning.'

Saffy nods, carrying Snowy upstairs with her. Lorna stands in the kitchen watching Tom as he replaces the lock, a knot of worry in her stomach. When he's finished he yawns. 'God, I'm exhausted.'

She tells him to go on up, saying she'll turn the downstairs lights out. She watches him go, then makes herself a decaf tea. She sits on the uncomfortable sofa in the living room in the half-dark, surrounded by mess.

She gets to her knees and reaches for a photograph that's been thrown near the fireplace, the one of her mother and the mysterious Daphne Hartall, who might really be Sheila Watts, standing in the back garden. It looks cold – they're wrapped up in scarves and coats, their smiles broad. She wonders who took the photo. Had she taken it?

'What am I missing?' she says, under her breath, to the two women in the photograph. '*What did you do?*'

36

Lorna

LORNA'S AWAKE EARLY THE NEXT MORNING. SHE'D fallen asleep on the sofa, still in her tweed jacket, Saffy's Puffa coat acting as a duvet, the photograph of Daphne and her mother pressing against her cheek.

Sunshine spills into the living room through the badly fitted curtains, spooling onto the floor and highlighting the dust motes that float in the air. Lorna glances at the watch on her wrist. It's gone nine. She sits up and stretches. Every muscle in her body aches. There is no movement from upstairs. She doesn't want to wake them. They need the sleep. She's thankful it's a Saturday and they don't have to get up for work. Her heart plummets when she notices the mess on the floor, and everything that happened yesterday comes rushing back. This won't do. She needs to take action.

She gets up and pads into the kitchen. The slate tiles are freezing under her bare feet. She's relieved to see the chair is still in place, tucked under the door handle.

Lorna opens the fridge. There's no milk. She'll walk down to the village and get in some supplies. That's one thing she can do. For Saffy and Tom. Practical things to take the burden off them.

Lorna throws on fresh clothes, then grabs her bag and quietly lets herself out of the cottage. As she does so she meets the postman, an elderly man in Royal Mail's regulation shorts. He smiles kindly at her as he hands her a padded envelope. Her phone. She's been lost without it. She takes it with thanks, turning it on. There's hardly any charge left. She notices ten missed calls from Saffy. She shoves it into her bag.

The clear blue skies are deceiving: the breeze has a chill to it. She's careful to keep to the middle of the road as she navigates her way down the hill, so as not to be dragged into any bushes. Every time a twig snaps behind her the hairs on the back of her neck stand up, but it's only a dog-walker, or a couple on a morning stroll. She's letting her imagination run away with her. She can't do that. She has to be strong, for her daughter. At the bottom of the hill she passes the Stag and Pheasant. A young couple are sitting at one of the bistro tables outside drinking frothy coffees and they nod to her as she passes. They look all loved up, like they've come away for the weekend, and she thinks of Alberto. She loves the idea of him more than she actually loves him. She finds that she doesn't care that he's probably moving his stuff out of the apartment right now.

As she walks through the square she notices the church. it stands opposite the market cross and behind a tall iron gate that's ajar. It's a beautiful old one, with a spire, stained-glass windows and a small cemetery with elaborate old tombstones at the front. She hovers by the railings, looking in. She feels the sudden thud of familiarity. A memory surfacing. Of walking with her mum. And she's upset. There are tears on her cheeks. The memory fades, like an apparition, and Lorna stands at the gates for a while, trying to summon it back. But there's nothing, only a heavy feeling that settles inside her, a deep sadness. Had they been at a funeral? Had somebody they knew died? Lorna fights back tears while telling herself she's being ridiculous. It's just a feeling – she has no idea why she feels so grief-stricken all of a sudden.

She takes a deep breath and moves to the little café across the square where she orders a latte, pleased to see that Seth is serving. She tries to quell the melancholy that's descended over her, instead asking him anodyne questions to take her mind off it. An older woman is at the counter with him today. She must be eighty at least, with a plump face, three chins and rosy cheeks. She's stocky and sprightly despite the walking stick she's leaning on while watching Seth. She is wearing little gold spectacles and her thick grey hair is gathered up in a clip. She smiles a greeting at Lorna.

'I'm Melissa, Seth's great-aunt,' she says. 'I used to own this place forty years ago. It hasn't changed much over the years.'

Lorna stands up straighter, adrenalin pumping through her as she introduces herself. 'I'm visiting my daughter who lives up at Skelton Place. My mother used to live there, a long time ago now. Back in the late 1970s.'

'Oh, who was your mother? I've lived in the village all my life, so I might have known her.'

'She's called Rose. Rose Grey . . .'

Melissa's mouth falls open. 'Lolly?' she gasps.

Lorna swallows. 'Yes. Have we met before?'

Melissa claps her hands together. 'Yes. When you were a little girl. Lots of times – oh, it's so lovely to see you. Tell me, how is Rose? It was so sad I never had the chance to say goodbye to her. And to you. You both left in such a hurry.'

'Did we?' Lorna wonders if it had anything to do with the bodies.

Seth hands Lorna the latte. 'Small world,' he says, with a chuckle, as Lorna pays him.

'A lot of people have lived in this village for decades. Generations,' says Melissa. 'Seth doesn't understand that. His mother moved away years ago. He's only here to do a holiday job because I know the owner.' She pats him affectionately on the back and he grins.

But Lorna is still reeling. Here is a woman who knew her mother when she was young. She can't believe it. 'What was she like, my mum, back then? Do you know why she left so suddenly?' she asks, determined to get the conversation back on track, not wanting to let this opportunity pass.

'She never even said goodbye. She just upped and left. She was such a closed book. And very jittery. A nervous thing, really. Always worrying about you. You once wandered off, on Christmas Eve, and, honestly, I thought Rose was going to have a heart attack. But then she got that lodger and it seemed to change her. She was happier. Thick as thieves they were.'

'You remember Daphne Hartall?'

'Daphne! That's it. I couldn't remember her name until you said. Yes, Daphne. Attractive woman. Used to work up at the farm.' She lowers her voice and looks around furtively even though there are no other customers in the tiny café. 'I heard about the bodies up at the cottage. Bad business. They're saying one was identified and died in 1980. I was shocked to read that.'

'Yes,' says Lorna. 'My daughter only found out the other day. Do you recognize the name Neil Lewisham?'

She frowns and shakes her head. 'No. I don't think he was local.'

'Mum was living at the cottage back then.'

'Well, yes,' she says. 'But I can't believe Rose would have known anything about it. She wouldn't have hurt a fly. And she had you, of course. A little girl in the house – she wouldn't have done anything to put you in danger.'

'Oh, I know that. But I imagine people will talk.'

'They will. But a lot of them won't remember Rose. I knew her. I always felt protective towards her. How is she now, anyway? I bet she can't believe all this, can she?'

'She's . . . Well, she's sadly suffering from dementia and is in a care home.'

'Oh, I'm so sorry,' says Melissa. 'She seemed a lovely woman. You remind me of her, you know. Darker, of course.'

Lorna smiles even though deep down she's always felt she looks nothing like her mother. Rose is fairer-skinned, paler-eyed, taller, less curvy. She assumes she must take after her father. 'Did she ever mention my father?' she asks.

Melissa shakes her head, her chins wobbling. 'No. She was very closed about her past. I think everyone assumed she was a widow although I didn't believe it.'

'Really?' Lorna is surprised. 'That's what she always told me. That he died before I was born.'

'She was pregnant when she first arrived in Beggars Nook. And she was definitely alone then. But she was so secretive.'

'Did you know much about Daphne? What happened to her?'

'No. Not really. She'd come into the café on occasion but she was as closed as Rose. More so, even. They kept themselves very much to themselves. Particularly later on.'

'Later on?'

'Yes, before they left.'

'Did Daphne leave before my mother?'

'I always assumed they'd left at the same time. Moved away together. I did wonder . . .' She pauses. 'No. It's not my place. I'm not one to gossip and it was all such a long time ago anyway.'

Seth lets out a harrumph and Melissa chides him good-naturedly.

'Wonder what?' presses Lorna.

Melissa glances at Seth bashfully. 'It's such a different world now. These things are just much more open. But they were . . . *feminists*.' She whispers the word like it's something to be ashamed of.

Seth rolls his eyes at Lorna. 'These old folk.' He laughs. Lorna doesn't see the big deal. She likes to think of herself as a feminist. Why does Melissa make it sound so sinful? And then it hits her.

'Do you mean you think my mother and Daphne were lovers?' she asks.

'Well.' Melissa's ruddy complexion deepens a few shades and she crosses her arms under her plump chest. 'I'm not saying that, but there was talk, of course. There's always talk in a village like this.'

Lorna sips her latte to cover her smile.

'So you don't know what happened to Daphne?' Melissa asks.

'No. Mum never mentioned her. It's only recently we found out about her.'

'Well, give Rose my love, won't you? I was fond of her. And you. It's lovely to see what a beautiful woman you've turned out to be.'

Now Lorna blushes. 'Thank you, that's kind.' She scribbles her number down on a napkin and slides it across the counter to Melissa. 'If you remember anything . . . it's hard to ask Mum now, what with the dementia, but any information you might have . . . I'd love to find out what happened to Daphne.'

Melissa nods. 'Sure,' she says, pocketing the napkin in her thick cardigan.

Lorna buys some croissants, then ambles over the bridge to the corner shop to get milk. As she walks back to the cottage she wonders about her mother and Daphne. Were they in love and did they fall out? Was that why Daphne was never in their lives after they left Beggars Nook, and why they left so suddenly? As far as she's always been aware, her mother had never had a boyfriend. Why did she feel she had to hide her sexuality from Lorna for all those years?

There is so much about her mother she doesn't know, she realizes. Had never bothered to ask, even when she was an adult. Was she that self-obsessed, refusing to see what was behind Rose's frumpy, self-contained façade? Not even bothering to care? She'd just accepted there was no father in her life. Accepted her mother's version of events. In hindsight she can see there were inconsistencies in her mother's stories. She kept things simple, never elaborated. Not that Lorna had really asked. She'd never been a particularly inquisitive child.

Guilt and regret wash over her. All those wasted years when she could have really got to know her mother.

When she reaches the cottage the front door is flung open and Saffy stands there, anxiety radiating from her. Something's wrong.

'What is it?'

She's still in her pyjamas. 'The police rang about speaking to Gran again. They want to do it today!'

37

Saffy

MUM HAS TRIED TO PERSUADE ME TO STAY BEHIND BUT I can't. I have to be there when the police speak to Gran. I need to protect her as best I can. I'm driving and Mum is in the passenger seat, tension emanating from her. I knew the police would want to talk to Gran again but the fact it's such short notice concerns me. Now they know Neil Lewisham died when she lived in the house, is she a suspect?

'I just can't believe Gran knew about this, can you?' I say, as we head towards the motorway. Mum remains silent and I bristle. 'Can you?'

'I don't know. I don't think so, honey, but '

'But what?' I snap. 'You can't possibly think Gran is capable of murder.'

Mum snorts. 'Of course not. But that doesn't mean she doesn't know *something*. She could have been there when it happened. Maybe even helped cover it up.'

I refuse to believe it. 'Gran is the most staid, law-abiding person I know. There's no way.' Mum clenches her jaw and I feel irritation bubble within me. 'I can't believe you can even doubt her. She's your mother!'

'She's not perfect. She's human, just like the rest of us.'

I grip the steering wheel tightly, not trusting myself to speak in case all the resentments I've felt towards Mum for so many years threaten to spill out of me.

'And,' continues Mum, 'she does mention a Jean hitting someone over the head. Did she witness something?'

'Of course she didn't! She's just coming up with random names!'

'She was right about Sheila, though, wasn't she? She's real. I've already told you what Alan said – and how I think Daphne's really Sheila Watts.'

'We don't know that for definite. Next you're going to tell me you think Daphne's the other body in the garden . . . Do you think Gran killed her too?'

Mum doesn't say anything.

'You think it's Daphne?'

'I'm not saying that. But I spoke to Melissa earlier, and she said your gran and Daphne moved out at the same time. I don't want to think badly of my mother any more than you do but we have to face facts.'

'That's ridiculous. Just because you have no faith in Gran. Just because you've never bothered –' I stop. I've said too much.

Mum's silent for a few seconds. Then, 'What do you mean?'

'Nothing. Forget it.'

'No. If you've got something to say to me, I suggest you say it.'

I turn to Mum. Her mouth is pressed into an angry line. We haven't argued for years, not since I was a teenager and she'd shout at me for my messy bedroom.

'Okay, then. I think you've been a bit . . . neglectful.'

'Neglectful?'

'Yes. You buggered off to Spain. Left a lonely old lady by herself. Hardly visited. How many times have you actually seen Gran in the last six years? Once or twice a year?'

'That's not fair.'

'It's true. And me? How many times have you seen me? And when you do come and visit you bring along one of your many hideous boyfriends. And don't pretend you're happy about this baby.' I'm on a roll now and I can't stop even though I know I'm being a bitch. 'I could see by your face how disappointed you were when I told you! Just because you regretted having me so young it doesn't mean that I'm the same. Just because you couldn't wait to get rid of me every summer so you could go out and act like a teenager, leaving Dad and going off with other men. And you wonder why I'm closer to Gran!'

There's a shocked silence. I can't quite believe I've said it. I dare not look at Mum. I'm not a confrontational person. It must be my pregnancy hormones. Even so, I know that's how I really feel and have felt for years. It's actually a relief to get it out.

We continue driving in a tense, uncomfortable silence. My legs are trembling. From the corner of my eye I see Mum wipe a tear from her cheek and I'm consumed by guilt.

'I'm sorry,' I say. 'I didn't mean all that.'

'Yes, you did,' says Mum quietly.

'It's my hormones. I just feel so, so   *angry*!'

'I know.' She flashes me a watery-eyed smile. 'And I agree I haven't always been the best mother. I've made mistakes –'

'Mum, don't!'

'It's true, and you will too. Whatever you think now. But I never regretted having you. Not for one second. I'd hate you to think that.'

I swallow the lump that's formed in my throat.

By now we've reached Elm Brook and I pull into the car park.

As I push the gearstick into neutral Mum covers my hand with hers. 'Are we okay?'

'Of course,' I say. If I feel trepidation at the thought of having a baby at twenty-four I can only imagine how scary it must have been for my sixteen-year-old mother. I should never have said those awful things.

Joy greets us at the door with her usual harassed air. She looks more stressed than normal, but I can appreciate why. She's probably never had to contend with police coming over to interview one of her residents before.

Mum is sombre as we gather in the lobby. The ugly swirly carpet is making me feel sick.

'Are the police here?' Mum asks Joy.

'In there.' Joy indicates the room we were in last time. 'I'll go and get Rose. She's still in her bedroom at the moment. She didn't have a very good night. I'll bring some tea.'

Anxiety pools in my stomach. 'In what way didn't she have a good night?' I ask.

'She kept waking up, crying out. It happens sometimes. They forget where they are. Anyway, if you don't mind going in there,' she pushes the door open and stands against it so we can go past her, 'I'll get Rose now.'

DS Barnes is already in the room, with someone else this time, a woman around my age. They are seated in the same armchairs at either side of the fireplace and stand up when we enter. He introduces the woman as DC Lucinda Webb. She has a coppery mane that spills over the shoulders of her patterned blouse. I notice Joy has put out only two extra chairs this time.

'You sit here,' says Mum, indicating one of the chairs. 'I'm okay to stand.'

'Are you sure?'

'Of course. Sit!'

We're being unnatural with each other. Ultra-polite but I do as she says.

There's an awkward silence and I'm thankful when the door opens and Joy escorts Gran into the room. The sight of her brings tears to my eyes: she looks so frightened, like a shy little girl. I want to wrap her in my arms and take her away from all this. She seems thinner in her pink knitted jumper and pleated skirt, and I'm worried she's not eating enough. I notice she has on a gold necklace and matching earrings that I recognize and I wonder if one of the carers put them on for her this morning to make her look nice. She sits next to me, blinking rapidly like a baby bird.

I reach over and take her hand. 'Gran . . .'

'Who are you?' she says, and I feel like I've been stabbed in the heart.

'It's me, Saffy,' I say, trying not to cry.

Before she can respond Mum has crouched down by her side. 'Mum,' she says. 'There's no need to be afraid. The police just want to ask you a few more questions.'

'Why?' Gran asks, then turns to me, bewildered, but there is recognition in her eyes. I squeeze her hand.

'It's okay, Gran,' I say reassuringly. Mum stands up and hovers behind me, making the hairs on the back of my neck stand up. I wish there was a chair for her. Why didn't Joy bring one?

DS Barnes has his sleeves rolled up. It's not as hot as last time but even so there is a sheen to his forehead.

'Hi, Rose,' he says. 'It's nothing to worry about. Like your daughter said, we just want to ask a few questions. Is that okay?'

'I suppose,' she says, folding her hands across her stomach. Joy returns with an extra chair and Mum sits in it.

DS Barnes looks vaguely irritated by all the disruption. When Joy has left the room he continues: 'Rose, does the name Neil Lewisham mean anything to you?'

Gran turns to me and I smile encouragingly.

'I don't think so,' says Gran.

DS Barnes pushes a photograph across the wooden table towards us. Gran stares down at it, her hand still in mine, fine-boned and delicate. I lean forward to get a better view. A man with short fair hair stares out at us. He's plain, ordinary. There is nothing about him that would make him stand out. He has on a long black overcoat; one hand is thrust into a pocket and the other is holding a cigarette by his side. 'This is the man who was found dead in your old house, Rose,' he says gravely. 'We think he died in 1980, while you were living there.'

Gran's eyes are wide with fright.

'It's okay, Gran,' I say softly. 'What do you remember about this man?'

'He was after us,' she says, turning back to DS Barnes.

I stare at her in shock. I assumed she wouldn't know him. I can't look at Mum. I haven't told the police about Sheila's file and the article in it with Neil Lewisham's byline in case I end up implicating Gran somehow.

'What do you mean, Rose?' probes DC Webb, her voice gentle, and I realize that's why she's been brought along today. A woman's touch.

My mouth is dry and I'm still exhausted after last night's events. I notice Joy hasn't brought in the tea she promised.

'Did you hurt him, Rose? Or did Daphne?' Lucinda Webb's voice is soothing, like honey in warm water on a sore throat.

Gran takes her hand away from mine and reaches into her mass of white hair. 'I don't remember . . .'

'Was he having a relationship with you? Or with Daphne?'

'No, I don't think so . . .'

'Did he come to the house, Rose? Do you remember?'

'He was angry,' says Gran. She seems calmer now, her hands resting in her lap. 'He was angry.'

'Why was he angry?'

I stiffen. Can Gran really remember? Or is she confused again?

'He tried to hurt us.'

'Why would he do that?' asks DC Webb.

'Because he found out about Sheila.'

I notice Mum has gone quiet. I don't know whether to say something. What if it lands Gran in trouble?

'Who's Sheila?' asks DC Webb, in that same soothing voice.

Gran stares into her lap silently.

Mum glances at me, then turns her gaze on the detectives. 'I . . . think she might be talking about a woman called Sheila Watts. I recently found out that she might have stolen the identity of Daphne Hartall.'

Both detectives lean towards Mum. 'Go on,' says DS Barnes.

'A Sheila Watts drowned back in the late 1970s. My mother had an article about it in her things. I did some digging and, to cut a long story short, it appears that Sheila Watts could have faked her death and stolen the real Daphne Hartall's identity.'

A flicker of irritation crosses DS Barnes's craggy face. 'Why didn't you mention this before?'

'I'm sorry, a lot has happened over the last few days. I meant to.'

DS Barnes looks a little shame-faced. 'Of course.' He addresses Gran again, his voice grave, like that of a newsreader about to impart doom. 'Neil Lewisham was an investigative journalist. He often went on benders and, according to his son, had a turbulent relationship with his wife. Did he come all the way to Beggars Nook that day to see Daphne because he found out she was really Sheila Watts, Rose?' There is urgency to his voice, as if he knows time is running out before Gran reverts back into herself.

Gran doesn't say anything. Her mouth a stubborn line.

'Did Neil Lewisham find out about Daphne?' probes DC Webb, to Gran, in her smooth, liquid voice. 'That she was really Sheila?'

'No,' says Gran, looking up at the detectives and fiddling with the necklace at her throat. 'He found out about Jean.'

38

Rose

April 1980

THE DAY BEFORE NEIL LEWISHAM TURNED UP ON OUR doorstep everything had been perfect.

Easter fell on the first weekend in April. We had a wonderful time celebrating it, just the three of us. Daphne boiled some eggs she'd been given at the farm and we sat at the kitchen table painting them, you giggling at the funny faces Daphne drew – she was surprisingly good. On Easter Sunday we hid little hollow chocolate eggs in the garden, the colourful foil wrappers glinting beneath the plants and bushes. It was a sunny but crisp day. I'll never forget the delight in your eyes and your squeals of excitement as you hunted them out, Daphne and I standing by the back door of the cottage, proudly watching you.

Later that night, while you slept, Daphne and I sat up talking and drinking wine by the fire. And then she turned to me, her eyes huge in the firelight. 'I – I want to say something to you, Rose. But I'm scared it will ruin our friendship.'

I moved closer to her. Hoping she would say everything I felt.

'You could never tell me anything that would ruin our friendship,' I said softly.

She took my hand and moved towards me so that our faces were mere inches apart. She brushed the hair tenderly away from my face. I leant towards her, my heart fluttering as her lips brushed mine and she pulled me close, kissing me deeply. She took my hand and led me upstairs to her bedroom where I stayed until the early hours of the morning, creeping back into my own bed so that you wouldn't be alarmed when you came looking for me when you woke up.

I wish I'd drunk in every wonderful moment of that day, scrutinized each second under a magnifying glass: Daphne's throaty laugh, your squeals of delight, the way the sun bounced off the little foiled eggs, the smell of chocolate and pollen on the breeze. I'd give anything to relive that day on a loop, over and over again.

Because the next day everything changed.

He arrived on Monday evening, just as I was putting you to bed.

I could hear voices in the hallway but they were muffled, although I was sure one of the voices was male. My heart began to beat faster. We never had callers. I finished tucking you up and closed your bedroom door behind me, sweat pooling under my armpits at the thought of who could be at the front door. Was it the man Daphne was so afraid of? Had he found us?

I rushed downstairs, different scenarios playing out in my head. But Daphne wasn't with anyone, she was alone.

'Who was that?' I asked quietly, not wanting to scare you. 'I heard you talking to someone.'

She shook her head and walked into the living room. I followed. She stood in the middle of the room, wrapping her arms around herself. Her face was so pale she looked as if she might faint. 'It's him,' she whispered. 'Oh, God, Rose, he's found me. He's found me . . .'

Coldness washed over me. 'Where . . . where is he now?'

'He's gone around the side. To the garden. I said I'd talk to him there. I didn't know what to do.'

'We need to call the police.' I headed for the orange phone by the sofa. But she stopped me before I could reach it.

'We can't. Don't you see? That will make no difference. It never has before. They didn't help me then. Why would they now?'

I hung my head.

How I wished I had just called the police. Then maybe none of this would have happened. Fear. It makes you do strange things. It clouds the brain. And I had been so scared for so long. You have to believe me on that.

Daphne put her hand on my shoulder. 'I need to talk to him, try to convince him to leave me alone. I don't know if it'll work.' She let out a small sob. 'I'm scared, Rose. He . . . he's not a nice man.'

Her words conjured up images of your father, and the things he did to me. What would I do if he decided to turn up here, unannounced, like this Neil?

I pulled Daphne into my arms, kissing the top of her head. 'It'll be okay. I won't let anything happen to you,' I said fiercely. 'We'll sort this out together. Come on.' I pulled away from her and took her hand, leading her into the kitchen. I could see a man standing in the garden, smoking. I didn't think about my safety, or even, I'm ashamed to admit, yours in that moment. I told myself Neil wasn't interested in us. It was Daphne he wanted. Daphne he had been looking for.

I opened the back door and Daphne stepped in front of me and out onto the patio.

'Hello, Jean,' he said to her. Light spilled from the kitchen, il-luminating his face. He was very fair with translucent eyelashes. He had on a black Harrington jacket with a white T-shirt under-neath and jeans. He smelt of stale alcohol.

Jean?

'Who's this?' He inclined his head towards me.

'My best friend,' she replied, turning back to look at me. Her eyes locked with mine and something unsaid passed between us. We were two thirty-something women who had known each other for four months – I hadn't had a best friend since school – yet it was still not enough to encapsulate the intensity of my feelings for her.

'You'd better be careful,' he said to me, his eyes narrowed, but a smug expression on his face. 'Don't you know what this woman is capable of?'

Here we go, I thought. Trying to make out that Daphne was the bad person. The one in the wrong. I'd seen a black-and-white film about it once. What did they call men like him? Gaslighters?

I stood there, shivering in my cardigan and long skirt, not saying anything, just glaring at him in response. He took a puff of his cigarette and blew it out slowly and deliberately in my direction. I felt an intense hatred towards him in that moment. Daphne moved towards him, but I grabbed her hand and tried to pull her back. 'You don't have to,' I said.

She shook her head. I was surprised at her compliance. After all her talk of standing up to men. She shrugged me off, walking towards him. She looked thin in a cotton jumper and flared jeans. She had on her trusty boots and they sank into the grass as she stood next to him, their backs to me. I could smell the hint of a bonfire from a neighbouring garden and, other than the light from the kitchen, it was pitch black outside, the kind of darkness you only get in the countryside with no pollution, hardly any lights and the thick, dense wood at the back. The hedges on either side were high, eclipsing any views from neighbours.

Was I thinking of it then? Planning it? I think on some level I must have been.

I waited by the back door. Watching. Listening. Like an animal ready to pounce. Their voices floated towards me.

'After all these years,' I heard him say. I could see the tip of his cigarette; a dot of amber against the darkness, like a firefly. 'I knew I'd find you. Even with that fucking ugly hairstyle. You can't hide from me. *Jean.*'

'My name is Daphne,' she said firmly. I noticed how her shoulders tensed. Her neck looked long and elegant with her hair so short. 'I don't know why you keep referring to me as Jean. I'm not who you think I am.'

He lowered his voice but I could still hear him. 'We both know you are.' His words sounded threatening although I wasn't sure why. Not then anyhow. 'Exposing you is going to make my career.'

I wondered what he meant. And then it made sense. He was a policeman. No wonder Daphne didn't want me to ring them. He was one of them. Men who abused their power. Men others automatically believed.

Like Victor Carmichael.

Victor was a piece of scum masquerading as an upstanding member of the community, a doctor no less. Nobody would have believed me over him. He'd tried to ruin my life and it looked like Neil had done the same to Daphne.

'I'll just run away again,' I heard her say, her voice sounding small in the darkness.

'And I'll always find you.'

'Not this time.'

'Faking your death. That was clever, I'll give you that. But you're not clever enough, Jean.'

My blood pounded in my ears. I didn't want Daphne to leave. I loved her, I realized. She made me happy. I didn't want to live a life without her. I wanted it to stay the way it was, the three of us living in this cottage, safe – or we were, until Neil had turned up, tainting our lovely world.

Was it the idea of Victor and the way he had treated me that made me do it? Was it the thought of Daphne forever running away, never able to be with me, with us? I was so angry, so fed up with being powerless. For once I wanted to be proactive. Not passive. I wanted to be the one in charge.

I just wanted to make it all go away. Make *him* go away.

I watched as he trailed a finger down her cheek and neck, his face too close to hers. Then he gripped Daphne's upper arms and pushed her back against the wall of the cottage. 'You're a liar,' he snarled. I saw the fear in her face and it took me right back to the time Victor had first hit me. When I realized that not all men were kind-hearted like my father had been. A naive little fool.

But I wasn't that person any more. You had changed me. Daphne had changed me. I needed to protect her and the life the three of us had.

'Leave her alone,' I called from the doorway.

It was like snapshots flashing before my eyes: Daphne's fear, the sneer on Neil's face, as though he was enjoying the power.

I don't remember snatching the breadknife from the block on the counter.

I don't remember striding across the patio and plunging it just below his ribcage in one swift movement.

It was all so quick.

I let go of the knife in shock at what I'd done, stumbling backwards, catching sight of the horror on Daphne's face.

'You bitch,' Neil rasped, dropping to his knees on the lawn. 'You fucking bitch.'

He clutched the handle of the knife where it protruded from his stomach.

My hands flew to my mouth. Oh, God, oh, God, *what had I done?*

Neil flopped backwards onto the grass, his hands still around the knife handle. Blood soaked the front of his T-shirt: a bloom of crimson against white. There was so much of it. I started to gag in horror.

Daphne was by my side in an instant, her arm around my shoulders. 'It's okay,' she said gently. 'It's okay . . . oh, Rose, Rose . . .'

'The police. I need to ring the police.' I felt like I'd been winded.

Neil was now lying prostrate on the ground, his pale eyelashes fluttering. Daphne bent down and pulled the knife out of his wound. But it seemed to make things worse, the blood pumping out faster than before, gushing over his fingers as he held on to his stomach, groaning.

I took off my cardigan. 'Quick, let's try to stem it with this,' I said.

She shook her head. 'He's dying, Rose.' Her voice was clipped, matter-of-fact, emotionless.

'I need to tell the police,' I sobbed.

'No. No, you don't.'

'I do. We could save him!'

'You want to save him? A man like him? A bully, a nasty fucking piece of shit.'

'I –'

We were interrupted by moaning coming from Neil. I knelt down and pressed my balled-up cardigan against his stomach. As I did so he grasped my hand with such force that he unbalanced me and I toppled backwards. 'Now you're both murderers,' he hissed, spittle flying out of his mouth and landing on his chin. 'You're both the same.'

A jolt of shock. 'What?'

'She's Jean Burdon,' he said, his finger pointing towards Daphne, who was standing behind me. 'Jean Burdon.'

'Shut up,' I hissed, my mouth dry. 'Stop talking. I'm trying to help you.' I got back on my knees and leant over him. He repulsed me but I couldn't let him die. Panic engulfed me. 'Daphne,' I shouted behind me. 'Call an ambulance.'

She knelt down beside me. 'I'm not calling anyone, Rose,' she said calmly. I felt her hand on my shoulder. 'We need to let Neil die.'

His eyes were closed now and his face had a sheen to it. Was he already dead? I was shaking uncontrollably. I couldn't take my eyes off him, this waxwork man lying on my lawn.

Daphne grabbed my arm and pulled me up. 'If we call the ambulance the police will be notified and you'll go to prison,' she whispered. 'Lolly will be taken away from you. You won't be able to see her ever again. You don't want to go to prison, Rose. Believe me.'

What did she mean? Was she talking from experience?

I closed my eyes. What would become of you if I went to prison? When I opened them Daphne was staring at me, her beautiful face serious. She held my hand, grounding me, calming me. She smoothed the hair from my forehead, kissed my face, my lips. 'Please, listen to me, Rose.' Her voice was low, soft. 'This is for the best.'

We turned back to Neil, standing over him as the life seeped out of his body.

He was somebody's son. Somebody's brother, perhaps. Maybe a husband. Father. And I had *killed* him.

I'd had the chance to try to save him yet I did nothing. I stood, with Daphne, our arms around each other, too shocked even to cry, and we waited until we were sure that he was dead.

'What do we do now?' I said.

'I think we need to bury him,' she replied.

'Bury him?' I gasped. 'Bury him where? In the woods?'

'No. Not the woods. That's too dangerous. Someone might see us. We need to do it here. In the garden.'

I clamped my hand over my mouth. 'I can't,' I said, through my fingers. 'Not here, not where Lolly plays. Not where we hid Easter eggs . . .' I started crying then, hot tears cascading down my cheeks.

'Rose,' she said gently. 'You're not a bad person. You were protecting me.' She put her hand up to my face and gently wiped a tear away. 'And I'll owe you for that for the rest of our lives. I'll never forget what you've done for me. But now you need to be strong. For Lolly.'

I nodded. She was right. What choice did I have?

That's what I told myself anyway.

It was only later – much later, after we spent hours digging and burying a full-grown man along with my bloodstained cardigan – that I allowed myself to think about what Neil had said as he was dying.

You're both murderers now.

39

Saffy

'WHAT DO YOU MEAN, GRAN?' I ASK. 'WHO IS JEAN?'

'Jean Burdon,' says Gran, a tinge of impatience in her voice. 'Neil Lewisham thought Daphne was Jean Burdon.'

I notice the detectives exchanging shocked glances and I hear a gasp from Mum.

'Who is Jean Burdon?' I ask, confused. Why does that name ring a bell? And then I remember that article in Sheila's file: it had been about a Burdon. Was the first name Jean? I'd only scanned it. I hadn't recognized the name and assumed it had ended up in the wrong file. I could kick myself. I should have read it properly. If I'd seen it had said Jean I would have remembered Gran's ramblings.

Jean hit her over the head.

'Have you heard of Mary Bell?' asks DS Barnes.

I nod. 'She was a convicted child killer?'

'Yes, and Jean Burdon's case was similar but about ten years before. When she left prison as a young woman she was given a new identity and was never heard of again.' He addresses Gran:

'Is that who you mean, Rose? Jean Burdon who killed her friend back in the early 1950s? In east London?'

I feel shaken. I notice Mum is looking at Gran in horror.

Gran nods, folding her hands in her lap.

'And was she?' DC Webb asks, sitting forward in her seat. 'Was Daphne really Jean Burdon?'

'I . . .' Gran wrings her hands.

'Rose,' says DC Webb, resting her elbows on the table. 'Did Daphne kill Neil Lewisham?'

Gran purses her lips together. A shadow passes across her face and I wonder what she's thinking. 'Who is Neil Lewisham?' She turns to me. 'Who are these people?' She waves her arm in the direction of the police and Mum too. My heart sinks.

'I think Gran's had enough,' I say, reaching for her hand.

'Rose, can you remember if Daphne killed Neil Lewisham?' persists DS Barnes. He sounds desperate to keep the interview going but Gran is shaking her head, staring at him blankly but refusing to say anything else.

The detectives exchange resigned glances.

'We'll have to pick this up another day,' says DS Barnes, to me and Mum.

It's not until we're leaving the room that I hear DC Webb mutter to her colleague, 'I think we need to look into the other body being that of Daphne Hartall.'

'Have you heard of Jean Burdon?' I ask Mum on the drive home. The tension between us is still almost palpable after our earlier argument.

'Yes, of course,' she says crisply. 'You'd be too young, perhaps. The Jean Burdon case was overshadowed by Mary Bell.'

'Who did Jean Burdon kill?'

'Another little girl. Jean was only ten when it happened. And so was the girl she killed. Obviously it was before my time but I remember reading about it.'

I feel sick. 'God, that's awful. Imagine finding out that about your lodger.'

Mum nods grimly.

'Do you think Daphne killed Neil Lewisham because he found out she was Jean Burdon?' I ask.

Mum looks pained. 'It's possible. Especially if he was a journalist. It makes sense.'

'But then,' I say, my mouth dry, 'if Daphne is the other body, who killed *her?*'

When I arrive back at the cottage Tom is out with Snowy. I go straight to my study and look again at the article Dad sent me from Sheila's file. It's a short vox-pop-style piece written by Neil asking whatever became of Jean Burdon and interviews with some of the public about possible sightings.

Then I type Jean Burdon's name into Google and a number of entries pop up, mostly newspaper reports accompanied by a grainy black-and-white photo of a young chubby-faced girl with a bob. I click on a link.

17 February 1951

THE DAILY MAIL

GIRL, 11, CONVICTED OF MURDER

AN 11-YEAR-OLD girl has been sentenced to life after being found guilty of murder at the Old Bailey.

Jean Burdon remained composed and expressionless as the guilty verdict was read out after a four-hour deliberation by the jury.

Jean Burdon is said to have 'struck the temple with a blunt object' of 10-year-old Susan Wallace in an unprovoked attack on 20 June last year. Susan was found dead in a derelict bomb-shattered building by two passing boys.

Mr Justice Downing described her as a dangerous risk to other children and said she will be held in a secure unit for 'many years'.

Mum walks into the study carrying a mug of tea. 'Here we are. Red Bush,' she says, placing it carefully on my desk. 'I don't know how you can drink that stuff. The smell turns my stomach.'

'Look at this,' I say, and Mum reads the article over my shoulder. 'Do you think Daphne Hartall could really have been this person?'

'Well, it's possible that Sheila Watts was the new identity given to Jean Burdon.'

'And Gran found out?'

'She must have done. She mentioned a Susan Wallace too, didn't she? Do you remember? When she was talking about Jean?'

'You don't think she's just confused because this was a high-profile case and she remembers it from childhood?' I ask hopefully.

Mum glances at me with concern. 'I don't think so,' she says. 'I'm sorry.'

I feel tears pressing. 'The police are going to think Daphne killed Neil Lewisham, aren't they? And that Gran found out and killed Daphne. They've got a motive now.'

Mum pats my shoulder. 'They'll need more evidence before they can go down that route, don't worry,' she says, but she doesn't sound convinced.

'Do you think the private detective is working for Daphne/ Sheila/Jean, whatever her name is? That's if she isn't the other body, of course.'

'What makes you say that?'

'Well, Davies said his client is looking for some important paperwork and you said he called it evidence. What else could he mean? He's obviously some kind of thug. And whoever he's working for sounds desperate.'

'I've told the police everything we know about Glen Davies. Hopefully they'll talk to him and make him tell them who he's working for.'

'Daphne would be old now, though . . .' I say doubtfully, rubbing my temple. I can feel a headache coming on.

I think of Gran, not how she is now but how she was when I was growing up. Strong, dependable, kind but private. She obviously had more secrets than Mum and I ever realized. But she was so fiercely loyal, so protective, like a lioness. If Daphne is the other body and she was really Jean Burdon, she could have been dangerous, unhinged. Could Gran have killed her to protect her daughter? I place my hand on my bump, remembering how protective I felt last night after coming back from the hospital.

'I can't believe Gran might be a killer,' I say, thinking aloud. I turn to Mum who has taken a seat on the little cocktail chair in the corner. She doesn't look as if she's listening. 'Mum?'

'We need to talk . . . about what you said in the car.'

I turn back to my computer. 'We have more pressing things to think about.'

'I don't want there to be any bad feeling between us. I love you so much.'

'And I love you too,' I say. 'Please, can't we just forget it? It was a silly argument.'

Mum opens her mouth to say more but we're interrupted by a knock at the door. We stare at each other. My first thought is that it's him, Davies.

'Stay there,' Mum says, getting up and going to the front door. I lean back in my chair to see her peering through the glass. 'It's a young couple,' she says, sounding puzzled.

'Not journalists?' It's Saturday afternoon. Who else would be calling at this time?

'They don't look like journalists.' She opens the door. I get up and stand beside her, wondering who it is. I'm surprised to see a couple in their late twenties or early thirties standing there. A small, pretty woman with a bun curled like a pineapple on her head and a tall guy with a mass of dark floppy hair and warm brown eyes. He has a friendly, handsome face and a dimple when he smiles. He's almost as tall as Tom and looks relaxed in a T-shirt and jeans.

'Hi,' he says, blushing slightly. 'I'm Theo Carmichael and this is my wife, Jen.' She smiles a hello. 'I know this sounds crazy, and I hope you don't mind us showing up like this . . .'

I stare at them, perplexed. Are they neighbours? Jehovah's Witnesses?

'. . . but I found this article on my dad's desk the other week.' He hands the article to me and I scan it. It's about the bodies found in the garden and someone has underlined my name and Gran's. And at the bottom, in sprawling writing, are the words *Find Her.*

'How weird,' I say, handing the article to Mum. 'I'm Saffron Cutler and my grandmother is Rose Grey. You said you found this on your father's desk? What's his name?'

'Victor Carmichael. I think he must have known your gran.' He has a slight Yorkshire accent.

Victor. I'm too shocked to answer right away.

'My grandmother talked about a Victor. We didn't understand who she meant as she couldn't remember his surname. She has dementia now,' I add, when he looks at me with a bemused expression. I survey them both. 'Do you want to come in?' I find myself asking.

They nod gratefully and step into the hallway. I guide them to the living room.

'What are you doing?' Mum mouths.

'They seem fine,' I whisper back. 'We need answers.'

Theo and Jen take a seat on the sofa and Theo drops his backpack to his feet.

'Can I get you a drink?' Mum asks, as I sit in the armchair by the window.

'We're okay, thanks,' says Jen. 'We're staying at the pub down the road and had a late lunch.'

'We've come all the way from Yorkshire,' says Theo, as Mum perches on a chair by the fireplace. 'Look, I'll cut to the chase, but I think my dad is hiding something. He's been acting really weird. Well,' he gives a short laugh, 'weirder than usual. He wouldn't tell me why he'd written *Find Her* on the article, or give me any information when I asked. He was very defensive and prickly. And then I found a folder hidden in this secret space of his in a cupboard. It was filled with photographs of women. I was wondering if one of these is your gran.' He offers me the phone and I get up to take it from him. Still standing up I flick through them. They are all of pretty young women. One is heavily pregnant. By the fashions and haircuts it looks as though they span a twenty-year period. 'No,' I say, handing him back the phone. 'None of these is Gran.' I sit back down.

'Oh.' He looks disappointed. 'You said your gran mentioned a Victor? What did she say about him?'

I throw Mum an awkward look. 'Um . . .' I say, turning to Theo. 'She said something about how he wanted to hurt the baby.'

Theo looks shocked. 'Hurt the baby? My dad is a doctor. He might be many things,' his expression darkens, 'but . . . hurting babies?' Jen reaches for his hand.

We plunge into an uncomfortable silence until Mum pipes up, 'How old is your dad? My mother – Rose – is in her seventies.'

'My dad was old when he had me. My mum was much younger. Dad is seventy-six.'

'So they're the same age. Could they have been together at some point?'

Theo shrugs. 'I really don't know. Did Rose say anything else about my dad?'

'She gets really confused,' I say, as explanation. 'She mentions lots of names. She mentioned Victor a few times but when she did she seemed, well, scared . . .'

Theo pales. 'Scared?'

'Maybe scared is the wrong word.' I frown, trying to remember. 'Agitated. She definitely said he wanted to hurt the baby. She made him sound – I'm sorry, this is a bit blunt – but she made him sound like he wasn't a good man.'

Theo and his wife exchange a glance. 'I don't think he is a good man,' he mutters, suddenly looking vulnerable and my heart goes out to him.

'It's all been so strange since the bodies were discovered,' says Mum. 'Have you heard of a Daphne Hartall?'

Theo shakes his head.

'She was Mum's lodger and lived here in 1980 as well. We think she was also known as Sheila Watts.'

'Not heard of her,' says Theo. I notice his hand is still in-
tertwined with Jen's. I can tell they're as desperate for answers
as we are.

'We're trying to find her – well, the police are,' says Mum.
'There's something else too. A man approached me and Saffy
over the last few days saying he's a private detective, although
he grabbed me off the street when I was walking home one
night –'

Jen gasps. 'That's awful.'

'It was horrible,' Mum says, 'but he did say that his client
hired him to find some paperwork that my mother has. He
called it *evidence*.'

'Evidence?' Jen frowns.

'Yes, he didn't elaborate and I was terrified.'

'What was this man's name?' asks Theo. 'Did he say who he
was working for?'

'No,' says Mum. 'He refused to say but he did give his name.
Glen Davies.'

'Wait. What?' Theo sits up straighter. 'Glen Davies?'

'Yes, that's what he told me,' says Mum. 'And we think he
broke in here looking for this so-called evidence.'

'I know a Glen Davies,' says Theo, his face draining of colour. 'He works for my father.'

40

Theo

'HE WORKS FOR YOUR FATHER?' CRIES THE YOUNGER
woman. Saffron. She looks incredulous, her big brown eyes
wide. Theo feels sick to his stomach that his father's henchman
(as he's always thought of him) has been here and terrorized
these women.

'Yes,' Theo says, crossing then uncrossing his legs. He
wishes he'd now taken them up on the offer of a drink – his
mouth is so dry. 'He's known my father for years. I don't even
know how. Before him there was another guy – a similar type,
ex-military – but he retired. I do know this much, though. Glen
Davies is definitely not a private detective.'

'Then what does he actually do for your dad?' says the older
woman. Laura, or was it Lorna? He's hardly been able to take it
all in since he got here.

Theo shrugs. What does he actually do? He's never been
sure. 'I've always assumed he's like my dad's security. He comes
to the house now and again. Assesses the burglar alarms. Gives
Dad advice, that kind of thing. My dad's a wealthy man. Successful in his field.'

'Well. Glen Davies is a fucking bully, that's what he is,' says Laura. No: Lorna. He's sure her name is Lorna. 'He broke into the house when my daughter had to go to the hospital. It's like he was waiting outside, waiting for us to leave. All of this.' She stands up and paces the room, throwing her arms wide. Theo watches her, mesmerized. There is something very familiar about her. Like he's met her before but he can't think where. 'It has to have something to do with your father. And those photos . . .' She stops and rounds on Theo, holding out her hand. 'Can I see them?'

He does as she asks. They all watch expectantly as she flips through them. Then she makes a growling sound of frustration and passes the phone back to him. 'I don't recognize anyone. I was hoping my mother would be there.'

'I've already looked,' says Saffron.

'I know. I just wanted to see.' Lorna throws her daughter an apologetic smile and Theo feels a pang of longing for his own mother.

He takes back his phone. He feels Lorna's frustration. 'Can you remember anything else Glen asked you? That night when he . . . grabbed you?'

'Just about the evidence. That was it. Oh, and he threatened me, said he'd hurt me, or Saffy . . .' she flinches '. . . if I told the police.'

Theo swallows, trying to quell the panic growing inside him. Has his father got something to do with the murders that took place here? Maybe he's on the wrong track with the folder of women. Unless they're victims of his.

'I think my mum was running away from someone. A woman who knew her back then remembers her as being jittery and secretive, and she was apparently pregnant when she first arrived here,' says Lorna, sitting down again. She fizzes with nervous energy, like a firework that's about to go off.

'And you think she was running from my dad?'

Lorna glances towards her daughter, then back to Theo. 'I'm beginning to think so now. My mum was always so cagey about my dad. She said his name was "William" but never showed me photos, never talked about him. It was like she wanted to forget him.'

Theo thinks of Cynthia Parsons. Was Rose a victim of his too? An ex who was running away from him because she was scared? An ex who was pregnant?

'Babe,' says Jen, gently, placing her hand on his arm. He knows what she's going to say. He's been thinking it too. Lorna looks just like his dad: the same curly dark hair, the wide nose, the shape of the eyes and chin. The reason that Lorna had seemed so familiar when he first walked into the room was because looking at her is like facing himself in the mirror.

'I think Victor might be my father,' says Lorna, before he can voice his suspicions.

Saffron's hands fly to her mouth. 'Oh, my God,' she exclaims, standing up. 'Of course!'

'I think so too,' says Theo, slowly. 'You're so like him.'

There's an awkward pause before Lorna says, 'So the baby he wanted to hurt, that was me? And if he wanted to hurt me did that mean he wanted to hurt my mother as well? Why did she run away from him?'

Theo feels shame rising in him – shame by association. He wants to tell them he is nothing like his shitty father. 'I think he was abusive to my mum. I saw . . . bruises. He was controlling, manipulative.'

'Is he still with your mum?' asks Lorna.

He clears his throat. 'She died. She fell down the stairs.'

'I'm so sorry.'

Saffron is still standing up, staring at them with her mouth hanging open. *My niece*, he thinks.

'So your dad must be the client that Glen Davies was talking about?' asks Lorna. She's still sitting forward in her seat, her shapely eyebrows furrowed, elbows resting on her knees. 'And if that's the case, does that mean he's involved in the murders?'

Theo shuffles his weight on the uncomfortable sofa. Fuck. The bodies in the garden. The newspaper clipping. Hiring Glen Davies to put the frighteners on these women, his own family. It's just the kind of despicable thing his father would do if it meant protecting himself. But murder? In his wildest nightmares he hadn't expected that.

Theo is exhausted by the time they get back to their room at the Stag and Pheasant. He flops onto their four-poster bed. From the sash windows they have views of the woods. His throat is sore from all the talking he's done this afternoon.

Jen climbs up onto the bed next to him. 'I can't believe it,' she says. 'You have a half-sister.'

'And my dad is a potential murderer,' he replies. He still feels sick at the thought. 'Why else has he hired Glen Davies? What did he do? What does he so desperately want Glen to find?'

'Oh, babe,' she says, leaning into the crook of his arm and resting her head on his chest. 'I'm so sorry. Do you think your dad knew he had a daughter?'

'I'm not sure. I can't work out if he had that newspaper clipping because the bodies had been discovered and he was close to getting found out for something, or because it told him where Rose is now. Murder, though?' groans Theo. 'It's another thing entirely. And it —' He stops, unable to voice what he's really thinking.

'What?' Jen says, sitting up.

He takes a deep breath. 'If my dad is capable of murder, it puts a whole different spin on my mum's accident.' He sits up too, facing his wife. 'Jen, what if my dad killed my mum?'

41

Rose

April 1980

I COULDN'T GET OUT OF BED FOR TWO DAYS. IT WAS LIKE I was having a breakdown. I wanted to block it all out, the image of the knife going into his side, the horror on his face, the blood that gushed out of him, the hole we dug in the garden, the smell of the wet soil, the worms that squirmed inside, the thud of his body as he landed in the makeshift grave. It seeped into my dreams, turning them to nightmares. My act, his death, had opened up a floodgate of all the old feelings and fears.

Daphne was brilliant. She took care of you, taking you to playschool, picking you up, cooking for you, washing your clothes, keeping you safe. She was the only other person in the whole world I trusted to do these things, apart from maybe Joyce and Roy next door.

'Rose, darling,' she said, sitting on the edge of my bed the next evening, 'you need to eat something.'

It was dark and you were fast asleep, tucked up in bed.

Daphne had brought you up earlier to say goodnight and I had hugged you to me, as though your innocence could mend my dark, dark heart. And then I'd listened to your giggles from down the hall as Daphne read you a story in your bedroom, taking ages to do all the funny voices.

She had a cup of something in her hand. 'Drink this. I've put some whisky in it. You're in shock, that's all. You'll be as right as rain in a few days' time.'

As right as rain. That was such an un-Daphne thing to say. And I realized she was as out of her depth as I was.

'I'm a murderer,' I said, sitting up and taking the mug. 'I've crossed a line, taken a life. I'm never going to get over this.' I couldn't stop thinking of the mound of fresh earth near our patio slabs, the patch of brown in the grass that marked out his grave. How could I ever go into the garden again? Or look out of the kitchen window without that constant reminder?

'You have to,' she said, her voice stern. 'You can't stay up here feeling sorry for yourself, Rose. You're a mother. That's the greatest gift. You've cleansed the world of one evil man. It's a shame we can't do the same with the others.' She laughed then to show she was joking but something in her eyes made me think if I suddenly agreed she would do it. Two thirty-something vigilantes.

'I haven't got the stomach for it,' I said, trying to force a chuckle.

She smoothed the hair back from my face tenderly. 'I know you haven't. You're too sweet. Too kind.' She kissed my forehead.

'Will you stay with me tonight?' I asked. 'I don't want to be alone.'

'Of course.' She climbed into bed with me, fully clothed, pulling the duvet over us both, propped up by pillows. I could feel her socked feet against my bare legs. I sipped my tea, the whisky warm as it travelled down my throat.

'Every time I close my eyes I can see his face.'

'I know,' she soothed.

'I just want those images to go away.'

'They will.'

'Really?' I turned to assess her. 'You seem to know a lot about it.' I hesitated. I needed to ask her. But I was terrified of the answer. What would I do if Neil was right?

I took her hand in mine, her bones fine underneath my fingers. You and she were the only two people I loved in the whole world. 'Please just tell me the truth. I can't bear lies. No more lies. But I need to know. Was Neil right? Are you Jean Burdon?'

She looked at me for the longest time, her pupils massive in the fading light, obscuring most of her iris. Just when I thought she wasn't going to answer, she said, 'Would you still love me, Rose?'

Would I? I had you to think about. Maybe if I hadn't just killed a man I might have kicked her out there and then.

'I need to know the truth.'

Her eyes filled with tears. 'I didn't mean to do it,' she said, in such a small voice that I had to strain to hear her. 'It was an accident. I was ten years old. My childhood – it wasn't good, Rose. But I've never hurt anyone else. You need to believe me.'

I stared at her. She'd been a child. I couldn't imagine her hurting anyone now. I was the one who had killed Neil after all. And I was so in love with her I would have believed anything she told me.

We sat up most of that night, talking. She opened up to me for the first time since we'd met. She told me the story of Jean Burdon – the little girl the newspapers had dubbed 'evil', of how she was neglected and physically abused by her father, left to roam around the abandoned bombsites of east London. 'And then I made a friend,' she said, her face ashen in the moonlight. 'And I was so happy that I'd found someone who actually cared about me. I wasn't emotionally intelligent. I didn't understand about relationships, particularly with other kids. I had this rage inside me . . .' She gave a little sob and I squeezed her hand in reassurance. 'Anyway, when Susan – that was her name – decided she didn't want to be friends with me any more I saw red. They said I picked up a brick and smacked her over the head with it. But I can't remember doing that. I think I might have pushed her, though, and she fell and hit her head.'

'Oh, Daphne.'

'I went to prison – of course. Well, it wasn't an adult prison. A secure unit. I was rehabilitated, thankfully by well-adjusted kind adults who taught me the rights and wrongs my own parents never did.' She pulled the quilt up to her chin and shivered as though remembering.

'It must have been awful,' I said.

'It was less awful than the house I was brought up in.'

I couldn't even imagine. My own upbringing had been lovely, the only child to two kind, attentive parents.

I let Daphne talk that night about her childhood, her life. How she was given a new identity as Sheila Watts, how she'd had to steal the identity of Daphne Hartall from her friend Alan when she realized that the journalist, Neil Lewisham, had discovered who she really was.

I didn't tell her my story. Not then. I'd kept it a secret for so many years that to speak it out loud would have felt too much.

And I didn't want things to change between us. Daphne might feel uncomfortable if she knew my history. I continued to let her believe I was a widow, that my 'husband' had died before you were born.

I hadn't even told her about my last girlfriend.

Audrey and I were together a long time. We didn't hide our sexuality: there was nobody to hide it from. My parents were dead and she came from a very liberal, cerebral family. Her parents were academics. Even in the 1970s, with free love and the sexual revolution, there were still those who judged us, who thought nothing of telling us of their disapproval.

But when I turned thirty I wanted the one thing Audrey couldn't give me.

A baby.

And that was when I met Victor.

42

Lorna

'WE NEED TO RING DS BARNES,' SAYS LORNA, FIRST thing the next morning.

'Should we disturb them on a Sunday?' asks Saffy from the sofa, wrapped in her velour dressing gown the colour of aubergines, looking a little peaky. Tom is still in bed. They were up late last night, talking for hours after Theo and Jen had left. Lorna was wide awake at 7 a.m. and has already been on the phone to her boss back in Spain to tell him she'll need more time off. He was surprisingly understanding.

'Absolutely. This is important,' she replies firmly.

Although it's still early, the sun is already streaming through the windows and it cheers Lorna up. She needs it after last night's revelations. The only good thing to come out of it is that she might have a half-brother. But the rest – Victor Carmichael being her dad, and the despicable things he might have done. What kind of man would send a thug like Glen Davies to frighten her? His own daughter? The murdering kind, she thinks. Could he have had something to do with the bodies in the garden? Is he now panicking because the past is catching up with him and worried he'll be found out all these years later? What 'evidence' does her mother have against him?

And then there's Saffy. She glances at her daughter, who is staring into the middle distance, biting at her thumbnail. All the resentment Saffy has been harbouring, things Lorna wasn't even aware of. Has she been a bad mother? Her daughter's words still feel like a wound to her heart. She doesn't know how to make any of it better.

Lorna picks up her mobile from the coffee table. 'Would you mind putting the kettle on, honey? And I'll phone DS Barnes.' She's already had two cups of coffee this morning and feels jittery. Saffy comes to reluctantly, gets off the sofa and heads into the kitchen. She can hear her clattering about opening cupboards and plonking mugs onto the worktop.

DS Barnes answers straight away. She launches into an account of last night's events, talking so fast he has to ask her to repeat herself.

'Wow, good work,' he says, when she's finished. 'We'll send someone to talk to Victor Carmichael today.'

'He lives in Yorkshire . . .'

'That's not a problem. And now we know who Glen Davies works for it shouldn't be hard to find him either,' he says. Lorna feels a wave of relief. She's been on constant alert since he grabbed her off the street. She hopes they can lock him up. 'As you can guess,' he adds, 'the card he gave you wasn't legitimate. The number is probably a burner phone and it rang out when one of my officers called. We can organize a DNA test. When is Theo returning home?'

'He's staying until tomorrow. I've got his number – I'm sure he won't mind me giving it to you.'

'Great. I'll keep you updated.'

He ends the call and Lorna joins Saffy in the kitchen. She's staring into the fridge. 'We've run out of milk. Again. How are we getting through so much?' she wails.

'I'm sorry,' says Lorna, remembering. 'I used the rest of it for my coffee this morning. Why don't you go back to bed? I'll pop to the village and get some more.' She rubs her daughter's arm, the velour soft like a teddy bear under her fingers. 'I'll make something nice for dinner tonight. Something nutritious.'

'Thanks, Mum. Would you mind taking Snowy with you?'

Lorna agrees and watches as Saffy pads down the hall and up the stairs, like she's got the weight of the world on her shoulders.

Lorna is coming out of the corner shop clutching a plastic bag when she bumps into Melissa.

'Lovely to see you again,' she says, smiling brightly at Lorna. She has a pair of reading glasses on a chain around her neck. Lorna wonders what it must be like, living in the same village for all of your life. She's not even been here two weeks and she's already starting to feel oppressed.

'After meeting you the other day I've been thinking a lot.' Melissa lowers her voice as she leans on her stick. 'About Rose. And Daphne . . .'

'Oh, yes?' Lorna tries not to get her hopes up. It was nearly forty years ago. What could Melissa remember that would be useful?

'Would you like to come for a cup of tea? My cottage is only down there, by the river.' Beside the market cross she can hear a toddler crying and a woman's voice, coaxing.

'That would be lovely,' she says. She senses that Melissa is probably lonely and wants a trip down Memory Lane. It will give Saffy and Tom some time to themselves. And she'd like to know more about what her mother was like when she was younger. As well as the mysterious Daphne. She needs a distraction until she meets up with Theo and Jen later.

'Do you mind dogs?' she asks, untying Snowy's lead from the lamppost. 'He's my daughter's.'

'Of course not.' Melissa hitches her carpet bag over her shoulder. She walks slowly, resting heavily on her stick. They cross the little bridge and follow the river for a bit, Snowy stopping to sniff the trunk of a weeping willow, until they get to a row of cottages at the opposite end of the village to Saffy's house. Melissa's cottage is smaller, terraced, but with the same Cotswold stone and all of the character that Lorna has come to expect from properties in Beggars Nook.

She follows Melissa through the door and straight into a sitting room with low beamed ceilings. It's old-fashioned, with big-armed floral sofas and plates on the wall, but it has charm. And it's clean and tidy, which is important to Lorna. She can't abide mess. She wonders if Melissa ever married or had children of her own.

'Make yourself at home,' she says, indicating the sofa. 'Cup of tea?'

Lorna says that would be lovely and offers to make it but Melissa is having none of it. She's fiercely independent and, obviously feeling more secure in her own cottage, props her walking stick against the wall. Lorna settles herself on the sofa with Snowy by her feet.

Melissa returns with two mugs and hands one to Lorna, then sinks her large frame into a faded armchair opposite, by the little leaded window.

'Gorgeous fireplace,' says Lorna. It's wrought iron with a guard around the outside. The mantelpiece is cluttered with figurines and photo frames. She can't help wondering how long it would take to dust it all. But it's spotless, not a dust mote in sight.

'Thank you. We have them in all the rooms. Although I never used the bedroom ones. I doubt anybody does, these days, but the cottages were built before central heating.' She chuckles.

'Gives character, though,' says Lorna, sipping her tea and thinking of the fireplaces in Saffy's cottage. She wonders if the ones in the bedrooms have been used since her mother lived there. 'Anyway, so tell me, what were you about to say outside the shop?'

Melissa sets her mug on the side table next to her and purses her lips, her chins wobbling. 'Well,' she says, 'seeing you and reminiscing about Rose brought it all back.'

'Brought it all back?'

'That strange autumn.'

Lorna shrugs off her jacket. It's a warm day but Melissa has her heating on and the room is stifling. Her lower back is starting to feel sweaty.

'The autumn of 1980?'

'Yes.'

'In what way was it strange?'

'Well,' she folds her arms across her stomach, 'that's when I started to notice something wasn't quite right. With Rose.'

'Really?' Lorna leans forward to place her cup down. The tea is making her feel hotter.

'Like I said before, she was always quiet, kept herself to herself. It was obvious she was a devoted single mother. She never mentioned a husband. She always seemed jittery and on edge, overly worried about your safety. Anyway, I'm repeating myself, I've told you that before. But although Rose did all of those things, she still tried to help out in the community. She volunteered at the church café twice a month. She was in the WI. And then, around early summer, she stopped. She cut herself off completely from all of us in the village.'

'And what about Daphne?'

'Oh, we still saw Daphne about. She worked for a bit at the pub and then at the local farm. Occasionally we saw the three of you together, so we knew Rose was okay. I think she felt she needed nobody but Daphne. They were so . . . self-contained.'

'And you thought they might have been in a relationship?'

'I think so, yes. Although they didn't advertise it. Different times.'

'So what did you mean about that strange autumn?'

'Well, it was the weirdest thing. But Rose came to me. I remember it was Bonfire Night. There was an event in the village – up at the farm, fireworks and the like. I'd seen her there with Daphne and you. Rose seemed even more on edge, but I wondered if it was because it was a big event. I don't think she liked crowds. Perhaps she didn't feel safe. Anyway, later, much later, she cornered me and told me she was scared for her life.'

'Oh, my God,' gasps Lorna. She hadn't been expecting that. 'Did she say why?'

'It was after I told her that someone had come into the café looking for her. She asked who but I didn't know the man's name – at that time I'd never seen him before. But I did see him a few times after Rose moved away, just around the village but then he must have left too, because I never saw him again. Anyway, she said she had done something and she was scared they'd take you away from her. She was in a bit of a state, to be honest. It was all really strange. I tried to calm her down but she was so cagey, so worried about telling me anything.'

Was it Victor she was so scared of? Lorna picks at one of her gel nails. Had he found her and that was why she'd left in such a hurry? Without saying goodbye to anyone?

'Did the man give his name?'

Melissa shakes her head. 'No . . . not that I can recall . . .'

'And did my mum mention the name Victor to you?'

Melissa frowns. 'I don't know . . . maybe. It was all such a long time ago. I just remember her being really scared after I told her someone was looking for her. Why? Who is Victor?'

'I think he's my father. And she was running away from him.'

'Oh, that's awful. It makes sense now. She seemed very scared that night. Like I said before, we just assumed she was a widow when she first arrived in the village.'

Lorna shuffles in her seat. 'It can't be a coincidence, can it? She finds out someone is looking for her and then runs away.' She sighs. 'I don't remember much about living here, or Daphne,' she says. 'So they must have parted ways at some point when I was still young. Me and my mum, we lived in Bristol after moving away from here.'

'They seemed so close.'

'As much as I love her, my mother is a funny one. In all the years I can remember she never had a relationship. With a man or a woman. She concentrated on me and then, when I left home, on my daughter.'

'Something really seemed to scare her on Bonfire Night, though,' says Melissa, wistfully. 'She said . . .' she looks towards her fireplace and frowns '. . . something really odd.'

'What did she say?'

'She said, "If anything bad happens to me, look in the fireplace."'

Lorna frowns. 'The fireplace? Which one? Yours?'

She laughs. 'No. I don't think mine. I assumed hers. But I don't know . . .'

Lorna's heart starts to race. The fireplace. She must be talking about the evidence that Victor has been so desperate to find. Is that where it's been all this time? 'And . . .' she can barely contain her excitement '. . . did you ever look?'

'No. No, I didn't think much about it, really. After she left I'd heard that she still owned the house and was renting it out. So it's not like anything bad had happened to her. If it had – if, I don't know, she'd been found dead in the house or anything like that – well, then, yes, yes, I would have done as she asked, but she left, other people moved in. About ten years after she left, around 1990, I bumped into an estate agent who was looking at the house and asked him about Rose. He said she still owned it, that she rented Skelton Place out. I assumed she'd outrun the man she was so frightened of.'

God, thinks Lorna, tears blinding her vision when she thinks of her mother, alone and scared, bringing her up by herself.

'The bodies in the garden,' says Melissa, suddenly. 'Do they know who they are yet?'

'One was a journalist called Neil Lewisham. And the other, they still don't know. But I've been wondering. Maybe they didn't split up and the other body is Daphne's.'

Melissa breathes in sharply. 'But who would have killed her?'

Lorna looks down at her hands. 'I'm worried the police will think it's my mum . . .'

'No, no, that's not right,' Melissa says emphatically. 'Rose would never have hurt Daphne or let anyone else hurt her, not without calling the police, or doing something.'

'Unless it wasn't my mother who killed her,' says Lorna, swallowing.

43

Saffy

'What are you doing?' asks Tom, as I get out of bed and start to dress hastily. 'I thought we could have a lie-in.' He raises his eyebrows suggestively. 'What with Lorna out for a bit.'

'I'm sorry, I want to go and see Gran. I just feel I need to see her. To spend time with her.'

'We're meeting up with Theo and his wife later, remember. Will you be back in time?'

'Yes.' I throw on a T-shirt I haven't worn for about two years, some jogging bottoms, and scrunch my hair into a messy bun.

Tom sits up. He's bare-chested and I feel a flicker of desire but just as quickly it's gone. My mind is too full of other things. 'I'll come with you. I haven't seen your gran for ages and –'

'No,' I bark, then realize I sound a bit harsh. 'No,' I say, more softly, 'it's okay. I think Gran might talk more if it's just me.'

He stares at me, concern etched on his face. 'I'm worried about you, Saff. This is all a lot to take in and now you're going to hare off to Bristol.'

'I won't be long.' I sit on the edge of the bed pushing my feet

into trainer socks. 'I want to ask Gran about Victor. Now that I
know more. And it might be easier without . . .'

'Without your mum there?'

I nod guiltily.

He takes my hand. 'Is everything okay between the two of
you? I noticed some tension yesterday when I got back. I know
you'd just had an intense meet-up with Theo and found out
about Victor but . . . there was something else, like something
brewing between you.'

'We had a bit of an argument. I said some things I shouldn't
have said.'

'Oh, Saff.'

'I know. It's not my proudest moment. Mum tries her
best. And I do love her, but . . .'

'Hey,' he holds up his hands, 'you don't have to explain it to
me. I know it's complicated between the two of you.'

'My gran was just so much less complicated, you know? Or,'
I laugh ironically, 'so I thought.'

He pulls me towards him and kisses me. 'Drive carefully,'
he says. 'And don't be too long or your mum might have reor-
ganized the whole house!'

When I arrive, Gran is in bed. Joy tells me she's had a bad night
and I try to quell the swirls of anxiety in the pit of my stomach
as I head down the corridor to her room. Millie, Gran's lovely
nurse, warned me that one day she may not recognize me at
all, that the little pockets of lucid moments will be rarer until
they're non-existent. We've been lucky up until now, I know.
One day she will be gone completely and in her place will be an
old lady who doesn't remember who she is, let alone who I am.
An old lady with no memories, past or present.

She's sitting up in bed, propped up by two massive pillows,

the blankets tucked underneath her armpits. Her hands, folded across the covers, look bony and frail, her skin like rice paper, criss-crossed with blue veins. Her eyes are closed and I stand at the door and watch her for a while, her translucent eyelids, her lashes, once long and dark but now sparse, dusting her weathered pink cheeks. She looks a lot older than her seventy-six years, a shrunken figure in the large bed. On her table is a framed photograph of me when I was a teenager, taken in the garden of her Bristol house underneath the apple tree, hugging her black Labrador, Bruce. I haven't been in her room since she moved in last year and the sight of the photo brings a lump to my throat and I have to concentrate on not crying. I don't want Gran to see me upset. Quietly, so as not to wake her, I sit in the chair next to her bed. Opposite is a large window and I can see a tree in blossom outside, the pink petals obscuring half of the glass. She'll like that, I think, as I take one of her frail hands. I wish I could go back to a time when she wasn't suffering from dementia. All those years when I sat in her living room, just the two of us, all those missed opportunities to talk, for me to find out about her past.

There is a tray over her bed, as if she's in a hospital, containing a jug of water and a glass. I pour some for her, just in case she'd like it when she wakes up. And then I sit with her. Enjoying it being just the two of us. As it used to be.

I'm on my phone, reading the work emails I'd missed during the week, when I hear a cough. I look up to see that Gran has woken up. She lies there just staring straight ahead for a few moments, as though trying to get her bearings, until she notices me and then her eyes widen. 'Who are you?' she whispers, her voice croaky.

I hand her the glass of water and she puts it to her lips, her hand trembling. 'It's me, Gran. It's Saffy.' I point to the photo. 'Your granddaughter, remember?'

But there is just confusion in her eyes. Confusion and fear.

So I start to talk. About Skelton Place, about Snowy, about Mum, the house in Bristol with the pebbledash and the greenhouse, anything to help her remember who she is.

'And you used to show me your tomato plants in the greenhouse, remember? You taught me how to plant seeds and radishes.' I have to stop to swallow my emotions. 'And now I'm going to have a baby of my own.'

'A baby.' She smiles and it lights her whole face and she's my gran again. My wonderful, kind, quiet-mannered gran, who loved knitting and gardening and watching daytime TV and dunking custard creams in her over-stewed tea.

I lean forward to take her hand. 'You'll be a great-grandmother, imagine that,' I say, trying to keep my voice light.

'Imagine that,' she repeats, her eyes glistening. She hasn't got her teeth in and it makes her look so much older, the bottom half of her face like a Punch and Judy puppet. And then her eyes cloud. 'You'll be a good mother, won't you? You'll look after the baby?'

'Of course I will. And Tom will make a good father.'

'Tom . . . Tom . . .' she says, then recognition flashes across her face. 'Tom is a good man.'

'He is.'

'You're very lucky. Neil wasn't a good man. And neither was Victor.'

Victor. I'm relieved she's brought him up. This is my chance. 'Is Victor your ex-husband, Gran?' I ask.

She lets out a snort of laughter. 'Of course not. I've never been married.'

'But Victor is Lorna's dad. Lolly's dad?'

Her big hazel eyes meet mine. 'Yes . . . yes, I think he is.'

'You think?'

Her face crumples. 'Everything is so foggy . . . my memories. They aren't always clear.'

'I know,' I say gently. 'I know, Gran.' Her eyes fill with tears and mine immediately follow suit. 'It's okay,' I say. 'It's okay.'

'It's not,' she says, as a tear falls from her eye and snakes down her crinkly cheek. 'Even after all these years I miss her.'

My heart aches. 'Miss who, Gran?'

'I miss her.'

I wonder if she's talking about Daphne. 'What happened to her?' I ask, although I'm not sure I want the answer. What if she confesses to me right now that she killed her and buried her in the garden alongside Neil? What would I do with that information? She's an old woman now and I love her. I want to protect her. What good could come out of a confession? For the first time since all this began I'm not sure I want to get to the truth. Maybe secrets really are best buried.

'Did Victor hurt her, Gran?'

She nods, tears on her cheeks. 'Yes, he did. He's not a nice man.'

'I know,' I say. 'He doesn't sound it.'

'He tricked her,' she says now.

'Tricked Daphne?'

She shakes her head. 'No, no.'

'He tricked you?'

She looks at me and blinks. Then she reaches out and cups my hair behind my ears. 'I love you,' she says.

'Oh, Gran, I love you too.'

'And I love Lolly. Don't let Victor find her,' she says, closing her eyes again. 'Keep her safe.'

'Gran, Victor is an old man now. He won't hurt her.'

When she opens her eyes I can tell that the Gran I know has gone, replaced by a stranger. 'Who are you?' she says, as though the conversation we've just had has never taken place.

So I sit patiently and repeat everything I said earlier, hoping she'll come back to me.

As I'm walking to my car later I receive a phone call from DS Barnes.

They've found Glen Davies. He's been arrested.

44

Rose

Summer 1980

IT WAS GETTING WORSE, MY FEAR AND PARANOIA. EVERY TIME THERE
was a noise I'd think it was the police at the door, coming to arrest me. Every time I walked into the village I worried people
were talking about me, that they somehow knew. An article had
appeared in the newspaper about Neil Lewisham's disappearance, and when I saw his face staring out from the pages I had to
walk out of the shop, panic engulfing me. I wasn't coping well,
mentally, with the fact I had killed a man. Even if I tried to convince myself I had done it for good reason.

Daphne was amazing. Over the next few months she became my rock. She had some paving slabs delivered from a local stonemason and told me she was going to 'make over' the
garden. But I knew what she was really doing. She was length-
ening the patio so that it covered the area where Neil's body
was buried. So that I no longer had to look at the patch in the
grass that didn't match the rest of the lawn.

'Where did you learn how to do all this stuff?' I asked one day, when she came into the kitchen after laying the slabs, a smudge of dirt on her cheek.

She glanced around to make sure you weren't in earshot. 'I learnt a lot in prison,' she said, her cheeks reddening, and she looked vulnerable then. 'I was there for a long time.'

'Oh, Daphne.'

I tried to remain strong, for her and for you.

But the nightmares continued and I would wake up during the night covered in a film of sweat. Neil's face morphed into Victor's and I was convinced he would find us. After all, Neil had.

I still hadn't told Daphne about Victor, but the deeper in love we fell, the harder it was not to talk about my past. Not that she ever asked, or pushed. She didn't talk about her time as Jean either. It was as though we both just wanted to live in the here and now. As though we didn't exist before we found each other.

'You must stop torturing yourself over Neil,' said Daphne, on the many occasions when I had gone to her, shaking and crying, guilt and fear taking me over. She'd pull me into her arms and kiss me and reassure me that it would all be okay. 'Nobody will ever know,' she said, but that just made me feel worse. Out of control and vulnerable.

It puzzled me how Daphne didn't seem to worry about Neil and the fact his rotting remains were buried in our garden. His disappearance had made the papers, after all. He had been married with a young son. The guilt of that ate away at me. Even with the new paving slabs I hated going out there, and every time I did, the memories of that night flooded back. It was hard, especially during that hot summer as you wanted to be in the garden all the time. 'I'll go with her,' Daphne would say, touching my arm gently. And I'd watch, like a prisoner, from the kitchen window as she sat with you as you dug your little spade into the soil and made a small rockery, trying not to wince that the body of the man I had killed lay less than twenty feet away. At night I'd dream of going downstairs and seeing the paving slabs taken up to reveal the hole in the ground, empty, his body gone. Other times I worried that we hadn't dug deep enough and something, a neighbouring dog or fox, might accidentally dig it up, exposing the corpse. Or that he was still alive, he'd survived the stabbing and was intent on revenge, still wearing his bloodstained T-shirt.

'No animal can dig it up now I've laid the slabs. Don't worry,' Daphne would reassure me, when I confided in her. Most nights she crept into my room, after you were fast asleep. It was comforting to have her warm body next to mine. I didn't feel so alone with my dark thoughts. One hot sticky night in July, as we lay in each other's arms with just a white sheet covering us, she said, 'Do you think you're bisexual?'

I sat up, leaning on my elbow to look at her, the moonlight highlighting her sharp cheekbones. 'Why do you ask?'

'Well, you were married.'

'Um, actually I've never been married.'

Her eyes looked huge in the half-light. 'What? But Lolly's father . . .'

'I'm not a widow. I ran away from him. He was . . . is . . . a psycho.'

I felt her stiffen beside me. 'I did wonder if you were running from someone too. You always seemed so . . . cagey. Like me, I suppose. Although we were both running from very different situations by the sound of it.' She reached out and touched my cheek. 'But then I thought maybe you were just shy.' She took her hand away and pulled the sheet up over her chest. Her arms were tanned after so many days in the garden with you. 'So he's still out there, Lolly's dad?'

I nodded. 'His name's Victor.'

'Victor.' She sounded the name slowly. 'That sounds posh.'

'We were never in a relationship. Romantically,' I said, to try to put her mind at rest. 'It's . . . it's complicated.' I didn't want to tell her about Victor and what he'd done to me. I didn't want it to sit between us, like an evil presence, tainting what we had. 'Before him I was with a woman for a long time. Audrey. What about you?'

She chuckled in the darkness. 'I've had sex with men but it never felt right. Then I realized I preferred women.'

I felt a throb of jealousy. 'We shouldn't put labels on it anyway.'

'I'm not. I was just wondering about Lolly's father, that's all. I've always wanted children but I'm forty now.'

This surprised me. She looked younger. 'Really? You don't look it.'

She smiled in response. I nestled back down on the bed so that we were both under the sheet, facing each other. Shadows danced on the walls behind her.

'Does it ever go away?' I whispered into the darkness.

'Does what?'

'The guilt? For taking someone else's life?'

She didn't say anything at first and I wondered if I'd offended her. Then she said, her voice sad, 'I'll never forgive myself for what I did to Susan. I've paid the price. I did my time. I ruined my life. But I'll never get over it.'

'You were just a child. What's my excuse?'

'Love,' she said softly, finding my hand under the sheet. 'You did it for love.'

45

Lorna

SAFFY STARES AT HER MOTHER WITH HER MOUTH HANGING OPEN. 'IN the fireplace? Which one? We've got four in this house.'

'I've already looked in that one,' says Lorna, sheepishly, indicating the fireplace in the living room, then showing Saffy her dirty palms.

'We used that one regularly when we first moved in,' says Saffy, her lips twitching. 'Anything left there would have been incinerated a long time ago.' Tom ambles into the room and hands them both a mug of tea. Lorna's drunk so much her mouth feels furred, but she accepts it anyway. Saffy takes hers from Tom and then he joins her on the sofa. Saffy's looked sad since she came home from seeing her gran. She said she's getting worse, and Lorna feels a tug of guilt that she didn't accompany her today. She knows she needs to return to Spain soon: her boss won't keep her job open for ever, not to mention her apartment and the unfinished business with Alberto. On the other hand she doesn't want to leave Saffy and her mum. Her daughter's words still sting when she thinks about them. She'd hate Saffy to think she was abandoning her.

Saffy jumps up. 'Let's check upstairs,' she says.

'We can't be long,' says Tom. 'Didn't you say we're meeting Theo at two?'

'We've got half an hour,' says Saffy. 'It's important. Come on.'

Lorna is about to get up from the chair but then hesitates. 'What will this evidence be? A murder weapon? A knife?'

Saffy puts her hands on her hips. Lorna can now see the clear outline of a bump. 'Don't be silly, Mum. He said some kind of paperwork. That's what we're looking for.'

Tom frowns but stands up too. 'Why would Victor be so desperate to retrieve old paperwork? What could it possibly say that would tie him to a murder scene?'

'Well, let's find out,' says Saffy, impatiently. She grabs Tom's hand. 'Come on.'

Lorna follows Saffy and Tom up the stairs, Snowy at their heels, barking excitedly, picking up on their adrenalin. They go into Saffy and Tom's room first. The bed is unmade and Tom's clothes from yesterday are thrown over the chair by the window. Saffy goes to the small wrought-iron fireplace.

'I'll do it,' says Tom, rushing forwards. 'I don't want you straining yourself.' Saffy and Lorna watch as he stands on tiptoe and feels around inside the chimney breast. Saffy shrieks and jumps backwards when he dislodges an angry-looking spider. 'Nothing here,' he says, shaking dust and cobwebs out of his hair.

'Let's try yours next,' says Saffy. 'God, Mum,' she adds, when they walk into Lorna's immaculate bedroom, 'you can make a mess, you know.'

It's a smaller fireplace than the one in Saffy's room and has a wooden mantel, carved with flowers. It doesn't take long to work out that there is nothing there either. 'The little bedroom . . .' begins Lorna, but Saffy's already off down the landing.

The little bedroom is empty save for the boxes in the corner. Lorna can see where Tom's made a start on removing the wallpaper. 'It's funny that this was my room.' She goes to the window and looks out onto the garden. She tries to imagine her mother there with Daphne, digging away, burying a body. But she can't. It's like imagining Snowy with a human head.

'Doesn't look like there's anything here either,' says Saffy. Lorna turns to see her daughter feeling around the hearth, and above her Tom reaching up into the chimney breast. They look like they're performing some comedy act. 'Do you think Davies found it?'

Lorna sighs. 'Maybe Melissa remembered it wrong. It was a long time ago.'

Saffy comes and stands next to her and Lorna snakes an arm around her shoulders, even though she has to reach up to do so. They stand like that for a while, in the room that used to be Lorna's, staring at the fireplace as though it has all the answers.

They are just about to leave the house to meet Theo and Jen when Saffy's phone rings.

She reaches into her bag and answers it, mouthing that it's DS Barnes.

Lorna's stomach turns over. What does he want now? Have they spoken to Victor?

'Okay,' Saffy is saying, throwing them both a worried look. 'I see. And, you're sure? Right . . .' She pushes a curl behind her ear. 'Yes. That's fine. Thanks.'

She presses the end button on her phone and places it back in her bag.

'What is it?' asks Tom.

'Forensics checked the other body against the dental records they have for Jean Burdon from when she was in prison, and the results have just come in. It isn't a match. It's not her.'

46

Rose

September 1980

THE TROUBLE WITH LOVE IS THAT IT BLINDS YOU. AND I was so blinded by my feelings for Daphne that I felt like I had vertigo.

I broke my one rule since fleeing Victor – to keep myself to myself.

But one thing nagged away at me.

Daphne knew too much about me.

And I, in turn, knew too much about her.

Her stolen identity, her infamy as Jean Burdon, her incarceration.

I knew I loved her but would our crimes bind us together? Make it hard for us to part in case one of us told on the other?

What would happen to her if her true identity ever became public knowledge? She'd be vilified by vigilantes. Her new identity after leaving prison had been Sheila Watts. But she'd shed that skin the day she 'drowned' herself so now there were no probation officers keeping tabs, no officials making sure she didn't kill again. Not that I thought she would. I trusted her. After all, we were both killers now. And she had been an innocent, a child, neglected, abused, lashing out. I should have known better at the age of thirty-six.

No, if anything, Daphne had a hold over me. She could literally direct the police straight to the body.

But I assured myself that it was worth it because our love was the real thing: it was raw and true and for ever. That it would never come to the stage when either of us had to use our knowledge as a kind of emotional blackmail to make the other stay. Daphne wasn't manipulative. She didn't play games. I didn't have to worry.

Daphne wasn't like Victor.

At least, that was what I told myself then.

It was a beautiful morning in early autumn when the trees were just beginning to shed their leaves. You loved kicking through them on your way to playschool; the village looked so pretty, surrounded by red, gold and brown. It was brisk outside but sunny, and after I dropped you off I decided to walk the longer way home through the woods. It was peaceful, the sun slanting through the trees, and as I dug my hands into the pockets of my sheepskin coat I felt awash with happiness. As I rounded the corner on the path that led to the back of the cottage I noticed someone standing in our garden, by the stone wall that separated it from the woods. I stopped, hiding behind a thick tree trunk. It was Daphne. And she wasn't alone. She was with a man. My heart fluttered, my stomach turning over. Who was it this time? Not another journalist intent on finding out Daphne's true identity?

I wondered if it was Sean, one of the farm hands. I'd never met him but Daphne had become quite pally with him at work, by all accounts. It sounded like he gave her things – spare eggs, the odd tin of paint, a pint of milk. I hoped he wasn't taking these things illegally but Daphne said he was 'all right', which, from her, was quite high praise. It did cross my mind that he might fancy her, but I trusted her. I knew she loved me.

But as I peered closer I could see it was Joel.

Their voices floated towards me on the breeze. 'I think you should go,' I heard Daphne say. I went to step out from behind the tree. Was he bothering her again? But his reply rooted me to the spot.

'I don't understand why you've made up these lies about me,' he said, throwing his arms out in exasperation. I could see, even from my position, that he looked genuinely confused. 'Rose and I were friends and now she hasn't spoken to me in months. If I see her in the street she avoids me.'

'That's her prerogative.'

'You turned her against me by making out that I'm some – some lech.'

'Don't be ridiculous.'

'I never came on to you. I never harassed you. The only thing I did was tell you how I felt about Rose. Is that why you did it? To stop us getting together?'

'Get it into your thick head, she's not interested and never will be, whatever I might have told her,' she hissed. The anger on her face surprised me. She was usually so serene, so care-free. I'd always admired her patience, her kindness. I mean, of course, she wasn't a saint. She was a worrier, like me. She got angry about injustices and inequality. She was independent and capable. But she was never petty or unfair – or so I'd always thought. But if Joel was telling the truth, if she had lied about the advances he'd made on her, then that was a very manipulative thing to do.

'But you didn't know that, did you? Not then. You thought she might like me too and decided to put a stop to it. You might have fooled everyone else around here, Daphne, with your butter-wouldn't-melt façade, but I can see through you.'

'Why don't you just fuck off?' she snarled. 'Leave us alone.'

I inhaled so sharply my chest hurt. I waited for Joel's reaction. But he just shook his head sadly. 'I hope you're not using her. She's a good person.'

'Of course I'm not.'

He looked towards the cottage. 'You've got a good set-up there. A roof over your head. Love. A ready-made family.'

She folded her arms across her chest. She was wearing a baggy fawn-coloured jumper and cream jodhpurs I'd bought her for her birthday. Her hair was starting to grow out and was now at her shoulders, but she kept it dark. I liked it that way. Her cheeks were red from the cold and her eyes burnt with intensity. She looked beautiful.

'I love Rose.'

'I hope you do.'

'You sound jealous.'

'Perhaps I am.'

She toed the ground with my wellies, which she wore to work. 'Well, she would never have been interested in you, no matter what I said.'

He sighed. 'But at least we would still have been friends. Or do you not want that either?'

'I don't know what you mean.'

'Does Rose see anybody apart from you?'

'She's always been reclusive. That's not my fault.'

He shook his head. 'Melissa told me Rose hardly ever does the bell-ringing at the church any more. Or the WI.'

'That's her decision. Not mine. We just want to spend all our time together. Can't you remember what it's like? That first flush of love when all you want is each other? Stop trying to make out it's something else. I'd never stop Rose doing anything she wanted to do and vice versa.'

I couldn't stand by and listen to any more of this. It didn't feel right. I stepped out of the shadow of the tree and made my way to the back of the garden. I climbed over the wall and jumped down onto the grass. The shock on Daphne's face was so comical I had to suppress a laugh.

'What – what are you doing?' she gasped, as I walked over to where they stood.

'Sorry, I sometimes come back this way. I like walking alone in the woods. I thought you were supposed to be at work.'

Her face coloured a deep crimson. 'I . . . Yes, I'm just going. Joel popped over.' I could tell she was trying to work out if I'd heard their conversation. But I kept things light.

'Is everything okay?' I asked Joel.

'It's all good.' He flashed me a warm smile. 'Glad to see you're looking well, Rose. If you ever need anything,' he threw me a meaningful look, 'anything at all, you know where to find me, right?'

'Um, sure . . .'

'Good. Then I'll be off.'

We stood and watched as he strode across the lawn, disappearing around the side of the cottage.

'What was all that about?' I said, wondering if Daphne would tell me the truth.

But she reached up and kissed me deeply in response, pulling me against her. 'I've got half an hour before I need to be in work. Let's make the most of Lolly not being here,' she replied, as she pulled away, taking my hand and leading me back towards the cottage. But I couldn't shake the feeling that settled inside me. If Daphne had lied and manipulated me over Joel, what else hadn't she been honest about?

47

Theo

ON MONDAY BEFORE HIS SHIFT THEO DECIDES TO VISIT his dad. He needs some answers now he knows about Lorna and Rose. He hasn't seen him since his dad stormed out of his restaurant last week. He waits a few minutes, annoyed with himself that his heart is beating faster than normal. And then he hears the thud of footsteps coming down the hall and the door is thrust open. His dad stands there in a pastel diamond-patterned golfing jumper and chinos. 'What do you want?'

'You need to let me in.'

'I don't want to speak to you. Was it you who sent the police over? I might have guessed. Always so suspicious.' He's about to shut the door in Theo's face, but Theo sticks his foot in the crack before he has the chance.

'Actually, it wasn't me. And if you let me in then I can explain,' says Theo, trying to sound more forceful than he actually feels.

His dad stares pointedly at Theo's trainer wedged in the door. 'Doesn't look like I have a choice,' he says, stepping backwards. He turns on his heel and walks stiffly down the hall.

Theo follows him into the kitchen. It's immaculate as always. Not one thing out of place. His dad stands at the counter in the corner and switches the kettle on. 'Be quick. I'm due at the club.'

Theo wonders, in that moment, if his dad has the capacity to love. He can't imagine ever talking to his own child in the way his father speaks to him.

'What did the police say?'

'Nothing much. Just asked me a few questions.'

'What about?'

He doesn't say anything, just stands there blinking at Theo.

'I know about Rose Grey. I know that she has a daughter – who is possibly my sister.'

He continues to stare at Theo coldly.

'I know that you have that thug Davies threatening the family. Threatening your own daughter, for fuck's sake. What is wrong with you?'

His dad looks taken aback. Theo has never sworn at his father before. And the good boy inside him, the kid that always aims to please, flinches as he says it.

'I don't know what you're talking about. You are so like your mother. Letting your emotions run away with you.'

'At least I have some, unlike you.'

'I loved your mother. And I loved Rose,' he replies. Theo wants to laugh. He's sure his dad doesn't know what love is. He's confusing possession with love.

'So, who was Rose to you?'

'She was . . . someone I once had a relationship with.' His dad's eyes flicker, and Theo gets the impression he's not telling the truth.

'And what happened?'

'She was living with me and left when she was pregnant.

I tried to find her, but it wasn't so easy back then. No mobile phones, no tracking, no internet. She just . . . disappeared off the face of the earth. And then I met your mother and Rose seemed less important.'

'And your daughter?'

'I wasn't even sure if Rose had had the baby. She was around your age when I met her. She'd been around. She was only six months pregnant when she left me. And she was so . . . flighty.'

This doesn't tie up with what Lorna said about her mother. 'Are you saying you didn't think the baby was yours? Well, I've got news for you, Dad. She is. The resemblance to both you and me is unmistakable. Is she who you were trying to find? Is that why you had that article on your desk, or is there more you're hiding from me?'

His dad puts a hand to his head looking pained and, in that moment, less like the authoritarian control-freak Theo was always scared of and more like an old man. 'It's complicated. I asked Glen to look into it for me.'

He says this as though he's discussing something as anodyne as the weather.

'What does Glen actually do? He made out he's a private detective but that's bullshit, isn't it? Is he just a conman? I don't know what the police said to you earlier, but if you're linked with him it won't be good for you.'

'Don't be ridiculous.' He turns away from Theo to make tea. But something doesn't sit right about all of this: his dad's responses are purposefully evasive.

'What about the evidence?' asks Theo.

His dad doesn't say anything but Theo notices a stiffening of his shoulders. A hesitation as he dunks a teabag. 'Evidence?'

He's playing for time, Theo can tell. 'Yes. Apparently, when your *henchman* accosted Lorna – your own daughter – in the street,' he spits this sentence out, hoping his father will hear the disgust in his voice, 'he said something about Rose burying some evidence. What did he mean?'

His dad still has his back to Theo. 'I have no idea,' he says but Theo can hear the lie in his voice.

'And then Davies broke into the cottage. Nothing was taken, funny that. But he was obviously looking for something.'

His dad turns to face him and hands him a mug. 'I know nothing about that.'

'Of course you do,' says Theo, taking the tea. 'Davies never does anything unless you say so. Is this what you were like with the police? They'll see through it, Dad. You're tied with Glen now.'

His dad regards him over the mug. It's one Theo bought him for Father's Day with a golfer on the front mid-swing. Theo detects a flicker of something in his father's eyes: guilt, perhaps? Remorse? Fear? He's not sure. He's always been so hard to read. So closed.

Theo sips his tea. His dad is still intimidating, he realizes, as he watches him. But he's a pensioner now. He can no longer hurt Theo. He has no control over Theo's life. Theo is totally self-sufficient: he has never expected anything from his father. The things he did for him, they were born out of a sense of duty, and love for his mother. It was always drilled into him as a kid to love and respect his father – but it should work both ways. He felt he *should* love his dad when he was growing up so never questioned it. But now, if he's really honest with himself, he has no such feelings for him. He swallows his tea. 'And those photos of the women you had in your study?'

'They're just women I helped. I like to keep a record, that's all.' His father's voice sounds strained. 'I told you this at the restaurant.'

'Taking photos without their knowledge.'

'It's not a crime. I wasn't hurting anyone.'

'Then why hide them?'

His dad empties his tea down the drain and almost throws his cup into the sink, where it clatters. 'I've had enough of the third degree. I need to get going.' He stalks past Theo. 'Let yourself out,' he calls over his shoulder, as he picks up his bag of golf clubs by the door and hoists it over his shoulder. 'And don't bother sneaking around my study. You won't find anything.'

'What about murder, Dad?' he says, following him down the hallway. 'Is that why you sent Glen to find the evidence at Rose's cottage?' It's on the tip of his tongue to question him about his mother's accident too, but he decides not to. For now.

His father stops, his stance rigid, then turns slowly to Theo, his expression menacing.

48

Lorna

LORNA IS IN THE KITCHEN COOKING A VEGETABLE CAS-serole. It was her mother's recipe, and slicing and chopping calms Lorna, stops her mind racing. She has so much unwanted noise in her head: the bodies, Victor, her mother.

She's hardly seen Saffy all day: she's locked herself into her study saying she needs to get on with her work.

She sticks the casserole into the oven. Lorna misses meat. She hasn't eaten any since staying. She notices Tom just eats fish too, to please Saffy. She could really do with a fat, juicy cheeseburger.

When she goes back into the living room she's surprised to see Saffy on the sofa. 'Finished work?'

Saffy rubs her eyes. 'I'm shattered. I've been at my desk for eight hours straight with just one break.'

Lorna feels a punch of concern. 'You have to take it easy . . .'

'How can I?' she wails. 'This has all been such a distraction! I'm behind. I can't afford to get sacked.'

Lorna presses her lips together, not wanting to say anything

to annoy her daughter. Saffy was always so even-tempered.
Lorna knows this must all be getting to her, not to mention the
hormones flying around.

'I can't stop thinking about what the police said yesterday,'
says Saffy, with a sigh. 'About the body not being Jean Burdon.'

'It could still be Daphne. Perhaps your gran got it wrong
when she said Daphne was really Jean. Or Daphne lied to her.'

'But that file of Sheila's. It had a report about Jean Burdon
in it, written by Neil Lewisham. That's a link. And Dad rang
earlier to say someone at his newspaper deciphered the shorthand and it was notes about Jean and Sheila being one and the
same.'

'The police will figure it out,' says Lorna. Her stomach rumbles as the smell of the casserole fills the cottage. 'We need to
have faith in them. In DS Barnes.'

Saffy sighs. 'As soon as the police do figure it out, the journalists will be back with a vengeance, like wasps. I know they're
only doing a job, but this is our life.'

'I know.' Over the last few days they have lost interest, but
Lorna has been keeping Euan updated by text, and he warned
her that it's often the way. And then a new piece of information
will come to light and the journalists will be back.

They hear the front door bang and Lorna notices how Saffy
stiffens. Then Tom pokes his head around the living-room
door. 'Something smells good.'

'You're home early,' cries Saffy, happily, and Lorna feels a
stab of envy at how she runs to him and he wraps her in his
arms. It used to be her she ran to as a kid, when it wasn't her
gran. Now it's Tom. He's still wearing his helmet. It's white and
looks like an egg. He removes it and shakes out his hair. It's
slightly damp.

'I'm starving,' he says, throwing his helmet onto the chair. Lorna fights the urge to pick it up and hang it on the peg in the hallway.

'Only another half an hour –' She's interrupted by a rap on the door. Tom goes to the window and peers out. It's still light outside, the sun just starting to descend behind the trees, the kind of evening Lorna loves, where the heat of the day still lingers. 'It's an old woman with a young guy,' he says.

Lorna joins him at the window. 'Oh, that's Melissa and her nephew, Seth.' She darts to the front door, opening it. 'Hi, come in,' she says. She ushers them into the living room and introduces them to Saffy and Tom.

Melissa is beaming. She hands an envelope to Lorna, then glances around the cottage, at the modern sofas and the wooden floors. Then her attention is back to Lorna. 'After our chat I remembered I had these photos,' she says.

'I told my aunt to wait until tomorrow but she insisted,' grins Seth, thrusting his hands into the pockets of his jeans.

'I thought you'd like to see them,' adds Melissa. 'It's when Rose was bell-ringing with us all at the church. She used to love it.'

'She was a bell-ringer?' asks Saffy, raising an eyebrow in surprise. 'She never mentioned that.'

Lorna wants to add that there were lots of things her mother never mentioned but thinks better of it. She flicks through them. A group of about six women, including a much younger Melissa, are grinning at the camera, each holding a length of rope in what looks like the inside of a church tower. It must have been taken in the late 1970s, judging by the haircuts and fashions. Lorna scans the women but can't see her mum. 'Is she in these?' she asks, frowning.

Melissa peers over her shoulder. 'Yes, there she is.' She points to a woman with long wavy hair. The photo might be old but Lorna can see straight away it's not her mother. 'That's not her. She looks vaguely familiar but . . .'

'What do you mean?' says Melissa, snatching the photos from Lorna's hand. 'Yes, that's her, there. And in this one . . .'

'Let's see,' says Saffy, walking over and taking the photo from Melissa. 'Wait. That's not Gran.' She turns to Lorna, eyebrows raised. 'That's – that's the other woman in Gran's photos. That's Daphne.'

Melissa laughs. 'Don't be ridiculous. Daphne hadn't moved in when these were taken. In 1978. That's Rose. I should know what Rose looked like.'

A cold hand clutches Lorna's heart. She dashes to the box that is still in the corner of the living room, the one they still haven't finished sorting through. She retrieves the photos and shows them to Melissa, her hands shaking. 'That other woman, in those photos . . .' she says.

'This one?' Melissa says, pointing to the tall one with a dark elfin haircut and pale skin. Her mother.

'Yes. Who – who is that?'

Saffy is by her side. 'Mum, I don't understand. You know who that is. It's Gran.'

Lorna grabs her daughter's hand and squeezes it. 'Who is that?' she asks Melissa again, stabbing the photo with her finger, her voice urgent, nausea rising.

'Why, that's Daphne, of course,' says Melissa, looking at them both as if they're stupid. Oh, so, so stupid. 'That's Daphne Hartall.'

PART FOUR

49

Daphne

MY NAME IS ROSE. THAT'S HOW I THINK OF MYSELF BUT this damned illness makes me forget things, makes me confused, distorts things in my mind. All I have is my memories and they're fading like a picture left too long in the sun. I've been Rose for nearly forty years. I've been Rose longer than I've been anyone else.

But this past year things have become foggy. Faces I once recognized have turned into strangers. And when I forget the present, I think of these other identities as separate people, like they aren't part of me at all. Jean, Sheila, Daphne. Particularly Daphne. I liked being her the best because she had love.

I had a terrible childhood. That's no excuse, I realize that. Lots of people have terrible childhoods but don't go on to become killers.

I was born Jean Burdon on 3 August 1939 in Stepney Green, London. The only child to two parents who hated each other — and couldn't give a shit about me. My father was a drunk, my mother a prostitute, and I knew too much too young about men and sex. Most of the time I was left to my own devices, roaming the bomb-shattered East End streets, trying to keep out of my father's way or I'd get a beating just for breathing. My psychologist at the secure unit said that the bullied often turned out to be bullies. And that was the way for me.

Susan Wallace was my first friend. My only friend. She was pretty and sweet, and for one glorious summer we were inseparable. Her parents were kind to me: they let me stay for tea and, even though Susan's family were also poor, they tried to help me by giving me a jumper that Mrs Wallace had knitted, or an extra piece of bread and jam or an apple when they had it. And then one day Susan decided she didn't want to be friends with me any more. She had found a new best friend, she said. A little girl who had moved in next door to her. The rejection was like nothing I'd ever experienced before and I was filled with a white-hot rage. I hadn't planned to kill her. I just wanted to stop her leaving.

The judge at my trial was hard and unfeeling. He ruled me a psychopath. But I don't think that's true. I've read up on psychopaths since leaving prison and they are incapable of love, of compassion, of empathy. I feel all those things. My problem has always been that I love *too* much.

Yes, I was Jean Burdon for nearly thirty horrifying years. And, yes, I couldn't wait to escape her, to become Sheila Watts. I left prison, rehabilitated and armed with a new identity at the age of twenty-eight. And I tried to turn over a new leaf. I really, really did. I kept away from other people, tried not to form relationships or attachments, tried to remember all the things my psychologist had warned me about. And it worked for a while. I moved to Broadstairs, in Kent, and lived there quite happily for a number of years. But then that journalist started sniffing around – had somehow worked out who I really was. And I could have told the truth to my probation officer and they would have rehoused me, given me another identity, but I found that faking my death and taking Alan's sister's identity to be the much simpler option. That way nobody would know who I was, not the prison service or the probation officers. I'd finally be free. Finally be the person I'd always wanted to be – fiercely loyal, free-spirited, feminist, don't-take-any-shit Daphne Hartall.

So I moved to the West Country, first Cornwall, then Devon, and eventually to a little village called Beggars Nook.

And it was there that I made my biggest mistake and broke all my promises to myself.

I not only fell in love with Rose but with her daughter, Lolly.

50

Lorna

LORNA'S HAND IS SHAKING AS SHE HOLDS THE MUG. SHE'S drunk so much caffeine these last ten days she feels like she's swimming in it.

Sitting opposite her on the sofa, next to Saffy, DS Barnes is wearing an earnest expression as he hunches over his notebook. 'Are you sure?'

'Yes,' says Lorna. 'We think the body you found belongs to Rose Grey. My . . .' She swallows. 'My real mother.'

'I'm so sorry,' says DS Barnes, looking up at Lorna, his bright blue eyes full of sympathy.

'I . . . Thank you.' She's not sure what he's sorry for. The fact that it seems like the woman she's always thought of as her mother is a murderer, after all. Or for the fact her real mother is probably dead.

Saffy has hardly said a word. She's sitting with her hands in her lap, her face pinched, her dark eyebrows knitted together in worry. Another blow for Saffy, thinks Lorna, with regret. How much more can she take?

'Rose . . . *Daphne* . . . she could still be innocent, you know.

She might not have killed the real Rose Grey, if it is indeed Rose's body that was found,' he says. 'That still could have been Victor Carmichael, and it's something we'll be looking into, rest assured.'

'But then why steal her identity?' asks Lorna.

'It might have been the opportunity she needed to keep you safe. If Victor is your father and she was scared of him for some reason . . .'

'I suppose,' says Lorna, a flicker of hope igniting inside her, although she's trying to douse it. She doesn't want to be disappointed.

DS Barnes leaves at the same time Tom returns from his walk with Snowy. It's dark now and it's begun to rain. Snowy's fur is furrowed around his face, like wrinkles. Lorna watches as Saffy embraces Tom, burying her head in his chest as though she's trying to erase the last few hours from her mind.

'So,' says Tom, walking into the living room, 'what did the police say?'

'They've already taken Mum's DNA because of Theo,' says Saffy, bestowing on Lorna a watery smile. 'So they'll take DNA from the body to see if it's a close enough match to Mum's . . .' She moves away from Tom to stand by the fireplace. Lorna is worried about her. All this can't be good for the baby.

Tom slumps onto the sofa and scratches his head. 'Shit, this is just . . . shit.'

'I know,' Saffy says, joining him. She glances at Lorna, her eyes shining. 'But even if Gran isn't really my genetic grandmother,' she clutches her heart, 'I still love her. Is that wrong?'

'Of course not, sweetheart,' says Lorna, fighting back tears. She sits on the other side of her daughter and pulls her into a hug. 'I don't really remember my real mother at all. Just images and only since being here. It's more of a feeling somehow. Like grief. And I wonder . . .' she blinks back tears – she can't cry now '. . . if maybe it's the memory of grieving for my real mum. Who knows? All I remember is her . . . *Daphne*.'

'You were so young, Mum. Not even three. I need to go and see Gran tomorrow. Will you come with me?' she asks, looking up at Lorna with her big, dark eyes, reminding her of the little girl she once was.

'Of course. But, honey, don't expect any answers.'

When they reach Elm Brook the next day, they are told that Rose is deteriorating and is in bed. Saffy sits on one side of her, Lorna the other, and they watch as she sleeps, her eyelids flickering, as though she's in a dream. Another world where she's Daphne Hartall, perhaps.

'She looks so small,' whispers Lorna. 'Every time I see her she looks smaller. And if she is Daphne Hartall – Jean Burdon – then she'd be nearly eighty.'

Saffy doesn't say anything. Instead she stares down at the woman she's known all these years as Gran. Lorna watches as Saffy reaches over and takes her gran's hand. She feels conflicted: this woman is no relation to them at all, yet she's the only mother she's ever known. The only grandmother that Saffy has ever known, and their bond is still there, still so visible.

'I wish I could remember my real mother,' says Lorna. There is a heaviness in her chest. 'It's like . . . she, *Daphne* . . .' she almost spits out her name '. . . has wiped my memories all clean.'

'Mum!' Saffy looks shocked at the anger in Lorna's voice.

Lorna gets up. 'I'm going to get us a drink,' she says. She doesn't know if she can do this. Sit by this woman's bedside, knowing that she lied to them for all these years and perhaps even killed her real mother. Lorna's just about to move towards the door when Rose's eyes flutter open.

'Gran, it's me, Saffy,' says her granddaughter, gently, lovingly.

It's obvious she doesn't recognize them today. She seems to shrink further into the bed as though scared of them.

'It's okay, Gran, it's me,' says Saffy, in a soothing voice, still holding the older woman's hand. 'It's me, Saffy.'

'Hello, *Daphne*,' says Lorna. She can hear Saffy's sharp intake of breath, feel her disapproval. 'We know who you are. Who you *really* are.'

But the old woman in the bed just stares at each of them, eyes filled with terror. 'Who are you?'

'She's your daughter, Gran. She's Lolly.'

'Lolly?' She reaches for Lorna's hand. 'Is that really you? You look so grown-up.'

'What happened to Rose?' asks Lorna, crisply, refusing to take her hand. This woman who is no longer her mother. 'I know she's the other body in the garden.'

But she just blinks at her, confusion written all over her face. 'My name is Rose,' she says. 'My name is Rose. My name is Rose.'

Goose bumps pop up along Lorna's arms. It's as though repeating it mantra-style will make it true. 'No, it isn't. It's Jean. You're Jean Durdon, aren't you? You can admit it now. We know everything.'

'My name is Rose.'

'Stop it,' snaps Lorna. 'You owe us the truth.'

'Mum!' Saffy's voice is hard. 'You're scaring her.'

'I can't do this. I just . . . can't.' Lorna walks over to the door. She needs to leave. She'll wait for Saffy outside. Everything she believed in. All of it. It was one big lie.

'Lolly.'

They both turn towards the bed. Her mother is struggling

to sit up but her eyes are firmly fixed on Lorna. 'I'm sorry,' she says, her voice desperate. Lorna's shocked to see tears running down her creased cheeks. 'I'm so, so sorry.'

'Why?' asks Lorna, her voice thick and cracked with emotion. 'Why did you do it?'

But the old woman in the bed just stares at her blankly, regarding Lorna as though she's a stranger once again.

51

Rose

October 1980

SINCE JOEL'S VISIT THE DISTRUST HAD BEGUN TO CREEP in. Slowly at first, like rust on a car, but then spreading insidiously, eroding and tarnishing our relationship. I needed to trust someone completely after Audrey and particularly after Victor. I'd wake in the morning, Daphne's face next to mine on the pillow, and I'd experience a dropping sensation in my gut. Disappointment. Maybe I expected too much from people, from her. It was hard to know. But lies. How could you ever truly know someone, love someone, if they lied to you?

All I could think about as I sat and watched her sleep was what else she had lied about.

She'd lied about Neil Lewisham. She'd made me believe he was an angry, violent ex-boyfriend. But had I been so different? I'd let her think I was a widow when we first met. And, looking back, she'd never actually said Neil was an ex. I'd assumed. And now I had killed Neil. Had she manipulated me into doing that? Had I done the dirty work for her? She'd killed before – she'd admitted that herself. Although she said that was an accident, that she'd pushed little Susan Wallace in a temper after an argument and she'd fallen and cracked her head open on the discarded bricks of the bombsite they were playing in. I'd never looked into it, never had any reason not to believe her. But after she'd lied about Joel I decided to drive out to the library in Chippenham while you were at playschool. There, I was able to access all the old newspapers on microfiche – I read through all the reports of the trial, how she'd deliberately and, according to the barrister summing up, brutally struck Susan Wallace over the head with a brick, not once, but twice in an unprovoked attack.

I sat there, with the evidence in front of me, frozen to the spot.

She'd lied about that too.

I wanted to run away with you right there and then. Leave the cottage, leave Beggars Nook and run, run, run. But I couldn't. The cottage was mine. It was the only asset I had. I didn't even have a job. I couldn't just leave.

No, Daphne would have to be the one to go.

I paced the house, planning what I was going to say while I waited for her to come back from the farm. Then I noticed you playing with your Sindy dolls on the fluffy rug in the living room. You looked so happy, so innocent. I couldn't row with Daphne in front of you.

When Daphne arrived home, just half an hour later, you rushed into her arms. She dropped a bag at her feet before enveloping you. 'Daffy!' you cried. And then you grabbed her hand and pulled her into the living room before she'd even had the chance to take off her coat. She giggled, allowing herself to be dragged along, and my stomach turned over.

She smiled uncertainly at me over your head. I knew she was worried that I was slipping away from her since I'd found out about Joel, trying to reassure me that he'd got his wires crossed, still maintaining that she felt uncomfortable around him and that he had been trying it on with her.

But I no longer believed her. Joel had sounded too genuine.

I walked into the kitchen, knowing she'd follow. Which she did, slipping off her coat and dumping the carrier bag on the worktop. Her cheeks were flushed from the cold. 'Hey, you,' she said, coming over to kiss me. But I moved away before she could. Her shoulders slumped with the rejection. 'Are you still mad at me?'

'I don't know,' I lied.

'I don't understand . . .' She hung her head, her fringe falling into her eyes. She looked so frail standing there that my instinct was to go over to her and wrap her in my arms. But I couldn't. Instead I turned my back on her and put the kettle on the hob.

'What's in the bag?' I asked instead.

'Oh.' She opened it. 'Sean gave me this joint of beef.'

'He's giving you a lot of things lately. Are you sure he's allowed?'

'Mick, the owner, has loads of leftover produce. He doesn't mind.'

I felt uneasy about it. What kind of farmer just gave away his produce for free? Was it another thing Daphne was lying about?

Later that evening, when you were in bed, we were both sitting on the sofa together, each at either end like we used to do when we first met. Usually we'd be huddled up, a tangle of arms and legs, like a two-headed, eight-limbed creature.

'I've got something for you,' she said, handing me a small

leatherbound book. I took it, reading the title in gold embossed into the leather. *Love Poems.* 'Open it,' she urged.

I did as she said and was surprised to see a pressed red rose between the pages.

'I love you so much,' she said. 'Please forgive me.'

'So you did lie?'

'It was stupid. I just wanted to see if you liked him. Or if you liked women. Well, me . . .'

'Daphne, you have to be honest with me. I can't carry on being in a relationship with you unless you're totally truthful.'

'I am.' She inched up the sofa towards me. 'Of course I am.'

'And what about when you were a kid? You said killing Susan Wallace was an accident.'

'It was.'

'I read the news reports.'

She sprang back as though I'd slapped her. 'What? You were snooping around on me?'

'I have a two-and-a-half-year-old daughter.'

The hurt on her face crushed me. 'You think I'd ever hurt Lolly?'

'No.' I'd gone too far, I could see that. I knew she loved you like you were her own. 'No, of course not.'

She rushed to my side, kneeling at my feet and taking my hands in hers. She kissed them and looked up at me. My heart lurched. She was so beautiful. 'Rose, I'm sorry for lying about Joel. It was stupid.'

'I . . .'

She pulled me onto the floor with her and ran her hands through my hair, her eyes intense. 'I love you. I've never loved anyone like I've loved you. You have to believe me.'

'I do.'

Her eyes filled with tears. 'You can't leave me. I'd be lost without you.'

'Daphne . . .'

'You promise. You promise me, Rose. You can't leave me.'

I hesitated, thinking of how I'd been so determined to ask her to move out. But I knew I was just angry. I loved her so much. 'I'm not planning to leave you.'

Relief flooded her face. 'Oh, good.' She kissed me, wrapping her arms around me, the book of poetry she'd given me sliding off my lap and onto the wooden floor beside us. She pulled away, cupping my face with her hands.

'I know too much about you,' she said, her face serious.

'And I know too much about you.'

'Then we're stuck together, aren't we?' She laughed to break the tension but it did nothing to dispel the unease that crept through me.

And maybe we might have been okay. Maybe we could have moved past this.

If it hadn't been for Sean.

52

Theo

IT'S DARK AND RAINING WHEN THEO LEAVES THE RESTAU-
rant. Since May turned into June it's done nothing but piss
down and he has to sprint through the rain-slicked street to his
car, his jacket over his head.

It's been ten days since the weekend in Beggars Nook. Ten
days since he met Lorna and Saffron, his possible family. Lorna
has texted him a few times – like him, she's still waiting for the
DNA results. He has such mixed feelings: happy that he might
have a sister – he's always wanted a sibling – but also the gut-
churning fear his dad might be a murderer.

His dad had been furious, as he'd known he would be, when
he'd asked him about the bodies. He'd shouted, told Theo he
shouldn't let his imagination run wild, and had then slammed out
of the door. He hasn't heard from him since.

It's late, nearly midnight, and the street is empty. His Volvo
is parked under a lamppost, the halo of light illuminating the rain.
He slides behind the wheel, slamming the door against the bad
weather. The sound of the rain hammering on the car roof is
deafening and he's soaked through, exhausted, as he turns on

the engine and whacks the heating up. He's just about to pull away when his phone vibrates in his wet jacket.

He fishes his mobile from his damp pocket. An unrecognized number flashes up on screen. Who would be calling this time of night?

'Hello,' he says tentatively.

'It's me.' His father's voice is gruff at the other end of the line and Theo is so surprised to hear from him that he can't speak for a couple of seconds.

'Hello. Are you there?'

'Yes. Sorry, Dad. I'm here. What's wrong?'

'I've been arrested.'

So it's finally happened. His dad hasn't been able to wriggle his way out of this one. Even so he still feels sick.

'That bastard Davies is trying to pin everything on me. All his crimes.'

Theo's stomach plummets. All his crimes? How many have there been? The realization sends a jolt of shock through Theo. 'You mean he's confessed? He killed those two people in Beggars Nook in 1980?'

'Yes. No. Not that. Other stuff.'

The dark night seems to close in on Theo as he sits in his car, the rain slashing against the windows. He shivers. 'What, exactly?'

'He's trying to imply that I'm responsible for your mother's death.'

Theo feels like he can't breathe. He pulls at the collar of his top. 'And?' he manages.

'Of course it's not true. I've done nothing wrong. I was at work that day. You know that. I've got an alibi.'

The alibi obviously doesn't hold up, thinks Theo, if they've arrested him. He could have pushed his mother in an argument perhaps, then snuck off to work and pretended he'd been there all day.

'Why would Davies know if you killed Mum or not?' Something doesn't add up about this. Did Davies find out somehow and hold it over his dad? Or did Davies help him cover it up? Davies was working for his dad back in 2004 in myriad roles. He's been introduced as his dad's legal adviser, accountant and head of security over the years. And now, suddenly, he's a private detective. Theo has never been able to work out what his actual role is.

'And now . . . now they're questioning me about Cynthia Parsons's suicide. They think it could be foul play.' He doesn't sound sad or remorseful: he sounds furious. 'But I had nothing to do with that.'

Theo rubs his hand across his face, rage bubbling inside him.

'Look, get me a lawyer. Ralph Middleton. His number is online. He's – *Wait a fucking minute, I've not finished,*' he shrieks to – Theo assumes – someone behind him. 'Look, son, I've got to go. My time's up. Call him. Please.'

The line goes dead. Theo stares out of the rain-blurred windscreen onto the empty street. An image of his mother's lovely face appears in his mind, so clear it's like he saw her only yesterday. Why would his father want to kill her? Was she planning on leaving him? Had she found out about the sexual assault? Or the women in the folder? Or the bodies at Skelton Place? My God, he could have been killing for years. Theo feels as if he wants to throw up. He slams his palm against the steering wheel, a sharp pain searing through him. Fuck. Fuck. Fuck.

And despite the loathing he feels for his dad, Theo can't help the emotion that sits heavy on his chest, suffocating him until he's forced to let it out in sobs. He sits there for a while, his forehead resting on the steering wheel of his cold little car, and lets the tears flow. He doesn't really know who he's crying for. Definitely not his father, who he hopes will rot in jail. Definitely for his mother, whose young life his dad had stolen, and partly for himself for being robbed of his lovely mum.

He sits back in his seat and wipes away his tears. His mobile is still in his lap and he sees there's a text from Lorna, sent hours ago, which he'd never noticed as he'd been so busy at the restaurant. He presses the screen and it lights up, illuminating the inside of the car.

It simply says: *It's official. You're my brother.*

53

Saffy

I FOLLOW TOM INTO THE COTTAGE, STANDING ON THE threshold to shake out my umbrella. It's cold and damp for June. From behind the hedge a man steps out and I exhale sharply, expecting it to be Davies, somehow released from police custody. But it's just a pensioner walking past with his dog. When he notices me he tips his cap in greeting and I wave half-heartedly before turning and closing the door.

We've just come back from dropping Mum at the airport. She suddenly announced yesterday that she'd booked a flight for today, that she would love to have stayed longer but it's been two weeks and she had no choice but to return. There was so much left unsaid between us as we hugged goodbye. There never seemed the right time to continue that discussion we had in the car, or for me to reassure her that I love her. After finding out Gran is really Daphne, everything between me and Mum just got buried underneath it. Mum can barely process what she's feeling about all of that, let alone dredge up our past.

'Right,' says Tom, bending down and unclipping Snowy

from his lead. 'Shall we order a takeaway for tea? I could murder fish and chips.'

'I'm going to miss Mum's cooking,' I say wistfully, kicking off my trainers and slipping out of my Puffa. The cottage suddenly seems too big and quiet without her. I hang my coat on the rack by my study. Tom follows suit. We were drenched during the dash into the house from the car.

'I know. I'm going to miss her too. She's a force to be reckoned with.' He heads towards the kitchen.

'Do you think she'll be okay?' I ask, going to the kettle and smiling to myself to see that Mum has moved the toaster into the corner. She never could leave things alone. 'It must be a shock for her, finding out her mother isn't actually her mother.' I glance out of the window at the garden. We're still waiting for confirmation that the body does belong to the real Rose Grey. DS Barnes said we should get the results tomorrow.

'It's the same for you,' says Tom, gently. 'You thought Rose was your grandmother all these years.'

'I still love her. I can't . . .' I gulp, tears springing to my eyes '. . . I can't just stop loving her. I can't forget everything we've been through together – everything she's done for me, you know? But then I think she could have killed my actual grandmother . . .'

'I understand' He comes over to me and wraps his arms around my waist. 'I can't believe – whoever she is – that she's a killer, though. There could be some other explanation if the body does belong to the real Rose.'

'She killed when she was ten years old. All the things I thought I knew about Gran were wrong.'

Tom falls silent as we digest this. 'We've read all the reports from the time,' he says, after a while. 'She had an awful upbringing . . . she was abused herself. And she was rehabilitated.'

We've had this conversation many times since we found out about Daphne, of course. And we always end up in the same place. Because there is no getting away from the fact that Rose, Jean, Daphne, whatever her name really is, was the best grandmother in the world. People can change, reverse their circumstances, adapt to a new way of life. 'I think all of this has fucked Mum up,' I say. I shiver, feeling cold to the bone, and Tom holds me tighter. 'I think she's repressed memories from that time. She was nearly three. It's not like she was a baby when it happened. I think it explains why she's always running away. Like now. Once again things get tough and she scarpers back to Spain. We moved around a lot when I was a kid. I was born in Bristol, then we moved to Kent and then out to Brighton, back to Kent and then she moved all over Europe. I don't think she even knows what she's running from.'

'Saff,' he says gently. 'She couldn't stay here for ever. She has a life in Spain. An apartment. A job. She had to go back some time.'

I sigh. 'I wish Mum had seen Gran to say goodbye before she left. Gran isn't well. I'm worried she'll die and Mum will never have the chance to apologize, to . . .'

'Babe,' says Tom, pulling away, 'you can't expect Lorna to forgive your gran just because you do.'

'I know . . .'

'She's been lied to all her life by the person she trusted most in the world.'

I hang my head. He's right. I can't blame my mum for being so angry with Gran. But I also know she'll regret it if she doesn't have a chance to put things right before it's too late. Even if it's only to hear Gran's side of things.

'Mum and Theo have a lot in common, don't they? Both with parents who lied to them?'

'But that's the thing,' says Tom, pushing back a curl from my forehead. 'Your gran isn't Lorna's mother. Shit, I can't imagine how that would mess with your head.'

'I suppose. It is messed up. It's just . . . I can't be angry with a frail old woman, Tom, I just can't.'

Tom moves away from me to make the tea and I stand and watch him. My emotions are so conflicted. I can understand why Mum is so upset, but every time I think of Gran lying in her care-home bed, her eyes wide and frightened, I think of the woman who looked after me every summer, the woman who didn't expect me to be someone I wasn't, who allowed me to be awkward, shy, gauche me. Gran loved me like I was her own grandchild, I have no doubt about that. She was always so kind, so gentle. Nurturing. To me, to her plants and her animals. No . . . there's no way she murdered the real Rose. I refuse to believe it. All she's ever done is protect me and Mum.

'It saddens me that she couldn't be honest, though,' I say, taking the mug of tea from Tom and wrapping my hands around its warmth. 'From the book of poems we found, she obviously loved Rose. Maybe she never got over her.'

'It's actually really sad,' says Tom, thoughtfully, sipping his drink. 'She pined for her all these years.'

My heart contracts. 'To think they stood here, Tom. Right here in this kitchen.' I walk over to the window and place my hand on the leaded glass as though doing so connects me to them, to the past, as though my hand is touching the invisible prints they left behind. 'Do you think she killed Neil Lewisham?'

'I think maybe one of them did. And the other protected her.'

'God.' I breathe in deeply, the glass cold beneath my fingers, watching as the raindrops cascade down the window. Outside the deluge has caused the sky to mist, obscuring the woods in the distance, but through the glass I imagine them out there, two ethereal creatures in the garden, Daphne and Rose, burying their secrets.

Later, after we've eaten our fish and chips, which we had to drive to the next village to collect, and I've spoken to Mum, who assures me she's arrived in San Sebastián safely, I escape upstairs for a bath. Ripping out the old bathroom was one of the first things we did when we found out the house was ours, then put in a claw-foot bath and walk-in shower. I touch my stomach. The baby kicks regularly now, little bubbles beneath my belly. I'm halfway through my pregnancy. We have another scan booked for next week. Sometimes I can't believe we've got this far. I can hear the murmur of the TV downstairs. Tom is watching some football match. I get out of the bath and wrap myself in my towelling robe. And then I go into Mum's room. She's left it neat, stripped the bed and bundled the sheets into the washing machine before she left this morning. There is nothing to say she was ever here apart from a faint whiff of her musky perfume. I don't know if it's my hormones but I ache for her in a way I've never done before, not even as a child left with my grandmother during those long summers.

Then I go into the little bedroom at the back, the room that will belong to the baby. The room that used to be Mum's when she was Lolly. Whoever rented it from Gran obviously never used it, except as a junk room. I go to the fireplace, remembering our mad dash around the house looking for the evidence that Davies was certain we had. I touch the warm wood. It's like the mantel in Mum's room – pine and engraved with delicate flowers. It's covered with dust. I'm surprised Mum didn't come in here to clean. I go to move towards the window but as

I do so I trip on a nail sticking out of the floorboards and grab hold of the corner of the mantelpiece to stop myself falling. I right myself, my hand still on the mantelpiece, when I notice it's come away slightly at the wall. I peer closer. My heart quickening in excitement, I pull it. There's something hidden beneath it. Like a hole where the fireplace meets the brick. It's concealed by the mantelpiece but I can tell something's there. Something hidden. 'Tom!' I yell. 'Tom!'

I hear his feet thundering on the bare staircase and he darts into the room, breathless. 'What is it? Are you okay? Is it the baby?'

'I think I've found where Gran may have hidden the evidence,' I say. 'Quick, help me lift this up.'

He rushes to my side and together we lift the mantelpiece. It comes away from the rest of the fireplace to reveal a hole in the chimney breast. He carefully lowers it to the floor, coughing as the action dislodges dust. In the hole a brown envelope is covered with cobwebs. I reach in for it, not caring about spiders or bugs or any of the things I'd usually be worried about. 'I can't believe we've found it,' I say, looking at Tom in shock, holding the A4 envelope as though it's the Holy Grail. And then my vision blurs. 'I wish Mum was here.' I'm suddenly nervous of what this might reveal about either Gran or the real Rose.

I drop to my knees and Tom does the same so that we are both sitting on the rough floorboards. I take out the contents of the envelope. It's a leatherbound folder, with clear sleeves. I tentatively open it and gasp. Naked women. Photos taken with what looks like a Polaroid camera. The women all look like they're asleep. Some look like they have hospital gowns on, pulled up to reveal their naked bodies. My stomach heaves. 'Oh, God,' I say, handing it to Tom.

He recoils. 'What the hell is this? It looks like each photo has a number.' He snaps the folder shut. 'Look, here, on the front of this folder. It has the name of a clinic.'

I lean over to see. In gold writing are the words Fernhill Fertility Clinic. 'Do you think this is Victor's clinic? Is this something to do with what Theo found in his father's study? Remember all those women? Some were pregnant. Shit. Tom, do you think the real Rose went to this clinic?'

'Artificial insemination?'

'It makes sense, doesn't it? Gran and the real Rose were lovers. Maybe Rose and Victor never were in a relationship . . .' The implication of this suddenly hits me.

'You need to call Theo,' says Tom, gravely.

'This must be the evidence that Davies was on about. It's not about the murders after all. But about something else. Something to do with Victor's clinic.'

'How did the real Rose get hold of it?'

I shake my head. So much still doesn't make sense. Why would someone take photos of these naked women? Are they consensual? Somehow I sense not. It looks too clinical, the women asleep . . . or anaesthetized, legs in stirrups as though mid-procedure.

I put my hand to my heart. It's racing underneath my dressing-gown. And then I notice something else inside the envelope. A smaller one. White. Sealed. The type you'd send a letter in. I turn it over. On the front are just two words in flowery writing: *For Lolly*.

54

Rose

November 1980

AND SO, IT SEEMED, HE'D FOUND US. I SUPPOSE IT WAS
inevitable. We couldn't hide for ever, you and I, Lolly. It was
only a matter of time.

Nobody messed with Victor Carmichael and got away with it.

But I was blissfully unaware, going into November. Things
had settled down between Daphne and me. I still woke in the
night sometimes, my pyjamas clinging to my sweaty body, my
heart racing after dreaming of killing Neil. And when that happened Daphne was by my side, my angel, soothing and shushing
me until I fell back to sleep. I had come to terms with the fact that
the guilt would live beside me for ever, my shadow. And that was
the price I had to pay.

I still had my doubts about Daphne, of course I did. But I
loved her. And I wanted to believe in her. And, for the most
part, I did. Since the Joel incident she never gave me any reason
to doubt her. Even if she did lie sometimes, about silly things,

like how she'd got things for 'free' from the farm – or more particularly, from Sean – nothing worth a lot of money, items like eggs and milk, but still it didn't sit well with me.

One day, she rang me from the farm asking if I'd pick her up in my Morris Marina. She had been given a couple of leftover boxes of tiles, she said. She looked so joyful when she got to the car, carrying them. That weekend she knocked the ugly brown tiles from around the cooker and sink and I watched, in awe, as she fastened the new ones to the wall. 'What?' She'd laughed when she saw the amazement on my face. 'You wouldn't believe the skills I acquired in prison.'

It was a stark reminder of her past and I swallowed the uneasy feeling that lodged in my chest every time she mentioned prison. Not that she did often. And never in front of you.

You loved the new tiles – they were very country cottage with cartoon pigs and sheep on them but they brightened up the dingy kitchen.

The next day, a Wednesday, Daphne came with me to walk you to playschool because it was her day off. There was a fireworks display that evening and she was desperate for us to go. I was a bit worried about taking you – you'd never seen a firework before and I was concerned they would frighten you – but Daphne convinced me that it would be fun, even though I hated large crowds.

We watched you skip in with Miss Tilling.

'Listen, Daph, about tonight,' I began. 'Do you think Lolly's a bit young –'

We were interrupted by Melissa, who was heading out of the café and barrelling towards us with a polystyrene cup in her hand. 'Hello, ladies,' she said, and looked pointedly at our held hands. Embarrassed, I moved away from Daphne, although she was wearing a defiant expression. I know she would have continued to hold my hand, not caring what Melissa thought. Melissa could have been no older than late forties yet she was so old-fashioned in her outlook on life. She'd never understand our relationship.

'Rose, I'm glad I caught you,' she said, ignoring Daphne completely. 'A man came into the café on Monday looking for you.'

My heart stopped. 'Really? Did he . . . give a name?'

She shook her head. 'No. He just asked if I knew you.'

'What did he look like?'

She seemed to consider this for a few seconds. 'Well, handsome, I suppose. Dark hair. Tall.'

Victor. It had to be him.

'Did you tell him . . .' I swallowed, my throat dry '. . . anything?'

She gave me a pitying look. 'No, of course not.'

'Thank you,' I said, in a rush of fondness towards her. 'Thank you so much.'

She patted my arm reassuringly. 'Seemed very charming too. But,' her expression clouded 'he appeared determined to find you, Rose.'

I fought back tears. I sensed Daphne moving closer to me. 'Please,' I said, my voice shaky. 'Please don't tell him anything about me.'

Melissa searched my face with her currant-like eyes. 'Of course I won't,' she said seriously.

I thanked her and walked off before I could hyperventilate in front of her.

'Do you think it's Victor?' Daphne whispered by my shoulder. She had to run to keep pace with me.

'Who else is it going to be?' I snapped, then felt guilty at the hurt on her face. 'Sorry, I'm sorry. It's just . . .' I let out a sob '. . . he's found me. After three fucking years he's found me.'

'Rose, calm down, you're scaring me. Stop!' She grabbed my arm. 'Stop,' she said again, gentler this time. By now we were halfway up the hill towards the cottage. There was nobody else around but I shuddered as though Victor was behind us. 'Listen, it was two days ago now. He's probably gone home. Where does he live?'

'Yorkshire,' I said, wiping away tears. It was where Audrey and I had lived, to be near her family. I'd been happy there until I met him.

'Right. So maybe he came here, but nobody said anything so he went home again.'

'I – I don't know, but that doesn't sound like Victor. If he thinks I'm here he won't give up.'

She took my hand. 'Come on, let's get home and talk about it. If you want me to pick Lolly up later I will. He won't know what I look like, will he?'

I nodded and let her lead me home. Once inside she sat me at the pine kitchen table and made me a cup of tea. 'We can move, if you want?' she said, handing me a mug and sitting beside me. We still had our coats and boots on.

'I can't sell the cottage. Especially now with – with . . .' I couldn't bring myself to say Neil's name. We were trapped there.

'We could rent it out then? Move somewhere else. A city. Easier to hide in.'

'What if someone found . . . *him*?'

'If we rented it out we wouldn't let any tenant dig up the garden. We'd put that in the lease.'

Nausea washed over me. 'Daph, I need to be honest with you. About Victor.'

She pushed her fringe out of her face. 'What do you mean?'

'He . . . We were never romantically involved. We never had sex. He was my doctor.'

'Your doctor? I don't understand.'

'He was my fertility doctor. But he . . .' I gulped. I'd tried so hard to put him out of my mind these past three years. The betrayal I'd felt. The fear. It was all still so raw. The threats he made to take you away. 'He did something awful.'

She reached across the table for my hand. 'What – what did he do?'

'He tricked me.'

'How?'

It was a relief to reveal the secret I'd been hiding all these years. So I told her everything.

Nearly four years ago Audrey and I had gone to Dr Victor Carmichael's clinic in Harrogate for fertility treatment. He'd seemed so nice, so caring as we explained our predicament, assuring us he had helped same-sex couples before. Once an anonymous donor was chosen he booked me in for the procedure. Audrey and I had always agreed I'd be the one to carry the baby.

Looking back to those sessions in Victor's office it was obvious that he'd taken a liking to me. I thought, naively, that he enjoyed my company as we were around the same age. It wasn't until later I realized that wasn't the case.

I got pregnant quickly, even though, at thirty-three, I was older than what was considered normal for the mid 1970s. It was expensive and I'd had to use some of the money my parents had left me, but I was so happy that it had worked.

And then Audrey broke my heart.

She should have been ecstatic that I'd fallen pregnant so quickly, but as my stomach grew she retreated until eventually she admitted she couldn't face being a parent after all. That it wasn't what she wanted. She walked out and moved in with her parents. I was devastated, scared, alone and four months pregnant. At my next appointment with Victor I broke down and admitted everything to him. We became friends after that. He'd pop over to see me, to make sure I was eating properly and to take me out – trips to the theatre, dinner at restaurants I'd never have been able to afford. I enjoyed his company. He was a clever, charming man. And I didn't think of it as crossing any patient/doctor line, although I see now how guileless I was. But I was so heartbroken, so lonely, I was grateful for his attention. After all, he knew I was gay. When it came to renewing my lease on the flat he invited me to lodge with him instead. 'I've got this lovely big house,' he'd said. 'And I'm single. Let me look after you. You shouldn't be on your own at a time like this.'

I was surprised that he was still single. This handsome, eligible man must have had women flocking around him. But when I asked him he joked that he was a workaholic and didn't have time for a wife and children, not while he was building his practice. His house was stunning and on one of Harrogate's most salubrious streets. I couldn't say no. Maybe if I'd had my parents around or friends in the area – we'd only moved up a few months before I got pregnant to be near Audrey's family – then I might have resisted. But I was grief-stricken and terrified and, oh, so naive and I looked up to Victor. Respected him.

Unfortunately he hadn't respected me.

It went well at first. We rubbed along together. But then he became possessive: when I went out he asked where I was going and with whom. I worked as an usherette at the local cinema, handing out ice creams after the B movies, and when I made friends with this woman he started to act jealous. And that was when I realized my mistake. I might not have had any romantic feelings for Victor, but he did for me. Other things I began to notice: he started telling me what I should be eating, wearing, how much sleep I needed. I couldn't breathe. And if I didn't take his 'advice' he would spend the next few days ignoring me, slamming out of rooms and giving me the cold shoulder.

One night, after I returned late from work, he rounded on me, accused me of being flighty, and said I ought to act like the mother-to-be I was. I'd stared at him in shock. We were supposed to be friends but I felt like I was in a controlling relationship. We argued and I told him to mind his own business, that he was my friend not my lover and certainly not the dad-to-be.

I'll never forget how he looked at me. Smug, like he knew a secret that I didn't.

'Actually,' he'd said, his lips twisting cruelly, 'I am.'

'What do you mean?' I'd asked, but a cold hand had gripped my heart as it hit home exactly what he had done.

'Why use an anonymous sperm donor when you could have me?' he said. He made it sound so natural. Inserting his sperm into my cervix without my consent. 'Why are you looking at me like that? It's not illegal.'

I screamed at him, told him he had violated me, lied to me. He watched me rant, his eyes cold, as though I was nothing more than a toddler overreacting. I raced upstairs and began packing my stuff, running through my mind as to where I could go. I'd stay in a hotel and buy a property – I had the money in savings and was planning to do it with Audrey anyway. I couldn't face it after she left, but I couldn't stay there. As I packed I heard the key turning in my bedroom door. He'd locked me in.

'I'm not letting you leave,' he'd called through the door, his voice calm, sinister. 'You're carrying my child.'

I was the most terrified I'd ever felt. He brought me food, told me he was doing this for my own good, that he loved me, wanted to marry me. He wouldn't listen when I said I could never think of him in that way.

'I'll never let you go, Rose,' he said. And I realized I had to be clever. Trick him, like he'd tricked me. So I pretended that I'd think about it. When he trusted me enough to leave me in the house without locking the doors I planned my escape. First I would try to find some kind of 'insurance policy' in case he ever found me. A man like Victor, I thought, must have made mistakes in the past. I searched his study and when I thought I'd never find anything that was when I saw it. A file in his desk drawer. It looked innocuous enough, with the heading of his clinic blazoned along the front. But when I opened it I dropped it in shock. They were photos of women, legs akimbo in stirrups in one of his consulting rooms – the room I'd been in myself. The photos looked like they had been taken with a Polaroid camera and without the subjects' consent: the women were all in hospital gowns, as though he'd been halfway through a procedure and decided to photograph their genitals for his own personal use. It wasn't something a normal doctor would do. The women all looked drugged. I was sickened – he was every bit the monster I had come to expect. I wondered if I was one of them, but I didn't want to look. My stomach churned and I had to concentrate on not throwing up.

I considered going to the police there and then. It was obvious from those photos that he'd be struck off the medical register, might even go to prison. But I was scared and intimidated by him. I couldn't risk that he might try and wriggle out of it. He was a respected doctor, and he might have destroyed all the proof that I'd been artificially inseminated. He'd lie, manipulate, say we had been in a relationship and that the baby was his.

I had no choice but to run as far away as I could, taking the file with me.

The next half-hour was the most frightening of my life as I frantically packed my belongings into two suitcases, leaving a lot behind. And then I called a taxi and asked for it to pick me up two streets away. All the while my heart pounded as I expected Victor to turn up at any minute and stop me. As I ran down the streets, pulling my suitcases, I thought of him chasing me, my heart beating wildly. I only felt safe when I got into the taxi, and then when I boarded the train, knowing that each mile was taking me further and further away from him.

I didn't come to Beggars Nook straight away. I stayed in a bed-and-breakfast in Chippenham while I trawled estate agents until I found a property cheap enough for me to afford: 9 Skelton Place.

Hidden away.

Or so I thought.

Until now.

55

Lorna

THE APARTMENT LOOKS BARE WITHOUT ALL OF ALBERTO'S THINGS. Lorna walks around it forlornly. More years of her life wasted with the wrong man. Her heart feels heavy but she knows it's not for him. It's for the daughter and son-in-law she's left behind in England. She's had enough of flitting from country to country and from man to man. She wants to be near Saffy and the baby, when he or she arrives. Put down roots for once. Theo and Jen flash into her mind. A brother she never knew she had. She wants a relationship with them, too, despite the dark secrets that lurk in the past. And more than anything she wants to make it up to Saffy for not always being there when she was a kid. Her daughter's words occasionally worm their way into her mind when she's going about her day.

She could rent a little place somewhere on the Bristol Channel so she's not too far away from Saffy. Yes, she resolves, as she perches on the edge of her bed and kicks off her boots. Yes, she'll do it. First thing tomorrow she'll put the plan into motion: the lease here is a rolling one. She can leave more or less straight away. She's suddenly energized at the thought.

She takes out the photograph of Daphne and Rose standing in front of the cottage with their flared jeans and tank tops. Daphne – the taller of the two – has her arm slung around Rose's shoulders. Saffy had given it to her before she left. She can't stop staring at it, at her real mother's beautiful face, searching for some resemblance. Ever since they found out the truth, she's been dreaming about her, the pretty, petite woman with the golden-brown hair and the chocolate eyes – eyes like hers and Saffy's. Snapshots of a life come to her in her subconscious when she's asleep: walks through the woods holding her real mother's hand, standing in the village square listening to Christmas carols and drinking hot cocoa. She doesn't know if they're memories or her brain imagining scenarios she wishes were true. The sadness she'd felt in Beggars Nook when she tried to remember her past. That had been real. She'd been grieving her mother – the real Rose – and hadn't even known it.

Earlier she'd heard from DS Barnes. The DNA results were in.

He told her the DNA taken from the second body was a close enough match to Lorna's to suggest it was her mother's.

It hadn't been a surprise but Lorna had still burst into tears when she got the news.

As she places the photo on the side table, her thoughts are interrupted by her mobile ringing. Saffy's name flashes up on screen and her heart lifts.

'Hi, honey, you okay?'

'Mum!' Saffy sounds breathless. 'We've found it! The evidence that Davies was looking for. The evidence Rose hid in the fireplace. It's . . .' she gulps '. . . it's a folder with photographs of naked women.'

'What do you mean?'

'It looks like Victor sedated his victims when he was about

to perform some kind of procedure on them. And then took photos of them. Naked.'

Lorna's stomach turns over. 'Oh, my God.'

'I'm sorry.'

Lorna feels dizzy. 'Have you contacted the police?'

'We're about to. But . . . I also found something else.'

'Okay . . .'

'A letter. With your name on it.'

A letter from beyond the grave, from her real mother. Lorna stands up and paces her room. 'Open it!'

'Are you sure?'

'Of course. Of course. I need to know what it says.'

'Okay, hold on.' She can hear the rustling sound of the envelope ripping open and then Saffy's back on the line. 'Right, well, it's a long letter.'

'How long?'

'Five pages or so. Of A4 paper. Front and back.'

'What does it say?'

'You want me to read the whole thing?'

Yes. 'No. No, don't do that. It'll take ages.'

She can hear the flicking of pages. 'Shall I read it and then – Oh, my God!' Saffy gasps.

'What? What is it?'

'Rose says here she killed Neil Lewisham. Mum, it's a confession.'

Lorna sinks back onto the bed, her legs weak. 'You're going to have to show it to the police. You need to tell them everything. And give them the folder from Victor. Shit, I knew I shouldn't have left. I shouldn't have come back here.'

She hears Saffy's sharp intake of breath. 'Oh, Mum,' she says, her voice sad. 'I'm only scanning, but in the letter, Rose . . . It sounds like Victor found her.'

56

Rose

Bonfire Night, 1980

I DECIDED TO HIDE THE FOLDER UNDER THE WONKY mantelpiece in your bedroom. It had never fitted properly because of the missing bricks behind it. I didn't tell Daphne where I'd put it. Better that nobody knew.

'Tomorrow,' she said, standing at the range, stirring a saucepan full of carrots, potatoes and broccoli, 'let's look into renting Skelton Place out. And we can find somewhere to live in Bristol. A big city. It will be easier to blend in.'

'Okay,' I agreed. A busy anonymous street where all the houses looked the same. A place where nobody knew our names. I should have done that from the beginning. I shouldn't have come here to Beggars Nook.

'But tonight,' said Daphne, angling her body towards me, wooden spoon in hand, 'let's go to the fireworks display, and act normally. For Lolly. Okay?'

I nodded.

'Good,' she said. 'Good. We can do this. It will all be okay.'

I didn't feel so sure. It was like my world was closing in so that I felt claustrophobic in the village. In the cottage. In the place I'd always felt safest.

'I think you should wear my old wig,' she said suddenly. She was standing in her familiar flamingo pose, the sleeves of her jumper halfway over her hands. 'Hide that lovely wavy hair of yours.'

I laughed. My hair was mousy – it didn't exactly stand out. 'I'll just wear a bobble hat. It'll be cold and dark, so if Victor's there, prowling about, it'll be hard for him to recognize me.'

She surveyed me, a frown creasing her brow.

'What?' I asked, suddenly feeling self-conscious.

'Nothing.' She shook her head. 'It's just you're stronger than you think, Rose Grey.'

'I don't know . . .'

'You are,' she said, her voice softer now. 'The way you escaped Victor. Really, I'm impressed.' She blew me a kiss and turned back to her cooking.

There was a feeling of anticipation in the air as the three of us made our way to the village that evening. You were walking between us, as usual, holding each of our hands, while Daphne chatted away to you about toffee apples on sticks. I glanced over your head at Daphne. She looked carefree and happy. Not worried at all. Whereas my stomach felt like the inside of a washing machine, and every time I heard a shout of laughter or a dog barking I'd flinch. It wasn't just Victor I was worried about. It was the thought of starting a new life away from the village with all its familiarity. I was beginning to doubt moving to Bristol. It was something Daphne had always wanted to do. I think she was worried that if we stayed here someone would eventually come looking for Neil – and find out who she really was. But I'd never liked big cities even though I grew up in London.

But Daphne was right about one thing. If Victor had found me, we had no choice but to move away.

The firework display was being held in a field near the farm where Daphne worked. It was a bit of a trek, for you especially, but you didn't complain. You were too excited at the prospect of sugary food and fireworks. We followed the throng of people through the village square, over the bridge and towards the farm.

'At work yesterday Sean told me there's going to be hot dogs and a bonfire,' said Daphne to you. You squealed in excitement and clutched our hands tighter. You were too young last year to go to any display.

Sean again. Daphne talked about him a lot. He lived in Chippenham and travelled in every day. She said she saw him as a younger brother, but I worried he wasn't a good influence on her. Ever since he started at the farm she'd been bringing more items home. Things I wasn't sure Mick would be very happy about if he knew. She was allowed friends, of course. I never wanted to be a controlling partner. But I couldn't help my unease. It felt safer to keep our circle as small as we could. And even though I'd never met Sean I'd already made up my mind that I didn't trust him.

'It's quite crowded,' I said, trying to keep the anxiety from my voice.

'I think neighbouring villages might have got tickets too,' she said.

I bristled.

I couldn't enjoy myself. I watched Daphne lead you around the field, going from one stall to another while I hovered behind, like a bouncer on high alert, still terrified that Victor might be looking for me. It was dark with a fine drizzle in the air. I could see your pink and red bobble wobbling as you followed Daphne around, your hand tightly in hers. 'Make sure you don't let go of her hand,' I said to Daphne. I must have sounded stern because Daphne's eyes widened in surprise and hurt, as she said that, yes, of course she would. 'I'd guard this child with my life,' she said.

I lurked behind you both when you stopped at the toffee-apple stall. 'Shouldn't she have a hot dog first?' I said, leaning over, but Daphne was already placing the toffee apple in your eager hand.

'Sorry,' she mouthed over her shoulder, not looking sorry at all.

I felt too wound up to eat so wasn't bothered when Daphne bypassed the hot-dog stand, snaking her way through the crowd with you, to the front. The huge bonfire was already lit, the smoke billowing and dispersing into the damp night. People jostled next to us, clutching polystyrene cups, and I could hear the faint tinny music coming from one of the nearby stalls. You leapt up and down in front of us, your excitement palpable, until I had to put my hands on your shoulders to stop you. 'You'll wear yourself out.' I tried to laugh but it stuck in my throat.

Daphne leant into me and whispered in my ear, 'Shall I get us a drink? A hot chocolate or something? It's freezing and we might be waiting a while.'

'I . . .' I stood on tiptoe to peer around anxiously. 'I don't know. You might lose us.'

'I'll find you, don't worry,' she said. And then she was gone, moving effortlessly through the crowds in her patched velvet coat and her crocheted beret, and I was reminded of the night, nearly a year ago, when I'd first spotted her in the square and my heart had sung.

I turned back to you. 'Daffy's just going to get a drink,' I said, not sure if I was trying to reassure you or myself. I held your hand tightly.

'No,' you said, letting go. 'Don't want.'

'No, hold my hand,' I snapped and then instantly felt guilty. 'Please, Lolly, I don't want you to get lost.'

You turned away from me to continue eating your toffee apple but you let me hold your hand. Where was Daphne? She was taking too long. I wished we were at home, safe in the cottage.

'Hello, hello,' said a voice beside me. It was Melissa, clutching a flask. 'Isn't this exciting? And what a great turnout.'

'Hmm,' I said, glancing over her shoulder to see if I could spot Daphne. Then I turned back to Melissa, with an idea. 'Actually, I'm glad I've bumped into you. This is going to sound strange,' I lowered my voice and angled my body away from you so that you couldn't hear, 'but the man who came into the café looking for me, I'm worried it's someone I used to know. Someone I . . . escaped from.'

'Oh, lovey, I'm sorry, I didn't realize.'

I held up my hand. I needed to get this out before I changed my mind. 'I've done something stupid, really stupid. My life,' I said, 'could be in . . .' I mouthed the next word so that you couldn't hear ' . . . danger.'

Melissa's eyebrows shot up. 'What do you mean?'

'If something happens to me —'

'Why, nothing's going to happen to you, dear, don't be silly!'

'Listen. Please. If something did, the evidence is in the fireplace. Can you remember that? It's very, very important.'

She looked horrified. 'I – I will. But I'm worried for you. Is there someone I can call? The police?'

'No!' I almost shouted. You turned and I smiled at you.

When you looked back to the bonfire I said, in a hushed tone, 'No. Please, no police. I'm sure it's fine, but just in case.'

She threw me a look of concern but agreed. 'Oh, there's Maureen. Sorry, lovey, I need to go.' She turned away from me, probably with relief that she'd found someone more normal to talk to. I craned my neck to see if I could spot Daphne. She was taking ages with the drinks. And then I spotted her, over by the hot-dog stand, talking to someone. My heart started racing. It looked like a man. Tall, dark. Was it . . . was it *Victor*? No, no, of course it wasn't. This man looked younger, dressed in wellies and a waxed jacket. Daphne was smiling, and so was he from the way he was throwing his head back and touching her arm. Jealousy shot through me. Were they *flirting*?

'Mummy, when is it going to start?'

I turned my attention back to you, unease growing in my gut, like bacteria. 'Soon, sweetheart. Really soon.'

'I feel sick.' You thrust the half-eaten toffee apple into my hand.

'Not surprised,' I said, trying to keep my voice light. 'Ooh, look! Look, it's starting.'

You were distracted by the rocket that ripped through the sky and exploded over our heads in rays of pinks and purples.

And then I felt a hand on my shoulder. I jumped but it was only Daphne. She pressed her cold cheek against mine. 'Sorry,' she said. 'Here.' She handed me a polystyrene cup and I dropped the toffee apple on the ground, stifling the guilt I felt at littering, so that I could take it and still hold your hand.

'Who were you talking to?'

She frowned. 'No one. Why?'

'I saw you. With a man.'

'A man?' She looked confused for a few moments before she apparently remembered. 'Oh, yes, that was Sean.'

'What was he doing here? He came all the way from Chippenham?'

She shrugged, like it was no big deal. It crossed my mind that she hadn't brought him over to introduce us. Did he even know about me? About us? I told myself I was being silly. Of course she would have told him. Unless he thinks she's my lodger and nothing more.

She giggled. 'I think he fancies me a little bit. But it comes in handy.'

I stared at her in shock. What had happened to all her feminist principles? To the 'we don't need men' conversations we frequently had?

'What?' She laughed, sipping her drink. 'He helps me carry the heavy stuff.'

'God, Daphne.' I turned away from her.

Her next words were drowned in the explosion of fireworks and I bent down so that I was on your level. I didn't want to look at Daphne. You were watching intently, your mouth open in surprise as a banger burst into a riot of gold and yellow, but you covered your ears with your hands.

'Are they too loud?'

You shook your head. 'Pretty.'

I ignored Daphne for the rest of the show, not even sure why I was so cross with her. Was I jealous that she was flirting with a man? Or was it because she seemed so totally unconcerned that Victor might be here and that I could be in danger? When she was worried about Neil I was there for her. I *killed* for her. And in return she was acting like my situation was just one big joke.

When it had finished I clutched your hand and turned, expecting Daphne to be behind us. But she had gone.

57

Rose

Bonfire Night, 1980

I SCANNED THE FIELD FOR DAPHNE. SHE COULDN'T HAVE gone far. I'd obviously upset her with my frostiness. We rarely argued. We never really had much to argue about, living in our safe little house with you. Even with the spectre of Neil hanging over us. But now that Victor was potentially in the area, everything had turned in on itself. I was once again on full alert.

'Mummy, tired,' you complained, as I frog-marched you across the field. People were dispersing, and we wove in and out of them, searching for Daphne but also hyper-aware of Victor. You were still slurping at your hot chocolate although my cup was empty.

'Sorry, honey, but we need to get home as quickly as we can,' I said, trying to hide the fear in my voice. Why had Daphne gone off and left us when she knew I was scared about Victor? As we attempted to leave the field there was a bottleneck as everyone tried to get through the gate at the same time and we had no choice but to stop and wait. I glanced around anxiously: we were penned in on all sides by people who stamped their feet impatiently and complained loudly about the holdup. I studied every male face in case it was Victor's and I clutched your hand tightly. 'Don't let go,' I said to you, in my sternest voice. Finally the crowd gave way and swarmed forward and I breathed a sigh of relief as people scattered, but thankful that there was still enough of a throng to protect us if Victor was there.

But as we walked along the high street and up the hill towards Skelton Place everyone else had melted away and it was just the two of us.

'Bit scared, Mummy,' you said, gripping my hand tightly and my heart broke. You must have sensed my fear because you were never normally scared. You looked around at the high hedges and the woods that encompassed us with wide, terrified eyes. Somewhere far away an owl hooted.

'It looks later than it is because the moon is hiding behind the clouds tonight,' I said, trying to keep my voice jolly. 'It's only eight o'clock.'

'I'm tired.'

'We're nearly home, not far now, just up the hill a bit. What about a piggy-back?'

You nodded eagerly and I bent down to allow you to climb up. You wrapped your little arms around my neck and I grabbed your ankles. 'Giddy-up,' I said, trying to pretend to be a horse as I jogged up the hill, even though I thought my legs would buckle from exhaustion. Fear that Victor might suddenly appear from behind a bush gave me the adrenalin to keep going.

'Where's Daffy?' you asked, as the cottage came into view. My heart sank when I could see there were no lights on.

'We lost her,' I said, my voice sounding small in the darkness. 'But don't worry, she won't be far behind.'

You jumped off my back as I opened the front door.

The cottage was cold and dark and empty. I felt uneasy, as if someone was about to jump out at me. I turned on the light in the hallway. Daphne's coat wasn't hanging up. Where was she? An image of her and Sean flashed through my mind and I pushed it away.

I turned on all the lights downstairs. The windows were opaque. Was someone out there, looking in?

I shivered. A firework exploded overhead, making me jolt.

'Come on, Lolly, let's get you to bed,' I said, taking your hand and leading you upstairs.

I tucked you up in bed and read you a story but you fell asleep before it was finished. And then I kissed your forehead and stroked your lovely curly hair away from your face.

Another noise outside made me jump. It didn't sound like a firework this time.

It was coming from the garden.

Carefully I got up from your bed and went to the window, pulling aside your pink gingham curtains.

I froze with fright.

There was a man on my lawn looking up at the house.

It was Victor.

58

Theo

'Okay,' says Theo, into the phone, glancing across at Jen, who's pushed her sunglasses onto her hair and has raised her eyebrows questioningly. She's lying on the sun-lounger in their little garden, her bare legs stretched out in front of her. 'So he's been charged?' He's standing on their patio, the sun beating down on his neck. 'And,' he lowers his voice, 'he's now been transferred to Wakefield prison?' The French windows that lead into their living-dining room are open and he walks into the shade, worried the neighbours might hear him. There has already been a storm of press interest.

'That's right,' says Ralph, his father's solicitor. He has a deep voice and Theo imagines he's the kind of person who enjoys a fine wine and nights at the opera, although he's never met the guy. 'Because of the seriousness of the charges. He's on remand until the trial. He's been charged with murder as well as sexual assault.'

'And what about the fertility fraud?' Theo still doesn't have all the pieces of the puzzle, just what they've managed to fit together from the evidence Saffy found.

'Yes, that looks likely too. Although it's more of a grey area. Thanks to all the press interest, a number of women have come forward to the CPS. He's been doing it for years.'

Theo feels sick. Those women's photos he'd found in his dad's study had been a catalogue. A way for him to remember exactly whom he'd artificially inseminated with his own sperm. The other women, the ones in the folder Saffy found . . . He can't bear to think about that.

Ralph must mistake Theo's silence for concern because he says, 'I'm sorry, it doesn't look good for your father. I've advised manslaughter when it comes to Caroline as he says he didn't mean to kill her, that it was an accident. That they'd argued, she was going to leave him, and he'd pushed her in anger. She'd stumbled and fallen down the stairs. If he pleads guilty, there'll be no trial, but you know what your father's like.' Theo feels a lump in his throat at the sound of his mother's name. It hadn't taken his father long to admit his crime. It had surprised Theo. He'd believed his dad would go to his grave protesting his innocence. But it seems that the evidence had been too much for him to deny: Glen Davies's testimony of a confession, his alibi not holding up to more scrutiny and a neighbour remembering talking to his father that morning, later than the time he said he'd left for work.

'What about Rose's murder?'

'Police are still combing through the evidence on that one. In the letter that Saffron Cutler handed in, Rose writes that she was scared Victor had found her, that she saw him in the garden on Bonfire Night. But the letter ends after that. We can assume, of course, that he did find her and that was why she'd never had the chance to finish the letter. But obviously that might not be enough for the court. However, a witness, a Melissa Brown, has said that a man fitting Victor's description had been looking for Rose in the days before she disappeared. We'll keep you updated.'

'And what about Cynthia Parsons?'

'Not enough evidence to suggest her death wasn't suicide,' he says.

At least he's admitted to causing Mum's death, thinks Theo. If only he'd admit to killing Rose, Lorna and Saffy would have peace of mind.

'He's asked me if you'd like to visit him,' says Ralph, his voice suddenly tentative.

'He killed my mother,' says Theo. 'I hope he rots in jail.' From the garden Jen is watching him intently although he's not sure if she can hear what he's saying.

'I know. But I had to ask. Anyway, I'll keep in touch and let you know the court date when your father enters his plea.'

'Thanks for letting me know,' Theo says, ending the call. The truth is, he just wants justice. He wants his dad to pay for his crimes. He sinks into a chair, phone still in his hand. A shadow looms over him and he looks up to see Jen standing in the doorway, obscuring the sun.

'Are you okay, babe?'

Theo nods. His hands are clammy and he drops his phone onto the table.

Jen hops onto his lap and throws her arms around his neck. She smells like coconut sun cream. She doesn't say anything. She doesn't have to.

'I'm related to that bastard,' he says, with a sigh.

'You're nothing like him. You're all your mum. Remember that. And you're not alone. Lorna must be feeling the same way now she knows he's her father.'

'True.' Thank goodness for Lorna. He's spoken to her every few days on the phone since she texted him that night to tell him he's her brother.

'Davies has been charged with a number of crimes too,' he says, pulling Jen closer to him. 'I get the sense he's cut some kind of deal but he's charged with assault and intimidation, not just to Lorna and Saffy but to other women as well. Fraud, pretending to be an officer of the law, breaking and entering – the list goes on.'

He feels Jen shudder.

'Do you think you'll go and see your dad?' she asks gently. 'Even if it's just to ask why he argued with your mum? And if it's true that she was planning to leave him?'

'I never want to see him again,' he says with feeling. 'I hate him. And he'll never be honest. He'll never offer up an explanation as to why he did these things. He'll make excuses, try to blame Mum.'

'I'm sorry. I can't even imagine what it must be like.'

At least he's got Jen, this wonderful woman, Theo thinks. Who's always been so supportive and whom he trusts implicitly. 'I think I might call Lorna, update her on all of this.'

'Sure.' She squeezes his shoulder affectionately, then jumps down from his lap. 'I'm going to carry on with my tanning.' She grins at him over her shoulder as she heads back into the garden. Theo watches her go. Her shoulders have already started to turn red. He knows she won't be satisfied until she's sat out there for another hour, at least, despite his warnings of skin cancer. A doctor's son, after all.

Later that afternoon Theo goes to visit his mum's grave. The cemetery is busier than it usually is on a Saturday, which he puts down to the weather. Couples are strolling through the grounds arm in arm, families with young children and buggies. His heart contracts. He wants it so badly for himself and Jen. It's a cruel irony to him that his dad illegally fathered all those children when he, Theo, can't even get his wife pregnant. He wonders why his dad did it. He'd read up on other cases of doctors performing fertility fraud – he'd never heard of it before. A God complex is usually one reason. That sums up his father perfectly.

When he reaches his mum's grave he kneels down to take the old flowers out of the vase and replaces them with the fresh roses. 'They got him, Mum,' he says, as he arranges the roses in the vase. 'He's admitted to pushing you and I think they'll get him for Rose's death too. I'll . . .' his voice catches '. . . I'll never understand what happened that day. I'll never understand *him*. But I promise, Mum, I promise that if I'm lucky enough to be a dad I'll be everything he wasn't.'

He touches the glossy marble tombstone, remembering the last time he'd seen his mum: the weekend before she died. She'd stood on the doorstep, pressing a bag of homemade cottage pies and lasagnes into his hands. She was the one who'd made him want to become a chef. She'd given him a huge hug, almost as if she knew it would be the last. And then she'd stood waving until he'd reversed out of the driveway, her smile hiding the pain she must have been feeling. 'I'm sorry,' he says, a lump forming in his throat. 'I'm sorry I never knew what he was capable of. I'm sorry I couldn't save you.'

59

Daphne

August 2018

TWO WOMEN COME AND VISIT ME TODAY. THEY HAVE dark curly hair, although one is older than the other. The younger one is wearing denim dungarees and looks like she might be pregnant. The older of the two is in an orange sundress. They are both beautiful. But all young women are beautiful to me, with their youth and their agility and their hips that don't ache when they walk.

'Gran,' says the younger one, sitting beside my bed. I've been in bed a lot lately. My body doesn't feel strong but I don't know why. I cough and the younger one's face crumples with worry. She's chewing her bottom lip. The older woman looks hostile. She reminds me of someone. The expression she's pulling, the disappointment in her eyes. She reminds me of Rose. 'It's Saffy,' says the pregnant one. Saffy. Saffy. The name rings a bell. She's calling me Gran. She must be my granddaughter. The other has to be her mother: they look so alike. But I've never had children. I know that. I'd remember that. The younger one is crying. I don't know why. Tears are slipping down her face and falling onto the denim trouser legs, creating little dark splodges. Who are your tears for, my dear? I long to ask her. But my mouth won't move. The words won't come.

The older woman stands behind this Saffy and squeezes her shoulders. 'Mum,' she says, looking at me. 'It's Lorna. Lolly.'

Lolly. Of course it's Lolly. My Lolly, my love.

'I wish you could remember,' she says softly. 'I wish you could remember what happened to Rose, why you took her name.'

Of course I remember. 'To keep you safe,' I suddenly say, and their eyes widen in surprise. My voice is croaky. I sound like an old woman. The hands folded over my sheets are wrinkled and veiny. I am an old woman. Of course I am. Why do I keep forgetting that?

Lolly comes around the other side of the bed and places her hands over mine. 'I want to forgive you, so much,' she says. Her hands feel warm on top of my cold ones. 'Especially now. We'll never really know what happened that night,' she says to me. I stare back at her. I'm not completely sure which night she's referring to. I close my eyes. It hurts to keep them open. My chest aches and so do my lungs. I can hear their voices although they sound very far away but they're talking about Skelton Place. And Rose.

My Rose.

I realize they're talking about an upcoming court case. And Victor Carmichael. They're talking about the night Rose died.

And despite the pain in my chest and the ache in my lungs I begin to talk.

I could feel Rose slipping away from me. It was the same feeling I had when I was a kid. When I was Jean. Susan pulled away from me too, and I knew the same thing was happening with Rose. It began after she killed Neil, looking back. She wasn't a murderer. She didn't put the bad things she had done in a box in the deep basement of her mind, not to be looked over, dwelt on, again. Not like I did. It was a gift. It helped me move on. But Rose couldn't do that. Rose needed to believe she was a good person, that she was kind, that she'd go to Heaven one day. I loved that about her. That innocence. It was refreshing after what I'd come from. But sometimes it could also be unbelievably annoying. She expected too much from people. Nobody was all good or all bad but Rose was very black and white. And I could tell, after she found out who I really was, she began to re-examine her feelings for me. She got past it because she had killed too – but she could console herself that she'd done it out of loyalty and love. Out of protection and self-defence. Mine had been out of anger, and fear, and that deep-rooted sense of abandonment.

I don't know what I thought I was trying to achieve by flirting with Sean. I never fancied him for a second, but I wanted to make Rose jealous, I suppose, to make her realize she loved me. She needed me. And then, at the fireworks display, I noticed the way she looked at me. It was cold, detached. As though she'd had enough of me. I was so hurt by it that I couldn't stand to be near her. So I walked away, got lost in the crowd. When she noticed I was gone she didn't even seem that concerned. She just took Lolly's hand and moved through the crowds towards home.

I walked around the village for a bit, trying to gather my thoughts, hoping that Rose would miss me, would realize that we were right for each other. I hoped by the time I'd got back she'd be so scared about Victor she'd agree we needed to leave together. A new life away from there.

When I eventually returned, Rose was pacing the little

kitchen, her face white. She had a knife in her hand. She looked like a beautiful but unpredictable horse that was about to rear or bolt.

'There you are!' she hissed, as soon as I walked in. 'How could you just leave me like that? You know I was scared with Victor on the prowl.'

'Rose,' I said, gently, walking over to her, my hand out to calm her.

'I saw him!' she cried. 'He was in the garden.' She waved the knife around.

I walked over to the kitchen window. The garden was empty. As I'd known it would be.

'Rose. Darling. Put the knife down. There's nobody in the garden.'

'You . . . you . . .' Her jaw was clenched and she was shaking with fear. Or was it rage. I couldn't tell. 'Where did he go? What did you tell him?'

'We need to leave, Rose,' I said instead. 'Now Victor knows where you are . . .'

'You know that's not true,' she hissed, her eyes flashing.

'Please, Rose. You're overreacting . . .'

It was the worst thing I could have said. She began to accuse me then, of lying, of manipulating her. 'I should never have trusted you,' she said. 'Joel was right.'

I was so hurt by her words. 'But we love each other.'

'This was a mistake,' she spat. 'I have to put Lolly first. You need to leave. You and Sean . . .'

'There's nothing between me and Sean. What are you talking about?'

'It's over. I want you to leave. Now!'

'I . . . What?' I couldn't believe what she was saying. 'Are you ending things with us?'

'I don't trust you,' she said sadly, but she put the knife down on the worktop with a shaky hand. 'I'm sorry, Daphne. I love you but I don't trust you. I think you lie. And,' she wiped tears away from her eyes, 'I can't do this any more.'

This couldn't be happening. I'd thought I'd found the happiness I'd always craved. The family I'd always wanted. To lose Rose was one thing, but to lose Lolly as well? I loved that little girl like she was my own.

'I'm not letting you leave me,' I said, coming over to her and pulling her into my arms. 'We love each other.'

'I think I need a clean break. Start again.'

'You can't,' I wailed. She pulled away from me and swiped at her eyes. Her wavy hair fell over her shoulders. She was shorter than me by about two inches and she looked small and frail in that moment. I was desperate. I needed her to see that she was making the biggest mistake of her life. 'We know too much about each other,' I began.

'Oh, don't start that,' she said. 'That's not going to wash with me any longer. You can't prove that I killed Neil.'

Then she started accusing me of all sorts. Manipulation and lies about Sean. She had guessed, my clever, sweet Rose. I'd underestimated her.

I knew then that she'd never forgive me. That I'd lost her.

It was an accident.

Just like Susan Wallace's death had been an accident.

She pushed past me. She went to walk away.

And all I knew was that I couldn't let her go. And I couldn't let her take Lolly.

Red flashed in front of my eyes. It happened in one swift movement. I grabbed the kettle, the cast-iron one we used for the hob, and swung it against the rear of her lovely head. She fell backwards, as though in a faint, her eyes open in surprise as she collapsed in my arms. Too late I realized what I'd done. And I held her as she died. I held her and I cried and I told her I loved her. Over and over again. Because it was true. And apart from Lolly, and then, years later, Saffy, I never loved anyone else.

When I've finished talking Lolly is staring at me in horror, her mouth hanging open and tears rolling down her cheeks. And I realize I've said it all out loud. I've told this lovely woman, this amazing person, whom I love like my own daughter, that I killed her real mother.

Saffy – my kind, thoughtful granddaughter – is holding my hand. And despite everything I've just told her she doesn't let go. I can see Rose in her. The same guile and innocence and faith. And I hope that I haven't destroyed that in this sweet child.

'I'm sorry,' I say, my mind painfully, awfully lucid in this moment.

Because the truth of it is, my mind has always been more lucid than I gave them reason to believe. Don't get me wrong, I have dementia: my brain is foggy and forgetful, and I don't recognize people I know, people I love. But when I do have those clear, perfectly sharp moments, I remember a lot more about the past, about what I've done, than any of them have ever given me credit for.

And now they know. They know the truth – *my truth* – before I slip further into myself, because one day I won't have control over how I reveal it. And I wanted them to know I'm not a cold-hearted killer, I'm not a psychopath, that the judge was wrong about me all those years ago. I was a good mother and grandmother.

And that, despite everything, I loved Rose.

I really, really did.

60

Epilogue

One year later

LORNA OBSERVES HER FAMILY, GATHERED IN THE GARDEN of 9 Skelton Place. The bi-fold doors to the new kitchen are flung open and Snowy sits just inside, in the shade, enjoying the cold of the new slate tiles, his head resting on his paws. Sometimes, especially on hot summer days like today, it's hard to believe what went on here nearly forty years ago.

Occasionally, when she closes her eyes at night, she has visions of Daphne kneeling in the garden, prising up the patio slabs to bury Rose alongside Neil. Sometimes it's so sharp that she wonders if it's a repressed memory and that she had witnessed it. It's something she's working on with Felicity, her psychiatrist. No wonder Daphne never sold the cottage and why it stood empty for a while before she rented it out. She couldn't risk anyone finding the bodies.

But she won't think of that today. Because today the scene in the garden is a happy one. The sun is high in the cloudless sky and there, on the lawn, fussing over their nine-month-old daughter, Freya, are Saffy and Tom. Tom's laid out her colourful playmat on the grass and she sits, like the queen she's become to them all, in her little yellow dress, surrounded with stuffed toys and teething rings. Saffy is lying beside her, propped up by her elbow. Lorna knows Saffy has surprised herself by how much she loves her little girl. And it's given her a new confidence, a bloom that Lorna is proud to witness. Next to them on two sun-loungers, smiling indulgently, are Theo and a pregnant Jen. They got lucky on their first round of IVF and Jen is due in eight weeks' time.

It's worked out well for them all, she thinks, glancing around, a cold glass of Pimm's in her hand. And she's pleased for them, she really is. She's happy to be living in England, has, for once in her life, put down roots in Portishead. She has even bought her own apartment overlooking the marina in the same block as the flat she rented when she first moved back from Spain – and sometimes, especially on a hot day, it feels like she's abroad. A homeowner at last. And she's closer to Saffy than she's ever been. After Saffy gave birth they had a real heart-to-heart.

'I love her so much it hurts,' Saffy had said, holding her newborn daughter in her arms in her hospital bed. She'd stared at Lorna with tears in her eyes. 'I'm sorry. I'm so sorry for the things I said, doubting you. You're the best mum in the world. And now I know . . . the love I feel for Freya. God, I'd die for her.'

'Like I'd die for you.'

And they'd smiled at each other over Freya's tufty hair. A smile of understanding. Mother to mother.

They meet at least once a week: sometimes Saffy drives over to Portishead or Lorna will come to the cottage. They are close in a way that Lorna never was with Daphne. There was always a gulf between them that she could never explain. But now she knows why. On some unconscious level she must have known that Daphne was an imposter.

She has been seeing Felicity once a fortnight, and she's been great at helping Lorna work through her issues, mainly her worry about being the child of two murderers, not that she puts Rose and Victor in the same bracket. And Felicity has made her see she doesn't have a dark heart, that it's not genetic. But she has made Lorna understand that she does run away from her problems and she does have trouble forging romantic relationships. So that's something she's going to work on in the future. There is still a spark between her and Euan – he's even been to stay with her in her new place. She doesn't know where it will lead – if anywhere – but she's excited to find out.

'So,' says Theo, lifting his glass. Tom is standing at the barbecue in the corner, a pair of tongs in his hand, which he raises instead of a glass. 'To justice.'

'To justice,' they all echo.

'And to the future,' says Lorna, and Jen strokes her bump, reaching for Theo's hand.

Yesterday they found out that Victor's trial, which had gone on for weeks, had finally come to an end. Victor refused to plead guilty to murder; his plea of manslaughter was turned down. So a trial went ahead and he was found guilty of the murder of Caroline Carmichael, as well as sexual offences against the women in his folder. Twenty different women. He'll be sentenced next month. Lorna knows Theo has never gone to visit him and she won't either. She has no interest in getting to know her so-called father.

There was never enough evidence to charge Victor with

Rose's murder. Lorna's heart feels heavy when she thinks of Daphne, lying in her care-home bed, admitting to what she had done. It was the first time she really felt the woman she had always thought of as her mother was telling the truth. Neither she nor Saffy told the police about Daphne's confession. Maybe they would have if Victor had ever been charged.

She died a few days later. Pneumonia. Saffy took her death a lot harder than Lorna did. Saffy had found it in her giant heart to forgive Daphne but Lorna is unsure if she ever can. Daphne robbed Lorna of her real mother, a mother she can barely remember, and that breaks her heart.

It's still a blank – what she must have gone through after the real Rose suddenly disappeared. She hopes Felicity will be able to unlock some of the memories, however painful. When did she start calling Daphne 'Mum'? She must have cried for her real mother. She must have felt abandoned and confused, and she can never forgive Daphne for that. Even if Daphne did dedicate her life to looking after her. The betrayal is something she'll never get over.

She downs her Pimm's and goes into the kitchen to get some water. She can't drink too much: she's driving home after this. She wanders across the kitchen – it's been transformed: beautiful Shaker-style units in a pale grey with white stone worktops. She knows Saffy feels guilty – she often says that this house is truly Lorna's. But Lorna is happy for Saffy to have it. She's content in her apartment overlooking the sea. She's found work as a manager of a local boutique hotel in Bristol and has made some new friends. When Daphne died Lorna inherited the rest of her money – there was more than she'd thought. Money she'd obviously taken from Rose by pretending to be her. It had been enough for her to buy the apartment outright.

After Victor's arrest Lorna did wonder if Saffy wanted to stay at Skelton Place. But her daughter said she felt close to Rose, living there. And to honour her she planted a rose bush at the end of their garden. It's started to grow nicely – the top has reached the stone wall.

'Are you okay, Mum?' Saffy appears beside her, Freya on her hip sucking the ear of a plastic giraffe. When she sees Lorna she reaches out her chubby little arms and Lorna gladly takes her, enjoying the warmth of her granddaughter's little body against hers. 'You seem a bit . . . wistful today.'

Lorna pulls funny faces at Freya, then turns back to her daughter. 'I'm just thinking about everything, that's all.'

Saffy walks over to the big American-style fridge to fill Lorna's glass with water. 'Why don't you stay tonight? You can have Freya's room and she can sleep with us. Theo and Jen are staying.'

'I know, but . . . I'm going to read the letter tonight. I think it's time, don't you? I've been putting it off for long enough.'

Saffy smiles sympathetically and nods. 'There's something I need to tell you about that,' she says, looking sheepish.

The letter. She'd kept it in a drawer, unable to face reading it. She knows it will be upsetting, but now she feels ready.

'What's that?'

'The last page. I didn't give it to the police at the time. I'm sorry. You'll see why when you read it. When they returned the letter to me I made sure to put the last page back before giving it to you. It was before . . . well, before Gran told us what she did. I was worried it would implicate her. It was wrong of me.'

Lorna frowns. 'I don't understand.'

'You'll know when you read it,' says Saffy. 'I was just trying to protect Gran. I really loved her.'

'I know you did, honey. And I did too. I must remember that.'

They stand together, their arms linked with Freya between them chewing her toy.

'I like to think that Rose is here,' says Saffy looking out onto the garden. 'The real Rose. Looking over us.' Lorna smiles at her daughter. Always the romantic.

But she hopes it's true, all the same.

Later, when she's back in her apartment, she pours herself a glass of wine and goes to the balcony. The sun is going down and she watches as couples and friends, all dressed up, head out for the evening. She can hear the laughter and chatter of people sitting at tables in the restaurant opposite. Yes, this is what she likes, she thinks, as she settles down to read her letter. She likes to feel she's in the middle of things. That around her couples are on their first date, or their last; friends are celebrating or reminiscing. She wonders what sort of person she would have become if her real mother had lived.

She takes the letter out of the envelope. It's written on sheets of lined A4 paper, yellowing with age, with two horizontal creases, and she stares at it for a minute, at her mother's flowery writing, imagining her sitting down to write it, almost like a diary. She runs her fingertip tenderly over the word 'Lolly', her eyes landing on the first sentence:

The village never looked prettier than it did the evening I first met Daphne Hartall.

As she reads she can almost hear her mother's voice, melodious and soothing, as though she's sitting right beside her, and she's reminded of all those bedtime stories that she thought she'd forgotten. And as the sun fades and the stars come out she sits, entranced in her mother's world, as she learns about her love affair with Daphne, her fear of Victor, and the night of the fireworks. The night she died.

And the last page, the final piece of the puzzle that Saffy had kept from the police in a misguided attempt to protect the woman she'd always thought of as Gran.

When she's finished she clutches the letter to her chest and stares out at the moon reflecting in the water of the marina, tears on her cheeks, feeling she understands everything at last.

So now you know, my darling girl, my Lolly. You know everything. My confession. My sins.

And if you're reading this, if you've found this, along with the evidence of the man I ran from, then I fear it means something bad has happened to me.

Because, you see, I no longer trust the woman I love. I found out tonight that she'd manipulated and lied to me in the worst way, and I think she has throughout our relationship. She said she loved me and, in her own twisted way, I think she does. And I have no doubt that she loves you. But tonight she has sunk to a new low. I fear that nobody walks away from Daphne Hartall with their life.

I'm writing this next to your bed as you sleep, your toadstool night-light glowing in the darkness, your eyelids flickering as you dream. I don't want to leave you, my precious daughter. The thought of being without you hurts so much. And I never would willingly be apart from you, please know that.

Just now, after the fireworks, I thought Victor had found me. But I was wrong. When I felt brave enough to look again out of your bedroom window, I saw that the man on my lawn wasn't Victor at all. I recognized him from the fireworks display. It was Sean. And in that moment it hit me what a fool I'd been to trust her. He resembled Victor from afar, as Daphne no doubt knew.

And I suspect Daphne had told him to stand there to frighten me, to make me think Victor had found me. I think she also sent him to Melissa's café, knowing Melissa would tell me someone was looking for me. Maybe she wanted my fear to bring us closer together, to push me into moving to the city with her. I think she knew I was having doubts about her. That I was on the verge of telling her to leave.

And I am — as they say — between a rock and a hard place. Because to involve the police would mean I'd be arrested for the murder of Neil Lewisham and you'd be taken away from me. So I have decided to stay and fight.

And if it goes wrong, if I don't win that fight, I want you to know how much I love you. I love you more than anything in the whole world. I really have tried to be the best mother I could be. To keep you safe. I've made some stupid decisions. But I'm not a bad person, please believe me.

Be strong, my darling, my girl. You are not a product of me or Victor. You are your own person. Be the woman I wish I could have been, my beautiful Lolly.

All my love, for ever,
Mummy ×

ACKNOWLEDGMENTS

I STARTED WRITING *THE COUPLE AT NUMBER 9* DURING the first lockdown when everything was so uncertain and scary. I was homeschooling two children and wondered if I would ever be able to concentrate long enough to finish a novel. The decision to set this story in 2018 when we weren't in the midst of a pandemic, and having this other world to escape to helped me mentally, and for that it and the characters of Saffy, Lorna, Theo, Rose and Daphne will always be special to me.

This book wouldn't have been possible without the following people. First, Juliet Mushens who is not only a brilliant, intelligent (and best-dressed) agent, but a special person, friend and fellow cat lover! There has been no one better to help steer my writing career and I feel very lucky to be part of Team Mushens. Also I'm indebted to Liza DeBlock at Mushens Entertainment for being so patient with my lack of organization!

To Maxine Hitchcock, my wonderful editor, who has made this book a thousand times better than it would have been, with her thoughtful, clever and insightful editing, her encouragement and kindness. I can't wait for another Bath meet-up! And also to Clare Bowron – the cutting queen – for all the help on the second and third edits. A huge thank you also to the rest of the brilliant team at Michael Joseph: Rebecca Hilsdon, Bea McIntyre, Hazel Orme, Lucy Hall, Ella Watkins and everyone in Sales, Marketing and Art for all their hard work and creativity. I'm so grateful for everything you all do.

To my foreign publishers, particularly Penguin Verlag in Germany, Harper in the US, Nord in Italy and Foksal in Poland for their continued belief in me.

To my brilliant writing friends, the West Country crew, Tim Weaver and Gilly Macmillan for the Zoom calls, pub lunches, texts, laughs and advice, and to Gillian McAllister, Liz Tipping and Joanna Barnard for the funny memes and WhatsApp messages and encouragement. And to my other friends for all your continued support – I won't list you all here for fear of missing someone out but I'm looking forward to those nights out in the future!

Thank you as always to my family and my in-laws, especially to my mum and sister for reading my drafts before they are published and my mum's meticulous proofreading! To my husband Ty for brainstorming plot points with me and being totally honest when he feels something won't work, and my two children, Claudia and Isaac, who I'm so very proud of. Love you all so much.

A massive thank you to Stuart Gibbon at Gib Consultancy for patiently answering my questions on police procedures surrounding decades-old buried bodies, and how detectives would treat a vulnerable suspect.

To all my readers. Thank you so much for buying, borrowing and recommending my books, and for all the social-media messages. It brightens my day to hear from you.

ACKNOWLEDGMENTS

To the bloggers and reviewers for all your support, for the blog-tours and for taking time to read and review my books. I'm so grateful.

And finally to three amazing women who are sadly no longer with us. My great-grandmother Elizabeth Lane, my grandmother Rhoda Douglas and my great-aunty June Kennedy. All three were important women in my life and all sadly ended up with the cruel disease Alzheimer's. And although – I'm pleased to say – they never had bodies buried in their gardens, their strength and spirit inspired me to write about Rose.

ABOUT THE AUTHOR

CLAIRE DOUGLAS HAS WORKED AS A JOURNALIST FOR FIF-
teen years, writing features for women's magazines and national newspapers, but she has dreamed of being a novelist
since the age of seven. She finally got her wish after winning
Marie Claire's Debut Novel Award for her first novel, *The Sisters*,
which was one of the bestselling debut novels of 2015. She lives
in Bath, England, with her husband and two children.

DON'T MISS THESE OTHER NAIL-BITING THRILLERS!

"Douglas is a true must-read thriller author."
—*PopSugar*

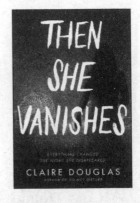